THE LYNMARA LEGACY

THE
LYNMARA LEGACY

Catherine Gaskin

BOOK CLUB ASSOCIATES LONDON

This edition published 1976 by
Book Club Associates
by arrangement with William Collins Sons & Co. Ltd.

Printed in Great Britain by
Richard Clay (The Chaucer Press), Ltd.,
Bungay, Suffolk

FOR VIOLET

Author's Note

The skeleton—the bare bones—of this story was published nearly thirty years ago under the title of *This Other Eden*. When I wrote it, I was, literally, a schoolgirl, living in Australia, with no factual experience or knowledge of the world I wrote about. Over these past few years the feeling has grown in me that I would like to revise it. When, in fact, I began the task I quickly realized that a simple revision was not enough. The characters expanded and developed; they demanded true motivations for their lives and actions; I no longer saw them with the eyes of a schoolgirl, but with the experience of thirty years in between, and the knowledge of the various places I had lived in, and visited, during that time. When finally I presented what had grown into a long narrative story, with a much larger canvas than the original, the opinion of my publishers was that it was not so much a revision of an earlier story as a new book. It was as a new book that I gave it the title, *The Lynmara Legacy*.

C.G.

Contents

Prologue

February 28th, 1974

The woman looked towards the house, and then at her watch. They would soon be coming. Although the days were lengthening at this dead end of winter, this day had been overcast and showery: the dusk was drawing in. She had come, dressed in a raincoat and wellingtons, to take her usual afternoon walk. It looked as if the rain would be on her again before she reached the house.

It had been rotten weather for an election, she thought. A week of mild, spring-like weather, and now this sudden return to winter. And what a winter it had been. The rumble of discontent in the nation's throat had been an audible thing—the endless strikes, the picketing, the scarcities, the unheated rooms; even the television sets, which the people had come to rely on to soothe and sedate them, had, for a time, been blackened early. And then the politicians had realized that that move had been the most unpopular of all, and had hastily cancelled it. Politicians didn't change much, the woman thought. It had been, quite certainly, the winter of England's discontent. She was in a mess, but unlike all the other messes she had been in, there seemed this time no will to get out of it. No one seemed to know the way.

The woman moved briskly across the sodden grass. She didn't intend to see any of her children until the drink period before dinner, when she would be changed and ready to face them. She had decided what she would wear, and it would be her most becoming. She would even wear some jewels. They would come, her children, and they'd sit up most of the night, first watching the returns on TV, and then when that closed down, they'd sit with the radio on, half-asleep until some new result was flashed, and there would be pleasure or gloom, depending on which of her children it was. They'd probably drink quite a lot, and arguments would start. Between two of them, at least, insults would be traded, as one day, she expected, they would trade professional insults across the aisle of the House of Commons.

This election had come just too soon for either of them to have been adopted as a candidate for any constituency. By next election, she guessed, they'd be in the thick of it, each fighting for a seat, and each scorning and hating the political philosophy of the other. The others would go about their various businesses, making the most of whatever came their way, even profiting from times as black as these because they had an eye for the main chance, and they might even pick up fortunes in their time. Her only daughter, Judith, with a First in Economics from Cambridge, was potential Cabinet material, someone had told her, even though she had yet to fight her first election. 'Brilliant and beautiful women in politics are a rare combination,' was what had been said. And this one had been born with battle in her blood.

Well, they would all be there, growling at one another to-morrow because they'd had too little sleep, and because they were divided about 'what to do about Mother and the house.' This weekend had been arranged as if it had been happen-stance, and because it was her birthday; and yet she knew it was the result of much telephoning among them. It had been some time since they had all been there together. They had sounded too casual as they'd each telephoned saying they'd like to come this weekend. '. . . dying for a break in the country after all this electioneering, Mother . . .' But whichever way the election swung, there was a sense of an end and a beginning. Things could not go on as they had been going with the country. It seemed to be much their idea that things also had to change with their mother and with the house.

The woman smiled to herself with a touch of grimness. Well, they would have a few shocks before the weekend was out. They were beginning to understand the state of the family trusts, and they feared that the trusts were not going to support the house any longer—not with death duties to pay. She, their mother, would be settled comfortably, and they would take care of it all; but their care didn't extend to the house. 'An anachronism,' Judith called it. 'I'm ashamed to say I've ever lived here.' The others were less blunt because they weren't Socialists, and they weren't ashamed of ever having lived here. But they were wor-ried about those interlocking trusts, and how their own pockets were affected; they might try to close ranks to see that no more money went into the endless sump-hole of the house. But what wasn't in the family trusts, wasn't theirs to order. They knew nothing about the other money. They thought they could order and arrange it all, and between them, they represented a formidable array—the Establishment itself, yes, even Judith with her dogmatic espousal of Socialism was part of the Establishment. Among them they represented the Army, banking, law, the Church, and all with strong political leanings—this had always been a political house. She had bred a brilliant clutch of children, and she had bred them *for* this house. Well, they were going to have a job to shift her from here. And for the first time in their lives, they were going to hear why she wouldn't be shifted, and how the money was there to make sure she could bargain.

Election Day in the winter of Britain's discontent. Well, she'd lived through other times when it had seemed Britain could never make it, when things like this house were to go for ever—bombed, or simply taken over by the conqueror, or taxed out of existence. She remembered very well those other times. They had once stood on the very edge, almost plunged into the blackness of defeat. It hadn't happened then; she couldn't believe it would now.

The rain started to fall again, and the woman quickened her step. Then she saw that the first of the cars had arrived, and she frowned. She hadn't meant to be caught in a raincoat and old headscarf. She didn't want to look like an ageing woman, which she was. They were going to hear some surprising things, these children of hers, and she planned to make the maximum effect on them. She had made a special effort with the food for this long weekend. Even brought down extra help from London so that everything should function as smoothly as possible, the way it had once been—in the days before the war. The way they never remembered it. And she had brought out her jewellery from the bank, so that she would outshine the wives, dazzle them perhaps, while she told them where the money was coming from, the money that would keep this house and its treasures intact.

She had had two great passions in her life. One had been for one man only, and the other for this house. The house still remained, and with it, a part of England. So long as she could fight to prevent it, she'd be damned if she'd see it dismantled, taken from her.

11

Part 1

Anna

CHAPTER 1

February 28th, 1931

It was raining. A venomous wind tore at the tattered awning of the drugstore and rattled a loose trash-can lid. Piles of dirty snow still lay around from the last fall, and in the gutters the rain was turning it into freezing slush. Nicole Rainard paused on the steps leading from the subway and looked out into the dimness about her. The rain, blown in gusts, swept the sidewalks, and showed itself in slanting torrents against the light from the street lamps.

Nicole glanced down at her shoes. They'd get soaked, and perhaps ruined; the walk to Mrs Burnley's was a long one. She shrugged, and decided she couldn't wait here. Fastening the collar of her coat high about her throat, she bent her head against the driving rain and stepped out from the half-shelter of the subway entrance. As she turned the corner at the end of the block, she was shielded from the wind, and the rain seemed to slacken. She quickened her pace a little. It was getting late. Anna would be annoyed with her for being on the street at this time. Anna was particular about things like that. Glancing up at the dingy buildings that lined the street, most of them showing lights through an assortment of curtains like eyes in an ageing battered face, she reflected that this part of Brooklyn, shuttered against the rain, with newspaper and rubbish mixed in the heaps of soot-laden snow, was one of the ugliest places she knew. At the best of times it was never a beauty spot, but in bad weather, she thought contemptuously, it was like the end of the earth. She sighed, hoping that Anna would be reasonable about her good news. If she was, there was a chance to leave this behind—they could get away from it. Yet, at the back of her mind she was doubtful. Anna was not an easy person to reason with, nor was she easily swayed. Nicole knew it would be difficult to make her understand that it was time she left school behind her and began to make her own way in the world.

15

Tomorrow was her sixteenth birthday, and at that age most girls who lived in this neighbourhood were already working. Anna had been unmoved by this observation last time they had talked of it. She told her tersely not to worry about what anyone else did. While the school fees could be paid, she must think nothing about a job; her education was only halfway through. It made Nicole uneasy. Anna seemed to expect so much from her, demanding to know, and to have demonstrated, what Nicole had achieved at the end of each term. She was hard on poor results, and only partly satisfied with good ones. She would often ask Nicole to read aloud to her—in English or French. Anna could speak and read French fluently herself, though with an accent. Her English was correct, though here also the accent was obvious, and even after all these years away from Russia, she still listened to English carefully, and attempted to correct her own mistakes of pronunciation. For Anna, language was like music, and to hear it badly executed was painful to her ears. So she listened to her own voice, and listened to Nicole's, and she was savage with any trace of the Brooklyn accent which might creep in. For some reason she refused ever to teach Nicole any Russian. 'That's all finished—a long time ago. You'll never go to Russia. Forget it.'

Nicole's shoes were wet through and she was cold when she reached the narrow, shabby brownstone which was rented in small apartments by the owner, Mrs Burnley. There was no one in the dingy front hall. She remembered that most of the tenants played poker together in the Lynches' apartment on Friday nights. She could hear the murmur of voices as the door closed behind her, and the sound of the wind was muted. As Nicole mounted the stairs, she noticed that there were three broken steps now; there had been two when she had been home for a few days at Christmas. This area was fringing Bedford-Stuyvesant and going down steadily in the world. Mrs Burnley either couldn't or wouldn't spend money on repairs. She reached the second floor and knocked on the door of the rear apartment. After a while when there was no answer and no sounds from inside, she tried the handle. It was, of course, locked.

'You lookin' for your mom?'

Nicole swung around. Mrs Burnley stood at the foot of the stairs. 'Yes,' she said.

'Well, she ain't here.' Mrs Burnley smoothed the front of her soiled dress delicately. Nicole recognized the gesture. It was one Mrs Burnley used when she was trying to draw information.

Nicole thought of the locked door. Anna might not be back for hours. She did not relish the thought of sitting on the stairs waiting for her. 'Do you know where my mother is, Mrs Burnley?'

'Sure. She's at Lucky Nolan's this time of night.'

'Lucky Nolan's?'

'Sure, the joint where she works.'

Nicole winced, and hoped it didn't show. She came to the head of the stairs. 'Have you any idea when she'll be back?' she asked quietly.

The woman shrugged. 'Who knows if she'll come? These days she usually only comes Sundays.'

'Sundays . . .?'

'That's what I said. Don't know why she bothers to keep this place on. Must have something closer to Lucky Nolan's, I'd guess. Them nightclubs don't close until all hours, y'know. Like I said, she only uses this place Sundays and when you're around.'

Nicole gripped the banister. The words seemed to spin around in her brain. Anna in a nightclub! It was ridiculous. The old fool didn't know what she was talking about. Yet Mrs Burnley had a nose for information, and it seldom proved wrong. But Anna in a nightclub. Why?—she had a perfectly good job as a receptionist with a law firm, with some overtime when they needed extra help with routine filing. But Nicole felt an uneasy sense of having been fooled by this façade of a receptionist's job. The woman standing below her had no need to fabricate such lies; they were too easily denied. Suddenly Nicole realized that it might be time to question what she had never questioned before—things like her mother's reluctance ever to talk about her job. 'It's boring and dead-end, Nicole. There's nothing to talk about; and the fact that she had given strict instructions that she must never be called there except in a case of extreme urgency. 'They don't like personal telephone calls.' Nicole realized that while she had a telephone number, she didn't know the name of the firm for which Anna worked, nor the address. 'A Wall Street firm,' was all Anna had ever said. She wondered if the nightclub job was something extra—extra to make more money. But that didn't make sense. No one could work all day and half the night as well. Mrs Burnley was watching her closely. If she was waiting for her to express surprise, Nicole decided that she was going to be disappointed. 'Do you know where this Lucky Nolan's place is, Mrs Burnley?' she asked casually.

'You ain't figgerin' on goin' there, are you?'

Nicole nodded.

Mrs Burnley shook her untidy head slowly. 'I wouldn't do that if I was you, kid. Your mom might get kinda upset if you was to turn up sudden-like. If I hunt around, I'll probably find that telephone number she gave me to call if anything was wrong. I could call from the drugstore. Then she'd be sure to come home if she knew you was here.' Her tone grew a little more expansive. 'You can sleep in Spike's bed if you want. Ain't seen him for near two weeks now, so it ain't likely he'll come strollin' in tonight.'

Nicole eyed her with distaste. She had only seen the roving Spike once or twice, and she had no intention of sleeping in his bed. 'No, thank you. I want to find my mother. Do you know where this place is?'

'Sure I know where it is. But I don't reckon you should go there. It's gettin' late.'

'I'll be all right.'

'You're sure anxious to see your mom, aren't you? Reckon it must be somethin' mighty important to bring you all the way down from that school.'

'Yes, it is important.' Nicole held her tone even. She mustn't insult this woman, but she wouldn't tell her what she wanted to know.

'You could tell me what it is. I'd see your mom got the message.'

'I must see my mother myself.'

Mrs Burnley shrugged her fat shoulders. 'I guess it's not much use arguin' with you. Got a mind of your own. Don't say I didn't warn you if your mom's all upset with you.' She dragged a greasy lock of hair back and tried to tuck it into her knot at the back of her head, jabbing aggressively with a large hairpin. Nicole thought Mrs Burnley would have liked to jab her. 'Well —you take the subway from Rafferty's corner. The B train. That'll get you straight across to Manhattan. Get off at Times Square. Then ask someone—better ask a cop—where the

Arthur Keenan Theatre is. It's somewhere about 44th–45th Street. Lucky Nolan's is in the same block. You won't miss it. It's a big place.'

'Thank you, I'll find it.' Nicole started down the stairs. When she reached the bottom, Mrs Burnley laid a restraining hand on her shoulder. 'Better let me call, kid. Your mom's going to be mad as hell with me for lettin' you go there. They might not even let you in—you bein' so young. There's laws about things like that. Look—I've got a pot of coffee just made. You sit awhile and have some while I hunt about for that telephone number ... Then *you* can go to the drugstore and call. Yeah, better do it that way, kid.'

'No, thank you, Mrs Burnley, I'll go now.' Nicole brushed past her and opened the front door. She managed to squeeze out 'Thank you,' before she shut it firmly behind her.

The standard reply 'You're welcome,' died on Mrs Burnley's lips. For a second she watched the girl's shadow on the door, heard her steps on the stone stairs; and then the sound of the rain took over. To hell with her, she thought. Stubborn as hell, and too damned high and mighty to condescend to a night in Spike's bed, or even a friendly cup of coffee. Well, let her take what was coming. She licked her lips a little at the thought of the confrontation. Mrs Burnley knew all about the supposed job at the law firm; she also knew a good deal about Lucky Nolan's. She was sorry she was going to miss the row between them—the mother and daughter. They were both stuck-up as all get out, only the mother had learned where it was good to keep a few friends. The kid had the looks of a fighter, but she had a lot of learning to do.

Nicole hurried along the wet sidewalk, her cold hands thrust deep into the pockets of her overcoat. The brush with Mrs Burnley had left her angry and disturbed. The place, this Lucky Nolan's, must be something special, or else Mrs Burnley wouldn't know so much about it. It was hard to be told about it by Mrs Burnley, instead of Anna. Nicole knew very well Anna would be annoyed when she appeared. She disliked being questioned. But it seemed to Nicole that the time had come for questions. There were too many things that had been let go, year after year, no questions asked, so no answers needed. She wondered suddenly why she had been content to allow things to drift on like this without ever asking. Because it was easier not to? Her own thoughts accused her. She and her mother spent so much time apart. They were not companions, not friends—just mother and daughter. Nicole was now aware of a need to draw closer to Anna. This whole scheme she had come to discuss had this nub of need at the heart of it. She looked up at the crumbling brownstone as she walked. She had been eight years old when Anna had sent her away from here, and in the years between it had reached the stage of decay when it could rightly be called a slum. She had hardly noticed. It was just a place she came to for a few days over Christmas, and again at Easter. Every year, for two weeks, she and Anna went to the same place in Maine for a vacation. Anna had made it easy for her, and had somehow kept her a child. She was aware that the kids who lived here year-round didn't stay children long. Out of her memory she dredged the sounds from childhood—the family fights, the crying babies, the women quarrelling, and the sometimes heartbroken sobbing in the night. She could remember all of it, the sprawling, teeming life that erupted about her, and before it could touch her too deeply, or put its mark indelibly on her, Anna had sent her away to the convent. So she was younger now than she would have been if she'd stayed, and suddenly her youth was screaming out for experience, for life. But Anna had seen to it that it would not be this sort of life. For the first time it occurred to Nicole to stand back and view her mother from this angle. Seen from here, Anna was a very strange person.

She began to run because the rain was becoming heavier. She felt the drops splashing coldly against her face. The rim of her absurd school hat was bending under the onslaught. She was very cold on this February night, the night before her sixteenth birthday, running along the frozen sidewalks in the wrong part of Brooklyn.

Head down she turned the corner and almost collided with a police officer.

He caught her by the shoulder. 'Hey, wait a minute. Where do you think you're going in such a hurry?' He swung her around so that the street light shone full in her face. 'It's you— the Rainard kid? Right?'

'Yes,' she said.

'What are you doing here? I thought you were at school this time of year. You haven't left, have you?'

'No—not yet,' she answered, freeing herself from his hold.

'Lookin' for your mom?'

'Yes.'

'She'll be at work now.'

'Yes,' she said, making it sound as if the fact didn't surprise her. 'That's where I'm going.'

'Well, I don't think you should.' His voice wasn't unkind, just firm. 'They rightly shouldn't let you in there. And your mom wouldn't want you running around this time of night.' It stung her that he, like Mrs Burnley, seemed to know so much about what should have been her business, but hadn't been, until this night.

'I couldn't get in at home, Officer.' She had remembered, from a long way back, his name. O'Neil. He had been on this beat a long time. She could remember seeing him on the steps of the church at Christmas and Easter. Not that she and Anna attended his church; they didn't seem to have any part of any of the melding religions of this area. Suddenly, that was strange too.

'You're going to Nolan's then?'

She nodded. The rain beat on O'Neil's cap; she watched it running in little streams down his oilskins.

'Look—I finish in a half-hour. Suppose you just wait at Mrs Burnley's and I'll pick you up there after I leave the station. See you down into the subway—make sure you get into a coach with a few decent-looking ladies in it. Your mom—well, she's a real nice lady, and she would want me to look out for you ...'

Nicole broke in with cool logic. 'But if I do that it will just be that much later—and in the time while I'm waiting I could be there, almost. I think I can take care of myself. I'll be careful.'

He peered at her closely. Suddenly his mouth widened into a grin. 'Yes, I guess you can take care of yourself. Only just move right along. Keep well in the light. If a man comes near you— scram. Well ...' He straightened himself. 'S'long, kid. I'll be seeing you again sometime. Easter, maybe.'

Nicole smiled, and suddenly O'Neil seemed to be looking at a different person. 'Good night, Officer.'

He watched her as she went. 'Good night, Officer.' From any other kid in the neighbourhood it would have sounded like cheek, but from her it was quite natural. He felt as if he had

21

been dismissed, but in the nicest possible way. Rainard. The mother was foreign, of course, but there was no trace of it in the way the kid spoke. But she didn't speak much like an American either. Her accent was clipped, almost English. He searched his memory for more facts about her, but there were surprisingly few, considering how long Anna Rainard and her child had lived here, and how little privacy was possible in this sort of neighbourhood, especially if you rented from Mrs Burnley. The kid had been sent to some school in Connecticut, he remembered. They seldom saw her after that, and saw little enough of the mother, either. Kept to themselves. Gave no one any trouble. Paid their bills. That in itself was out of the ordinary. He couldn't even remember seeing Anna Rainard in the company of a man, and she didn't have visitors to her flat, either. That was all he knew. His curiosity stirred, he reminded himself to ask about her at the station. Someone had to know where the mother spent all the nights she didn't return to Mrs Burnley's. Someone always knew.

He kept his measured pace, automatically glancing at the shuttered store-fronts, trying a few locks, watching for the figures of drunks slumped in doorways. The rain had driven them into the holes. The bars would soon be emptying. It didn't occur to him that what he saw was ugly, as it had to Nicole Rainard. It was just as it always was. He didn't think about it. He had lived with it most of his life.

But something warmed him as he walked. He kept remembering the smile of the girl, and the way she had looked up at him from that fringe of dark lashes. There hadn't been much else to see—just a skinny kid in a dowdy school coat and a drooping rain-soaked hat, a kid with pale, pale skin and big eyes, grey or kind of purplish-blue—he couldn't remember. And the way that face had been transformed by her smile. There was a kind of power in the way she used those eyes and granted that smile, as if she were bestowing some kind of favour. Something else had been there in the face, the expression of the kid, something one glimpsed occasionally in the face of a woman, and if she had it, it hardly mattered whether she was beautiful or not. The kid was too young to be beautiful, but she'd got whatever it was—that power to stir and arouse. Easy, O'Neil, he told himself—easy. Lie down, boy. She was only a kid. He felt a vague shame that he should think of her in this way, but he continued to enjoy it. He told himself it was all right to enjoy the half-promise in that look and smile, to enjoy it only because she was no longer with him, standing beside him. But he also told himself he wouldn't want to tangle with whatever that power was when the kid was no longer a kid.

CHAPTER 2

Nicole did as Mrs Burnley had directed, and found her own way to Lucky Nolan's. She didn't want another encounter with a policeman who might tell her to go home. The marquee of the Arthur Keenan Theatre was visible from Seventh Avenue, and just beyond it was the neon that heralded Lucky Nolan's. It was discreet enough, and it looked expensive. She waited some time, judging the type of people who went in. They were in evening dress, and several came in chauffeured cars. It was the kind of sight you could still see in a country in the midst of a depression. There was still money about, and people wanted to spend it. She didn't think she wanted to present herself, as she was now dressed, to the uniformed doorman. There was, however, a smaller door farther along, with a tiny sign which indicated it also was Lucky Nolan's—Trade Deliveries. She rang there. After a while a small grilled space in the door opened, and she found herself under scrutiny. 'Well,' a man's voice said, 'what do you want?'

'Could I ... could I speak to Anna Rainard?'

'No one of that name here. Beat it kid.'

She suddenly remembered the name she had seen, in very small letters, under the banner of the big-name band, at the doorway. 'Well ... er, Anna Nicholas.' Nicholas had been her mother's maiden name.

There was a much longer, silent scrutiny this time. 'She expectin' you?'

'Yes.' She lied without blinking. 'Yes.'

'Can't let minors in. Against the law.'

'I'm her daughter.'

'Her daughter ...?' The small grille snapped closed, and the door itself was partially opened. What the man saw outside was the dripping, huddled figure of a young girl. He saw an embroidered crest on her hatband, a dark tie slipped about the

24

collar of a white blouse. He saw the identical crest on the pocket of the streaming raincoat.

'Hey, you could be a trap from ...' He had been about to say 'from the vice squad,' but the words died on his lips. If the vice squad had ever employed anyone like this, he had yet to hear about it. Besides, the upturned face, in the glare of the spotlight above the door, with the rain pelting past it, was remarkably like the woman she claimed as her mother.

The door opened grudgingly, farther. 'I guess you can come in. But make yourself small, will you, kid? You can't see her now. She's about to go on ... And listen, if you see a cop, beat it!'

She squeezed past him, out of the rain, into the warm and dimly-lit corridor. He was a very tall man, dressed in evening clothes that seemed too small for his frame, and worn uneasily. 'Band's just ready for a break,' he said, prodding her forward ahead of him. 'Anna's going on.' As he spoke the final bars of a popular number went into their crescendo. There was a burst of applause, and then the clatter of heels as about six scantily-dressed girls rushed past them, heading for dressing-rooms down the passage. There were curious glances at Nicole, the strange figure she cut in the drooping hat; but the fact that the tall man stood with her seemed to make them hurry past. 'Hi, Danny,' one offered with a touch of bravado. Danny's popularity didn't seem to be his strongest asset.

'You want to hear her?' the man said. Nicole nodded. 'Over here.' He led her along the passage to where a space opened up and she could see the men of the band leaving their positions behind their music stands. For a moment while they passed, Danny stood in front of her so that she was hardly seen. Then when they were gone, he moved aside. She smelled whisky and brilliantine from his closeness. She wished he would go away. 'You can listen, kid, but don't let anyone see you. You don't exactly look like something from the chorus line. Well ... there's Anna now.'

In trying to move away from him she had missed the moment when Anna had emerged from the other side of the small stage. Her arrival caused no great stir in the crowd. Anna seated herself at the piano. By moving just a little bit sideways, Nicole could now see part of the closely packed room. Smoke swirled in the lights. The people gave orders to waiters and went on talking.

25

There was a smell stronger than Danny's brilliantine and whisky; it was the smell of the rich out to enjoy themselves. It was the first time Nicole had ever smelled it, and she was never to forget it. At that moment it was hard to believe there was not only a depression in America, but there was a Prohibition law too. In this gathering, neither seemed to exist.

Anna began to play. It wasn't what Nicole expected—but then she hardly knew what to expect any more. Remembering Anna's insistence on her studying classical music from the time she had been four, to hear Anna herself take up a steady jazz beat was a shock. She couldn't tell if Anna was good—she didn't know enough about it, and the people gathered at their tables seemed to pay no attention. She risked a further, longer look out into the room, trying to judge better the reaction of the audience, but they weren't really an audience, and Anna's music was just a background to their talk. Then she felt Danny's hand on her shoulder. 'O.K. kid. That's far enough.'

She turned and looked up at him, while obediently moving back. 'Do they like her?' she said.

He shrugged. 'They don't have to. Anna just fills in while the band takes a break. Got to give them time to order more drinks, get a bit of food into them. Well ...' he was studying her face, and perhaps saw that it registered disappointment. 'Anna's O.K. Duke Ellington she ain't, but she's O.K. Keeps them happy enough. Top class entertainer would want them all nice and quiet and that ain't good for business. She does well enough. Now look, kid, I don't have all night to stand here yakkin' with you. Got to keep my eye on a few things. You'll have to wait while Anna finishes. I'll see she gets the message that she's got a visitor. And you'd better wait in Lucky's room. Any cop sticks his big nose in here, he'd better not see you. We don't pay off to the cops and the rackets for havin' minors on the premises. You'd better come with me ...'

He led her to a smoothly carpeted, windowless room, where the sound of the piano and the crowd hardly penetrated. It was a curiously impersonal room, with a large desk, armchairs, panelling, a decorator's room which the occupant had never disturbed. 'Wait here,' Danny said. 'She'll be about fifteen minutes.'

In that time Nicole had a chance to recover herself. The room was warm; she took off her dripping hat and wet coat. She didn't want to lay them on any of the upholstered chairs, so she folded them neatly and put them on the floor. It was a schoolgirl's gesture, which she recognized, but was powerless to change. It was enough, for one night to be sitting here, a very long way from the school she had left that afternoon, trying to bring into focus a mother who wore a totally different aspect from the one she had adopted through the years. Nicole had a resentful feeling of having been tricked, and yet she had to acknowledge that she had only been tricked because she had been a willing dupe. She hadn't wanted to ask questions. Now she couldn't avoid them.

Anna came at last. Nicole had heard the applause, rather perfunctory, and had braced herself. Anna came in and closed the door quickly behind her. There was no greeting except the tense words, 'What are you doing here?'

'I had to see you.'

'Something's wrong?'

'Nothing wrong. I just wanted to talk to you.'

'It couldn't be that important. You could have written. I've told you always to write.'

'This time I didn't. Perhaps it's just as well ...'

Anna came closer, and her face loosened a little. 'Yes, perhaps just as well. It makes it easier if you see it all at once. Saves a lot of explaining.'

'Was it necessary? I mean—couldn't I have known a long time ago? I felt a fool tonight. I went to Mrs Burnley's. She told me where to come. And then I ran into Officer O'Neil. *He* knew where you worked.'

Anna managed a tight smile. 'Well, it looked better on the books of your school. I went to the Reverend Mother. I gave her the story. A respectable but not highly-paid job with a law firm. A tiny widow's pension—which I really didn't have, but it sounded good and I used it to explain the school fees. What could I tell her? A nightclub entertainer? She would have understood, of course. They're women of the world. But it mightn't have sounded nice to the parents of the other girls. That's what polite lies are all about, Nicole. And,' she added, 'it's your sixteenth birthday tomorrow.'

'You remembered?'

'Don't I always?'

It was true. She always did. She remembered meticulously.

27

There was always a birthday gift, something serviceable, like clothing, always of good quality, and something unexpected, but always in the same vein, like the beautifully bound folio of the Beethoven sonatas which had arrived last year, and which the nuns had exclaimed over. No one else in the school had anything like that. Nicole had seen it, though, as something she was expected to measure up to. It was a hard measure.

Anna ended the silence. 'Well, I'm still waiting. Why did you come? I'm surprised they let you travel alone—without telling me you were coming.'

'Sister Berthe was supposed to telephone the office—' Suddenly Nicole choked on the word. 'The number you gave. She's a little absent-minded. I didn't remind her. I suppose I was afraid you'd say I wasn't to come. I wanted you to hear it from me.'

Anna seated herself in one of the armchairs; she leaned back as if she was prepared to do a lot of listening, or a lot of talking. Nicole remained perched on the edge of hers. She licked her suddenly dry lips. Her mother had always been a remote figure to her, for all that they had shared rooms during all the summer vacations they had spent together. Until this moment the relationship had been of a mother to a child, the one who gave instructions rather than confidences. But Nicole knew that subtly she had passed over a line with Anna. Not yet an adult, but no longer a child; the relationship would and must alter.

'It's about a job,' Nicole said abruptly.

'What sort of a job?'

'Well, that's it. It's the sort of job that you ... well, I thought it was very like what you were doing, and since it's in Wall Street, I thought we ... well, that part of it doesn't make much difference now.'

'Yes ...?' The dark-red nails began to tap on the arm of the chair.

'It's with a very big Wall Street law firm—one of the vice-presidents had a daughter who had been to St Columba's. He likes the kind of girl they turn out. The job had been arranged six months ago, but the girl who was going broke an arm last week, and now she can't take the job. They need someone—someone with good shorthand and typing. I'd only be a very junior secretary in the beginning, but the man said there's plenty of opportunity. Mother Mary Helena asked me if I wanted to try. Sixteen tomorrow ... they always remember how old a girl is. And she must wonder how you manage to pay the fees ... the books, the clothes, the music. In fact she mentioned that to me. "It might be a good chance for you, Nicole, to start with a famous and highly reputable firm. And it would relieve your mother of quite a financial burden." You see, they *do* think of money. They know the school's expensive. They can't help that. But they're not unaware that some people find it rather hard going to get up the money—especially in these times. Almost everyone in that school comes from a well-to-do family, but there are a few, just a few, who don't. I think the nuns are aware of it, and try to help.'

'They should mind their own business. When the fees aren't paid is the time to start worrying.'

Nicole flushed. 'I don't think that's fair. Mother Mary Helena was only ...'

Anna gestured. 'Let's forget about what Mother Mary Helena thinks. What *I* think is this. That you'll forget all about a job. You're only sixteen, and you're not going to throw away whatever's been done for you—well, let *me* be fair, too—what you've managed to do yourself—just to rush at the first thing that offers.'

'I have to go to work some time.'

'Not yet.' Anna looked down meditatively at her hands, very beautiful hands Nicole was suddenly aware. Then her eyes came back sharply to her daughter's face. 'Nicole, would you like to go to college?'

'I don't understand.'

'There's nothing to understand. It's very simple.'

'Oh, yes there is something to understand. There's money. You know—tuition, board, books, clothes. There are millions of people looking for jobs. It isn't likely I'll pick up a job waiting on table to help out.'

'Who said anything about waiting on table? Forget about a job. Do you want to go to college?'

'I'd love it. But you haven't answered my question. Money. The question of *money*.'

A gleam of interest and humour flickered in Anna's eyes. 'Well, at last I begin to hear something. At last you want to know something about money. Perhaps you *have* grown up in

29

this last year. I've been waiting for it, and thinking sometimes it would never happen. I thought you might always be like your father. He was so charming, your father. And part of his charm was that he never thought about money. Money was a language he didn't understand, like ... well, let's say like Russian. Of course he'd never had to think about it when he was growing up. That was half the trouble. The rest was just a sweet, wilful determination *not* to think about it. If one didn't think about it, it would take care of itself. Perhaps that's what made him, at times, a very good salesman of very expensive cars. He always assumed that whomever he talked to had never thought about money either. All they were interested in was the very finest car in the world. Money was no object. It was surprising how many people he sold cars to, and how well we lived off his commissions. He never saved, naturally. That wouldn't be in his nature. And since he didn't let me handle the money, I had no chance to. He was one of those true-blue Englishmen. He knew how to wear a well-cut suit, and he had the right tie. He went to Harrow. Did you know that? You never asked. He even had a year at Oxford. Didn't last longer than that. He wasn't the academic type, and he liked games and girls too much. They asked him not to come back. Not expelled, you understand. "Sent down" they call it. Just told he was wasting everyone's time. A born drifter, Stephen was—and very, very sweet. Your father was a gentleman, Nicole. I shouldn't really have minded that he didn't have a head for money. One money-grubber in the family is enough.'

Anna glanced around the room before she spoke again. 'You don't like this place, do you, Nicole? Or the way I look. I don't blame you for that. That's what I've tried to put into you—a sense of what's class, and what isn't. But it doesn't do to be too much of a snob, you know. You're just the faintest bit snobbish about the source of money, where it comes from. Stephen was too. He didn't like where his father's money came from. But look a little harder at where the fathers of the girls you go to school with got *their* money. In about half the cases you'd find it wasn't old money. They haven't had it around for a few generations, which is usually what makes money smell sweet——' She frowned tightly as Nicole broke in.

'Is this lecture getting us anywhere, Mother? Mrs Burnley isn't "old money". Nor Officer O'Neil. They both knew where you earned your money. I didn't. And I didn't like it.'

Anna shrugged. 'I'm sorry you had it come to you like that. I should have moved away from there some time ago. I suppose I thought you'd stay a kid for a while longer. I got careless. I was going to put the whole idea of college to you at Easter, and if you'd wanted college, I'd have moved somewhere else. The trouble was always explaining how I could manage the fees and all the rest for the school on a trumped-up job as a receptionist. I cried poor-mouth a bit to Mother Mary Helena. There was a slight reduction of fees. I'm careful with my money, Nicole. I'm not like your father. I take a bargain where I find it. If you'd said "yes" to college at Easter, I would have found somewhere else before your last year at school. That part of Brooklyn isn't for girls who go to Radcliffe or Vassar.'

'But *you* don't live there, do you? Mrs Burnley told me you're only there Sundays now.'

A coldness closed on Anna's face again. 'So Mrs Burnley started talking, did she? I've always tried to prevent that happening—I've always tried to be there whenever you were.' Then she shrugged. 'Well, so you know. I *had* to have some address for the school, and for a long time I used to trail off to Brooklyn every morning just so that it looked all right. I'm getting older now. I don't care for the subway ride at five in the morning. And not in evening dress, either.' Her tone was deliberately crisp. 'For the last four years I've hardly used the Brooklyn apartment at all. Who can sleep during the day in a place where the kids are always crying, and the women slinging insults at each other up and down the stairs? It was coming to an end, in any case. I would have had to tell you. Perhaps I was waiting until you asked. Yes, perhaps I was just waiting until you woke up—and asked. I knew if once you asked, you'd be ready, almost, for the answer.'

'Perhaps I'm ready.'

'You'll just have to be.' Anna fingered the lamé of her dress. 'I won't even ask you to guess how much this cost. It cost plenty. The place where I spend my nights costs quite a packet each month, too. It's only a one-room efficiency, but it's on Central Park West, and the cab ride from here is not too long. I couldn't pay for that, Nicole—not the apartment and the dress and the other things I have to have in this job – and pay your school fees as well—on what I earn here. Hell, pianists are a dime a dozen.

There's a depression on. They'll work for eating money, these days.'

'Where does it come from—the money?'

'The name of this place is Lucky Nolan's, Nicole. Remember it. Lucky Nolan actually exists. He's a man. Quite a man. Oh, a little bit rough, but still quite a man. I've known him almost ten years. Eight years ago you went to St Columba's. He saw the point about not leaving you alone at nights—with just Mrs Burnley to look in on you. He's particular about things like that—and he knows the best costs money. He provided the money. It's as simple as that.'

'And you ...?'

'Find it hard to say? I'm his girl-friend—his mistress—whatever you want to call it. You see now why I kept on that Brooklyn address. Central Park West would have puzzled Mother Mary Helena. They're not such fools, those nuns. She might not have kept you.'

'This ... this Lucky Nolan ...?'

Anna's eyes grew angry. 'Don't say it like that, Nicole. You *are* a snob, you know. Lucky's a very decent guy. Not a gentleman, of course. Not like your father. But he's decent, and generous. He likes me. He's stuck by me all these years. And I've stuck by him. I'm not ashamed of it. He's paid up cheerfully for everything you've needed. He's that sort of guy. He's got a big family himself. Five kids. And he knows that kids cost plenty. A real family man, he is. Every Sunday he spends all day with them. After Mass he drives them all out into the country. Takes the whole of Christmas off to spend with them. And four days at Easter. He takes them to some big place in the Catskills for a month in the summer. That's when we—you and I, Nicole—go up to Maine. Yes, a good family man, Lucky is. That's why he's been so good to you.'

'Good ...' Nicole thought she would choke on the word. 'Good! What about his wife? Does *she* think he's a good family man?'

Anna's answer came swiftly. 'Nicole, I never ask. I just never ask. Lucky has manners, of his own kind. He's never discussed his wife. He never talks about any shortcomings. She may be an angel, for all I know. She may know about me—or she may not. Perhaps she prefers not to ask questions—just like me. There's no question of a divorce. I've never asked it, or expected it. I told you Lucky was a family man. He'd never give up his family. I'd be the one to go. I prefer to stay. I've no intention of causing trouble in his life. I once *did* have a receptionist's job. The money was far less than I earn here, and there was no Lucky to pay all the extras.'

'And you're going to put me through college on his money?'

Anna nodded, her gaze hardening at Nicole's tone. 'Yes.'

'I'm not going, then.'

'I rather expected you to take that attitude, Nicole. The trouble with you, you know, is that you're soft. I've sheltered you, and kept things from you all your life. That was how you seemed to want it. I've never encountered anyone who asked so few questions. If it weren't for your marks at school, I might even think you were a bit dumb. What you're dumb about, or afraid about, is reality. So far, nothing's ever hit you very hard, but after you've had a few knocks, you may learn to grab and hang on to anything that comes your way. I suppose you're more like your father than I thought. He was like you, squeamish about anything he thought was not quite playing the game.'

'Supposing I do go to college?—where does that get me? I still have to get a job in the end. If I'm as soft as you say, perhaps it's already time I toughened up.'

'Toughen up, by all means. The sooner the better. But do it in the right place. If you use your head and develop a little charm, you'll get invitations for the vacations. Then you'll know how confidence is acquired. I think you'll develop the feeling of being the equal of anyone—money or not—and that's pretty important if you're on view as a prospective daughter-in-law.'

Nicole dismissed this with a flick of her head. 'That's rubbish. If I ever do meet what you think is the right sort of man, and he falls in love with me, he'll marry me no matter what.'

'You think I don't know what I'm talking about, Nicole? Your view on this is quite as good as mine, since all you know about me is that I have a friend called Lucky Nolan, who will never marry me. You know something?—I do know what I'm talking about.' She gave a slight, rather grim laugh. 'That's one subject I do know quite a lot about. You've had a few shocks tonight, so one more won't hurt you too much, but it might make you see sense. Somehow I never thought I'd tell you about this. I never wanted to. It didn't seem any of your business. I didn't think I'd need to just to convince you about college and all the rest of it. But you're a stubborn, and in some ways, a rather arrogant little girl. Let me enlighten you.'

Nicole shifted uneasily. Suddenly she wished she had not come. She was learning too much. St Columba's seemed a haven which she should not have left. She remembered what Anna had said about having sheltered her. She felt a shiver of apprehension run through her. Was there always hurt concealed in truth and hard reality? Nicole didn't want to be hurt.

Anna was speaking. 'It was a long time ago,' she said. 'Perhaps all stories should start that way, but I wish it was even farther away, and I could forget about it. Even now when I think of it, it seems utterly fantastic that it could have happened. If I'd been older and more experienced, a bit more calculating, I might have thought I had somehow caused it to happen. But it wasn't that way. I was nineteen, and a real innocent, even if I was earning my own living, which wasn't very usual in those days—not unless you were someone's servant, or worked in a factory. I had never been either of those things— not in the true sense.'

Her tone became lower. 'I suppose it's better if I go back to the real beginning. You've never asked about that, either. What do you know about your grandparents?—nothing except that they were Russians who left Russia in 1907, stayed for two years in Paris, where your grandmother died, and then my father and I were in London for about two years when he died also. That's all you know because that's all you've ever asked. Your English grandparents—well, I couldn't tell you about them, since I never met them. Do you want to hear about Russia, Nicole—or do you think I'm going to produce some sweaty peasant saga which you'll be ashamed of?'

The girl in front of her squirmed, and said nothing.

'Well, I suppose my father was a servant in one sense, but a superior one, as things went in those days. He'd been born in St Petersburg, the son of a violin maker, and he studied piano at the Conservatoire. I suppose his father had hopes of him being a really great pianist, or even a composer, but he wasn't either of those things. Just a gentle, quiet man, with no real ambition except to get through life as best he could without hurting anyone. He married a young student at the Conservatoire, and both of them seemed delighted to be taken into the family of Prince

Michael Ovrensky, as music teachers. My father also doubled as a French master and my mother helped the English governess. Living in that way with a great Russian family wasn't at all like being a servant. They were part of the family, and so was I when I was born. Except that we ate and slept in our own rooms, we seemed no different to them. Yes, they had finer clothes, and grander presents at Easter and Christmas, but it didn't really matter. It never occurred to me, growing up, to feel jealous. I suppose we might have seemed like poor relations, but we were *relations*—not servants. The Princess Tatiana Fedorovna took as much care about my health as she did of her own daughters. She nursed my mother when she was ill. I shared the English governess with all the children, rode their ponies, went skating with them, went to their houses in Moscow and St Petersburg, went on holidays to the Black Sea. They were all very pious of course. The Princess used to pray for my mother to become pregnant again, because she knew she longed for another child, and if there had been another child, it would have been part of the family.

'Prince Michael's principal estate, Beryozovaya Polyaná, bordered on Count Leo Tolstoy's. The families used to exchange visits, and Prince Michael was very much influenced by Tolstoy. He was a happy madman, Prince Michael. He had about as much sense of money as a rabbit, and Russians as a whole never had been renowned for their money sense. He loved to gamble. It seemed a harmless pastime to him. The society in St Petersburg was a little fast, and gambling was a national mania. He had already freed his serfs, which cost him an enormous sum of money. He didn't seem to be aware of this part of it. Then one day he woke up to find he'd not only given away most of his fortune, but Tatiana Fedorovna's dowry as well. Gambled or given away, it hardly mattered. He was deeply in debt, and he had to close up the St Petersburg and Moscow houses, sell two estates, and half of the Beryozovaya Polyana estate. What would be left was barely enough to live on—for that family, at any rate. Since the children were almost grown, one of the economies was that they could easily do without the English governess and the music teachers. There was, by then, so little for my father and mother to do except to act as chaperones for the girls. I had been born at Beryozovaya Polyana. It was like announcing the end of the world to me when I was told we had

35

to leave. I was losing my brothers and sisters, my uncles and aunts. I was losing my whole world.

'Naturally Prince Michael was distressed at having to dismiss us, and he arranged with a friend that the three of us should immediately be taken into the family of good friends of his—a very rich family, where we would have had much the same position as with the Ovrenskys. My father was Russian enough not to want it. The Ovrenskys were *his* family. He would be with them, or with no one. That was when he determined to emigrate. He was going to America. It was the land of the free, wasn't it? It was the place where everyone was equal and had a chance to get rich—the place where there had never been serfs. Well—they weren't called serfs. There was much crying and embracing, many gifts when we left them. I don't think any of them envied us going. There'd been stirrings of revolution, of course, but no one ever imagined it would ever come to the overthrow of the Imperial Family and the whole system. Anarchists were appearing all over the world, not just in Russia. I remember crying myself sick when I left the Ovrenskys behind. It seemed such a cosy, familiar world—I can remember the samovars always ready for tea, the big stoves, the sweet cakes. I was certain that somehow the estates would be restored, the houses in St Petersburg and Moscow would be opened again. Everything would be just as it was. I was fifteen years old. It was 1907.

'We only got as far as Paris. My father had many introductions in Paris—and my mother was already ill from travel, and homesickness. Everyone seemed to need music teachers, and naturally we all spoke French. He taught music and we had rooms high up in a tall house overlooking Paris. It was pleasant enough, except that my mother didn't get better. My father had managed to have me accepted at the Conservatoire, and between lessons and practice and nursing my mother, there was no time for anything else. I remember my mother used to lie on her sofa and listen to me at my scales, and even when she was weakest she wouldn't let me skip one single half-hour of them. She died of tuberculosis when I was seventeen. She's buried in Père Lachaise cemetery.'

Anna looked sharply at Nicole. 'That's something you have always to remember. They say the tendency to it runs in the family. You must always have a proper diet, and plenty of rest.

You must never live in damp places. You must be very careful that colds never go to your chest——'

'Mother, you have other things to say, don't you? You know I'm as strong as a horse. I'm never ill.'

Anna seemed to have been brought rudely back to the present. 'It doesn't hurt to take care. Since I'm telling you about your grandmother, I might as well *tell* you. Just be careful, that's all. You don't *look* strong ...' Then she waved her hand. 'Oh, well. That's past. I hope for ever. My father seemed to think that way. He couldn't bear Paris after that. So we packed again, and he talked of America once more, but we only got as far as London. He took up teaching music again. It wasn't as good as Paris. There weren't so many Russian families in and out, coming for shopping, to see the sights, having friends there. In Paris we heard a lot of gossip from Russia. The Ovrenskys still wrote. They told us who was coming, and who we were to see. London was different. To start with, our English wasn't nearly as good as we had thought it. We learned, of course. It was necessary. My father took up his rounds, going from pupil to pupil. The best families. He had introductions from Paris. The houses were all in Belgravia or Mayfair. He had such nice manners, my father, and he never let anyone see that it hurt him to have to come in at the servants' entrance. He used to say "Ah, well, Mozart ate in the servants' hall." But he wasn't Mozart, and he was desperately homesick. We talked of going back to Russia, but kept putting it off. Then he took a chill, which turned to pneumonia. He didn't have the will to fight it. He hadn't really lived since he'd left Russia. The dream of America was just that—a dream. Russians are great dreamers, Nicole. The dream seemed to end with his death.

'I gathered myself up, of course, and went on. I'd been teaching a little myself, taking on pupils who were very young and ones he hadn't time to go to. My English had grown quite good. One learns more easily when one is young. I might have gone on just as he had done, but the pupils were not so numerous after he died. I had been accepted as a substitute for him because people thought some of his skill would rub off on me, but after he died the pupils seemed to drop away. Perhaps I wasn't as ready as he was to accept the things that I thought of as slights and insults from those terrible Englishwomen. I remember as I was leaving a house in Eaton Square one day, packing my music in the hall I heard one woman say to another in the drawing-room—I wonder why they always seem to think people like myself are deaf?—"My dear, she's far too pretty to have around any house where there are young gentlemen." I couldn't make myself go back to that house. You see, I had my time of being soft, too, Nicole. I was nineteen.'

Nicole thought her mother regarded her with more kindness in those moments. The memories of herself as a young girl had perhaps brought its own reaction. She was remembering that she was pure Russian, and she had been happy there. Looking at her mother's face, Nicole regretted the years that she had not asked for these memories to be shared. What had she been afraid of? Was Anna right in saying she had feared some peasant saga; if that was so, she was more than a snob, she was a coward also.

'It was then I was offered a steady job—more or less steady—with a small group who hired out to play at people's parties. Just a quartet—strings and a piano. Nothing serious either. Nothing more advanced than a waltz. Very genteel. It was 1911. We usually played behind a screen of potted plants. No one wanted to see the musicians. Everyone went to Ascot dressed in black. We found work rather hard to get. We were hired for small dinner parties at which no one danced, and for small balls for the débutantes who couldn't afford a really grand ball. It was a pretty lean time. Not everyone would have a lady pianist with the quartet, and then they called in someone else. I was running pretty low on the money my father had left.

'Around Christmas and New Year things picked up. People were giving parties. We were booked every night. It was New Year's Eve that I remember. I can remember everything about that house where we played. It was a dinner party for about twenty-four. We were to play in the hall. Noises off, sort of thing. They were going to a much bigger affair later, and we were going on to play at some other party. The dinner was over, I remember, and the ladies had gone to the drawing-room. The men were still having their port. The three others in the quartet had gone down to the kitchen to have their supper. I didn't go. I still wasn't used to eating in the kitchen. I suppose *I* was a snob, too, Nicole. Well, there I was behind the screen of plants, and a man came into the hall. He was looking around on all the chairs and the tables for his cigarette case. One of us had found it on the floor. We put it on the top of the piano, and I was to tell the hostess as soon as I could where it was. It was very heavy gold. I can remember how we all looked at it, and tried to figure how many nights pay for all of us it would have been worth. Well, there he was, and I guessed what he had come for, so I called to him. He came over and seemed surprised to find me behind the potted plants. I remember I was wearing the last of the good dresses Tatiana Fedorovna had given me. It was the best silk, but it had been made for a schoolgirl, and it was tight and too short. But he looked at me as if I were a queen, and from that moment the rest of the whole situation didn't matter. He asked me if I minded if he smoked, and he just sat there and talked to me. He asked most of the questions, and I found myself telling him all about Russia—at least the part I knew. He wanted to know more about the political side of things. All I could tell him was how things had been on the Ovrenskys' estates. All the world knew about Alexander II being blown to bits. He talked about the defeat by Japan in 1905 and about Bloody Sunday. He seemed to think there was something rotten in Russia, but I didn't agree with him. All I wanted was to get back there—to be with the Ovrenskys. I talked so much. I suppose I had become rather desperate for someone to talk to like that. He listened so well. He never went back to the dining-room, nor did he join the ladies in the drawing-room. In polite society, what he did that night was unforgivable. He even asked me to play for him—that was after I'd told him about being at the Conservatoire in Paris. I played "Für Elise"—it begins so gently, and I didn't want people to hear. Of course they heard. I can remember when I finished he was sitting there still as a cat on that chair, and the hostess was standing behind him with a face like a fury. "Really, Lord Manstone, I didn't know you had such a keen interest in classical music," she said, and he answered, "Neither did I, Mrs Tatenham. I'm just learning."

'The upshot of it was that I was invited—no, I was commanded into the drawing-room and ordered to play. The gentlemen had joined the ladies by then. They were all there, talking, talking, taking no notice at all of me. I think it was the hostess's idea to make me look ridiculous, and reprimand him. Well, I played better than I ever had before. I chose the Chopin "Military Polonaise." It was loud enough to rattle the coffee-cups, and by the time I was finished, a few of them had stopped talking, and a few were even decent enough to put their hands together in a little polite applause. "Really—quite an artiste, your little protégée, Lord Manstone. But I don't believe Miss—I don't believe this lady has had her supper. Her fellow musicians will be waiting ..."

'Well, I was out of the drawing-room like a slapped child, and this Lord Manstone was following me. He came downstairs, and that threw the kitchen into an uproar. The butler was furious, but he hadn't quite the nerve to order him out. He sat there while I ate, and then he drove me and the other three to the next party. He hadn't been invited to that party, but they let him in as if he were one of the musicians, until someone recognized him, and *that* seemed to be a great joke. It was five in the morning and very cold when he drove me home.

'I had about four weeks of that. When I was working, he would drive me to the house, and if he didn't know the people and couldn't get inside, he'd just wait in the car, freezing, probably. A few nights he said he was a friend just driving us all, and he was invited into the kitchen and the butler or the hostess never knew. When I wasn't playing, he took me to dinner. When I was playing, he waited and took me to a late supper somewhere. Heaven knows what he paid in tips to keep those waiters on their feet. He——'

'What was he like?' Nicole said. She felt the scepticism thicken her tone, and tried to stifle it. 'How old was he?'

Anna smiled. 'You think I picked up someone old enough to be my grandfather—just because he could drive me about and give me supper? It wasn't at all like that, Nicole. He was not only charming, with charming manners—at least to me—but he was twenty years old and unmarried. He was also extremely handsome. He was John Ashleigh, thirteenth earl of Manstone. I called him Johnny, and I fell very much in love with him, and, for a while, I do believe he was in love with me. At least he thought so himself—then. He asked me to marry him. I said "yes". Of course I said yes. What girl wouldn't have?

'I didn't know it, because I didn't read newspapers very much or society magazines, but we were the talk of fashionable London. Or the joke—both, I suppose. Naturally everyone assumed I was his mistress, though no one could figure out why I continued to go about and play half the night at little dinners.

I wasn't his mistress. We were as romantically in love as any two young people can be. We meant to get married.

'Then the talk must have reached his mother—his father had recently died. We were both summoned down to the family home in Kent. I suppose if I'd been English I might have known about Lynmara, might have heard it was one of the show-places of the country. I was used to something different, you see. The aristocracy in Russia were different. Extremely grand when it came to formal things and in their contacts with the Imperial Family, but on their estates and with their families, life was—well, it was chaotic. It seemed to be a mad mix-up of children, silver samovars, furs, jewels—and loads of debt which no one took seriously until they were forced into bankruptcy.'

Anna gestured impatiently. 'Oh, what am I trying to tell you? It's all there—it's there in Tolstoy and Chekhov. You can read all that. What it didn't prepare me for was my introduction to the English aristocracy. It felt then, in that prewar period when they were still masters of the earth, as if things were so ordered and orderly that they could hardly breathe out of rhythm. I wasn't prepared for Lynmara. I wasn't prepared for the Countess. I had expected Johnny's mother would be—just Johnny's mother. Instead, she was the Countess of Manstone. It didn't matter in the least to her that Johnny and I were in love. I was clearly totally unsuitable, and that was that.

'Perhaps I began to feel a little frightened when we drove past the gate-lodge of Lynmara. Lynmara was not at all like a country house in Russia. It was more like a palace. By the time Johnny stopped the car and the butler came to open the door, I had to clench my teeth to stop them chattering. I didn't actually trip up the steps, but I almost did that. Instead I dropped my hand-bag just as I was being introduced to the Countess, and I can remember being so ashamed of the few little things that fell out. I don't know why—there was no lipstick, no powder or anything like that. She stood and watched me and Johnny and the butler pick the things up—a comb, a few hairpins, a tiny bottle of perfume. How ashamed I was of that perfume. She stood and watched it all, that woman—I really can't think of her as Johnny's mother—and I think she knew right then that she had won.'

'Won?' Nicole said sharply. 'Won what?'

'There was a battle, of course. An undeclared war. She wasn't

41

going to let Johnny marry someone like me. And I'm ashamed to remember now that I didn't even fight very hard. If I had weapons, I seemed to forget how to use them. I was demoralized.'

'I don't believe it,' Nicole said. She couldn't imagine Anna routed, giving up without a struggle.

'There's quite a long way between a girl of nineteen and a woman of thirty-eight, Nicole. There's a big gap between a place like Lynmara, and this ...' Her gesture encompassed the room about her, the building, the low sound of the jazz band behind the heavy door. It even seemed to take in the world beyond that, the lights of Times Square, the noises. Most of all it seemed to acknowledge the crowd, the rich out there dancing to a jazz band, the gap that existed between this and the era of the musicians hidden behind the potted plants.

'The Countess made use of every opportunity to show Johnny how unsuitable I was. The place was always crowded with guests, and they would talk about things I couldn't know anything about. Worst of all were the jokes—their *private* jokes. My English seemed to get worse instead of better, my accent was thicker. My clothes were all wrong. I just didn't fit in. In the end I didn't have to be dismissed. I simply packed my bags and went. Johnny made some poor, weak protests, but they were only protests. He knew he was beaten, too. What I can't forgive him for was letting it happen at all. He should never have asked me to marry him. He was very young, of course—and that's about the only excuse I can find for him. He wasn't even twenty-one, and he would have needed his mother's consent for marriage. She had time on her side, and she used it. I had the happiest, and the worst weeks of my life all inside those two months. The only forgiveness I can find for Johnny was that in those first weeks he was happy too. And he was just as miserable as I was during that time at Lynmara. I think he was weak and foolish, and he should never have led me into that situation. But he was young ... You may think so now, Nicole, but the fact is that being young doesn't always mean being right. The young can be so unintentionally cruel. Johnny just failed to see past those first few weeks when we were in love.

'I couldn't stay in London. So I took up where my father had left off, and I went to New York. I actually got a job playing in the salon of the first class section of the ship I sailed on. I had

42

no money, so I didn't tell them I was going to leave the ship in New York. There were gales all the way—that time of year is bad for ships on the Atlantic. I was playing every afternoon and evening to an almost empty room. Funny, I didn't get seasick at all. Perhaps I was too sick in my heart to notice what my stomach left like. But one of the people who showed up day after day to listen and stand by the piano, and to buy me champagne at eleven o'clock in the morning, was Stephen. He was going, he said, to make his fortune in America, and it seemed to me he was going to spend a fortune before he got there. He was charming, eager, kind, and good fun. He laughed a lot, and that was what I needed. He had introductions in New York he said, and almost as soon as we landed he had got a job selling Rolls-Royces. He asked me to marry him, and I did. A sort of sea-change had worked in me. I put Johnny and the whole London thing behind me. I was the person I used to be, not awkward or miserable, or too young. I can't say I ever was in love with Stephen, but I did love him, and I was immensely grateful to him for giving me back to myself, for helping me to believe that I wasn't some sort of freakish fool.

'We had only a few years together. Stephen was kind and wildly extravagant with his money. He only got a tiny salary, and commissions, and he had a little money from his mother's will. He never told me how much. He insisted on spending and spending. He had me take piano lessons again, and he hired someone to work with me on my English. He was very good to me, Stephen. But the fact that I was pregnant in 1914 didn't stop him from rushing off back to England the second that war was declared. It simply never occurred to him that his place was anywhere else. Those English ...'

'Hadn't he a family in England? You've never told me.'

'You never asked, did you, Nicole? He had a father, with whom he'd quarrelled, a mill-owner somewhere in the north, and a sister. He didn't like to talk about either of them. But when he was in France, he began to write about perhaps taking one of his leaves in England and that you and I should come over. His father should see his only grandchild, he said. But he didn't do anything definite about it, and after the *Lusitania* was sunk, he thought it was too dangerous. He never took that leave in England, and he was killed in 1917. He never saw you, except in photos.

43

'The big shock was finding out about the money. There was hardly any left. He'd given me his Army pay, and the rest was made up from the inheritance from his mother. Then I found that that was almost gone. That's when we moved to Mrs Burnley's, and I went out to find a job. I started with Lucky Nolan's when it was a very small place, and I was part of the band. Lucky went up in the world, and you went to St Columba's. That's about it.' Anna shrugged slightly as she said those last words, as if a whole decade was in that gesture.

Nicole wished the maddening thump, thump of the band would stop. She didn't understand jazz, though the girls at school were crazy about it. The sound was outside, beyond them, and here in the room was the same quiet which had always existed between herself and her mother. This hadn't been a cosy chat, it had been revelation and was not going to be repeated. Anna seemed ready to return to the distant place she had always occupied in her daughter's world. Slowly, Nicole began to realize how much of a revelation it had been, what it must have cost Anna, even after these years, to admit to the defeat and hurt of that period. She had been in love, she said. Nicole didn't know what that meant. The way Anna described it, it sounded as if two people had lost their senses. Of course it had been a mistake, that whole episode. She judged her mother from her ignorance, and still found herself admiring her. She admired the slim, beautiful woman before her, the abundant self-control, the discipline which had fashioned a way of life for herself and her daughter when so many others would have gone under. She was shaken from her self-sufficiency into a kind of curiosity she was rarely visited with.

'Do you know what happened to him?—to this Lord Manstone? *Did* he marry?'

Anna almost smiled at this sign of awakening. 'Yes, I had often wondered. One day when I was passing the Fifth Avenue library it occurred to me to find out. I just went in and asked for Burke's Peerage. It was there. John Ashleigh, thirteenth earl of Manstone, married 1911, to the Honourable Cynthia Barrington, deceased. One son, David. Just about every year since then I've looked up the new edition. It hasn't changed. No second marriage. No other children. The strange thing is I can remember Cynthia Barrington. She was one of the people who frightened me most when I was at Lynmara. I don't think she meant to frighten me. But she was just so much the sort of person that Johnny should have married that the sight of her would set me shaking. She had money, good looks, and the right background. She was very much favoured by the Countess. If I'd never appeared, Johnny would have married her just that much sooner. I was only an interruption.'

Anna looked down at her carefully-tended hands. 'You said "*this* Lord Manstone". That's almost how I think about him now. He's hardly Johnny in my mind. I've lumped him in with the rest of the English. You'll have gathered I don't like them. Stephen was different. He wasn't very clever, and he had a charming way of admitting it. He said he was done with England too, until he went rushing off to save her. I've given a lot to England in my life, Nicole, and it irritates me to see how they conduct themselves right to this day. Still lords of the earth. Still the bland calm assumption that they're that much better than everyone else. Look at the fools women make of themselves over the Prince of Wales—a nice-looking little man, but hardly a god. He actually reminds me a bit of Stephen. But it's a sign of the way things really are that when Wall Street crashed, England went into a depression. The ermine around the crown is getting a bit moth-eaten. You'll say I'm bitter and prejudiced. I'll admit it. I never would have been any good as the Countess of Manstone. That part's hard to admit, but I do admit it. So you see ...' She stared directly now at her daughter. 'So you see why I'm telling you to forget about taking that job or any other job for a long, long time. I can't give you a social position. But I can give you an education. Your grandfather dreamed a dream of America, Nicole. It could come true in you. Education is the only way. I want you never to feel afraid of any situation, the way I was afraid. When you're through college, you'll have the sort of experience and confidence you can't even imagine now that you'll ever need.'

Nicole said slowly, 'Are you expecting me to make up for what you missed? That's——'

Anna cut her off with an impatient shake of her head. 'That's foolishness. You can't live anyone else's life for them. I won't try. I'm not asking to live my life again through you. I just want to make sure that whatever comes your way, you're ready. There's some old saying about "Fortune favours the prepared."

45

I just want you to be prepared. To leave school now would be sheer waste. Let's see what life throws in your way—and make sure you're prepared for it. And if you end up being a secretary, you'll be the best god-damned secretary there ever was. Presidents need secretaries, don't they? Don't set your sights lower than the highest. You may always have to come down a little, but a little down from the top is much higher than a long way up from the bottom.'

The unexpected profanity in Anna had slightly shocked Nicole. Her mother didn't speak like that. Or did she? How much of Anna was Christmas, Easter and summer vacation façade, just like the neat little white-collared dresses? A mixed feeling of admiration and resentment for this woman moved in Nicole like a drug in her veins. She felt inexperienced and clumsy beside her, and with this recognition she suddenly was aware of the full truth of what Anna had been saying. She *had* been afraid this evening. She looked down at the neat pile of her coat and hat on the floor and knew at once what it represented. A gauche schoolgirl had put them there. Someone a bit more experienced would, next time, no matter where it was, find some way to intimate that she was neither awed nor frightened by her surroundings.

'So I'll go to college?' Nicole said in a rush. 'And what will *you* do?' One slight gesture of her hand indicated the nightclub, Anna's dress, the whole lifestyle she had witnessed for the first time.

'Leave me to worry about that. We'll leave Mrs Burnley's. I'll look for some other place in Manhattan. Not too grand, but the right address. Lucky will understand. He's ambitious for his own children. He's got a big house in Bronxville. Perhaps by the time you're through college I won't be working here any more. You'll have to play a game of keeping *that* part of me in the background. If it weren't for the depression and jobs being so scarce, I think I'd even have a go at learning to do office work. Well ... I'll think about that, and hope that Lucky will stick with me. Sometimes I get afraid of what will happen when I'm forty ... and forty-five. But I try not to think too much about that. I try to be prepared in my own way. If Lucky will just go along till you're through college ...'

She straightened herself, and in an instant the small anxiety she had betrayed seemed to have been deliberately wiped from her face and voice by an act of will. 'Use your youth, Nicole. Use it hard. It isn't a time of wisdom, but learning comes easier. Learn everything you can. You'll never have so much energy again. Don't waste too much time in sleeping—or dreaming, either. And if you're hit—I suppose I mean by the sort of thing that's hit you tonight, try not to whine about it. It's better if the world only sees you laughing, no matter what's going on inside. Try to——' She broke off, because the absence of the sounds of the band had finally broken through to them. She looked at a little jewelled watch on her wrist. 'I've got to go. I'm due to fill in again. You'll have to wait until I'm finished here, and I'll go back to Brooklyn with you. It could be four o'clock before I'm through. I'm sorry, you'll just have to wait. I can't just blow out of here. I've got a job to look after.' She was rising, smoothing the folds of her dress. 'I'll ask Danny if he can get some coffee and sandwiches brought in to you. If Lucky wants to use the office, you'll have to wait outside. I'd prefer you didn't go into the girls' dressing-room, even if Danny wants to put you there. I don't think you'd get along with them somehow, and they already think *I'm* too big for my boots. I'll come and sit with you when I'm through this break. It depends on how long the customers stay how long we go on. In this business, there's no real closing time . . .'

She went quickly, her movements silent and efficient. Nicole waited, and very soon she caught the faint and seemingly far-away sound of the piano. She still didn't believe it was Anna out there. It was a stranger in a silver dress with painted lips and nails. Her mind slid back over the years with her mother, the years when she had first started to remember things, to notice things. It was true, she had an almost inborn caution about asking questions. Was it right that she simply hadn't wanted to know, that this self-protection had been deliberate? She thought of the Christmas and Easter holidays. Anna always had an arranged schedule for the few days Nicole spent with her. They ate their Christmas dinner at some good restaurant. 'Your Christmas treat' Anna always called it. The rest of the time was allotted to museums and galleries and the zoo, even when she had been quite small and had become easily bored and tired. On Easter Sunday she and Anna put on their best clothes and attended Mass at St Patrick's, watched, and were part of the Easter parade on Fifth Avenue, ate lunch at the St

47

Regis Hotel. Suddenly Nicole saw it all as part of Anna's plan for her. By observing the rich, you learned how it was done. It was a slightly different impression from the one she had gained tonight. She had never observed the rich drinking and dancing before. They were different from the Easter Sunday crowd. And then she thought of the summer vacations, the two weeks a year she spent away from St Columba's in her mother's company. They always went to the same place, a house at Hattonville, in Maine, which received only guests who could offer references and were willing to obey the rigid rules laid down by the owner, Mrs Whalen. Anna and Nicole were acceptable; they were, above all, quiet. They were never a second late for meals, they kept their room tidy, they didn't go out at night; they spoke little and offered no criticism of the food. Hattonville, Maine, was Nicole's total experience of the world outside of St Columba's and the carefully planned visits back to New York. It couldn't have been happenstance that Anna had chosen such a place. Like the breathtaking coldness of the water off Maine's coast, did she mean these vacation times to be a lesson in respect for the hard virtues of thrift and industry, of close-mouthness which these New Englanders set so much store by? The vacations had not been vacations at all, Nicole decided. They were periods of exercise, hard walking, piano practice, and sleep with the window wide open to the wind from the sea. Anna didn't believe in soft living, even for two weeks. When Nicole returned to St Columba's to spend the rest of the vacation months as one of the few pupils who stayed behind, she was each time a little more tutored in rules of discipline and restraint. Had Anna been trying to wipe out for ever the memory of the time, there in London, when she herself had allowed sentiment, and not good sense, to rule her emotions? Nicole was beginning to understand more of what Anna had been saying that night. She had once been wildly, disastrously in love. Love was a luxury she could no longer afford. It would never again swamp her good sense.

Nicole was hungry, and her head ached; there had been too much to learn in one night. It would be many months, perhaps years, before she understood and sorted it all into some tidy place in her mind. Her eyelids drooped, and despite the heat of the room, she shivered. She was about to ease off her wet shoes, but she knew that that would outrage Anna. The sound of the piano went on. She wished her mother would come back; she wished the coffee and sandwiches would come.

She must have had her eyes closed, because he was in the room before she saw him. He was a neat man, good-looking in a dapper way, of only medium height, with hair as thick and black as Anna's own; the sort of Irish face Nicole was used to from Brooklyn, a suit which looked as if it had been tailored for him, and immaculately manicured hands. Nicole didn't know whether to stand because she was still a child, or remain seated because she was a young woman.

The man solved her dilemma. 'Take it easy, kid.' He went to the desk and took a cigarette from a silver box. 'You smoke? No, I didn't think so. Anna wouldn't approve.' His movements were neat, like his body. Nicole realized she had been expecting, and dreading, someone who looked rather like Danny. He took his time lighting the cigarette, and drew on it before he spoke again.

'I'm Lucky Nolan. And you're Anna's kid, Nicole.'

'How do you do,' she said. It was a ridiculous thing to say, but what was the right thing to say when meeting your mother's lover?

He surveyed her thoughtfully. 'You're like Anna. Very much like her. Funny, I've never seen a photo of you. She didn't say you were like her.'

'Perhaps she doesn't think so.'

His eyes seemed to snap at her. 'Well, listen, there's no one you'd be better to be like than Anna. And I don't mean just her looks. That's the trouble with kids—send them to some snooty school and all of a sudden they're too good for you. Well, just you mind your manners. And remember that you've got one hell of a mother.'

His anger seemed to release something in Nicole. To her great surprise she found herself almost liking him, when she had expected to loathe him. 'She hasn't given me much time to learn that. She keeps me away from her most of the time.'

'Yeah—well that's for your own good. That's what she says. I say a kid should know something about life. Well, maybe we're all fools about our kids. Nothing too good for them, and then one day they suddenly decide to become big shots and tell *you* how things should be. I hope you don't make that mistake, kid.'

Nicole even managed a half-smile, but her hands, held tightly

49

in her lap, trembled. This was how it was done. All the way up, no matter where on the ladder you were, you had to make friends, not enemies. 'I've decided I won't make that mistake, Mr Nolan.'

'Smart kid. That's talkin' smart.' He pulled at his cigarette, and his voice was speculative. 'You shouldn't be here. It's not allowed, you know. And Anna's all upset about you being here. Why the big rush, all of a sudden?'

'I came here because I was offered a job. I wanted Mother to agree to me taking it. It was an office job in Wall Street. But she told me I should try for college.'

'College, eh? Well, that's where the smart ones head. Myself, I think it's wasted on a girl. Goes and gets married and it's all wasted. But your mother—I know she don't think like that. So . . . college, eh? It'll cost plenty . . .'

'I know that. That's why I thought a job . . .' Nicole floundered. 'I didn't know, you see . . . about this.'

'None of your business, was it, kid? Your mother's got a right to her own life.' He looked at her as if daring her to make some protest, to indicate by some gesture that she disapproved of the relationship between himself and Anna. Nicole decided that if he waited for that he was going to be disappointed.

'Not my business at all, Mr Nolan. What's my business is to see that the money——' she hesitated for just a fraction of a second, 'that the money *you* provide is well used. I've got to get the best marks in the class or it's not good enough. Value for money, Mr Nolan. I didn't know where the money came from until tonight, Mr Nolan. But now I do, I'm more than ever obliged to see that it's used properly. Taking means giving back something. I hope I don't cheat you.'

He stubbed out his cigarette in annoyance. 'Hell, you takin' things too far. Who said anything about giving anything back? The money I give Anna's hers. The way she spends it is her business. No strings.'

'*I'm* the string that comes attached to my mother, Mr Nolan. And you've always known it. All you've paid. Now I know. And since I seem to be accepting it all, going along with it, then I've got to turn in value for money. I hope it'll be a good investment, Mr Nolan.'

'For God's sake, kid, shut up! I've always said educated women were a pain in the neck. Except Anna. Here you are, a kid. And you're talking like an old woman who's seen all the action. Value for money! Say, listen, how old *are* you?'

Nicole looked at her watch. 'I'm sixteen, Mr Nolan.'

He shook his head. 'Then God help the man you get hold of when you're twenty-six. That's all I can say. God help him.'

CHAPTER 3

I

Nicole returned to St Columba's the next morning. She had an interview with Mother Mary Helena in which she told her that her mother wished her to remain at school, and to try, in the next year, to see if she could take college entrance exams. Her mother, she added, would be grateful for any advice as to which college might prove most suitable. Nothing more was said about a job.

The nun looked at her pupil across the desk, looked at the delicately-modelled features that were turning out to be quite beautiful, met the straight stare from deep-violet eyes. There were shadows of fatigue under those eyes, and the features, Nicole's whole demeanour, seemed subtly altered since the time she had sat there just yesterday morning. It irritated Mary Helena that with all her experience of girls, she could not quite put her finger on the precise nature of the change.

'College? It has never been mentioned before, Nicole. I will give it thought. You know, of course, that you will have to work very hard.'

'I will.' Just that. No more or less than a declaration of intent, but said with the kind of intensity which Mary Helena didn't like to hear in a girl of Nicole's age. She wondered, but would not ask, what had gone on between the child and her mother the night before.

A lesson bell rang, and Nicole was dismissed. Mary Helena was not teaching for the next hour, and she gave herself over to her own considerations about the girl who had just left. She did it, to more or less degree, with each of the hundred-odd pupils under her charge. This was not the first time that Nicole Rainard had puzzled her.

The overnight rain had turned to sleet early that morning,

and finally to snow. There had been radio warnings of a blizzard. Mary Helena, having made her routine checks that there was plenty of fuel for the furnace, that the kitchen was well-stocked with supplies they might need for a few days until the snow ploughs got through to their remote old mansion with its modern extensions far off the main road, relaxed into the enjoyment which the sight of snow falling, snow softly piling on bare branches, weighing down the green of the conifers, obliterating walks, disguising the little landmarks of the garden, always gave to her. She remembered also, that there would be those in danger from the snow, and those who would suffer cold and hardship, and said a prayer to be forgiven for having pleasure in what would be pain to so many people. 'But, Lord,' she said softly, speaking to a friend, 'it is hard not to love Thy beauty.' And then she slipped on a heavy black knitted shawl, gloves and boots, and gave herself over to the beauty. For a while, screened from the windows of the classroom by a row of pines, she walked in the falling snow, held her face up to it, and thanked God that at nearly seventy she could still enjoy it.

But as she paced, the thought of Nicole kept returning. She had always been one of the odd ones. St Columba's was an odd school, Mary Helena conceded. It had been founded as a branch of a High Anglican Order in England; most Americans thought of it as a rather fancy version of Episcopalian. But Anglican nuns were rare enough anywhere, never mind in America. Nevertheless, there were enough people who wanted to send their daughters to be educated by nuns and yet who didn't want to send them to a Catholic institution to keep the place well-tenanted and well-endowed. There was always a waiting list for St Columba's, and the academic standards were high enough that Mary Helena knew, as Nicole must have known, that if she could satisfy them, she could satisfy the entrance requirements of most colleges for young ladies. But St Columba's was still a religious order, and Mary Helena had strong views on maintaining a policy of admitting other than the daughters of the rich. Yes, it was an expensive school, but with a certain selected number of pupils, the fees were quite sharply reduced. That had been the case with Nicole Rainard. Mary Helena could still remember the letter that had come to the school from her mother more than eight years ago. It had been an honest letter, and yet not a begging one. Her daughter needed an education, she said; she needed a place away from Brooklyn. Anna Rainard had told the history of the family in Russia, in Paris and London. She had told of her English husband and her widowhood. She was particularly anxious that Nicole should study music, she said. The letter had sufficiently impressed Mary Helena that she had asked Anna Rainard to bring her small daughter for an interview, 'to see how we like each other,' she had phrased it ambiguously, at the same time pointing out that many others were asking for admission to the school. The meeting with Anna Rainard, and the slight, pretty child she had brought with her to St Columba's, had excited Mary Helena. The school, she had always maintained, needed a mixture of cultures—she was ahead of her time in thinking this way. She had deliberately introduced such ones as Nicole from time to time, hoping that some understanding of another background would rub off on the too-sheltered daughters of the rich who mainly made up her pupils. So Nicole had been accepted, and had arrived, her bags and uniform marking her as no different from other children who had started there that same September. But she had been different, and not in the way Mary Helena had hoped. There had been no explosion of Russian warmth and laughter, no rages and tears. She was one of the few Mary Helena could remember who, at eight years old, had stood silently and resolutely, and without even a quivering of the lips when the sounds of the taxi bearing her mother away had receded. She had gone on that way, closed, mostly silent except when asked questions, always obedient, well-behaved. That was what was wrong, Mary Helena thought. She and the other nuns had tried often to break through that cold little shell, and had not succeeded. Mary Helena thought of the English father, who had never seen his child. Could it be true that the English inheritance overrode the Russian? What did one do with a silent, always obedient child?

And then the cold, and the whirling snow began to be too much for Mary Helena. She returned, shivering a little, to the house, and the bell was ringing for the next lesson period.

In the months that followed Mary Helena had cause to call Nicole several times to her office, or to invite her to walk the spring-thawed gardens with her. Once they had gone together to pick daffodils in the long grass under the oaks. Mary Helena had used her time to try to probe the reason for what seemed to her Nicole's obsessive overworking, the habit of reading late at night, which was forbidden. Nicole promised she would observe the rules about lights-out, but no one could forbid her the morning light. One of the sisters had found her just after dawn, crouched by a window in her dressing-gown, hunched over a book. 'I have to go to college,' was her only reply. 'You don't have to get your degree all in one year, Nicole.' She went at her music in the same slightly fanatical way. She extended her practice periods until she had a row with the girl who was waiting to take over the piano in that music-room. The sisters, who were more used to having to persuade girls towards learning than keeping them from it, were at a loss. Nicole had been ordered to increase her time on the tennis court; she did this unwillingly. She wasn't good at games. But once told she must have more exercise, she threw herself into it until the tennis mistress had to tell her she was too wild. Then she began to practise her serves with the same kind of deadly patient quiet that marked the way she played her scales. She began to play quite a fair game of singles; at doubles, she could not co-operate with her partner.

The first break in the smooth façade came when the letter from Anna had announced that instead of their usual vacation in Maine, she had arranged for Nicole to attend, for the full three months, a summer camp for girls that was generally regarded as being for the rich only. At this news Nicole had finally broken, before Mary Helena, into a storm of passionate, weeping protest.

'I don't want to go. I've spent every summer here with you —except when I was in Maine. This is my last summer. I want to stay.'

In the end she went to camp as docilely as she had done everything else. She swam and rode and played tennis as everyone else did. The single difference was that her mother had made arrangements for her to go to a house nearby where she could have the use of the piano for two hours a day. They were early risers in that house, and they made no objection when that black-haired, pale-faced child, who should have been wearing the universal sun-tan of the camp, turned up for two hours of practice before breakfast. They didn't mind; her mother was paying them well for listening to scales.

When Nicole returned from camp, Mary Helena began to worry about her seriously. 'This is the last year,' she said. 'I have to get it all done now, or I've lost out.'

'You won't lose anything, Nicole.'

'I might. I have to be sure.' And she had flung herself into her work in a way that frightened Mary Helena. The girl wasn't looking well. She sent her for a check-up, and the doctor pronounced her fit. 'But you have to watch these high-strung ones.' Nicole said nothing about the cause of her grandmother's death, and she begged Mary Helena not to write to her mother. 'She'll worry. It isn't fair to make her worry when I'm perfectly all right. I promise I won't work longer hours than you say I may.'

Mary Helena had nodded and agreed, but she knew she couldn't temper the intensity with which Nicole now approached every task set for her. She would obey the letter but not the spirit of the rules. There was no promise which could change that.

For Christmas that year Anna booked a room at a fashionable country inn fairly near St Columba's. 'I thought I'd like a break from the city,' was her explanation, but Nicole knew that it was to keep her away from the Manhattan apartment. The deception of the apartment at Mrs Burnley's was over for ever. On Christmas Day Anna handed Nicole, after the presents she herself had given her, a small grey box with the name of a famous jeweller on it. 'From Lucky,' was all she said.

Nicole opened it, and drew out a fine gold chain, at the centre of which, neatly placed so that the open ends turned upwards, was a golden horseshoe. The fine engraving on the back of the horseshoe read: *Good luck. Lucky.*

Nicole sat down at once and wrote a note of thanks, trying to make it sound relaxed, and not quite succeeding. When Lucky read it he tucked it into his pocket and smiled wryly at Anna. 'Like a letter from a nice little lady. I wonder if the kid'll ever wear it ...'

Nicole took it back to St Columba's and hid it under her stocking case in the farthest corner of one of her bureau drawers. She would have liked to throw it away, but she lacked the courage.

II

In a stark, bleak Victorian mansion perched on a hill overlooking a mill town in Yorkshire, a seared and yellow man lay dying. He knew that he was dying, and the time left could not be very long. The pain, rather than the doctors, told him that. While his mind was still clear of the ultimate wash of the pain against reason, he struggled to think of what he should do. Or rather, he thought of the situation as what he *would* do. He had always been master of his house, and he remained so. For a long time, for a time until a few years ago, he had also been master of the town below him.

The solicitors, summoned here, had brought their reports. The last report had been brought directly from London by one of the partners of a firm his local solicitor had engaged to make the enquiries. It had all been done with great legal finesse, each deferring to the other, no one quite willing to say that enquiry agents had been engaged to do the work they needed doing. But the report, suitably dressed in decorous terms, lay on the bed beside him. Two hours ago it had been read to him, every last word of it; he had told them to leave it with him, and now they waited, downstairs, until they should be summoned again. He had pretended he still had the strength to read it again for himself, but that was not so. He touched that crisp legal paper, and the edges of it seemed to cut his emaciated hand. If he had had the strength to do it, he would have gone once more to look at the town below his house, the town that his father and himself had built. But he really did not need to do that; every line of the streets, the lanes, the alleys was drawn on his memory. All that was strange now was that the stacks of the mill chimneys did not belch their familiar smoke. That had gone, a little at a time, after the great stock market crash on Wall Street in '29. It was a fact that the man refused to recognize as a direct outcome of his quarrel with his only son, that when the crash had come, and the orders from all over the world for woollen goods had slowly dried up, he had no longer been the owner of those mills. It had not been his fortune which had blown away with the winds of world depression, but the fortune of the man to whom he had sold his mills.

What the doctors had hopefully talked of as a cure had been a period of remission. The disease had struck him again, and once again he had endured an operation. But this time even they did not speak hopeful words. He was a very tough man, was Henry Rainard. He was taking his own good time about dying, but he knew the time left to him now must be very short.

He thought with bitterness of his two children. Iris, his daughter, had been a disappointment. No more than that, no less. She had disappointed him because she had failed to produce the grandsons he had counted on, the ones he had thought of as he had laboured alone at the mills. He did not even concede that if there had been grandsons to inherit, undoubtedly, he would have held on to his mills, and he would now be nearly bankrupt. Henry Rainard seldom gave credit to anyone but himself, and by now he had, in his own mind, translated what had seemed to be the move of a dying man who had no one to carry on after him, into a stroke of financial genius. It was his great enemy, his arch-rival in the woollen business in Yorkshire who was now almost bankrupt, and, he, Henry Rainard, was held, in the local parlance, to be a very 'warm' man indeed. He had lots of brass, and no one to leave it to. Iris, of course, would have it. She expected to have it. She had, in these last years, made dutiful visits to this house where she had been born, and each visit they had been farther apart, and his disappointment in her childlessness more evident. He wondered if it were her fault, or the fault of that soft fool she had married, Charles Gowing. She had married his title, of course, but he was only a baronet. Henry Rainard had educated his daughter for better things than that, had settled money on her at eighteen, but after several seasons in London, all she had been able to catch as a husband was an amiable Army man, a man of impeccable family, and a small, heavily-mortgaged estate. It didn't matter in the least to Henry Rainard that Charles Gowing had achieved the rank of Brigadier during the '14–'18 war, and had won a clutch of medals. That he limped badly from a war wound was also against him. Henry Rainard had little time for those who were not successful—to be wounded was an evidence of failure. Mentally he dismissed Iris. He didn't want to think of her being the only one to benefit from his life of hard work; she had never done any work herself. She didn't know what it was about. To Rainard's way of thinking, she hadn't earned anything.

His feelings towards his only son were more deeply bitter.

Stephen had achieved the ultimate failure by getting himself killed. And he had not even been an officer, although Henry Rainard had sent him to Harrow and to Oxford, where he had lasted only a year. But that year had been enough to do the damage. Their great quarrel had come when Stephen had returned from Oxford, accepting at last that he must join his father in the mills. The fool had absorbed some half-baked ideas of Socialism at Oxford, and had actually objected to the working-hours and the wages of the mill workers, the conditions of their work. When Henry Rainard had coldly asked him how, if these things were changed, they would make their profits, Stephen had answered that their profits should be less. This was such blasphemy to Henry Rainard that he actually thought he had misheard his son. But the truth was that Stephen refused to set foot inside any of the mills until conditions were changed. The conditions remained the same, and his son had left, having only the money which his mother, a soft woman who had doted on her son and whom Henry Rainard had despised as a fool, had left to him of her own small inheritance. With that inheritance, which Henry had been unable to deny to Stephen, his son had gone to America, and here had uselessly wasted his life playing about with cars, and had married a foreigner, a Russian. A few letters had come from Stephen while he had been serving in France, with vague suggestions that they should meet, that his wife and child might join him in England. Henry Rainard had responded to only one letter, and that harshly. He thought he had plenty of time in which to let Stephen change his mind about how the mills should be run, and if Stephen came to his senses, he, Henry, would perhaps overlook his marriage to a Russian, with the thought that there would be more children, there would be sons. He had taken Stephen's death as a personal insult, in that it wrecked his plans.

And so the years had passed, lonely years for Henry Rainard, if he had been the kind to feel lonely. The illness was an affront to him; he had expected to live for a very long time. At the moment that he decided to sell the mills, he also ordered his solicitors to investigate the whereabouts and lives of the daughter-in-law and grandchild he had never seen. He could not have said why he wished to know about them; he just wished to know.

It was a surprise to learn that the Russian had not remarried.

That had pleased him, in an odd way. In that time she might have remarried, and her husband have adopted Stephen's child, who would not now be called Rainard. If that had happened, Henry Rainard would not have bothered further.

The reports had kept coming over the years, and were surprisingly comprehensive. The feelings of Henry Rainard about what he learned were mixed. He viewed with distaste the association of the Russian with a nightclub owner. He knew about the small apartment on Central Park West, and about Mrs Burnley's. Information came from all kinds of sources—from people such as Mrs Burnley and Danny at the nightclub, who would talk if money were offered. There was the other side of it which puzzled him. He had paid a great deal to have the school his grandchild attended investigated. He didn't approve of High Anglicanism—he was a Nonconformist himself. But at least the place was *English*, not Russian. He learned it was a place of outstanding scholastic note, and that his granddaughter did very well in her class. He knew about the special emphasis on music, which he thought a waste of time, but evidence of her skill. She played games, but was not good at them. He learned with surprise that Anna Rainard bought a copy of the *Wall Street Journal* every day. He also knew the opinion Mrs Whalen at Hattonville had of her. What he did not know, because no one else had known, was what had happened between his granddaughter and her mother on the night she had come to Lucky Nolan's, the eve of her sixteenth birthday. It was routinely reported to him that Anna Rainard had given up the fiction of living in Brooklyn, and that his granddaughter had spent the summer at an expensive camp for girls. He did not delude himself about where the money for such things came from. The reports even knew the state of Anna Rainard's bank account, and that, very oddly at the height of a depression, she had bought a few hundred dollars worth of very low-priced stock. The last piece of information in the report had been of the Christmas Anna Rainard and his granddaughter spent together in the country. It was January now, and the winds that brought the flying snow to the school in Connecticut where his granddaughter worked in the last months before her final exams, these winds blew from the east over the North Sea, and struck the house on the hill with icy roughness, found the tiny ill-fitting places at the windows, flapped the washing hung in the alleys of the town below, and made the man who was so near to death wish that just once he might feel really warm. Despite the fire that burned night and day, and the hot-water bottles laid close to his body, he was very cold, except when the pain drove out any other feeling. Iris telephoned each day, and asked to be allowed to come. He refused her. He and Iris had nothing to say to one another.

He listened to the chiming of the clock in the hall. The hours were passing, and down there, having eaten lunch, the solicitors waited on word from him. The short February day was drawing in, and still he had not made up his mind. For a second his hand touched the pages of the report, built up over these last years. He thought contemptuously of the Russian, and yet the report had no mention of any but that single man, Lucky Nolan. A nightclub entertainer. Just the sort of person Stephen would have got hold of, fool that he was. But his curiosity was about his grandchild, the child with the dark hair, the report said, a very pretty child, delicately made, but not given to illnesses. He wished just for one minute he could see that child; all he needed to do was see her, and he would be sure. But with the report there had been no photograph. A photograph would not have told him what he needed to know. He needed to look into the face of a living child to know if she was his kind or not.

His thoughts were interrupted by the arrival of the nurse—he had had them round the clock for the last months. He hated them all, bustling and cheery, knowing they were here until he died, and then they would move on to the next case. He made their lives as difficult as possible.

'Time for your injection, Mr Rainard.'

'Get it over with, then.'

The injection was skilfully given, but he winced at the very touch of the nurse. The time between injections was now shorter and shorter, and he knew the doctors had authorized any amount of drugs that he desired. It was perhaps just the act of the nurse going to close the curtains, the final ending of the daylight that decided him.

'Tell those fools downstairs that they are to come up now. I wish to see them.'

For five hours Anna Rainard rode the Staten Island ferry back and forth across New York harbour. All day long the skyline of Wall Street grew near and then receded; she watched the gigantic features of the Statue of Liberty take shape, and then dissolve, she listened to the muted commotion of the docking and undocking, the muffled thump as the ferry hit the slipway, the cars driving on and off. It was the middle of the day. There were very few people aboard, and none that stayed, trip after trip, as she did. Twice she went and bought coffee, but did not eat. She wasn't aware that a deckhand hovered near whenever she went on the outside deck. The ferryman had seen others like her before, those who rode the ferry hour after hour, and then at some point, slipped into the oily green water.

It was 29 February. Chunks of rotten ice came floating down the Hudson. Tomorrow was Nicole's birthday. Winter and Nicole's birthday were always intermixed in Anna's mind. The Statue was coming up again. To herself she quoted the lines first heard from her father, something that inspired his long, uncompleted trip from Russia, 'Give me your tired ... your huddled masses ... send these, the homeless, tempest-tossed to me: I lift my lamp beside the golden door.' There had been no golden door for Anna Rainard. One might now be opening for Nicole.

The letter from Fairfax and Osborne, and the six other partners listed, had reached Anna yesterday. It had asked her to call for an appointment at her convenience. She had never heard of these people before, and the curiosity and sense of fear aroused was no less in her than in anyone else. She had made an appointment for that morning at ten o'clock. When she saw the long list of junior partners, the size and muted air of importance of the office itself, she realized that here was one of the bastions of Wall Street. She had expected to be shown into the office of one of the junior partners, but it was to the corner office of William Osborne himself that she was shown. From that high window the Statue had looked quite small, of little importance beside the power that money had built in this land which had sent out its call to the poor of Europe.

William Osborne had also read every word of the reports which had reached Henry Rainard in Yorkshire, but the sight of Anna Rainard was still a surprise. He knew of the deception she had practised on her daughter, but when she seated herself, a beautiful, slim woman, neatly dressed, her face innocent of make-up, her nails, when she slipped off her black gloves, unpainted, he knew that he would have liked such a receptionist in his own office. She looked the part. But he said nothing about this. As briefly as possible he explained the terms of Henry Rainard's will.

They were simple and harsh, like the man. The only child of his son's marriage would receive half of his estate. The other half was to go to his daughter Iris, Lady Gowing. There was one condition only. Nicole's inheritance was to be placed in trust for her until her twenty-first birthday only if, and provided that, within six months of his death, Anna Rainard was to pass over her guardianship to Sir Charles and Lady Gowing, make a promise in writing that she would never see her daughter until she reached her majority, and after that, only at her daughter's instigation, and that Nicole's education should continue in Europe. For this act of signing over her rights in her child, for her written promise never to see her until the specified time, Anna Rainard would receive five thousand pounds, or its equivalent in dollars.

When Anna sat in the chair facing William Osborne, Henry Rainard had been dead for just three weeks.

'May I ask how you knew where to find me?' Anna said evenly. Her tone betrayed nothing, not shock nor outrage, nor dismissal. William Osborne, who was accustomed to scenes within this quiet office, was mildly surprised. 'There are ways of doing such things, Mrs Rainard ...'

'I'm to believe then, that Stephen's father has been aware of Nicole's existence—of mine, and our whereabouts for some time.'

'For some time,' he conceded.

'I see.' She asked a few more direct, very blunt questions. Had Mr Rainard known what kind of job she did?—had he known of her relationship with Mr Nolan?—had he known of the kind of school Nicole attended? William Osborne winced as he answered. Who would have expected such a quiet-seeming woman to be so indelicate? And yet he admired the soundness of the questions. She wanted to know exactly where she was; that was the whole point of law.

'Would my promise not to see Nicole extend beyond her twenty-first birthday?'

'*Your* promise would. Once your daughter comes of age, no one can stop her contacting you, if she so desires.'

'I see. Well—I must think about it.' She rose and began to put on her gloves. William Osborne was used to ending interviews himself and her taking over the situation annoyed him. 'You realize the extent of Henry Rainard's estate, Mrs Rainard?'

'No—I was waiting for you to tell me, Mr Osborne.'

He frowned. 'These things are subject to valuation, of course, but Henry Rainard's estate is mostly liquid. He sold his mills just before the crash.' At this he smiled rather grimly. 'Many of *my* clients might have prayed for his foresight. It is believed by his London solicitors to be in excess of three hundred thousand pounds. This, of course, is subject to death duties. The remainder after expenses and—er, the payment made to you, is to be divided equally between your daughter Nicole, and your husband's sister, Lady Gowing.'

'And if I refuse?'

'The whole estate will go to Lady Gowing.'

She stood for just a moment longer, seeming to stare vacantly out the window and across the harbour. 'Do you recall how old my daughter is, Mr Osborne?'

He glanced down swiftly at the folder of notes on the desk before him, but he had taken off his glasses, and standing he could not read them. 'Er ... I believe——'

'Tomorrow she will be seventeen.' She turned and walked towards the door. He had to hurry to open it for her.

'Isn't there any more you'd like to know, Mrs Rainard? I'd be happy to advise you ...'

'I know the facts, Mr Osborne. I will call for another appointment. Good day.'

He watched her slim black-coated figure walk down the corridor. She had not allowed him time to summon his secretary to escort her to the elevator, but she wasn't the kind to lose her way. Rarely, since his name had gone on the very bottom of the list of junior partners of the firm, had William Osborne been so dismissed. This might be one of the toughest clients he had ever dealt with, and his admiration for her was acknowledged, though grudgingly. She wouldn't blur any of the lines, this

64

woman. She would say yes or no, and mean it. He began to wonder what her daughter was like, and if Henry Rainard had not made a grave mistake.

The pain and anger which Anna would not betray before William Osborne rode all day with her on the ferry. She paced the deck and then wished that she might have stamped beneath her feet all the anonymous faces of the anonymous people who had brought herself and Nicole to this situation. The fierce February wind that blew across the harbour did not drive her to the warmth of the cabins. She pretended that it was the wind which whipped the tears to her eyes. She thought of a man, known only to her as a mill-owner who had educated his son to be a gentleman, and had married his daughter into the upper classes, and who could shape his will into such a cruel instrument. She thought of Lucky, who had been generous and easy, and who had given Nicole the things that made her what she was, the education that would make her acceptable to this man's daughter, Lady Gowing. Anna relived again, against her will, the hurt and humiliation of those few weeks when she had encountered the English at their haughtiest, their most inflexible, the few weeks of her love for John Manstone, and how it had withered and died beneath the icy stare of his mother. The English. How she hated them, all the tribe of conceited, overbearing, cold-eyed snobs. She thought of how the facts about herself must have looked on paper—the facts about the job, and Lucky and the small apartment on Central Park West. Well, where had Henry Rainard been with his money when Nicole had been a small child?—where had he been all these years? He was taking the product of Lucky's money, the product of St Columba's, and imagining that she could be fashioned overnight into a little English miss. Brigadier Sir Charles and Lady Gowing. God, it had a fine sound. But so did Prince Michael Alexandreovitch Ovrensky, order of the Grand Cross of St George. Had Henry Rainard's investigation gone as far back as that? Anna didn't think so. And yet it was there whence she felt herself to be sprung. The Ovrenskys were her family. She had had a family, even if she was called by another name. She wasn't sprung from the mud of the steppes. And yet she could hear Lady Manstone's voice again, 'My son tells me you are a Russian. How interesting,' as if she were some new kind

65

of insect. The English—once again they had shown very plainly that they did not want her.

She paced and paced the deck, and she was locked by the confines of the ferry and the rigid terms of Henry Rainard's will. The early lights began to come on in the skyscrapers at Manhattan's tip, and a sense of panic grew in Anna. The day was running out, and her sense of direction had deserted her. She had lost count of the number of times the ferry had made the crossing. The lamp in the Statue began to glow in the sky. The night was coming and tomorrow was going to be Nicole's seventeenth birthday. She recognized that she was herself responsible for what Nicole had become; it was she who had encouraged the latent spark of ambition in her, had aided the little snobberies, the trace of vanity. She had brought Nicole up thinking of better things, and higher places. Now, when she could have all Anna had urged her towards without struggle, why should she expect Nicole to choose the struggle, to risk the failure and to taste its bitterness? Put that way, the question answered itself. But it would have to be resolved with speed and a seeming heartlessness that left no time for second thoughts, speed that would inflict one savage hurt, not a lingering pain. There could be no goodbye to Nicole.

When the ferry thumped against the timbers of the slipway, this time Anna was ready to disembark with the other passengers. She bought herself a sandwich and a cup of coffee at the ferry terminal. For the first time Prohibition was a hardship for her. It would have helped to have a large glass of brandy to anaesthetize the pain of what she was going to do this night. She went out, found a taxi to take her to the offices of Fairfax & Osborne.

Back in William Osborne's office she insisted that it be done at once. He protested that the documents would have to be drafted, and typed; she insisted that she would wait until they were done, otherwise she would not sign them. So William Osborne, with some irritation, agreed; he and his secretary and a junior partner worked for several hours, while Anna sat alone in the waiting-room, not even pretending to read the magazines on the table. When it was done, she read it over carefully, twice, and then signed. She also received from William Osborne a paper which set out her right to the payment of five thousand pounds from the estate of Henry Rainhard.

'I'll be in touch with you, Mr Osborne. I'll let you know where to send the money.'

'You won't be at your New York address, Mrs Rainard?'

'No.'

The answer was so flat and unequivocal that it startled him. He was already dismayed by what had turned into a rather sordid business of making a legal document of a mother promising not to see her only child. He had dreaded tears from Anna Rainard; he found he was shocked by their absence. The woman who signed her name with such a steady hand seemed strangely numb. He asked her several times if she fully understood what she was doing. Her reply had been cold and full of impatience to have the act finished. She was preoccupied with thoughts that took little account of him, it seemed. She did not talk of going to see her daughter; she did not talk of her daughter at all.

This time, he escorted her along the silent corridors to the elevator. 'Mrs Rainard, if I can be of any help, please do call on my services. You may think of investing——'

She cut him off. The elevator doors opened: the operator stood waiting. Anna Rainard gestured to indicate the silent building, the whole world of tall and silent buildings outside, the world whose crash had sent shock waves through financial institutions and ordinary homes all around the globe. 'You people down here don't seem to have made such a good job of investing, do you? Thank you, Mr Osborne, I'll manage for myself.'

Anna returned to the apartment on Central Park West, and made a phone call to Danny at Lucky Nolan's. 'Danny?— you'll have to get a fill-in for me tonight. I'm not feeling well.'

She could hear him swear softly. 'Hell, Anna, this is a great time to be tellin' me. Where am I gonna find someone——'

She cut him short. 'You'll find someone, Danny. I can't come. Just tell Lucky when he gets in, will you?' She hung up.

Then she packed two suitcases, made a reservation at one of the big anonymous commercial hotels near Grand Central, and checked in. As soon as the bank opened the next morning she cleared the small sum she had in her chequeing account, and closed it. Then she went to her safe deposit box and took out the cash that was there, the few stocks she had bought, her passport, her naturalization papers, the photographs of her father and mother, the few she had of the Ovrenskys, the photos of Nicole as she had been growing up. There was a gold watch which had belonged to her father, presented to him by Prince Michael, and a watch of Stephen's returned to her after he had been killed. There was also the citation for bravery he had earned. For a few moments only she dwelt over the small pile of objects which represented a lifetime of history for her parents, herself and her daughter. Then she put them all into the hand suitcase she had brought, handed back the key, and instructed the bank official that she would not need the deposit box again. After that she collected her suitcases from the hotel, and went to Grand Central and took the first available train to Chicago. She didn't think she was going to stay in Chicago, but it was the first stage on a journey away from New York.

IV

William Osborne wrote first to Mother Mary Helena at St Columba's, and then followed his letter with a telephone call suggesting that he might send a car to pick up Nicole Rainard and bring her to his office. 'I'm sure you're just as experienced in these things as I am, Mother,' he said soothingly, 'but it has been my experience that with news to impart, either good news or bad, it is often better if it is given in an impersonal environment. This young lady has some shocks coming, and it might be kinder if she has the journey back to think about what has happened, and adjust herself. That is why I suggest I send a car for her. I don't want her to have to think about the trains, or anything else ...'

Knowing a little of what Nicole was going to hear, Mary Helena gave her permission with some misgivings. In a sense the man was right. Nicole was going to have to get used to a great deal more of what she would experience in William Osborne's office. She was seventeen now, and the time for shielding her behind the calm façade of the convent life was almost over. She decided that she would send Nicole to William Osborne's office, and she would send her without any companion—not one of the nuns who usually went with a pupil when there was any family problem; Nicole didn't have a friend among the pupils close enough that she could make a confidante. As solitary as her way had been all through her time at St Columba's, so it would remain until the end. Mary Helena would not visit on Nicole the indignity of the suggestion that she did not have the control to face what she must alone. Nicole had never been a girl for talk; she knew she would take this new development in silence, and a companion might be an unbearable burden.

William Osborne rose to his feet as Nicole Rainard was announced. He saw a very slight figure, of only medium height, in a school hat and coat which seemed to be a little short in the sleeves and length, as if she had shot up suddenly this unexpected inch or so. He guessed that Mother Mary Helena was careful of Anna Rainard's budget, and had not wanted to impose the additional expense of new clothes when Nicole would be finished at St Columba's in June. William Osborne gestured towards the leather-covered sofa and chairs at the end of his long office. 'Won't you take off your coat, Miss Rainard? Please sit down and make yourself comfortable.'

Rather slowly she removed her coat, revealing a school tunic, a white blouse and blazer. Then with a single swift gesture she pulled off her hat, as if it bothered her. She placed them neatly across the arm of the sofa, and then seated herself. William Osborne for the first time saw her face clearly. His immediate reaction was 'What a little madame!', and then, more soberly, 'What a beautiful girl.'

Whether Nicole Rainard was beautiful or not was debatable. She had a rather severe face, not the sort currently in fashion, the features were delicate, classical, a pointed chin, faint hollows at the cheeks; but when the gaze went to the eyes the rest was forgotten. While William Osborne took in all this, he also noticed her hair, a great fall of silken black hair caught in a simple ribbon behind her head, hair that reminded him of her mother's. She had white skin, like her mother's, and those odd dark upward slanting eyebrows. She certainly was not pretty in the conventional sense. Given those eyes and those features, she was either beautiful, or she was nothing at all. William Osborne decided that she was beautiful. He was one of many men who would ponder that question in the years to come.

She heard what Osborne had to say in silence, a silence that strangely disconcerted him. For only the briefest moment her lips parted, as if to utter a protest, when he explained the condition of Henry Rainard's will which meant that she was to be separated from Anna. But he never could afterwards be certain that it was a protest.

'It's all settled then,' she said when he had finished.

'There are details to be worked out. I am in contact, of course, with the solicitors for the estate of Henry Rainard, and Sir Charles Gowing's solicitors. I have made the suggestion that it would be unwise for you to leave St Columba's until you have taken your examinations in June. A shame to leave without seeing the results of your work ... After all, a few months doesn't make any difference in complying with the terms of the will.'

'I must see my mother.'

He shook his head. 'Not only has your mother already consented to the terms, but, I believe, she has left New York. We do not know her present whereabouts.'

Some colour came into the white before him. 'But she was to receive *money* ...'

'My dear, I wouldn't attach too much importance to that. The sum of money is not great. I believe Henry Rainard deliberately left it in that twilight area which constituted neither a bribe nor an insult. It was there, available. In these times there are few people who would have refused it. But I don't think it in any way influenced your mother's decision. She obviously intends to use it to make some fresh start somewhere. Your mother appears to me to be a woman of admirable will and purpose. She will keep her promise.'

'But I should have been *asked*——'

'Would it have been fair to consult you? To tell you that a considerable amount of money and the chance of further education in Europe was yours—but only on the condition that she did not attempt to see you? Very properly she did not consult you. She left something with me for you ...'

He went to his desk and brought an envelope and a silver letter-opener. The heavy bond paper was headed with the name of Fairfax & Osborne; Anna must have written the letter here in this office.

Nicole read it twice. It was phrased in Anna's careful, stiff English, as if she did not entirely trust herself writing in this language. 'Nicole—do as they say. Don't try to fight them. Not yet. I couldn't refuse this condition. Pride is a poor substitute for the reality of money. You cannot live off it, and you cannot eat it. This way, there is no chance that you will ever live at a Mrs Burnley's again. Do you understand? You will ask what my feelings are. I am angry and hurt, as I have been before. I recovered from that, and I will again. This action of Stephen's father is just what I might have expected from the English, but you will find them different, because the situation for you will be different. This is the second time the Engish have managed to throw me out. I do not intend they should ever do it again. How much I would like to be able to refuse that man's money, but that also would be stupid pride, which I cannot afford. I have uses for it, and it will be used. I will not burden you——' Here a few words were crossed out heavily, as if Anna had faltered. '—with all my hopes for the future. I cannot, I do not intend to try to live my life again through you. I wish with all my heart that your future will be a happy one. I think it is certain now to be a successful one—who knows, even brilliant.'

The flowing lines of the letter broke as if Anna had been shy of adding the last. 'I think, in our way, we have loved each other. I know we have not been very close, but that is the fault of neither one. We have respected each other. Remember this, please, and do not try to find me. Anna.'

It was so strange, that final signature. The letters had come all through the years to the school, and had always ended 'Your loving Mother.' Now the person behind that broke through. Nicole stared at the sheets of paper, conscious of William Osborne's eyes on her, and she was remembering so much that Anna's strong will had cloaked. She was remembering the organized Christmas and Easter holidays, designed to get her away from Mrs Burnley's as much as possible; she was remembering the sameness of the summer holidays in Maine, the long silent walks they took together, never having much to discuss, sharing no plans, few jokes, Anna never talking of the past, or of the future, until it had been forced from her that night at Lucky Nolan's. For the first time Nicole was conscious of having missed a great deal in not insisting on knowing her mother, in not breaking through that reserve and iron will. It could once have been done. It was not possible now. Suddenly the thought came to Nicole; she raised her head.

71

'When I'm twenty-one?—will I be able to see her then?'

William Osborne relaxed a little. The first flicker of something human had broken into that stony little face before him, the face that with its trace of childishness still left, still so much resembled the face of the older woman. The self-discipline in both those faces had almost repelled him. It was not natural that women should be this way. For the first time he began to feel easier about the situation, and relieved that he was not part of an instrument which had irrevocably separated this mother and her daughter.

'That will be your decision, or course. The terms of the will are only operative until you are twenty-one, at which time you will come into control of this money, and the right to decide whether or not you wish to see Mrs Rainard.'

'Will I know where she is? Will she keep in touch with you, even if she's not allowed to write to or see me?'

He shrugged. 'That will be *her* decision. If she chooses to communicate with us, we, at the proper time, will pass on whatever information we have.'

'I see.' It was said softly, with a kind of deadness of tone which Osborne hated. He talked further about plans for the future. Nicole gave monosyllabic replies, betraying no sense of curiosity about the people who were to become her guardians, about plans being made for her, where in England or Europe she might go to school.

'You don't seem interested,' Osborne said at last, driven to it by exasperation.

Nicole stood up. 'I'm not very interested, Mr Osborne. I have made application for admission to Vassar, Radcliffe, and Bennington. One of *those* places was where I was to go to school. I've worked for it. Do you expect me to get excited by places I've never heard of?' She reached for her hat and coat. 'May I go now? I'm sure you and Sir Charles Gowing's lawyers will fix up the details. There's really nothing for me to do, but do what I'm told, is there?' She pulled her hat on firmly, and he jumped to his feet, speechless, to help her on with her coat.

At that moment one of his two secretaries knocked, and opened the door. The other entered carrying a tray which contained William Osborne's idea of what a hungry young girl might like for tea. Nicole was already holding out her hand to him.

72

'But do stay and have some tea—an English custom I'm sure you'll get used to, and like.'

'Thank you, I think I would like to start back. There's a whole evening's study. So close to exams, one can't afford the time . . .'

And she left him, his secretary standing with her mouth just slightly open, bearing the tea tray with its little sandwiches, scones, tiny cakes. He had thought he was arranging a tea-party for a child, but this budding young woman was having none of it. Damn, he thought; she was so like that other woman who had compelled him to do things exactly as she wanted them done, and immediately. He hoped, against all practice, that when she was a grown woman, this girl didn't decide to give Fairfax & Osborne any of her business affairs to handle. He didn't want any more, either of Anna Rainard or her daughter.

When the chauffeured car William Osborne had hired for the journey drew out into the uptown traffic, Nicole said to the driver. 'I'll be making a stop, a short stop, on the way back.' She gave him the address on Central Park West, the apartment Anna had never let her see.

The driver protested. 'But I've had instructions . . .'

'That's all right,' Nicole said smoothly. 'It's all been arranged with Mr Osborne.' The man didn't believe that any kid wearing such a school uniform could lie like a veteran, so he did as she asked. The rest of the journey uptown was made in silence, Nicole desperately hoping that when they reached the address, the bluff would keep working. She said nothing but 'Thank you. I don't expect to be long,' as the driver held the door open for her at the entrance to the apartment block, which boasted a uniformed doorman, who hurried to open the door at the sight of the big chauffeured car, an apartment block which had no pretensions, was neither too shabby nor too grand. Nicole waited until the doorman let the door swing closed behind her before she spoke. She didn't want the driver to hear what came next.

'I'm Mrs Anna Rainard's daughter. She's staying near my school in the country and she's not well. She sent me to get a few things from her apartment. I realize . . . well, in the rush I forgot to bring the key. Can you let me in? I don't want to have to go all the way back.' She tilted her face upwards towards his, and gave the slightest smile. The man blinked rapidly, and wished she hadn't looked like that.

'Mrs Rainard's apartment? Well, we don't have any authority to let anyone ...' Another uniformed man was coming from behind a counter where a rack revealed apartment numbers and the mail sorted and waiting for the tenants. 'Mike, I'll handle it.' Then he in his turn looked hard at Nicole, and once again she used a rather wan smile. 'Mrs Rainard's sick, is she? Too bad. Sorry to hear that. And you're her daughter? Yes, she did go off a few days ago with bags and said she'd be gone for a while. Heard she had a kid ...' It took minutes more of talking before he produced keys, and took her up in the elevator. 'Against the rules, but, hell, you look so much like your mom, there couldn't be any trouble.'

'Yes, it was stupid of me to forget the key. And the note she wrote for you ... But she was so feverish with this 'flu ... and I didn't want to leave her too long. Thank you very much for your trouble ...' as the man opened the door of an apartment for her. Then, for the first time in her life she found herself passing over a five-dollar bill. 'My mother said to give you that.'

'Well, thanks. That's real nice of Mrs Rainard. She always was a real nice lady. Sorry about her being sick ...' He wanted to stay and talk, and Nicole found herself smiling again at him. 'I won't be long,' she said as she closed the door.

She hadn't known what to expect. It was nothing like Mrs Burnley's, of course. It didn't look the boudoir-like place she had dreaded, either. There was only one room beyond the small lobby, a room with a view of the park. There was a kitchenette, and a bathroom. It was comfortably but very simply furnished, neat and almost painfully clean. It told Nicole absolutely nothing of the woman who had lived here. There were a few books with Russian titles, but no piano. There were no magazines, no newspapers. Only the slight film of dust on the polished surfaces told her that no one had entered here for some days. There was no sense of disorder, or of anyone having left in a hurry. Nicole felt her throat tighten as she looked at it. Why had she come? What had she expected this place to tell her? Anna's final letter to her had been left with William Osborne. There was nothing for her here.

After a while she began to open closet doors, to open the drawers, searching for something of her mother. There was nothing identifiably hers. The dresses that still hung in the closets belonged to a nightclub entertainer, as did the astrakhan coat and hat. There was a satin-lined box full of costume jewellery, satin bags with silk stockings and lingerie neatly folded. Nicole had never seen underwear like this during the times she had shared a room with her mother. In the bathroom cupboard there were two bottles of perfume, and a whole range of cosmetics, three bottles of nail-polish. Nowhere could she find the neat dark dresses and coats Anna had always worn when she was with her. What remained in this apartment was what signified the woman, Anna Nicholas, the fill-in pianist who worked at Lucky Nolan's. Anna Rainard had gone.

Even the refrigerator had been emptied, and the current switched off, as if Anna had been careful of wasting electricity. Who would come, Nicole wondered, to take the rest of it?—the coffee, the tea and sugar, the tin of plain biscuits, the breakfast cereals? Where would the expensive evening dresses go? and who would use the perfume? Mr William Osborne didn't have the answers to everything. Nicole sat down in a chair, facing the open closet doors. Nothing, nothing at all. She had always known herself to be a solitary person, but she had never been absolutely alone until this moment. It was a shock to feel the tightening of her throat swell to a lump that could not be forced away. She seemed to have been a very young child the last time she could remember having wept. So now the tears that came, the blinding storm of tears, were totally unfamiliar, another and worse shock to add to all the ones these last days had given her. Nicole didn't recognize her own self weeping.

But she had stopped weeping, and leaned back in the chair, spent and exhausted, when she heard the door behind her open. She jumped to her feet angrily, thinking the man at the desk had returned. The words of protest died as she looked, for the second time in her life, at Lucky Nolan.

He removed his hat. He was wearing a dark coat over a dark suit. The slightly exaggerated cut of the coat, his dark, rather dapper good looks added up to someone who looked expensively, but just a little flashily, dressed. He looked what he was—a very successful nightclub owner.

'Well, kid . . .' he greeted her. 'Come to see if she left anything for you? Well, she didn't. I've been through it all.'

'How did you know . . .?' Nicole struggled for her words. The

75

winter afternoon had darkened, and she hoped this man would not see the signs of her weeping. But he switched on a table-lamp, and she blinked uneasily in the light.

'How did I know you were here?' he finished for her. 'The desk man downstairs called me. He's not quite as dumb as he seems. These apartment house guys, they know all the tenants' business. What else do they have to do all day but collect information? Sure he knew about me—what my name is, where to find me. He probably knows a hell of a lot more about you than you'd expect. Well, so he called me, and I came.'

'What for?'

He shrugged. 'Good question. I didn't know if there was may-be something I could do to help.'

'Do *you* know where she is?'

He shook his head. 'No, kid, and I'm not going to try to find out. It was quite a letter your mother wrote to me. She's a very determined woman. When she says it's over, I know it's over. Listen, you can't hold anyone—man or woman—when they want to go. She told me why she was going. You've always come first with her, kid. And I've always known it. She wanted every-thing for you. And now, because she thinks she's somehow going to get in the way when you might have a chance of marrying some big shot guy, she just ups and gets out. Don't ask me where Anna gets these ideas. Wouldn't be right for you to have a mother who was still working in a nightclub. She's too damn polite to say it wouldn't do to have *me* in the background either. So she leaves, disappears. She says "Thanks, Lucky, for every-thing. It's been swell knowing you." That's it.' He nodded to-wards the open closet doors. 'That's all of it. All that's left.'

He walked across the room and paused before the closet, running his hand along the row of dresses. 'Good taste, Anna had. Classy. That old fool of a grandfather you have, kid, he just should have seen her sometimes. He should have *seen* her.' He went to the open drawer and picked up a handful of the costume jewellery, and dropped it slowly back. 'I told you she wanted everything for you. Look, other dames would have had a few diamonds, a bracelet, earrings, things like that. No, not for Anna. She wanted your school paid. Sometimes, honest to God, I used to feel like a real cheapskate because she only had this junk stuff. But that's the way she wanted it. She used to say, "I don't need to get rich out of you, Lucky." Listen kid, when you find a dame like that, you hold on tight. But when she's gone, you know she's gone for good.' He banged the drawer closed. 'So she's gone.' He swung back and faced Nicole. 'So—is there anything I can do for you?'

'No,' she answered. '*They're* doing everything now.'

'Listen, kid, no use in being sore at me. That's the way things go. Yeah, I know you don't think much of me. But I gave Anna whatever she wanted for you. That old man, your grandfather, he wouldn't have been interested in some kid who'd come out of P.S. 43 in Bedford-Stuyvesant in Brooklyn. You can bet your boots he found out all about you before he decided to unload his money. Going to live with some fancy relations, aren't you— titles and all that? Well, it isn't my style, but Anna would have been all right there. Pity that old fool of a man never took the trouble to find out—*really* find out about her. Anna was the swellest dame I ever knew. They don't come like her much. I'll probably never see her again. But if that's the way she wants it, that's the way it's got to be. And listen, kid, if she ever gets in touch with you—if you're ever in touch with her, just say Lucky sends his regards. No—tell her Lucky sends his love.'

Nicole rubbed her face with a handkerchief, and buttoned her coat. 'I'm going now. I don't know why I came. There's nothing here——'

'There used to be quite a lot here for me.'

'*You!* If it hadn't been for you——'

'If it hadn't been for me you'd have been growing up like all the other kids in your neighbourhood. Don't forget it. The bad comes with the good, kid. I guess we'll both miss Anna ...'

She banged the door behind her and rang impatiently for the elevator. The man talked to her all the way down, and she didn't hear a word he said, didn't understand it. The driver was sitting in the lobby. 'It got cold out there, Miss. You said only a little while.' He opened the door for her. She didn't make any reply, and she bent her head so that perhaps the red puffiness of her eyes wouldn't be seen. All the way back to Connecticut she was silent. She decided that if William Osborne had telephoned Mother Mary Helena about her abrupt departure, and they wondered why she was so delayed, she would tell the truth, but only to Mother Mary Helena. She would say where she had been, but no more. Nothing and no one was going to make her talk about Lucky Nolan.

Anna Rainard moved on quickly from Chicago. She knew the letter to Lucky had been strongly worded, and that he usually respected what she said she must do. But there was a chance that this time he would not. So she moved on as far as San Francisco. She found a one-room efficiency apartment, put her savings into a chequeing account, sent a Post Office box address to William Osborne, and settled to wait until Henry Rainard's estate should be probated and the promised money sent to her. It would not be long, William Osborne had said; the payment to Anna Rainard was one of the first expenses the estate had to settle. She did not take or look for any sort of a job. Instead she enrolled at a secretarial school and dutifully spent half her day learning to type, which she found easy, and the other half struggling with the crypsis of shorthand, which she found extremely difficult. Most of the evenings she spent reviewing and trying to memorize what she had studied that day. It was a lonely existence; she was at least twenty years older than any other student taking the course. She ate her lunch-time hamburger alone, and fended off questions about herself. Wanting to be alone, she was left alone. Sometimes, as the spring advanced, she rode the ferries on the bay, revelling in the sight of what she thought was a beautiful city, liking, strangely, the patches of fog that came down suddenly, wetly, loving the eerily mournful sound of the fog horns. She would have liked to stay in San Francisco, but she was afraid that she might be traced there. So when in May the money came through from William Osborne, in the form of a treasurer's cheque, she paid her few bills, cashed the cheque which was in the name of Anna Rainard, and received in one hundred dollar bills from the hands of a vice-president of the bank, the price that Henry Rainard had been willing to place on her co-operation. The man was shocked that she took the money in cash and warned her about the dangers. She listened to him, nodded, and left. He sighed and supposed she was yet another whom the depression had taught to mistrust banks, and that it would go into shoeboxes in a closet somewhere.

Anna moved on to Los Angeles, found another one-room efficiency apartment in a small apartment block in Santa Monica and set about enrolling in another secretarial school.

Under the name of Anne Maynard she opened small accounts in banks scattered widely through Los Angeles, dividing up the money in amounts that would cause no particular attention to be paid to her. While she finished her secretarial course, she lived very economically, very sparsely. In San Francisco she had known the money she had saved would only hold out another few months. It had been a worrying time, when every job had hundreds of applicants, and the only thing she knew how to do was play the piano in some bar or nightclub—the sort of place where people who had ever seen her at Lucky's might recognize her, and report back to Lucky. So she held on to her money, and slaved at the shorthand. She finished the course first in the class in typing, and near the bottom in shorthand. Then she went looking for an office job. She found one, not very well paid, in the office of a small real estate broker who was just scraping by in these times when not many people were buying houses. She discovered the first day that no one was going to dictate at the rate of one hundred words a minute, and that the typing was minimal. She was left to mind the office and the telephone while her employer, Frank Hayward, was out driving round prospective clients. 'I need a neat, smart-looking woman like you, Mrs Maynard,' he had said frankly. 'This town is full of kids who want to be in the movies, and I don't want anyone like that in this office. Times are hard enough without having young chicks screw up the works getting messages wrong. Oh, and say, can you make any sense of cheque books? The office one's in a mess, and so is my personal one. There's a bit of back filing to be done when you can get around to it.'

She sat quietly day by day, taking what enquiries came in her correct shorthand, and typing them afterwards for Frank Hayward's attention. In a little while she was able to read the listings of the houses for sale as well as her own notes, and to turn them up while she held a person on the other end of the telephone line. She studied the map of Los Angeles so that she knew every district as if she had to fight a battle across its terrain. She asked Frank Hayward questions, drawing on his twenty-odd years in this still-infant city. The day that Frank Hayward sold an expensive house in Bel-Air which she had first recommended to a client as ideal for his needs, he gave her a slice of the commission. 'You've damn well earned it, Anne,' he said. He looked around the office, now as neat as the woman sitting at the typewriter. 'Don't know how I managed to get anything done without you. Listen, I'm taking the wife to dinner tonight to celebrate. You come along. Time you met her . . .'

She went, but unwillingly. The darkly subdued restaurant on Sunset Strip depressed her, reminding her too much of what she had left behind at Lucky's. She was uneasy, and the evening wasn't much of a success. Frank Hayward's wife, scrutinizing her, decided that it was a pity Mrs Maynard didn't make more of herself. She talked to her husband in the car on the way home. 'She could be stunning-looking if she tried. You know— go to the hairdresser instead of dragging her hair back that way. Wear a bit of make-up.' And then she added, 'Oh, hell, what am I saying? Who wants you shut up in an office all day with some siren?'

'Listen, honey,' he replied. 'I know a treasure when I've got it. I don't want to do anything to disturb that lady, and I don't want any distractions, either. Just thank your lucky stars.'

Anne Maynard, with the piece of the commission Frank Hayward had paid her, went and put a down-payment on a second-hand Ford. Then she needed to be taught how to drive it, so she hired the young boy who helped out at the used-car sales lot to give her lessons on Saturdays and Sundays. At first it was as difficult as shorthand. She began to realize that her time for learning such things was almost gone. The boy in the seat beside her winced as she crashed and scraped through the gear changes, shuddered as she went sailing through intersections, blushed when she held up traffic by stalling. But she did learn, eventually, and got the courage to drive by herself. The boy by then liked her and missed the lessons as much as the money. And Anne Maynard started on her deliberate, methodical search and scrutiny of every district of Los Angeles which until now she had only known on a map. Her weekends were spent on the road, driving at a sedate speed, only occasionally now crashing the gears, watching and noting the changes as she entered each neighbourhood, filing the knowledge away in her memory, making notes when she got home in the evening. It was a year before she had the courage to make her first purchase, a vacant lot on a corner of La Cienga Boulevard. In the meantime she continued to read the *Wall Street Journal* and to make very small purchases of very cheap stocks. 'Stocks!' Frank Hayward shouted at her when he discovered this. 'You're out of your mind!' The market'll never recover, Anne. You're just wasting your money, pouring it down a hole.'

'Perhaps,' she said, 'perhaps ...' And she returned to her struggle with the office accounts. After a while she looked across the office at Frank Hayward. 'Mr Hayward, I think I should take one of those night courses in accounting. I wouldn't ever pass the exams, but I might know the right column to post the figures in.'

He shook his head. 'Crazy, Anne, crazy. What do women need accounting for? And for heavens sake, just about everything in this country is going to be posted in red ink for a long time yet.' He shrugged. 'Well, it's your time ...' Then he added in an undertone, 'I can't understand why a woman like you isn't married.'

'I've been married, Mr Hayward.'

VI

In the months between March and June, Mary Helena was often troubled about Nicole Rainard. A kind of fierce energy seemed to burn in the girl; she worked as if she were possessed, as if entrance to a college would be her only salvation, and yet they all knew that in June, after her examinations were finished, she would go to England, and it wouldn't matter what her record was. At one time when Nicole had a cold, Mary Helena called the doctor. He spoke to her afterwards. 'There's nothing physically wrong with the girl except a bad head-cold. But she is in a fever over something. Whatever it is she wants, it it's in your power, give it to her. She's literally burning for something.'

There was a kind of anticlimax when she was accepted by Vassar, Radcliffe and Bennington. 'And I can't go to any of them,' she said when Mary Helena gave her the news.

'I didn't withdraw the applications,' Mary Helena said. 'I thought you'd want to know how you stood academically.'

Nicole shrugged. 'And in England they won't have heard of any of them. Well, it doesn't matter.' The fever was gone, replaced by a kind of apathy which made Mary Helena anguished to witness. Nicole Rainard was on her record one of the best students they had ever had at St Columba's. And still she was one of the most disappointing. Mary Helena had seldom witnessed a pupil leave with such misgivings. Perhaps her music professor had expressed it best. 'Technically, she's almost brilliant. But where is the heart? At the heart she seems dead.'

Mary Helena and another nun drove with Nicole down to the pier on 57th Street where the Cunard liners berthed. They saw her and her luggage aboard. They kissed her and there were small gifts exchanged. Mary Helena's to Nicole was a montage of the small spring flowers of the wood around St Columba's pressed and framed. 'Mine seems so unimaginative,' Nicole said as she passed over a specially bound volume of the psalms. The flowers in the glass entranced her and kept her from thinking of the moment of leave-taking. So many springs at St Columba's. What was an English spring like?

She waved to the two dark-garbed figures on the dock as the tugs pushed and pulled the Cunarder out of dock. She had almost expected that somewhere, somewhere in the background, she would see the figure of her mother, also dark-garbed, but splendid with a kind of rare beauty. But she was not there.

She went down to her stateroom. It symbolized the beginning of a new life because she was travelling first-class, and had a cabin to herself. She had two long dresses to wear to dinner, and she didn't know what to do with her hair.

A cabin-boy brought a huge vase of red roses, long-stemmed, the traditional American gift. 'The instructions were not to give it to you until after we'd sailed, Miss.' Nicole remembered to tip him, that also was part of the new life. Then she read the card.

'*Good luck, Lucky.*'

The thorns pierced her hands as she gathered the flowers savagely from the vase and carried them to the porthole. As she was about to thrust them through, she paused. '*Good luck, Lucky.*' What was the sense in throwing out good luck? She took them back to the vase and carefully rearranged them.

She brushed her hair and tied it in a loose knot, not chic, but something better than a schoolgirl. Then she went upstairs to arrange her place in the dining-saloon with the Head Steward. He had a note about Miss Nicole Rainard, travelling alone, but loosely under the supervision of a lady who was a friend of William Osborne; she was a niece of Sir Charles Gowing. He had been prepared to give her a pleasant, but fairly obscure table with the lady travelling companion. But when she stood before him, quietly asking where she would be seated, he swiftly rearranged his plans, so that she could be in the centre of the room. It would be a fairly dull crossing, and she would help to decorate the space.

On the way back to her cabin Nicole carefully watched to see what people were wearing. They said you didn't dress the first night out, but she wasn't sure. She had a lot to learn.

Part 2

Nicole

CHAPTER 1

I

Iris Gowing was a plain woman, who had never become reconciled to her plainness. In an effort to make people overlook her plainness, she had striven all her life to make them notice her in other ways, respect her, obey her. Too conscious that she was only one generation removed from the mill town her grandfather and father had created, she had put as much distance between it and herself as possible. She had been given as much education as her father had thought reasonable for a woman, she had been taught to arrange flowers, to manage a staff of servants, but she had not needed to be urged to climb the social ladder. Money had been her means; her father had made a generous settlement on her before she had married, another when her only brother had died, and she herself had found the men who could make more money for her. Her father had also advised her to get out of the market at the time he had sold his mills. He had never explained why, but she had obeyed him and the money was still intact. She now owned stretches of land under crops in the Midlands which she had never seen, streets of terraced houses in Manchester whose names she didn't know. She had shares in safe things which returned a safe income; she had three times the capital which her father had first settled on her, and a few good pictures she had been advised to buy. In her years of climbing away from the mill town in Yorkshire she had, through grinding hard work and single-mindedness, fought her way on to the committees of important charities. These absorbed most of her time. She sometimes forgot she was married to a quiet man with a limp, and when she did remember, it was with a shrug of impatience. Charles Gowing had been the last desperate straw at which she had clutched at the end of several seasons during which she had been mostly ignored by London society. She had suspected that he had married her because her money could help him to keep the place in Hampshire that he had inherited and which he could not any longer afford. It had given her a kind of satisfaction over the years to see that as little money as possible was spent on that small estate, until he had finally been forced to let the beautiful fourteenth-century house on a long lease, and retain only one of the lodges for his own retreat. Iris herself never went near the place; she had acquired a late-Georgian house in Surrey, conveniently close to London for weekend parties and just enough acreage to qualify as a country house. It was used only on weekends when she entertained. Charles's presence was then demanded, as it was when she gave dinner parties in London, or attended charity balls. The rest of the time she noticed him only in an absent-minded fashion; Charles was not a notable social asset. Like many other things in her life, and they included her own self, he had disappointed her. They rubbed along together, neither seeming to seek any alternative. It was a marriage not terribly different from many marriages she saw about her. The worst disappointment of all she never even discussed with her husband; she had no children.

It was with mixed feelings then that she waited for Charles to return from meeting the ship at Southampton which had brought her niece to England. She had learned long ago from her father that her brother Stephen had made a ridiculous match with some Russian in New York; there was one child he had never seen. And now this child was being thrust on her, this grown child who was not her own. As chairwoman of the committee of a well-known London society to aid orphans whose Patroness was a member of the Royal Family, she could not refuse what her father's will had thrust upon her. An unknown child was coming into her house, but the child was not her own. An American child, or that polyglot mixture which passed for American, would now be her responsibility. She hardly let herself remember how much she had wanted her own children as she filled the hours of waiting for the boat-train to come up from Southampton. She made telephone calls and worked steadily with the meek, dowdy, efficient little woman who came three times a week to help answer her mail. She asked the butler to wait when four-thirty came and Charles and the girl had not yet arrived. They would keep tea for an extra half-hour, she said, and went back to answering her letters.

It was over tea in the elegantly formal drawing-room, with its two Renoirs, at No. 14 Elgin Square that Iris Gowing first attempted an assessment of her niece. She was surprised, as she asked the usual questions about the crossing, the journey up to London, to find a faint stirring of jealousy in herself. It was unexpected. Who could be jealous of a child of seventeen? Not Iris Gowing, for so many years now secure in her social niche. And why? Was it because she herself wanted to be seventeen again, and most of all to look as this child did? Or was it because she had wanted so much to see her own daughter—or better, her son—sit where this stranger now sat?

What did she see? A girl, not a child. A girl with delicate but severely-cut features, strong eyebrows, and eyes which fitted no colour Iris could describe to herself. Not pretty, certainly not pretty. What else was there Iris preferred to leave unstated. But looking at her, observing her neat, confined movements, ambition which she had thought long dead began to grow again in Iris. 'Well, now, we must see what is to be arranged,' she said.

II

'I think, Iris, it's barely decent, when she's only just got here, to be planning to send her away. After all ... she's your niece. And your father's will expressly said——'

'A *European* education, Charles. The school in Paris is just what she needs to become accustomed ...'

'... accustomed to English ways in *Paris*.' His tone was acid.

'Charles, you don't understand. She's just out of a very *odd* sort of school. She's not *used* to anything. This school in Paris is filled with all sorts of girls—many English. They're all trying to get over the awkward stage before they come out. Of course ... well, she will be older than most, but one extra year doesn't matter. We're far too late for this season. Let's be in very good time for the next. I have to arrange a presentation at Court. That isn't done in five minutes ...'

Charles looked at his wife unhappily, but didn't argue further. Iris no doubt was right. She usually was, when it came to the ordering of the social scene. He thought rather bitterly that none knew it so well as those who had had to learn it. So he gave way, and retreated, as he had so many times before, into his newspaper, and left Iris to her letters, and her invitations.

But he didn't read the print before him. He was thinking of what these last few weeks had been. Before his eyes a young girl had responded to the passing show that was London. Because of her he had done things he had never done before. He had looked on the Crown Jewels at the Tower, had stood, his bad leg aching almost intolerably, for the time that it took to change the Guard at Buckingham Palace, had walked the halls of Hampton Court and Greenwich, had even, heaven help him, taken a punt out on the Thames at Marlow, and almost made a complete fool of himself. And all of this just to see some light of enjoyment, of recognition, of awareness come into that disturbingly calm little face. And his reward had been the beginning of a smile, and a quiet, 'Thank you, Uncle Charles.' And best of all, 'And what will we do tomorrow?'

So like a child she seemed, and yet she was no child. He hadn't missed the very nearly unconscious coquettishness in the way she sometimes talked to him, and the eyes of men which had followed her, of which she pretended to be unaware. She was either a fool, or a very clever girl, and he didn't think she was a fool.

And now Iris was proposing to pack her off in September to a finishing school in Paris. There, he supposed, she would learn the dreary things Iris had been taught—how to arrange flowers and cook. Iris had never cooked again in her life. And what did this young girl need to know of manners, when her own were so self-contained, so watchful that she would never put a finger wrong? When he had expressed this to Iris, she had a ready answer.

'That's the whole trouble, Charles, She's too watchful. She looks as if she's rehearsed something. She needs to learn to *relax* with people. She needs some confidence ...'

'And will she get it with a lot of giggling girls?'

'If she could learn to giggle just a little herself, she mightn't stand out so much.'

Charles privately thought it would be a pity if Nicole ever learned to giggle. 'Well, she says she wants to keep on with her music ...'

'Very admirable, I'm sure, Charles. Nice that she has some accomplishments, so long as they're not so formidable to frighten off the young men. Naturally I'm making arrangements for her to continue her music. But I wish ... well, I would have supposed she was past the time of those wretched scales. I wonder if it's really necessary to have to listen to them for an hour every morning?'

'I've always heard,' Charles answered, 'that all serious musicians play scales all their lives. You know ... exercising like a dancer.'

'My dear Charles, I hope you don't suppose Nicole is going to be a *serious* musician. Why, that would spoil *everything*—the presentation, the coming-out. Young girls like Nicole don't have careers. They marry.' She paused just a moment before returning to the correspondence on her desk. 'I wish though she'd play something ... well, something *entertaining* for a change. It won't do when she comes out to have to have everyone sitting around *listening* to her play. She should be able to manage the sort of thing young people dance to these days ... so amusing and helpful at a house-party, don't you think?' But she didn't wait for his reply, and he didn't offer one.

The weeks of the summer went swiftly for Nicole. There was one weekend when Iris entertained at Mowbray, the place so conveniently close to London. Nicole was part of the house-party, but there was no one of her own age there, and she was expected to stay in the background. Iris commanded her once to perform on the piano in the drawing-room which was just slightly out of tune, then dismissed her briskly. 'Nicole's not coming out until next season.' Nicole felt as if she had been put back in a bottle and re-corked. The next weekend party she asked to be excused from, and Iris rather too readily agreed. She found it disconcerting to have a silent girl around when the conversation flowed easily over the drinks. Yet she didn't want Nicole to talk; she was afraid of what she might say.

So Nicole and Charles fell into the habit of going down to Dencote Lodge, at the end of the back avenue of the estate which was leased, and might, he confessed, have to be sold. The weekends were the best time, better than the sightseeing in London, better than buying the new clothes with Iris. Here there was silence also; she and Charles didn't talk much. They drank wine together with their meals, and he read her bits from the newspapers. By the fire at night, or in the garden in the long twilights when it was warm, he sometimes talked about things

91

that interested him; he talked about money—not her money or Iris's money, but what he thought had gone wrong when the world money market had crashed, and why there were dole queues on the streets; he talked about the rise of dictators, the banning of books, the trouble brewing in Spain. Nicole listened in a growing wonder. She had never thought of these things, had never been asked to think of them. It was amazing to her that behind the shy, rather bumbling exterior Charles presented to the world, was a man who thought and worried about these things, who read extensively—the small lodge at Dencote was made almost uninhabitable by the bulk of his books—and had literally nothing else to do. He had given a good and honoured name to Iris and her great step up the social ladder. Nothing else was required of him, and no one seemed to need an ex-soldier when far younger men were walking the streets hunting for jobs. So they drank their wine and talked together and were companionably silent together. At last Charles said it.

'Do you want to talk about your mother?'

'I don't want to talk about her, but if you ask me, I will.'

She gave the details, very sparingly. She found she couldn't talk about Lucky Nolan. 'She said in her letter that it would be better if I told people that she was dead. It would save explanations.'

'Will you?'

'I don't know. It seems wrong. She isn't dead.'

'Will you try to see her again?'

'I'll try. If she'll let me. *She* will have to let me know where she is. My mother is a very determined woman. If she has decided to vanish for ever, I'm sure she'll make a very thorough job of it. That man—my grandfather—no, I don't want to talk about him. There's nothing good I could possibly say about him. If he'd only met my mother—just once. He didn't even give her a chance ...' She had got up then and poked the fire. There was no other light in the room. 'Uncle Charles, will you give me something? Will you give me a brandy? I've never had brandy before. I'll have to try these things. I would like the first time to be with you.'

He had hastened to do as she asked, pleased almost beyond his own believing that she had made the request to him. He also didn't want to talk of Iris's father, because the talk might lead on to Iris herself, and that was best left alone. He touched glasses with Nicole as she cautiously tasted the first brandy of her life, and already he was beginning to dread the coming of September, and the terrible gap which this not yet matured girl's going would leave in his life. He was quite aware that he had been lonely for many years, but when she was gone, there would be a special kind of loneliness. So he savoured the fleeting days of summer, and did everything in his power to bring the rare smile of pleasure to the girl's face, the enigmatic smile that was both innocence and terrifying knowledge.

CHAPTER 2

I

It was Charles who accompanied her to Paris. 'Really quite unnecessary, Charles. Nicole can be met at the station by someone from the school. She's quite of an age to travel by herself.'

'Oh, I don't know ...' he had answered vaguely. 'Hell of a long time since I've been in Paris, Iris. I thought we might go over a few days early. I wouldn't mind a spot of sightseeing. Taking Nicole around London has made me realize what I've been missing ...'

She had shrugged. 'As you wish, Charles.' Iris would be glad to have Nicole gone. For some reason the girl made her uncomfortable; Iris was not used to being watched, perhaps watched critically. The ambition she had once felt for her own self, and then for the children she did not have, might have flared again when she had seen Nicole, but that did not mean that she also had to like the girl. She simply wanted to make a success of her; that was something quite different.

So Charles and Nicole spent the first dusty, dry days of September wandering the boulevards of Paris, doing the obvious things that tourists always did. Charles spent a passive half-hour looking down on the tomb of Napoleon, reciting, with a military man's love of such names, the places of the great battles, the road of the long retreat from Moscow. 'He shook the whole of Europe, Nicole, and he almost had *us* at times. But at Waterloo we finally beat him—but only by the skin of our teeth. We don't admit it, but we only hung on by the skin of our teeth in the last war, too. And if our blockhead politicians have their way, we won't have any skin on our teeth by way of armaments when the next war rolls around.'

She had looked at him, startled. 'There won't be another war, Uncle Charles. There can't be!'

'There could be, there quite easily could be if people don't wake up.' He gestured to the faded flags of Napoleon's campaigns. 'There have always been wars, and men to wage them.'

One other thing was settled before Charles left Paris. On the appointed day they had gone to Madame Graneau's school near the fashionable Rue Martin. It was a splendid old house whose main doors opened into a courtyard which had once received coaches. The noise of the traffic now was remote. Nicole and Charles waited for Madame Graneau in a room decorated with long gilt-framed mirrors and Louis XV tapestry-covered chairs; here the windows looked into a smaller courtyard, where pear trees were espaliered against a sunny south wall. There was an air of calm and dignity about the place, and, to Nicole, the scent of money. That smell was now something tangible to her, and it differed—it was what she had experienced that night at Lucky Nolan's; it was the puckering of her nostrils when she had viewed the private beaches in Maine; it was the smell of flowers and Chinese tea in the drawing-room at 14 Elgin Square and the scent of wax in this hushed room and the pears ripening on a wall in the heart of Paris.

Madame Graneau entered, a handsome, tall figure whom Nicole knew instinctively would command respect from her students. She was dressed in black, but it was a dress that might have come from a quietly elegant salon of the *haute couture*. She talked in perfect, precise, almost accentless English. 'We shall concentrate on your French,' she said to Nicole, 'although I understand you are already quite fluent. You should also undertake some German—we have some German students here, who, of course, come to learn French.' She laughed a little. 'You will find us a mixed lot, all anxious to learn from each other. We like to send you from here a confident and well-rounded young woman. It is as important to know how to shop carefully in the market as it is to choose one's dressmaker. No one who leaves this school should ever be helpless in the kitchen, or unable to handle a needle, no matter how many servants there are at home.' She looked directly at Nicole. 'The world is a place of change. Fortunes rise and fall. We like to think we give our girls a chance to grow up. We hope they will be useful as well as graceful women.'

Charles nodded. 'Graceful ...' Spoken thus by this elegant French woman the word had a different meaning from the one he usually gave it. Grace implied a lot of things other than the lack of clumsiness; he suddenly sensed tranquillity in that word and in this woman, and he hoped with all his heart that when she returned to London, Nicole's tightly closed face might reflect some of this tranquillity.

Madame Graneau had had a report from St Columba's; she talked of Radcliffe, Bennington and Vassar. 'I understand that your special gift is the piano, and that you want to continue it.'

'Seriously,' Nicole said, speaking almost for the first time. 'It's very special.'

'We have an excellent music mistress here . . . but perhaps . . .'

It ended with the mistress, Mlle Boucher, being summoned to the room. Nicole was invited to play at the grand piano. After rubbing her suddenly cold hands to relax and warm them, Nicole chose the Chopin Ballade in G. When she had finished, Mlle Boucher nodded quietly. 'Do you have any Mozart from memory? That or Beethoven.' Nicole licked her lips and began the first movement of the Waldstein sonata.

Mlle Boucher interrupted when the movement came to an end. 'That will be sufficient for the time, Mademoiselle Rainard.'

She spoke quietly with Madame Graneau and Charles for a few minutes. The next day Nicole accompanied her to the Conservatoire. There she played, after waiting a nervous hour, for Professor Lermanov. He listened without comment as she played, gave her a sight-reading test, brought three other students to perform one movement of a Brahms quartet with her. When the ordeal was over, he merely nodded. 'I will accept you. Do you understand what that means, Mademoiselle? I know what sort of school you are attending in Paris. Excellent in its way, but not for professionals. I say to you this. I will have no dilettante wasting my time. Students are lined up. I will take only the most promising. Unless you are prepared to give more than you think you can, we will end this interview now. How hard can you work, Mademoiselle?'

'Very hard.'

His grey, seamed face almost relaxed into a wintry smile. 'I think you have yet to learn what very hard means. You will learn, or you will go.'

Charles was permitted to take Nicole to dinner that last

night, a night when most of the other students were arriving, and classes had not yet begun.

'Are you sure you really want the Conservatoire, Nicole? It's a damned hard bash to go through. It seems to me you play wonderfully now.'

She smiled, and he was glad to see some sense of excitement in her expression. 'I haven't begun,' she said.

She found that the girl she was to share a room with was English. She was thankful that it wasn't one of the German girls, whose language she didn't understand, nor one of the French, who seemed to her, for their age, strangely sophisticated—or was it that they had the ease of being at home, and speaking their own language? The girl's name was Judy Fenton. She was pretty in a soft blonde way, with a beautiful complexion and teeth, and strong, capable-looking hands. She seemed shy, and a little awkward, and her clothes were plain and sensible, rather than decorative. Quite unselfconsciously she put a photograph of a horse on the mantel. 'Do you mind?' she said to Nicole. 'Old Trooper reminds me of home almost more than anyone else. He practically brought me up ...' She looked at Nicole's side of the room, neat and almost bare, the new luggage, the new clothes. 'Haven't you any photos of your own? It's your room, too.'

Nicole found herself repeating the lie about her mother that Iris Gowing had told anyone who had asked. Her mother was dead; she was the ward of Iris and Charles. She despised herself as she listened to the words come out. She already seemed to have thrown her lot in with the twisted old man who had made that will, to have declared herself to belong to the English side of her. She felt herself flush with shame. Judy Fenton mistook it for distress, and her sympathy was instant and generous.

'Oh, I'm sorry. What a rotten thing to happen. You've hardly any family then, just this new aunt you hardly know.' She shook her head. 'I find that hard to imagine. I've got so much family—Allan and Richard and Ross. And cousins. I'm the only girl in the family. No wonder I look like a horse.' In an eagerness to share that Nicole found oddly touching, she dragged out the photo album. 'Well, might as well get it over ... Might as well bore you in the beginning.'

Nicole didn't find it boring. It struck her that all the years she had been at St Columba's she had never been able to share in this fashion in anyone else's life; it occurred to her that she hadn't wanted to share because of what they might ask in return. For this Judy Fenton she suddenly found she wanted to give what she could. It didn't at this moment, seem she had very much.

The album was pictures of people, dogs, horses, pictures of hunt meets and gymkhanas. There were many pictures of her mother, a beautiful woman generally wearing a battered straw hat and pictured in the garden, her hands busy among plants. Nicole was suddenly aware of the lack of photographs in her own life. There had never been a box Brownie on those summer vacations in Maine. She now remembered that the only photograph she had ever seen of Anna had been of the night-club pianist on the board outside Lucky Nolan's. Not a picture to display at Madame Graneau's.

The backgrounds of Judy Fenton's pictures were often of the house she lived in—a low, half-timbered house of the Tudor period Nicole thought, a house of rambling roofs and old brick chimneys, a house that looked as if it had been sunk in its earth for ever. 'It's called Fenton Field,' Judy said. 'It's mentioned in the "Domesday Book." Of course *this* house couldn't have been there then—it's sixteenth-century, they think. But there was probably a cow byre and a pigsty which belonged to some remote ancestor, and they wrote it down as Fenton Field.' And Nicole was aware, at that moment, of envy, almost jealousy, of someone who could speak, not boastfully, of ancestors who went back to the time of William the Conqueror. 'It's very old,' she said, and the words almost stuck in her mouth. 'Very beautiful.'

Judy made a face. 'Father's always complaining of how much it costs to keep in repair. But of course he'd do without anything else to keep it. He's a farmer. There's always something that needs improving, or rebuilding. He always wants to buy better stock, new equipment ... all that. And then he has this gang of children to bring up and educate.' She lowered her head and stared hard at the last picture of the house. 'It costs a lot for me to come here. Really more than Father can afford.'

'Why did you come, then?' Nicole asked. Judy's talk almost seemed to invite the question.

'Oh, hell, I might as well get it out now. I'm such a cry-baby.

If you find me in tears some day ... Well, look——' She produced the last snapshot, one inserted in the leaves of the album, not given a permanent place. '*Him*,' she said. 'Stupid, isn't it?' Nicole leaned forward to inspect the blurred photo of a masculine figure on a horse. 'You know, it couldn't be sillier,' Judy went on. 'I fell in love with him. A crazy schoolgirl crush. Only it doesn't seem crazy to me.'

'Well, perhaps ...'

Judy flung her head up. 'No "perhaps" about it. He's twice my age, he's married, and he's no intention of breaking up his life and mine to do anything about a thing so crazy as a puppy love. He was nice to me. He used to buy me drinks when we were having the hunt meet at some pub. He watched to see that I was all right on the field. At the hunt balls he danced with me. There was nothing more. But I ...' She gave a painful little gasp. 'I had to make believe it was something much more. On my side it was. It just became all too obvious. For the sake of everyone I just had to ask to go away somewhere. So Mother found this place. I'm supposed to be "finished".' She flung back her head. 'I intend to come out of here a perfectly grown-up woman, not a schoolgirl. And yet——' She snapped the album shut. 'I'm nearly dying from homesickness right now, and I've only just arrived. I'm a fool. I *know* I'm a fool. And Mother and Father were so good about it ...'

Nicole made some comment, something that seemed to reassure Judy, and once again she was conscious of a sense of envy. Even if it was, as Judy said, puppy love, at least she had had that. And she'd had parents who knew about it, and tried to help her. The strength this girl could call on from a family and a house, a way of living that had evolved over centuries, was something Nicole could only imagine, but not completely understand. She wanted this girl for a friend. Like Charles, she represented an anchor in a new world, and one which Nicole badly wanted. For the first time in her life she was ready to make changes in herself to try to accommodate someone else.

The weeks of the gusty autumn fled into the early winter. Judy got up early every day to go riding in the Bois; she had begun to take dressage seriously. Nicole got up just as early. They would have a cup of coffee and brioche, before going their separate ways. For Nicole it was two hours in the big graceful room, which was cold at that early hour, to practise at the grand piano. Another two hours were squeezed in in the late afternoon. In between were busy hours of cooking lessons, visits to galleries; there were evenings at the Opera, and the *Comédie française*. Despite the arranged visits to the kitchen of Maxim's, and the ritual eating of the dishes they were supposed to have cooked, Nicole never worked up much enthusiasm for cooking. Her dishes, if not downright failures, were never outstanding successes. More than the cooking she liked the weeks when it was her turn to accompany the housekeeper early in the morning to the market of Les Halles. She loved the smell of the food, the sense of bargaining enjoyed for its own sake, the onion soup with fresh bread when the shopping was done. She loved the armfuls of flowers; she had less enthusiasm for the long task of arranging them.

Nicole learned, to some degree, the art of small talk, and how to cover what she didn't want to talk about. At Madame Graneau's they dressed for dinner every night, as if this would be normal in the homes they returned to; they were invited to discuss the wines they tasted nightly, and what they had read in that day's newspapers. Nicole found herself inventing things that happened at the Conservatoire, or embellishing them, repeating little jokes. Judy talked about horses, and she and Nicole went, with six other girls and a mistress, to Longchamps. Nicole followed Judy's tips blindly, and knew a satisfaction she had never tasted before when she ended the afternoon with modest winnings. She and Judy bought champagne for the other girls with the winnings, and it was all gone. That night Nicole skipped her two hours of practice, and didn't feel guilty. And Christmas came.

'I wish you were coming to Fenton Field,' Judy said as they parted. 'Christmas is wonderful at home.'

Nicole went back to Elgin Square and then to a house-party at Mowbray over Christmas. Iris had taken trouble to include some people of Nicole's own age, and they all drove down into Kent for the Boxing Day hunt meet. Because of Judy, Nicole found she could murmur what passed for the right remarks about the horses—and the people. Everyone sounded suitably bored. At the party that night she was kissed with expertise by a man who danced her out into a dim passage. Ronnie someone . . . she couldn't remember his name. She felt it was absurd that it was the first time she had been kissed in that way. Next day she packed and went back to London, telling Iris simply that she couldn't miss any more days from practice. Charles came back before the New Year's Eve party which Iris had planned. 'Your aunt is very upset with you,' he said. 'I think we should both go down for the New Year's Eve party ...' Nicole, working on a Mozart piano concerto, had barely time to register what he said. 'I have to have this in pretty good shape before I go back to Professor Lermanov. He wouldn't hesitate to throw me out if he thought I'd spent weeks away from the piano.'

But she did go down with Charles for the party on New Year's Eve, and actually found herself enjoying it. For one thing, it was so crowded that it was possible to escape Iris's scrutiny. At midnight everyone kissed everyone else. Nicole joined in without feeling too foolish. Several men, without knowing who she was, offered to drive her home. She said 'yes' to all of them, and then made sure that she was with Charles for the drive back to London. The first pale light was creeping over the grey cold streets when they arrived at Elgin Square. 'This year I'll be eighteen,' Nicole said and yawned. 'What a long time it seems until I'll be twenty-one.'

Charles didn't reply, and Nicole sensed she'd hurt him. She didn't know what to say, but as she went up the stairs, almost stumbling in her weariness, she turned back to him. 'I hope it's a good New Year, Uncle Charles.'

Winter went, and spring came to Paris. Nicole was hardly conscious of the weeks passing. Her life seemed to be lived less at Madame Graneau's, and more at the Conservatoire. She was behind other students of her age; she had to hurry. She faced Lermanov with this one day when the budding of the chestnuts forced on her the fact that the planned presentation at Court in London, and the coming-out was almost upon her. Iris had even been over to Paris to make the choice of clothes for her, and left her to the ordeal of the long sessions of fittings. 'Professor,' she said, 'am I going to be any good? Am I too late with it all?— should I be much further on?'

'You should be, but you can afford to wait,' he said. 'Unlike some of my other students, some of whom have more talent, you have the money to wait. You may be better for a few more years of maturity before you make your début.'

She thought then that he hadn't the faintest concern or

notion of the début that was planned for her that year in London. The storm burst when she wrote to Iris and Charles and announced that she wouldn't be returning to London that summer, that the presentation at Court and the coming-out must be postponed, better still, abandoned.

Charles came over to see her. 'Your aunt is furious. She's gone to a lot of trouble, Nicole ... can't you just fall in with her for these few months?—and then you can come back here in September. She'll have her parties, and you'll still have your music. Humour her ...'

'I can't, Uncle Charles. If I take a summer away from music, if I get myself mixed up at this stage, I'll never come back. Lermanov won't take me. If I go now, it's all finished ...'

'But even Lermanov takes the summer off.'

'*He* does, but he doesn't expect his students to. A month perhaps, no more.'

Charles argued for hours, and then left her in peace. He privately thought her notion was an excuse for avoiding all the things that Iris had arranged, a declaration of independence that she had to make in order not to be turned into some object that Iris simply regarded as a vehicle for her own ambition. He explained as best he could to Iris, and found no understanding there.

'It's *outrageous*, Charles. She *can't* do it!'

'I don't see how you can make her do anything different. You would be hard put to make a case to the trustees of the estate that she wasn't furthering her education—exactly as her grandfather's will stipulated.'

'Oh, *you*!—you encourage her in this! Well, she needn't think I shall bother with her again until I've had an apology and her agreement that she will do exactly as I say.'

'It will be some time coming, Iris. Nicole has been doing, so far as I can see, exactly what she's been told all her life. One must expect at some time ...'

So Nicole didn't return to London that summer. She and Charles moved around the cities of Europe—Rome, Venice, Florence, Vienna. They did their daily stint of sightseeing, and at night there was the theatre and concerts. And always there was some place found where Nicole could hire a rehearsal studio for at least four hours a day. Charles wearily following her in the dusty heat of the Italian summer, wondered again where she found her energy. She could appear so perfectly, deliciously idle when she chose, such as the times when they sat at sidewalk cafés eating ice-cream and sipping coffee. None of the men who openly stared at her could imagine behind that smooth façade the driving energy that got her from her bed before seven every morning.

Judy Fenton joined them for the last month, when the August heat drove them to a chalet with a piano in the Alps high above the Rhône. 'It's no good,' Judy confessed to Nicole. 'I'm just not ready to be back permanently at Fenton Field yet. I still make a fool of myself over ... over *him*. I thought it was all finished, but if we happen to meet anywhere I still can't stop myself coming out in goose-pimples. It's so *stupid* ...!' She flung herself down in the long grass of the high meadow and turned her back on the view.

So Judy also was back at Madame Graneau's, but this year as an assistant teacher. She spent half her day working for the riding stable which took Madame Graneau's pupils on their morning ride in the Bois, and the rest helping to supervise the cookery classes and any other task she could be fitted to. 'I never imagined,' Judy said, 'I'd have any bent for Cordon Bleu, or help anyone to know how to stock a cellar. But I'm earning my keep, at least. Father doesn't have to pay for me any more. And they can tell people at home that I have a job in Paris. A *job* ... It sounds grown-up, the way I want to be. I'm not Little Judy Fenton any more. Come to think of it, you and I are the oldest here, Nicole. The odd ones ...'

Nicole didn't care; it didn't seem very different. She had always been odd, but she'd never had a companion in her oddness. When Christmas came around again there was an invitation to join Judy at Fenton Field, but no word from Iris. So she refused Mrs Fenton's invitation, and shut herself up with the piano in the mirrored drawing-room at Madame Graneau's, one of three other pupils who had nowhere to go that Christmas. She felt almost as she had felt during the holidays when she had remained at St Columba's. But this time it wasn't lack of money which was the cause, but the presence of money. She began to recognize that money was cushioning her from the worst that her decision to hold out against Iris might have entailed; she began, just faintly, to glimpse the course of her own rebellion. Charles came over to Paris for the New Year, and took her to Maxim's. 'Had enough yet, Nicole?' he said. 'Haven't you shown what you can do? You've made your point with Iris. Are you really *sure* you want to spend the rest of your life tumbling out of bed at the crack of dawn, travelling all over the world to play in strange concert halls, live in hotels, have managers and secretaries——'

She cut him short. 'I'd only have those things if I were really good. A *success*. I want to be a success, Uncle Charles.' She raised her glass to him. 'Happy New Year,' and she was thinking of her mother, who had walked out of her life so that she might sit in this very place, might be able to dream of giving concerts. She wondered if it was all because she had some ill-defined, confused idea of her name on a billboard in some city where her mother would see it. And suddenly the New Year champagne tasted flat. It was too flimsy a foundation on which to build a whole life. 'What shall I do, Uncle Charles?' she said simply. 'I don't know what to do.'

He shook his head. 'This time I'm not going to try to tell you. I wish you could be more like Judy Fenton. She'll doubtless be married, and have a family ...'

'We're on the outside of all that, Uncle Charles—you and I, and Aunt Iris. We don't know what families are all about.'

It was cold in Paris that winter, but Judy Fenton's mood was exuberantly warm. 'I'm going home for good at Easter, Nicole! It's all over. I can go back. I met *him* at two parties during Christmas, and he was at the meet on Boxing Day. I didn't turn a hair. But I'm not sorry about it—he's still nice. But he just seems like any other man now.'

'You're going to leave ...' Nicole said. A sense of loneliness engulfed her.

'I can't stay here for ever,' Judy said. 'I've been good, and learned things, and I'll be useful at home. But I'll never be Madame Graneau. I don't *want* to be Madame Graneau!'

Charles took Nicole to Cannes that Easter. A cold wind blew off the Mediterranean, and they bundled into thick coats to walk the promenade. At the end of four days Nicole said, 'I give in, Uncles Charles. I'm ready to come back to London now. I'll do everything Aunt Iris wants me to do. How do I tell her?'

'I'll tell her. *You'll* have to apologize.'

The letter was written, and a stiff answer came back. It was too late to start making arrangements, but it could be done, if Iris had Nicole's promise that there would be no further changes of plan. 'You have made me look a *fool*,' the letter read, 'I shall expect just that much more from you to compensate.' And Nicole had given her promise. She went back to Paris and the trees were starting to bud along the boulevards. It was, at last, her own springtime. A kind of formal reconciliation with Iris was made as they discussed the new clothes she would buy. 'You will be a rather *elderly* débutante,' Iris said witheringly. 'The dresses of a very young girl aren't suitable.' Nicole took her advice on most of the clothes, and affected subtle alterations in the style when Iris had returned to London.

The scene with Lermanov was memorable. His face went white with rage. 'You insult me, Mademoiselle. Who told you you could give up your studies? Did I tell you? *Did* I?'

'No—I just decided I wasn't good enough.'

'*You* decided! It is *I* who decide such things. Well then, you are right. You are not good enough. You have wasted my time. You are that worst of all things, a dilettante. You have taken the place of those more deserving than you, and now you come and say *you* have decided. No—don't apologize. I have been mistaken. I seldom make mistakes, but with you I have. You wouldn't have made it. You aren't big enough. So go off and play your little pieces in drawing-rooms. *Amuse* yourself. And you can always boast that you were a pupil of the great Lermanov in Paris. But for me, I never knew a Mademoiselle Rainard. Now please leave me to continue with my *serious* work. There are others waiting!'

Before she left Paris Nicole did what she had not had the courage to do before. She walked the cemetery of Père Lachaise until she found the grave of her grandmother, Katerina Andreyevna Tenishevna. She remembered that Anna had told her that even when Katerina lay dying she would never permit a practice session of Anna's to be missed. She laid the spring flowers that she had brought with her on the grave with a mute apology. She was the product of two generations of music students and teachers, and she had walked out on the great Lermanov. He would not forgive her. She wondered if those two women would have.

That was her last task in Paris, one she had not been able to steel herself to until the very moment of leaving. Then she went back to London and decided that there was something else she could be a success at. She could have a try at being a young woman enjoying herself. It couldn't be so hard. It was more than a year since she had seen the coast of England emerge from the mists of the Channel. She had capitulated to the English dictates. She could carry it all through with the grace Madame Graneau expected of her, and the lack of regret that Lermanov despised. She would not look back.

CHAPTER 3

I

Elgin Square seemed unchanged; the April leaves were in full spate on the plane trees, the last of the daffodils were in bloom, the square drowsed in the spring sunshine which showed the gleam of its shining paint and brass doorknobs and number plates. There was a scent of wallflowers from the window boxes. It seemed a world unchanging and unchangeable. Nicole felt a surprising surge of excitement as the cab came to the door, and Adams responded at once, welcoming her back, and seeing to her luggage. Charles was out on the pavement, and Iris stood, a rare gesture of welcome for her, on the top of the steps. It was close to two years since Nicole had first seen No. 14 Elgin Square, and had bottled her nervousness within herself. Now she approached it as if it were not precisely a friendly place, but at least a familiar one.

Inside there were a few changes—the hall a shade of Wedgwood green, the moulding of the ceiling picked out in white, the carpet on the stair had changed to a plain, darker green. Although it was an old house, it looked new. There was no sign of chipped paintwork anywhere, no curtain faded along its folds. As they passed the floor where Iris and Charles slept, Iris showed her the new bathrooms—two of them in the space of the single old-fashioned one that had been there, a new dressing-room for herself, and Charles's bedroom redecorated. Here were most of the regimental pictures she remembered, and the pictures of Dencote now banished from the library below. It seemed as if Iris had decided to put Charles and all his memories tidily into one room, where they didn't disturb her. On the next floor was the room Nicole had always used, but it was changed now. Here too, the bathroom had been modernized, all the porcelain fittings were in pink, and a dressing-room fashioned out of its original space. The bedroom itself had changed; everything done in shades of chintz to tone into the rose-pink carpet. Iris evidently didn't remember that Nicole didn't care much for pink. It was all soft, with silk fringed lampshades, and rose velvet cushions on the chintz sofa. There were white-painted bookshelves, mostly bare. There were matching antique covered bowls on the dressing table, decorated with sprays of roses; before the mirror stood a vase of tiny pink hothouse rose buds. There was an ivory-coloured telephone on a Louis XIV table by the bed, and a headboard covered in pink silk. The room was a sort of princess's dream; Nicole thought there should have been a golden-haired girl waking to life in that bed, all soft and pink herself. She could have laughed, but she did not. 'Thank you, Aunt Iris—it's very beautiful. Thank you ...' And she saw from the hungry tightness in her aunt's face that this was the room Iris herself had wanted as a young girl. Nicole now knew enough about the North of England, and the Yorkshire mill-owner who had been her grandfather, to know that there had been no such fairy-tale room for Iris. Iris had come from a world where the mahogany was solid, the curtains dark, the carpets were all turkey red, and nothing ever wore out. 'How kind of you,' she added. 'You've thought of everything ...'

'Well ...' Iris relaxed. She moved around the room, touching things here and there, explaining where this had come from, and that. 'Room for your own books, of course. I have the frames ready for the photographs ...'

'I haven't any photographs.'

'Your presentation photograph. Your coming-out ball ...' It was all arranged.

There was another change. Iris grew embarrassed and almost defensive as she led Nicole up another flight of stairs. This was the floor which would once have been the nursery floor; it was inhabited now by the cook and two maids. Adams had the top floor all to himself. Iris was a careful housekeeper and knew how to keep her valued servants; the carpet did not change to linoleum here, and the woodwork was as freshly painted as below. She led Nicole to the room farthest at the back, a small but well-lighted room overlooking the mews cottages far below, and towards the high roofs of the next square.

Nicole had never seen this room before. 'It used to be a box room,' Iris said, 'but one collects such rubbish ...' It was perfectly bare and white, except for the brown carpet. It had a writing table and a chair, and one easy chair. It also had a grand piano. 'Charles's idea,' Iris said. 'It's been sound-proofed—that is as much as one can manage in an old house.' She nodded towards the shelves. 'The piano people assure me they're the right size for music. There's just one thing. I must ask you not to play between two and four in the afternoon, and of course not unreasonably early in the morning or late at night. Adams has his quarters directly above here. I can't have him disturbed during his hours off ...'

Nicole stumbled over her words, and she felt her throat tighten. 'I don't know what to say ... How do I thank you? I've never had a room ...' She went to the only ornament the place possessed, a small wooden bust of Beethoven, touched it tentatively, thinking of Lermanov's scorn.

'Charles found that,' Iris said, as if to dissociate herself from anything so frowningly ferocious. 'It seems very bare, but no doubt you'll find your own things to put here. Of course, that doesn't mean you can't use the piano in the drawing-room, but Charles tells me you'll still wants to practise. The piano downstairs needs tuning ... the man was to have come this morning ...'

'I can do it, Aunt Iris,' Nicole said eagerly. 'You have to be able to tune a piano. It's part of the training——'

'That won't be necessary, Nicole. There are people to do that. You won't have much time to yourself, you know ...' Her glance swept around the bare room. 'Not much time for this. I'm sure ...' Now she looked back at Nicole with great directness, a plain woman, as she had always been, well but unimaginatively dressed, her hair sculpted into iron waves, the efficient, untiring chairwoman of half a dozen important committees, an ambitious woman seeing in this girl before her a chance to achieve a wish she thought long dead. 'I'm sure, now that you have decided to come back and have your season, you will be a success. A *great* success. It's quite hard work. Not much time for sleeping ...' And, she implied, not much time for what this room contained.

Nicole knew what she had promised. 'I'll do everything you want me to, Aunt Iris.'

Iris nodded briskly, indicating with that single gesture that the room was already paid for. 'Now we must go downstairs. Adams will have tea waiting.' She threw back over her shoulder as they went down, 'I've engaged a maid for you. During the season you'll be too busy to see to your clothes yourself. Her name is Henson. She'll take care of your unpacking . . .'

It was all arranged. All Nicole had to do was to keep her promise, and Iris would ask nothing else. At that moment it seemed an easy thing to do.

Charles was waiting in the library, and so was Judy Fenton. Nicole knew at once that this was another concession from Iris, possibly made at Charles's insistence. They looked at each other a moment, and then laughed in a kind of excitement that seemed to say that each recognized the difference in the other. Judy seemed older—and Nicole had never seen her so smartly dressed. She carried an air of authority about her that would never have belonged to the soft blonde prettiness of eighteen months ago. They fell into a rapid French exchange that seemed, after all the time at Madame Graneau's, quite natural, and then laughed and went back to English.

'Lady Gowing was kind enough to invite me, and Mother urged me to come. She thinks I should enjoy some of my "finish" while it's still on me.'

'You're not going to do the season, are you?' Nicole asked.

Judy grimaced. 'It would be a waste. An absolute waste. I've been invited to a few balls. Just as a sort of country cousin, though. I'm taking over a lot of things at home from Mother, and the horses——'

'You could share——' Nicole stopped short. She had been about to suggest that Judy share her own coming-out ball, and in time she had seen Iris's expression, and remembered her promise. Iris would not permit anyone else on the receiving line on the night for which she had waited so long. So Nicole stifled the impulse, and felt that she had begun, already, to betray her friendship with Judy. So she said, looking directly at her aunt, 'It will be all right if Judy stays here whenever she has to come to town for a ball, won't it?'

'Of course,' Iris said, gracious now that the threatened danger had been passed. 'No doubt they will be the same balls you've been invited to, Nicole.' She added, 'Would your pour please? I just want to run through the list of luncheon parties you've been invited to, and the ones at which you'll be the hostess. It's necessary, of course, to know a nucleus of girls and their mothers before the season starts properly. It's no use having balls where everyone's a stranger to each other ...'

The talk went on and on, or at least Iris's talk did. Nicole said 'yes' to everything, and often felt Charles's gaze of gratitude of her, and Iris's more appraising look, the careful scrutiny of the way she handled the tea-pouring, the replenishing of plates, even ringing for Adams when more tea was needed. Iris visibly relaxed during this time. She could scarcely recall the silent, nervous, little dark-haired girl who had sat here two years before. This one had even grown an inch or two, she talked and made little jokes, her hand didn't tremble as she held the tea-cup. Even being nineteen years old, Iris conceded, might be an advantage; she could make the seventeen-year-olds look rather silly. She nodded in satisfaction as she ticked off the long list. The two-year wait had been worth it. She almost persuaded herself that the extra year had been her own idea.

'Just a week, Aunt Iris,' Nicole said. 'Only a week. There's plenty of time after that for the rehearsals and the lunches. Nothing starts until May, and I'd so love to go to Fenton Field. Judy's finished her shopping, and I haven't any more fittings for a week ...' She stopped there. It was dangerous to push Iris too far.

'Well ... I don't see why not.' Iris had made her own enquiries about the Fentons. There was no real money in Judy's family—comfortable Sussex farmers was how Iris would have described them. But they were well-connected. Judy's mother was a first cousin to the Cavendish family. Fenton Field, she had been told, was a house locally famous for its beauty and its gardens. Quite a good friend for Nicole, and quite unlikely to outshine her.

'Marvellous,' Judy said. 'Then you can drive down with Lloyd and myself tomorrow afternoon. Richard's going to be home, too, so you'll meet all the family.'

'Who is Lloyd, my dear?' Iris asked. She was, like all ladies who were bringing out a girl, anxious for the names of suitable young men to swell the lists for the balls and dinner parties. There could never be too many young men, so long as they were presentable.

'Lloyd's one of my American cousins,' Judy said. 'We've got a whole branch of Fentons who went to Massachusetts—not quite with the *Mayflower*, though. That must have been a very overcrowded ship if you can believe all those who were supposed to be on it. They're in all sorts of things, but shipping principally. Used to be in the whaling business. Some of them lost a lot of money in that. I expect they're just the usual American family, spread out into all sorts of things, and very energetic about it, if the comings and goings to Europe are anything to judge by.'

'And this cousin—Lloyd?' Iris's voice was a shade warmer '—is in shipping?'

'No. Nothing to do with it. He's a doctor. He got a fellowship to Cambridge, and then he decided to stay and take up surgery. He's interested in neurosurgery, principally. That's why he's at St Giles's. It's supposed to be the best place for that.'

'Oh—a doctor.' Iris's tone was disinterested; all the same she had written his name on a list. Possibly a presentable young man, but not one to be taken seriously. Not when one was looking for marriageable males.

Lloyd Fenton came at a time close enough to the appointed one to be acceptable the next afternoon. He was shown into the library where they were having tea, immediately directing his apologies to Iris before turning to Judy. There was a warm embrace of affection. 'Judy, you're so grown-up it's positively frightening. You're becoming more sophisticated by the minute. I guess I'll have to stop calling you "my little cousin Judy." Sir Charles, nice of you to have me here, sir.' Then he turned to Nicole, looking upwards at her as she perched on the library ladder, the teacup suddenly rattling in her hand.

'There—let me give you a hand. Shall I take that from you? I suppose you *are* coming down?'

'Oh—oh, yes. Just hunting for a Dostoevsky novel Uncle Charles said was here.' Why did her voice tremble, and why did she look away from him?

'Dostoevsky?—rather heavy reading for someone who's just about to begin a London season? Interested in Russian stuff?'

'Oh, Nicole's got Russian grandparents, or something,' Judy said. 'It sounds a delicious mix—with the English side of her.'

'Russian—interesting. Judy said you're a rather good musician——'

He was cut short by Iris's question, 'Do you take milk, Dr Fenton? Is it *Doctor* Fenton, or Mister? I never am quite sure. Please do help yourself to scones or sandwiches. You're doing neurosurgery at St Giles's? It sounds rather formidable.' This was Iris doing her best to be charming, and quite determinedly turning the talk away from Nicole's Russian ancestry.

'In America it's Doctor, Lady Gowing. In England it's now Mister. We have a bad joke about working ourselves to death in the beginning for the privilege of calling ourselves Doctor, and then working twice as hard for the right to go back to plain Mister.'

The rest of the tea time passed in small talk, little questions and answers, at which Iris pecked away at Lloyd Fenton's background, his antecedents, his prospects. 'You were at Groton and Harvard. How interesting.'

Nicole found herself tongue-tied. She realized that for the first time she was actually in the company of the sort of young man her mother had thought one day she would meet—but meet on her own home ground in America. She felt a pair of quietly speculative eyes on her and the pleasant voice, with its slight New England flatness, was gentle. She didn't know why she felt, because this man was a doctor, that he somehow saw more of her, farther into her, than another man would. How did they, with hardly a word, evoke an air of omniscience? 'Do you know Massachusetts at all?—Boston?' he asked.

'No, not really. I've just passed through. We ... I used to spend the summers in Maine.'

It was partly the truth. She and Anna had spent two weeks each summer there. 'Oh, I suppose you're the Bar Harbor lot, are you? We people on Cape Cod thought you were far too posh for us.' He laughed as he spoke.

'No—not Bar Harbor.' And she said nothing more. His questions were ended. He talked a little of politics to Charles, and to Iris about a new association being formed to provide extra patient amenities at St Giles'. 'If we're lucky we'll get the Duchess of Kent as Patroness ...' It wasn't necessary to say more. Iris took it up eagerly, the hard work needed to organize, the difficulty of prying people loose from their money unless proper recognition as well as a good night out was provided. 'It would save so much money if they would just *give* ...'

'But that isn't human nature, is it, Lady Gowing?'

They were still talking when Nicole and Judy went upstairs to collect coats and handbags. They were in the hall as Adams loaded their suitcases into Lloyd Fenton's car. 'You might like to come to some of our dinners this season, Dr Fenton,' Iris said. An American doctor was not her idea of someone for Nicole, but he had the right background and manners and was an unattached male. 'Little dinners before everyone goes on to the balls, you know.'

'It's kind of you, Lady Gowing. Doctors aren't very reliable guests, though. Apt to get called away, or be on duty at an inconvenient time. But I'm sure I can manage. As a research fellow I usually know what my free time will be. I'm not so important that I'm often summoned in to save the situation. The "great surgeon rushing to the rescue" is still a bit beyond me.'

They all squeezed into Lloyd Fenton's sports car, Judy insisting on Nicole sitting in front. She and Lloyd kept up a stream of talk as they threaded their way through traffic. Nicole was allowed to remain silent. They were people of another world, almost. They talked of horses and dogs, of Judy's brothers, of a world that Nicole knew she could never possibly belong to because it had not been there always, it was not ingrained in her as it was with these two. They had grown up on each side of the Atlantic, and yet this world was well-shared, a world of security, of knowing where each belonged. 'You know, Judy, it might have done you better to have come over to Boston for a while instead of Paris. But I must say ...' He looked incautiously over his shoulder at his cousin, and had to brake rather sharply to avoid a bus. 'I must say the Paris sheen is remarkably effective.'

'Sheen!—you *do* know I took the Cordon Bleu! I can make a meal for a king out of scraps now. Mother's quite alarmed when I start poking around in the pantry. And I've started going through her account books. She thinks it's a bit much. I've even made three evening dresses for the balls I'll be going to. I just *couldn't* spend my whole clothes budget on some silly dresses I'll only wear a few times. I'm very useful these days, Lloyd. You don't know any young doctors who are brilliant but need an economical wife for those first difficult years until they start rolling in money?'

'I'll look about, Judy.' Again he risked a backward glance

and laughed. 'But you know, with all these marvellous accomplishments, you'll probably end up marrying a millionaire
and it'll be all wasted.'

'Millionaire! Rubbish!' Judy's laugh was genuine, and it
told Nicole that between her and Lloyd existed a relationship
of great affection which would never be more than the feeling
she had for her brothers. The teasing was of old friends, not of
potential lovers. She added, 'Now, if anyone's likely to marry a
millionaire, it's Nicole.' It was said with complete frankness
and without envy.

'So ...' Once again Nicole was uncomfortable under the stare
from those discerning eyes. He glanced sideways at her, back at
the traffic, and sideways again. The look and his speculative
answer seemed to take in every part of her. She was conscious
of the suit from Molyneux, the hand-made shoes, the handbag
bought for her by Charles in Florence—the whole carefully
polished appearance that was the result of nearly two years with
Madame Graneau and the ministrations of the personal maid,
Henson. She felt vaguely ashamed, and wondered why. Money
was meant to be spent, wasn't it? And why did the word
millionaire sound so strange on the lips of someone like Lloyd
Fenton? Men who worked to become doctors when their background suggested that they might have slid comfortably into a
Boston law practice, or into stockbrokerage, usually didn't care
too much about money. She realized that she had come up
against the patrician American, and that hardest of all to bend
or sway, or impress, a New Englander. As they came to the
outskirts of London and Lloyd Fenton was able to increase
speed, she found herself glancing occasionally towards him as
he had done towards her, and her gaze was as speculative as his
had been. She supposed he was very handsome; in the first dis-
comfort of meeting him she had registered general good looks,
but not much else. Now in profile he seemed more American
than ever, the craggy handsomeness of the New Englander
descended from a people who had made their own aristocracy.
He had a long, lean frame and long, strong hands on the wheel.
He was dark, with rather pale skin, and dark bushy brows. She
supposed his eyes were grey rather than blue. She wondered why
she bothered to analyse him this way, and answered the question
herself. He was an American, the first, apart from the few
American girls at Madame Graneau's, she had encountered

115

since she had left the States. He would be measuring her by standards that the English could not because he knew the small, fine points of style and manner that an American girl of the type she was supposed to represent would display. Suddenly all the years at St Columba's seemed hardly worth the trouble, and her mother's dream of turning out a facsimile copy of the well-bred, well-connected young woman, impossible. She shivered just a little because he had so easily been able to shake the confidence she had thought impenetrable. She found herself wishing very much that Judy had had no American cousins.

'Cold?' he said. Damn, did he know everything about her? 'Or did someone just walk over your grave?'

'Perhaps ...' How had his thoughts so quickly reached to what she wanted to stay buried?

'How morbid,' Judy said. 'And on a lovely spring afternoon. We're all going to live for ever, didn't you know? Everyone's young and fair, and England is back in her golden youth again. Yes, I know there are dark Welsh mining towns that don't look golden, and the men have no work. But when I get this close to home again, and it's a spring afternoon, I just somehow can't believe that everything isn't beautiful.' She gave a slight, embarrassed laugh. 'Forgive me, I'm being a fool. Or am I just young, Lloyd?'

'You're young, Judy, and rather sweet, despite the sheen. Believe all the beautiful things as long as you can. They don't come round the second time.'

He wasn't that much older, Nicole thought, not yet thirty. But he sounded as if he had seen through the golden dream, had experienced it once, and knew it would not come again. She wished he didn't make her so uncomfortable. She wished she could have been a friend, as Judy was, but that wasn't going to be. She knew it.

They turned off the main road, and started through the winding narrow roads of Sussex. 'Nearly home, nearly home,' Judy sang from the back seat. 'And the apple trees are in blossom.'

II

Fenton Field was, as Nicole knew from the photographs, the perfect English house. It seemed almost as old as the land it sat upon, and older than some of the oaks which ringed it. The wistaria hung about its half-timbered frame was in bloom, at its back, along the edge of the orchard, the rhododendrons were flaming scarlet, paling the apple-blossom almost to nothing. When the car stopped, there was the hum of bees in the sudden silence, and then almost instantly, the varied barking of dogs. They all came out, the rush of dogs, the slower emergence of people. They came into Nicole's vision as some remembered dream—the faces of people, middle-aged and young, and the swarm of dogs. She couldn't have ever seen it before, but she already knew it all in her heart.

'This is Nicole, of course. Welcome, my dear.' A beautiful, rather tall woman was looking into her face, perhaps sensing her sudden feeling of being an outsider. Margaret Fenton was not stylish, but she was beautiful. Age had only added to grace. Hers was the face Nicole remembered from Judy's album. Then came her husband, Andrew, who also offered his welcome. His hand felt hard in Nicole's. The hand of a farmer, not a looker-on, and yet a hand delicate enough to know what was happening to a horse, a dog, or a child. Judy's youngest brother, Ross, was there, a thin child, with too-big eyes of a blue he had inherited from his mother. Lloyd was received as if he were also a son. A man called Wilks, somewhere between a butler and family custodian began to take out the suitcases, and at the same time told Ross to go and wash his hands.

Upstairs, in the room which Nicole was to share with Judy, Judy flung the casement windows wide to catch the breeze blowing from the orchard. There was a scent—Nicole could not distinguish between the wistaria and the apple-blossom.

'It *is* the most beautiful place in the world,' Judy said.

And Nicole, crossing that heavy-beamed room, with its floor of handpegged oak shining in the spring sunlight, with its vision on an enchanted world of green lawn sloping off to orchard and oaks, with the sound of the bees and the more distant sound of a stream, came to stand beside Judy. Yes, she could agree that it was, it just could be, the most beautiful place in the world. And once more she had to choke back her envy of Judy's place in this tight little world of beauty, closed to those who did not inherit it.

The Fentons, with their easy manners, did all they could to

draw her into their world. 'You were a help to Judy,' her father said softly as he poured drinks before dinner. 'We could tell that she admired you. All we heard from Paris was how hard you worked. You made her want to keep up. We have to be grateful to you that she wasn't lonely. Her time there was a great success, you know.' And his gaze went fondly across the room to his golden-haired daughter.

'But it was Judy who did all that for *me*!' Nicole protested. At the same time she felt an exhilarating sense of pleasure. She couldn't remember when anyone had ever paid her such a compliment, nor so obviously meant it. So she was content to sit quietly and still while they had their drinks, indulging in family gossip, hugging her compliment to herself with pride and gratitude.

She had sorted them out now, knew one from the other; they were no longer faces in the album. The oldest was Allan, who would be a farmer, like his father. Nicole knew about the girl he was engaged to, Joan Brewster, and about the labourer's cottage, a mile from Fenton Field, which was being modernized and enlarged to be ready for the time that they would marry in September. Nicole smiled a little to herself at the slightly absent-minded way Allan had greeted her; he seemed to be at the stage of being in love where he didn't notice another female. Judy had said, 'He's been waiting so long for Joan Brewster to grow up, and to get over the couple of times she's fallen in love with someone else. She did finally, and she's turned right back to Allan, whom she's known all her life. And Allan acts as if he's planned it all that way. I think they're going to be very right for each other.'

Nicole moved her attention to the next son, Richard, and found him staring at her with a studied frankness. She stared back, knowing that this was not someone whose eyes would waver. He was almost impossibly good-looking, blond like all the Fentons, his mother's face cast in a masculine mould, but his eyes a deeper shade of blue, and with startlingly dark lashes and brows. She knew from the way he looked at her that he was used to girls flocking about him, girls waiting for his glances, his invitations. He even made a grace of the heavy cast he wore on his foot and ankle, the ankle broken in a fall he had taken while fielding at cricket. 'Watch out for Rick,' Judy had said. 'He likes to think of himself as a bit of a playboy. He's certainly broken a few hearts. He's supposed to be reading in chambers—studying to be a barrister, but he's not very serious about it. In a way it's a sort of a pity about that money a Cavendish great-aunt left him. She doted on Rick, and he used to see her quite often. She lived near Cambridge all by herself, with just a housekeeper. None of us had really any idea she was so well-off. Rick is unexpectedly kind at times, and I suppose he felt sorry for the old girl. He used to take her to cricket matches and things like that at Cambridge. Made a bit of a fuss of her. When she died she left quite a lot of money to him. He hasn't gone exactly wild with it, but since he's come down from Cambridge, he hasn't been exactly serious about his studies, either. I suppose he could live without working, but none of us would like to see *that* happen. Rick needs something—someone, perhaps, to *make* him be serious. He's just bought Potters, the farm adjoining Fenton Field. He's leaving it to Father and Allan to farm. There's a rather lovely house that goes with it. He's having it done up, and spending a lot of money on it. He says he's going to rent it, but we all expect he'll suddenly spring an engagement on us, and he'll live there when he's married.' A faintly worried frown had creased Judy's forehead as she had dressed for dinner, and talked to Nicole about the family. 'I do hope there *is* someone, and that she's right ...' she suddenly blurted. 'Rick's so charming, and things have come so easily to him. I'd hate to see him play the field, end up with the wrong girl, fritter his time away in chambers, just because he won't be serious.' Then she shrugged. 'Oh, well—what am I worrying about? There can't be many young men as blessed as Rick is. Fortune's darling ...'

There was Ross, seated at a chess table, scowling with ferocious concentration. Across the table from him was a man a few years older than Allan, Nicole guessed, someone called Gavin McLeod. Nicole noted the thinness of Ross's body, the sharpness of the Fenton features here too finely drawn; he had been absent from his prep school for almost a year after an attack of rheumatic fever. Every so often Nicole saw Margaret Fenton's glance go to her youngest son, and the beautiful cheeks hollowed a little, as if a constant anxiety gnawed at her. 'It's such a damn shame,' Judy had said. 'Ross was doing so beautifully at school, and he was jolly good at games. That's all stopped. They say he'll be perfectly strong in time, but he's missing so much. Well, thank heaven there's Gavin McLeod, even if we're all a bit scared of him ...'

Gavin McLeod was in his thirties. 'He's absolutely brilliant,' Judy said. 'He's a Fellow of Christ Church. He doesn't do any teaching, just pure research in physics. He's been an absolute godsend for Ross, just taking over as a sort of tutor, and Ross has made up for all the lost time, and is even ahead with his studies because he's so passionately attached to Gavin he wants to be just like him. If Ross ever does take to physics, or something like that, and ends up with a Nobel prize one day, it'll be because of Gavin McLeod. If only Gavin weren't so fierce ... Those Scots, you know. They're such an *awkward* lot ... especially when they're proud and poor like Gavin. The chip on his shoulder's so big you'd almost swear he kept it there deliberately to frighten people off. That ... and being so brilliant.' She shrugged, 'Well, he awes us, really, and yet we're so grateful to him ...'

'But what's he doing here? Shouldn't he be at Cambridge?'

Judy had put the final dab of powder on her nose as she answered. 'Well, that's a bit awkward too. You see, about seven months ago he was smashed up in a car crash ... concussion rather badly. A broken leg and arm ... that scar over his eye. And the awful part of it was that Rick was driving the car, and he walked away with a few bruises. Gavin said it wasn't Rick's fault—it was raining and they hit some oil patch. But Rick felt responsible. Don't ask me how they happened to be friends. They're such an unlikely pair, but they're both mad keen on rugby, and they'd been to watch a match together. Any rate, when Gavin came out of the hospital, he went up to Scotland to recuperate. He went back to his father's home. His father's living in a gamekeeper's cottage, and renting out his house and moors for the shooting in summer. Rick went up to visit him. He found Gavin in a terrible state of depression, quarrelling with his father over everything, making the old man's life, and his, a misery. The house was like an iceberg, Rick said. They live up north of Inverness, and the snow was piled everywhere. No way Gavin could exercise and start to get his leg right again. The upshot was that Rick had Mother invite him here. Rather to everyone's surprise, he came. Everyone was terrified of him, but felt they had to do it for Rick. The big surprise was when he took so strongly to Ross, and Ross to him. It was the biggest shock in the world for everyone to see a brilliant mathematician like Gavin going back to schoolboy algebra again, and brushing up on his Latin and Greek so he could help Ross. We're all so grateful to him. And he *is* better. There's only that trace of a limp there. Mother said he still gets frightful headaches from the concussion, and the doctors say that to give himself a chance, he shouldn't go back to his work for at least another six months. He's straining at the leash to get back. He thinks someone's sure to get further in their research and beat him to the post. But they're keeping his place for him at Cambridge. He works a bit by himself here, but it isn't the same as being at Cambridge, with his assistants, and everything. He's got a string of degrees ... and yet he's coaching Ross. Dr Gavin McLeod ... I wish I didn't feel such a fool whenever I'm around him.'

That left Lloyd Fenton. How dark he seemed now, beside these fair English faces. She wondered if it was true that conditions changed the way people looked. Lloyd Fenton had something more akin to Gavin McLeod in the cragginess of his features, both men dark, both seemingly stamped with the hardness of the places in which they had grown up, though for Lloyd Fenton it would have been a hardness cushioned by the comfort of money. But why did New Englanders so often look as if they were fashioned by their harsh winters, structured by the rocky land from which they had first scratched a living, and seen it grow to wealth. Lloyd Fenton was Harvard, and he looked it. Perhaps that was why he made her feel uncomfortable. Those kind knew their own; he would have recognized her as being from somewhere outside the fold. For the first time she sensed the wisdom of Iris's decision to send her to Paris. If she was going to stand out as someone different in this society, there would be acceptable reasons for her difference. But people like Lloyd Fenton would know that it was an unusual kind of difference. She found herself hoping that he would not stay long here at Fenton Field. When he was gone, she could relax into the person Iris wanted her to be. There would be no awkward questions about places, and 'did you know so-and-so?' or 'I suppose you spent your summers at Bar Harbor?' Yes, better when he was gone. She didn't want questions.

Then she turned her gaze back to Richard, and now that steady stare softened, a look of amused laughter came into his eyes. He smiled, as if he had seen everything of her little survey of the people in the room, perhaps partly guessing her summing-up. She could almost have sworn that his eyelid came down in a wink.

Wilks's voice at the door. 'Dinner is served, Madame.'

After dinner the Fentons took up their own diversions. Ross had been packed off to bed, and Gavin McLeod now sat reading, apparently oblivious to what went on around him. Margaret Fenton sat in the midst of her family knitting, making herself a deliberate centre to them. Andrew and Allan and Judy had maps of the lower pastures of Potters spread out on the floor, and they were discussing a drainage scheme. Judy perched on the arm of her father's chair. Richard was supposed to be part of the group; it was his land they were discussing, and his money that would go on the drainage. But he was bored, and uninterested, and he drifted away from them. He went to the piano, and soon a teasing little trickle of jazz came as an undertone to the conversation. Nicole, trying to interest herself in a magazine, and conscious that Lloyd Fenton was watching her while he talked with Margaret Fenton, lifted her head expectedly. With a sort of surprised pleasure she went to the piano. She had not expected the unserious Richard to be so good at anything. Not a connoisseur of jazz herself, she still could recognize style, and Richard had it. She didn't know what he was playing; it seemed to be totally improvisation, something she knew all good jazz pianists had to be able to do. Suddenly her thoughts went back to the only time she had heard her mother play jazz, and then she wiped out the thought. She listened for a while, standing beside Richard. 'I suspect you're very good,' she said when he paused. 'I wish I knew more about it.'

'I fool around,' he said. 'It amuses people—it amuses me.'

'Do you ever do anything seriously?'

'Not much. Why should I?' He looked around the room, examining all the people in turn as she had done before dinner. He had placed his glass of brandy on the piano. 'There are enough serious people around, don't you think? They can afford a few clowns.'

'I don't think you're a clown. That would be a serious business, too.'

'Clever, aren't you?'

'No, not clever. It isn't the thing to be clever.'

He patted the long piano seat, and shifted to make room for her. 'Judy says you're clever, and it's nonsense to want to hide it. Sit down and talk about it.'

'You try to hide being clever yourself. You just said so.'

'Did I? Well ... well.' She sat beside him as he had indicated. Vaguely she was aware that Lloyd had risen and come to stand behind them. 'Do you ever play anything—dare I say it—serious?'

'Like Beethoven and all that stuff? Used to, a bit. It isn't the done thing for an English schoolboy, you know. Not unless you go to one of the choir schools and make music your whole life. I never felt like that. I just ... I just fell into jazz because it sounded right for me. I could play around with things, make them up as I went. But I remember a bit ...' With ease, and no apparent effort to remember, he went into the opening bars of 'Für Elise'. The way he played it, so simply, those opening bars might have been a continuation of his light jazz style, the haunting, maddening little rhythm was something he made mockingly his own. Then suddenly Nicole couldn't stand it. She was remembering once again the night she had been at Lucky Nolan's, the story Anna had told her. 'I played "Für Elise"—it begins so gently, and I didn't want people to hear.' The pain and shock Nicole had believed was deadened and almost gone returned. Would she never get that night out of her mind? She put her hand on Richard's wrist. 'Would you mind? Not that, I'm sorry ...'

He didn't ask her to explain. He smiled instead. 'I'll turn it all over to you. I'd like to hear someone who's been studying at the Paris Conservatoire. I'd think you have to be very serious indeed for that.' He was flicking through some of the piles of music on top of the piano. 'Here—the Beethoven sonatas. You have to be in practice on at least one of them.'

But she reached instead for Book Two of the Bach preludes and fugues. 'Will you turn for me?' He nodded.

She played, at first mechanically, then as the pain of the remembered little melody of 'Für Elise' slipped from her, she forgot her audience, and she was serious about what she was doing. She settled herself more squarely at the piano, and gave her whole attention to the music, suddenly relieved of tension as the music took over for her, the counter-point powerfully demanding reason and logic, but with the astonishing core of poetry at its heart. Richard had risen from the seat to give her room to reach the whole keyboard; he turned the pages at her nod, but he was reading the music also. Then it ended to complete and utter silence in the room.

It was, finally, Gavin McLeod who spoke. He had closed his book and removed his glasses; he was staring accusingly at her, looking at her as if he had never seen her before. 'That,' he said, 'was bloody marvellous. Now why on earth would someone who can do that be starting out on something so silly as a débutante season?'

There was no way to answer him. Nicole closed the music, stacked it tidily on the top of the piano, and turned to Margaret Fenton. 'I'll go to bed now, if that's all right, Mrs Fenton. It's been a lovely evening. What time is breakfast, please?'

After she closed the door she heard Margaret Fenton's voice come gently. 'You were rather hard on Nicole, Gavin.'

'I can't say I'm sorry, Mrs Fenton. It's a crime when you see someone throwing away a talent. I wonder what other things that quiet little minx has tucked away——'

Lloyd broke in sharply. 'Whatever they are, they're her own. Don't you think you should leave them to her?'

Nicole, reflecting on what she had been told about people who eavesdropped seldom hearing anything good of themselves, found herself warmed by those words. Lloyd Fenton, she thought, was displaying the New Englander's regard for the rights of other people, privacy being one of them. But still she listened, and heard Gavin McLeod say, 'I'm sorry, Mrs Fenton. I have no right to use such language, nor speak that way about a guest. I apologize. I'll even apologize to Miss Rainard if you think I should.'

Lloyd Fenton's voice carried a hostile edge. 'I'd just drop the whole thing, if I were you, McLeod.'

'Part of the bedside manner, Fenton?'

'Surgeons aren't usually reckoned to have much of a bedside manner——' Nicole turned away and started up the stairs. How had she managed to inject hostility into a group of people like the Fentons? Why couldn't she ever take it the easy, the softer way?

Nicole found herself alone with Lloyd Fenton at breakfast.

'Everyone else gone?' she asked as she poured coffee for herself.

'Gone, I imagine. Unless Rick is still in bed. Andrew and Allan have had their second breakfast, being farmers. Ross and McLeod have started on the day's work. Judy's off riding. That leaves you and me.'

'Yes ...'

'You don't sound too pleased.'

'May I have the butter, please?'

He leaned back in his chair. 'Will it disturb you if I smoke?'

'Not at all.'

'I think ...' He paused. 'I think you don't like me much, and I wonder why not. Have I offended you in any way?'

She scraped butter thinly on her toast. 'Offended me? How could you possibly have done that? As for liking you—is that important?'

'It could be.' He lighted his cigarette and turned his head away as he exhaled the smoke. 'I've even a feeling that it's something to do with my being an American. Is it?'

'Why should it?'

He shrugged. 'All right. I'll give up. You don't like being asked questions.'

'Does anyone? What is it you want to know?'

'I suppose I just want to know you. And you skirt around me as if I were a prickly pear.'

With great precision Nicole added marmalade to the toast; she wondered why she did it—she didn't even like marmalade. 'What's there to tell you about me? I was born in New York. I don't know which hospital. I never asked.'

'Look I don't want to pry——'

She cut him short. She was going to say it, and be done with it, and then, perhaps, this Lloyd Fenton would stop making her feel uncomfortable. 'You said you wanted to know me. There's nothing very much to tell when you're nineteen. Nothing much has happened. So I'll go on with the facts. My father was killed in France during the war. I was born after he left for France, so he never saw me. My mother took ... took a job with a Wall Street firm of lawyers. There was some ... there was some money left from an inheritance my father had from *his* mother. My mother used it to send me to St Columba's, an Anglican convent in Connecticut——'

Lloyd Fenton nodded. 'I knew a couple of girls who went

there. Probably would have been before your time.'

Nicole sipped her coffee and hoped that he didn't notice the slight tremor in her voice. She had recited this tale before, at Madame Graneau's, the half-truth blended into the truth. Somehow it didn't become easier to lie. 'I stayed at St Columba's until I'd finished. I sort of hoped ... well, I wanted to go to Vassar. I got a scholarship there. But then my ... my grandfather died and left me some money, but he wanted me to be educated in Europe, and my Aunt Iris, his daughter, and Uncle Charles were to be my guardians. So ... I went to Paris, stayed for eighteen months, met Judy. And here I am. Is that enough, Dr Fenton? I told you there wasn't much.'

'You've forgotten something. Your mother ... what does she think of you living over here? Why are Sir Charles and Lady Gowing your guardians?'

She drew a deep breath. 'Oh—I assumed you knew. I thought Judy might have told you. My mother died. That's why I'm here. Now you *are* asking questions, aren't you?'

'Yes, and I'm sorry I did. I seem to remember telling off McLeod last night because he ... oh, well, never mind. But here I am, asking questions, when I vowed I wouldn't. I suppose ... I suppose when a person's very quiet, and yet you know darn well they're not dumb, you just want to get behind the barrier.'

'Barrier? I wasn't aware there was a barrier.' And yet she knew there was. The last lie, the lie about Anna's death was the biggest barrier. That was the one she wanted no one to cross. And every time she repeated that lie, Anna was gone that much farther from her. But Anna had made that choice herself. And even Lucky Nolan had known she wouldn't reappear. Nicole excused herself, and hated herself. But what else was there to say?

'You're not shy,' Lloyd Fenton continued, 'but you're possibly the most self-contained person—for your age—I've ever encountered. Perhaps I imagine a barrier that really isn't there. Well, shall I ask the questions myself and answer them?'

'What questions?'

'I asked questions, didn't I—all about you? I'll give you two to one, and ask and answer them myself. All about me. Will it bore you?'

'Not at all.' But she said it coolly. She hadn't bargained on trading histories with him.

'Nothing unusual,' he said. 'And nothing as isolated as your life. There was four kids in our family—all born in Boston, and we had grandparents on both sides born in Boston. The place was alive with cousins. It almost seemed if you turned over a stone you'd find a Fenton, or a half-Fenton. Some of them would object to me comparing them with something that crawled out from under stones, since they think they're pillars of society, all made in shiny marble. But we've had our share of black sheep, the less shiny ones. But our family was O.K....'

Nicole thought she could almost have recited it for him. He was a Boston Brahman. The Fentons had been there since the Commonwealth of Massachusetts had been founded. There would be Fentons sprinkled all over the professions of law and medicine, banking and stockbroking. Their histories would be interweaved with every other long-established family of the state.

'... three boys and a girl, Liz. Our mother was one of those champion committee women—perhaps a bit like your aunt. But she thought of it as her *duty* to go around raising money. She was very thrifty ... made us do without things just to understand what it was like not to have *anything*. Not a bad way to be, I suppose. It seemed an awfully lonely house after she died. We had a place out on the Cape. Most of the family had summer places there. The first summer after she died I didn't think I could bear it. But one does. It was the Wall Street crash that killed my father. We lost quite a lot of money, but I think what really killed him was that he'd advised a lot of people on investing, and they were all just about wiped out, as he was. He felt responsible. I was qualified by then. Suddenly there seemed not much reason to stick around Boston. Sam and Peter were married, and so was Liz. There was some residue of money in trusts, so we all had some income—not a lot. Sam took the house on Beacon Hill because we didn't want it to go out of the family, and we all chipped in to handle the expenses until things look up a bit. I took myself off to Cambridge. Then on to St Giles'. I've got a sort of summer shack out on the Cape near Sam and Peter. One of the uncles owned it and left it to me. They say about him that he died of a heart attack. But privately we all know he took an overdose because he was in much the same situation as my father. When you're older, it's pretty tough to learn how to do without money, being blamed by other people because you've lost their money for them. The clubs in Boston weren't very cheerful places in those days. The older ones took it hard when the bubble burst. I was lucky I had a profession, and somewhere else to go, something to build on. I suppose I have to say I thought I was lucky I didn't have a wife and kids because I couldn't have dragged them after me—wouldn't have dared to take the risk. But when I come down to Fenton Field and see what they make of their lives here ... when I remember how Sam and Peter's wives have actually seemed to give them strength to get through these last years, well ... I wonder. I do wonder. To be free's fine. It can be damn lonely, too.'

Nicole said slowly, laying down the toast because it had suddenly seemed too dry in her mouth. 'You'll build up again. All of you. Your kind does. You'll all help each other because it's always been that way. Families matter. Families ...' Her voice trailed off.

'Yes ... families ...' he prompted.

'Well, since I never had one, I don't really know, do I? I wish ...'

She never knew what she had been going to say to Lloyd Fenton. Perhaps she never could have found the words, or wanted to reveal herself by saying them. The barriers she built were of loneliness, a loneliness she would never confess to anyone. She probably would never have said it to him, but she never knew, then, what might have been said. She heard the sound of Richard's stick tapping in the hall outside, and her thoughts as well as her tongue froze.

Richard stood in the doorway, skilfully balancing himself while he closed the door behind him. He had the grace that even made the plaster on his foot an ornament. As he appeared, Nicole thought she heard the merest whisper from Lloyd Fenton. 'Damn ...!'

Richard's smile took them both in. 'Good morning. Hope I'm not interrupting. Anything left to eat...?'

Nicole found herself helping him to bacon and eggs and toast from the sideboard, and pouring coffee for him. With a deliberate refusal to move, Lloyd Fenton lighted another cigarette.

III

It was, Nicole thought, the best week of her whole life. It was a magical piece of time, suspended between the end of one sort of life and the beginning of another. She was conscious of many things happening within herself, a receptiveness, a willingness to see and understand, to let herself be swayed and pulled by different influences. She let herself float, making no effort to struggle against a delicious, lulling tide of peace, and the sense of serenity that pervaded Fenton Field. She felt herself open up to receive these influences. She found she smiled a lot, and there was much to laugh at, silly inconsequential things. And when she looked at her face in the mirror, some of the tight reserve had gone. She was no longer quite so guarded, so wary. To be able to trust was a wholly new experience.

Even the weather combined with the sense of ease. There was a whole week of perfect spring days, days with the breeze warm and scented, the sun already had the heat of summer. The sound of bees was constant, a sound of contentment and fullness. She learned the names of the dogs—one of them, McGinty, belonged to Lloyd Fenton. He had brought it, a stray he had found in London, down to Fenton Field two years ago. Margaret Fenton accepted it as she had accepted Lloyd himself, as part of the family. She had an enormous capacity to embrace whatever came her way, to make room for it. Without seeming to, she stretched out hands to Nicole, and had them grasped. From that first hour Nicole knew she could never be a stranger in this house or among these people.

She went riding a little with Judy and Lloyd. Sometimes Ross and Gavin McLeod were with them. They played tennis and Nicole found she didn't mind at all that she was so bad at the game. There was time for croquet on the lawn, when Richard balanced skilfully on the heel of his plaster, and managed to beat them all. No one minded. There was no room for competitiveness in the easeful days of that week. Nicole often played the piano in the evenings after dinner, but not once did she put in a rigorous hour of scales.

'I can't believe it,' Judy said. 'You—slacking off ...'

Slacking off. To Nicole it suddenly had a delicious meaning. She felt herself trying to slow up the days, the hours even. She wanted to hold this piece of time, welcoming the early dawn chorus of the birds, waking just to revel in hearing it, hating to see the pink colouring in the west come to herald the beginning of the long spring twilight. For the first time she felt that she was grasping at the sense of what was England itself, what the poets had written about, what the soldiers who built the Empire had longed for, dreamed of returning to. She knew there were dole queues on the streets but for this one week she shut them from her mind, determined that nothing ugly should touch this little oasis of enchanted beauty.

The very essence of it all, the scene she would hold most strongly in her heart in the years ahead, came on the last afternoon, when already an impinging threat of the end of this idyllic dream touched her like a light cloud across the sun. They sat in the orchard where the bees droned about them and the daffodils which came as a flood in April had been left to die down among the long grass. Lloyd lay on his back staring into the trees above him. Judy plucked a long blade of grass and let it fall across his eyes; he brushed it aside lazily. Gavin McLeod and Ross had just joined them, bringing the latest MCC cricket score from Lord's. Richard sat with his back against a tree. He had selected it because it was the one Nicole was also leaning against, and Richard had made no secret in the past week that he liked to be near Nicole. Soon they would be joined by Andrew and Allan, and Wilks would carry tea to the table under the great oak from which there was the best view of the house. They were just waiting, doing nothing, perfectly content.

Then Richard reached for the book Ross had brought with him. 'They're still reading old Rupert Brooke, are they?' he said. He flipped the pages.

'Read "The Soldier", Rick,' Judy said. 'Read it for me.'

He turned the pages until he found it, and his low voice was accompanied by the sound of the bees and they melded together as if the poem might have been written in such a place.

> *If I should die, think only this of me:*
> *That there's some corner of a foreign field*
> *That is for ever England. There shall be in*
> *That rich earth a richer dust concealed ...*

The familiar words went on, and a sudden, almost unbearable pain touched Nicole. She wanted him to stop because he was speaking of things that threatened vaguely, dredging memories of a time she was too young to remember, too painful for this bright day. But the voice went on, remorselessly, to the end:

> ... Dreams happy as her day,
> And laughter, learnt of friends: and gentleness,
> In hearts at peace, under an English heaven.

It was Judy who broke the following silence. 'I shouldn't have asked for that. It's too sad for a day like this. I'm glad Mother didn't hear. She lost two brothers in the war.'

'And Nicole lost her father,' Lloyd said quietly.

'They lost almost a whole generation,' Gavin McLeod said, 'and if these fools don't wake up, they may lose another.'

'Stop it, Gavin!' Judy said. 'It can't ever happen again. The last war was fought so it couldn't happen again.'

'The last war hasn't finished yet, dear girl,' he answered. 'We're still manœuvring on the last battlefield.'

'And I,' Richard said, 'am learning to fly. If there's another war, I don't intend to be stuck in the mud in some fox-hole.'

Judy turned a startled, stricken face on him. 'Rick—*you're learning to fly!*'

'Yes, why not? It's fun! And it may come in useful some day, if Gavin's war turns up.'

'Oh, God—I hope you haven't told Mother. It would worry her.'

'Of course I haven't. And it isn't nearly as dangerous as ...' he stopped, and then as if he forced himself not to look at Gavin, he continued, 'It's not as dangerous as driving a car.'

Judy gave a soft, little cry. 'They couldn't be so stupid as to begin another war—they *couldn't!*'

'They just might,' Lloyd said slowly. 'The League of Nations is a shambles. Italy's eating up Ethiopa. Germany's bursting with illegal armaments. Hitler's ranting on ... And no one gets any wiser. Wars become more vicious, but no one gets any wiser.'

Nicole wanted to scream at them to stop, to finish this wrecking of the idyll. It was only men who ever talked of war. At this moment she hated them all.

And then, as if on cue, Andrew and Allan came from the direction of the stables, Allan rolling down sleeves over freshly scrubbed hands and arms. Margaret Fenton emerged from the house wearing her enchanting battered garden hat and carrying a tray of food. Behind her Wilks carried the heavier tray with the teapot and jugs of hot water. Ross scrambled to his feet and began to take the tray from his mother. For an instant Nicole held the scene as if frozen for ever—the figure of the woman walking on the clipped velvet lawn, the three male figures converging on her, the perfect house in its perfect setting, the deep shade cast by the oak.

It was Lloyd who spoke the lines as he extended his hand to help Richard to his feet:

> *Stands the Church clock at ten to three?*
> *And is there honey still for tea?*

His eyes met Nicole's, and she knew that somehow he had known and shared her longing that it should always be just as it was now.

The next morning under a dull sky Nicole drove with Lloyd back to London, and as they approached the outskirts of the city, it began to rain.

IV

The last fittings were made, the rehearsals were attended, everything went to a precise schedule mapped out by Iris. Nicole, dressed in the regulation white and with three ostrich plumes in her hair, went to Buckingham Palace to be presented. She could afterwards remember feeling nervous seated beside Iris as the car slowly moved up the Mall, waiting its turn to set down at the entrance where pale-faced débutantes, and the sometimes incredibly ancient ladies who were presenting them, were shaking out trains and adjusting long, white gloves. At the moment though of moving forward to make her deep curtsy, the nervousness departed. She knew the only terrible thing she could do at this moment was to fall flat on her face before Queen Mary, which at least would make her slightly more memorable than all the other girls similarly dressed. But she didn't fall; she had no intention of falling. It had all been rehearsed so many times. She twisted her right leg behind her in the approved fashion, went down sufficiently low, remained steady with a straight back. On rising she backed away and managed the train without awkwardness. It was over; she was free. Charles welcomed her back to Elgin Square with champagne.

'Very nicely done, my dear,' Iris said. It was the warmest praise she was capable of. 'And as a coming-out present, you are to keep the pearls. They will make a nice memento of the occasion.'

Nicole fingered the three strands of beautifully-matched pearls with the diamond clasp which belonged to Iris. She also wore a finely wrought diamond tiara which Iris had loaned to her. 'But—but what will you do without your pearls?' Iris was seldom dressed without them.

'Oh, it's always possible to buy more pearls, but I think it's always nicer if the first ones are given to you. In ordinary circumstances we would have been giving you pearls on each birthday until your necklace was complete. In your case——'

'Thank you, Aunt Iris. It's very generous of you. They're magnificent...'

And over her champagne glass her eyes met Charles's and she recognized the admiration and the sadness there. She felt she would have liked to stretch out a hand and say, 'It's all right, Uncle Charles. I'm not going away.' But that would not have pleased Iris. For her, the real satisfaction had not come on this night, nor would it come on the night of the coming-out ball next week. It would come when she could announce Nicole's engagement to a spectacularly eligible young man. The triumph of Iris's life would come when she could announce, arrange and preside over the wedding of the year. This presentation at Court was only the first step. So Nicole could not reassure Charles she was not going away. If she did not go away, did not achieve the marriage Iris expected of her, she would have failed. So she said nothing beyond thanking Iris again for the pearls.

Henson had a velvet-lined jewel box ready for them. 'Well, Miss Nicole, I expect that's only the first of many. You'd look very well in emeralds, Miss. I always say a lady needs a very white complexion for emeralds. They don't look at all well on sallow types.'

She brushed Nicole's hair out of the rather rigid *coiffure* needed for the tiara. 'Well, Miss, a time to remember all your life. Next thing we know you'll be presenting your own daughters at Court.'

Nicole closed her eyes wearily and for once was grateful for Henson's ministrations. Presenting her own daughters at Court ... was this what Anna had sent her here for? Was this the almost ruthless good sense in that final letter? She had expected no less of Nicole than Iris did.

Iris had new pearls for Nicole's coming-out ball, and she wore her tiara. Mowbray had been transformed for the party. To its straight Georgian lines a London designer had added two curving plywood colonnades hung with pink and white silk leading to two wall-less circular rooms capped with cupolas. These also were hung with pink and white silk, and with pink and white canvas ready to draw across in case the June evening should be chilly or wet. Each of the two rooms had its own orchestra. The inside of Mowbray had been converted into a series of supper rooms, and even a card room for those who didn't care to dance. Iris was determined that there should be people of every age, not just Nicole's at this, the best excuse she had had so far in her life, for a well-managed display of taste and style. She could not admit to herself as she scanned the bills which poured in, that she was at last having her revenge on the Yorkshire mill-owner who had given her a second-rate coming-out party at a London hotel, served bad champagne grudgingly, and severely limited her dress allowance for the season. The Yorkshire mills and the successful investment of the money which had come from them provided all this, and Iris did not count the cost. She surveyed Mowbray that night, just as the first of the bands began to play, and was satisfied. It was the perfect June evening. It would be daylight until almost eleven, when the specially installed lighting in the trees and through the shrubbery would come on. The manicured lawns were set with white chairs and tables with pink cloths. Great sprays of pink roses were set along the colonnades, and through the rooms. The herbaceous border had been specially replanted so that at this time only various shades of pink would be seen. Tubs of forced pink hydrangeas stood

134

about at any point which might seem to lack colour. The waiters wore pink jackets. Nicole looked at it all and thought, for Iris's sake, that it was a pity that she was not a pink and white English girl, with blonde hair, to go with all this spun-sugar fantasy. At least Iris had not insisted on her wearing a pink dress, though she had complained that Nicole's choice of a white dress was rather too simple and severe.

The cars began arriving. Iris, Charles and Nicole stood in the receiving line. The trickle of guests became a rush. Names were announced, Nicole smiled endlessly at people she could only vaguely remember having met before, and many she had never seen in her life. The music was very good, everyone said. How clever to get the two best London bands on the same night. Charles's relations seemed to have emerged from some back cupboard where they kept dirty diamonds and ancient boas. But they were a distinguished family, and so were able to wear what they liked, without regard to fashion. 'Handsome gel, Charles,' one deaf great-aunt shouted. 'Glad to see you've got something worth looking at this time.' Iris flushed at the remembrance of old snubs, but kept smiling and obviously was triumphant in at last showing Charles's family what she could do.

'Shouldn't be surprised if you make a good match, my gel,' the terrible old woman shouted. 'Good-looking fillies are short this season, they say. Watch out for the breeding lines, though. Always tells. Breed up, gel. The Rainard blood could stand some improving. Don't know about your mother's line. Americans are such a mix, aren't they . . .?' She wandered on to greet old friends, mothers and aunts and grandmothers of other débutantes. She and some cronies seemed to spend the rest of the evening dividing their time between the supper tables, and long enjoyable stretches seated out on one of the colonnades making cruelly sharp assessments of the dancers and the strollers on the lawns. Towards two o'clock when she took leave of Charles, the great-aunt shouted, 'She'll do very well, Charles. Has style. Bit out of the ordinary. But the young ones now can't touch what the girls used to be in my day. Then we had figures . . .'

Nicole danced with young men who seemed to look extra-ordinarily alike, and spoke of the same things. She went into three suppers, nibbling at pink salmon and delicately sweet strawberries. She drank champagne at one of the pink-covered tables with the eldest son of a duke. 'You mu-must come up to Scotland in Aug ... August,' he stammered. 'We've some ra ... rather good shooting ...' She watched Iris struggle to hide her supreme satisfaction when the Countess of Denby, one of the social arbiters of London, and with whom Iris served in a rather humble capacity on a famous charitable committee, said in a voice loud enough to be overheard, 'My dear, such a success. *Everyone's* here ...'

And Judy said, grinning at Nicole, 'Everyone's here—including the Fentons.'

Lloyd Fenton, however, was not there. Nicole guessed he had attended too many Bostonian Back Bay débutante parties to want to be drawn into any more. Richard danced with Nicole. With the cast off his foot he was supremely graceful. 'Now you wouldn't call *this* serious,' he said to her. 'And you look too beautiful for all this pink stuff. You'll never wear pink, will you, Nicole? You look like your pearls. Quite, quite beautiful.'

It seemed a number of people that night had told her that she looked beautiful, but she could only remember the time Richard had told her so.

At about five o'clock the bands packed up. A very few, very young people lingered at the pink-covered tables, and a few tired chaperones had fallen asleep in the drawing-room. One was stretched out snoring on the chaise-longue in the newly decorated pink ladies' cloakroom. Charles had limped upstairs. Iris was giving the last directions to the catering people, and deciding that those who had stayed could be served another breakfast. Nicole found herself wandering alone along one of the colonnades. The round dance-room was quite deserted, the musicians gone. The delicate pink roses had blown to fullness in the heat that the dancers had created. A crumpled pink napkin blew in from the lawn in the little breeze that was stirring in the dawn. The floodlights had been switched off, and the birds had begun to sing in the sudden quiet. A girl's laugh floated across the garden. Nicole went idly to the piano. Only one theme came to her restless fingers. She was calm and angry at the same time. How little of the money spent that evening would have kept herself and Anna comfortably in New York. There need never have been those all-night sessions at Lucky Nolan's—nor any Lucky Nolan either. All evening long she had played out the fraudulent role she and Iris—and Anna as well—

had devised. She had appeared to be what she was not. But what was she really? The theme her fingers had quite unconsciously wandered into was 'Für Elise'. She let it go on; she didn't try to stop herself. This was for Anna. She heard again the old deaf-aunt's words, 'Watch out for the breeding lines. Breed up, gel.' Her fingers became angry on the keys. She didn't play softly any more. And when she finished, one of the famous bandleaders was leaning against a silk-coated plywood column, sipping whisky.

'So you're a pretty good musician, Miss Rainard?'

She shrugged. 'Depends on what you like.'

'Play any jazz?'

'Not the way you'd approve. I haven't much . . .'

He smiled. 'Want to try "Jelly Roll Blues"?'

And without waiting for her answer he picked up his saxophone and gave out the first notes. She found herself following. The rhythm wasn't always right, but she fell in with him in a way she hadn't thought possible. For the first time she knew that the discipline of the classical knowledge, or else an inborn knowledge, was essential before one could seem to throw it away in this effortless fashion. The man led her on, and she responded. The notes wailed out over the dawn garden. Couples drifted towards the dance-room, not to dance, but to listen. It was afterwards said in London to those who had not been present, that the best time of Nicole Rainard's coming-out party had been that half-hour in the summer-morning garden, when an expert had led a beginner along, and they had made music together.

Charles had sighed over the newspaper and fashionable magazine reports and pictures of the party, which were lavish and detailed. 'I rather wish it hadn't got so much attention, Iris. It doesn't seem right, in times as hard as these, to be seeming to spend so much on a party——'

She cut him off swiftly. 'Nonsense, Charles. We're *creating* employment, aren't we? Where would the catering people be, and the florists and the dressmakers be if we all decided not to entertain? Walking the streets looking for work. Nicole can't go back and have her season ten years from now, when things may be prosperous again. What good will it do *anyone* if the money just stays in a bank, earning interest . . .?' Her ambition, he reflected, aroused once again by Nicole, had taken her a long way from the frugal strictures of the Yorkshire mill-owner. He could tell she was very pleased with it all. She was pleased with Nicole. She was especially pleased with the coverage in the *Tatler* which began, *'The surprise débutante of the year is undoubtedly American-born, Paris-educated Nicole Rainard, whose splendid coming-out ball was held at the Surrey mansion of her aunt, Lady Gowing ...'*

One of the gossip columns of an evening paper put it differently, *'There are those who wonder if the dark-horse entrant, Nicole Rainard, may not sweep past all the more likely entrants in the débutante stakes this season ...'*

To coincide with her coming-out party Nicole had had the usual full-page portrait in the front of the *Tatler*. At first the society photographer had tried her in the usual poses, long dress, pearls and flowers. Something strange in her personality kept breaking through, and he knew that the photographs would not have the usual rather lifeless, but acceptable quality. He had shaken his head. 'Do you ride horses, or something? Perhaps we should ... ?'

In the end the photo was of Nicole, seated at the piano, in a very plain dark dress, without jewellery, hands wide-spread on the keys in a double-chord. She looked preoccupied, not with the camera, but with the music. *'Miss Nicole Rainard, niece of Bridadier Sir Charles and Lady Gowing, has temporarily left off her studies at the Paris Conservatoire ...'*

V

The mailman who served the small block of efficiency units in Santa Monica had often wondered why Mrs Maynard had subscriptions to several glossy English magazines, but then he wondered why she had subscriptions to other publications, like the *Wall Street Journal*. They were all in the name of Mr N. Maynard, who had been, he supposed, her dead husband. People often keep subscriptions on for sentimental reasons, he knew, without ever looking at the contents of the journals. He also noted that Mrs Maynard never received a personal letter—just what he recognized as the occasional bill, and the renewal notices for the subscriptions. It puzzled him a little because the few glimpses he had had of Mrs Maynard she had not seemed the sort of person who would be so completely alone that no one ever wrote to her. She was very attractive, he thought, though pushing forty now; she dressed quietly in inconspicuous clothes, and drove an ageing Ford. She gave him a generous present at Christmas, and always made sure that she spoke to him herself at this time, asked about his family, and wished him a good New Year. Her accent was nothing he could place—not English, not American, but with none of the betraying sounds of the Italians or the Germans. He liked her for her courtesy, and was therefore very disinclined to gossip about her with any of the other tenants of the efficiency block. She was obviously the sort who kept herself to herself, and so far as he was concerned, she had the right to.

She was now an expert driver of the old Ford. One weekend in the month she left behind the books and papers, the study courses she had set herself, and drove towards the great pass between San Bernardino and San Gorgonio which led out to the desert. Small cabins which could be rented overnight, and which they called motels were beginning to appear. She could never explain to herself why the desert fascinated her, and drew her constantly. It was nothing like what she had seen in the East; it had not the mysterious enchantment of the woods around the estate of Prince Michael Ovrensky, where she had spun childish fantasies. There were no fantasies left for Anna Rainard. She wondered if she loved the brutal harshness of the desert because it seemed to have come down to the very bones of life itself; with all softness gone, what beauty she found there was not deceptive; the long shadows on the mountains, the burning, blinding quality of the light, these were things she felt she could touch and almost hold. The seared emptiness of the spaces found an answer in her own aloneness. She responded to it as if it were a place of her own heart. It was almost a shock of deception each spring then, when the miracle of the carpets of wildflowers spread over the valleys and cloaked them briefly with softness. 'The false smile' she always called it to herself, and was rather glad when the familiar bone rock hardness returned.

But she also learned that the mythical oases of the desert existed. A clump of trees, at first like a mirage, would appear. When she drove the old Ford to them, there would be a spring and a green pool of sweet water, rocks cooled from the afternoon heat by the overhanging branches. She shared it with the creatures of the desert, the rabbit, the lizard, the prairie dog, the snake. Sometimes, when no other traveller shared that space with her, she took off her shoes and stockings and waded in the strangely cool water. Sometimes, at night, when the desert grew cold, she would return to these places and watch the stars blaze in the night sky with an intensity that the sun had had at three o'clock.

Occasionally she mentioned these journeys to Frank Hayward at the real estate office. 'For God's sake, Anne, why do you go trekking out into the desert? Isn't anything there. You sound as if you could get like these old prospector guys—rock happy, sun happy. Look, if you want a bit of sun, why not the beaches? Beautiful beaches all along this coast.'

'Other people have found the beaches, Frank,' she said, in much the same tone she had used when she had once told him that she had been married. 'It's the desert for me. I'm thinking about trying to get a few acres out there ...'

'For God's sake, Anne,' he repeated. 'You really must be crazy. That's Indian land. It isn't worth a dime. To get the rights to a site you'd have to track down the descendants of about a dozen Indian families. Take you years to get title ...'

She shrugged. 'Well ... I'm not in a hurry.'

Then she found a small wooden frame house, in a rather run-down condition, on five acres of land up off Laurel Canyon. There were no near neighbours, the road leading to the house was choked in red dust in the summer, and treacherously slippery for the Ford to negotiate in the rainy season. But it had a good well, and the makings of a garden. A Japanese living farther down the canyon promised to come and help make a vegetable garden for her and to tend it two days a week. She paid a down-payment and took out a mortgage on it.

Then Frank Mayward really exploded. 'For God's sake, Anne, what do you think you're doing? It's nothing up there but rattlesnakes and chaparral! What do you want to go and live in the goddamned wilderness for?'

She couldn't explain to him that it was the closest she could come to making her own re-creation of the sense of spaciousness lost to her since the family had left Russia. She bought a German Shepherd puppy whom she named Mikhail, but whom everyone called Mike, and she bought, and was taught to use, a gun. She became quite used to carrying it as she walked her acres in her desert boots, and she shot many snakes. The little house was painted and put in good order. No one came near her —the obstacles of the road, the dog and the gun were enough. In the silence there at night it seemed she was less alone than when she had lived in the efficiency unit in Santa Monica. She rarely now saw the new mailman; he put her few bills, the renewal notices, the newspapers and the glossy English magazines, months out of date, in the big mailbox by the gate.

Mike rode with her in the car to Frank Hayward's office every day, and on the weekend tours of the slow sprawl of Los Angeles. Her own private maps were now heavily marked, and she said nothing to Frank Hayward when she put a small downpayment on some parcel of land here and there which no one else seemed to want. The depression still lived with them; there were few people like Anne Maynard who had money in the bank and the courage to back an idea, a theory—in the last sense, a wild hope and belief.

Mike came with her on the weekends in the desert. The motel keepers had learned to know her, and accepted Mike in the beginning as a favour to her. Then they came to accept the two as inseparable, and made no more comment. Anna continued to visit the places in the desert where the springs of green clear water rose, and continued to talk to the people who could lead her to those Indians who were the true owners. She knew if it took her ten years, she would own one of those shaded places by the water, a place where she and Mike could sit together on a rock and no sound but the silence of the desert would be their companion. It was here in such a place, by a spring of water, that she opened her lunch-time sandwiches, carefully apportioned a piece of Mike, and opened the first of the pile of magazines which had come by the last English mail. It was there in the *Tatler* that she saw the photograph of Nicole at the piano, read the account of her coming-out ball. A little smile flickered on her features. After she had read every scrap of information about Nicole several times, and digested it, she went wading in the water with Mike, throwing stones for him, and singing, to her own surprise, a Russian melody that had seemed lost to her many years ago.

And the next day she sold a house that had been on Frank Hayward's books for almost two years—an expensive house in

Beverly Hills. It was sold to a man who thought he really couldn't afford it, but had come to make his pile in the burgeoning film industry. He bought it because Mrs Maynard, cool and convincing, had steered him cleverly through the tangle of his finances, had taken him to the bank which would give him a mortgage, and charmed him into believing he had got a bargain. Anna knew if he managed to hold on to it, if his Hollywood bets worked out, it was indeed a bargain.

For a day or two she kept the photograph of Nicole on her desk at her remote house in Laurel Canyon. Then, on the odd chance that someone might come by and remark the likeness between them, the shape of face, the high cheekbones, the dark, straight hair, she put it away in the fireproof filing cabinet where all her other treasures lay.

The acquisition of the house, the news of Nicole for which she had waited so long, seemed to mark the point in Anna's life at which she suddenly was aware of a growing sense of isolation within herself. It was not the remoteness of her house that troubled her, the emptiness which only her dog's presence even began to fill, but the gradual knowledge that she was deliberately pulling herself farther and farther away from people, creating barriers which need not be there. It was now more than two years since the night she had signed that agreement in the office of William Osborne, the night she had written her last letter to Nicole. The months had been so busy, the time so filled with her own striving to achieve some goal which she herself could not exactly name, that she had only been aware of the externals—the struggle to master shorthand, finding a job and helping to keep Frank Hayward's business going, the new house, the mastery of the elements of business practice, even the terminology of her new job. She had carefully built a new identity around herself leaving behind Anna Rainard, but the identity was a shell, and nothing seemed to live at the core of it. She realized with some alarm that she was on the verge of becoming an eccentric, whom people would talk about. She had never wanted that to happen, but it was difficult to stop it. She began to accept the repeated invitations of the Haywards to come to their house for dinner, to meet their friends. But the habit of reserve built up over the years when she had hidden so much from Nicole, could not be overthrown. She knew that people called her 'that nice, quiet Mrs Maynard . . .' and left it at that.

She had no family to talk about, no background that would stand investigation. She was aware that the few times she invited the Haywards and other people to visit the house in Laurel Canyon she struck them as odd, and the life she led as odd. There was no hiding the books she had collected. The books on economics in their sombre bindings, the Russian writers that no one had ever heard of—'They belonged to my father,' she lied, and knew that it was recognized as a lie. She bought some records of Duke Ellington and a second-hand record player. She didn't buy a piano.

She had one or two dates with men she encountered in business, and they weren't very successful. If they were divorced, or widowed, they carried the stamp of their first marriages indelibly, and Anna knew she did not want to cope with a shadowy past, did not want to reveal her own. If they were still unmarried, they had hardened into a kind of selfishness she was beginning to recognize in herself—the mould of pleasing oneself becoming harder month after month. She had no enthusiasms she wanted to share. It didn't attract men to talk about the state of Wall Street or real estate. She never wanted to go near a restaurant or nightclub, the movies mostly bored her, and she was beyond the stage of caring to be pawed in the back seat of a car.

'Let's face it, Mike,' she said to the dog as they worked in the vegetable garden, he digging with a rock and ruining the new lettuces, she with a hoe, her head protected by a big hat like those the Japanese wore against the blazing sun. 'I'm not much of a success socially. I don't care enough. So, better suit myself and let people wonder. I hope—I hope Nicole finds the going easier.'

It was about then that she bought the Russian icon from a Pasadena antique dealer. She had seen it in the shop more than a year before, and had not allowed herself the extravagance of buying it. It was not very valuable, but she had been so used to making her money buy only what was useful that the purchase had a sense of a wild breaking with the identity she had tried to build up about her, and had failed. She was beginning to recognize that she could be nothing but what her life had made her, and if that meant being remote and alone, of finding the daily reports of Wall Street more interesting than the movies, of being more comfortable in her own company than pretending to be interested in a man who bored her, then that was how it would be. Triumphantly she hung the icon in her living-room, and didn't care who saw it, or who might ask questions about her Russian background. There were numbers of Russians who had followed the film industry to its capital in Hollywood. They had emigrated from the New York theatre, to act, to design, to write the music for the films the studios were now churning out. To be Russian was not so strange in America. She felt better when she had hung the icon there. She was giving recognition to a past she had tried to bury since the rebuff and the hurt she had suffered in England. At the date of the Russian Easter, she even sought out a Russian Orthodox Church, closed her eyes as the chanting went on, smelled the incense, and for a time was back in the small wooden church at Benyozovaya Polyana. Tatiana Fedorovna was there in her furs, and her mother was coughing her soft, apologetic cough. It was not entirely a success, that sharing of the Orthodox service. She started out for the desert at once, telephoning Frank Hayward that she needed a few days off, and thinking how much the hot dry air would have helped her mother. That was the time when she drove to Desert Hot Springs and started a real search for land to buy. It wasn't easy. People were beginning to discover the desert; weekend shacks were beginning to appear. Palm Springs had already been discovered, and was out of her price range. She hunted the edge of the great Joshua Tree National Monument, knowing that it was land which could never be built on. She found a piece of land at Twenty-Nine Palms, thirty acres of it. And then with a madness that surprised her, she bid for, and got, five acres at Desert Hot Springs itself. She couldn't afford to build a house on it, but it was a place of her own, a piece of land. As a Russian she broke at last from the tight strait-jacket she had placed on herself since the time she had left, defeated, the arena of battle to the triumphant Countess of Manstone. She loved her earth in the way a peasant loves it, values it, guards it. In that time the woman who had been born Anna Nikolayevna Tenishevna began to found her true links and bonds with the American earth. For the first time since she had left the birch woods and the cornfields of the Ovrenskys, she began slowly to develop, to feel, the sense of belonging.

CHAPTER 4

I

Afterwards the sequence of events in the crowded weeks that constituted the London 'season' were never clear in Nicole's mind, and certainly the names and faces were never properly linked. Young men were called Thomas and George and Charles and John and many other names she forgot; some were on Iris's list as eligible, others were present at dinner parties and balls only because they had the right family connections, the right manners, and the right clothes. Sometimes Iris grew impatient with Nicole's failure to distinguish between the two. 'Yes, but *which* Thomas Hamilton did you have supper with? You know, there's one who wouldn't be suitable at all ...'

'Aunt Iris, am I really supposed to fall in love and find someone to marry all in the space of two months? It isn't very likely——'

She was cut short. 'You may mock at this sort of thing, Nicole, but there are fresh faces appearing each season, and there's nothing quite so wilted as last year's deb. I advise you to make use of your time, and remember who is who. And as for falling in love ...' Iris's face twisted a little, and she took up her pen to check once again a dinner-party list. 'I wouldn't count on it. People marry—people in our circles marry because they seem suited to each other. It is a better foundation for a marriage than some wild fancy which is in tatters after a year. And don't,' she added, 'suppose that because you're said to be pretty and intelligent that you can have your pick of all the young men you meet. Your fortune is only very modest by the standards of some of the other girls who are still unmarried, and, while we're being honest about it, we might as well admit that you don't bring great family connections to a marriage. I hope you understand. Marriage is a serious business. You're far more likely to be satisfied and content with the rest of your life if you take the business seriously now. I advise you to look at it that way. The time goes very quickly for a young woman. If you're still unmarried after a season or two, people will begin to think you're on the shelf.' She bent over the list, and the last words were muffled. 'I hope you heard that, Nicole. I know all about how cruel people can be in those circumstances.'

Nicole knew she wasn't meant to reply, and she left Iris alone, going to the only place in the house in Elgin Square which seemed to give her peace and rest, the music room high up where the sounds she made hardly reached the rest of the house. She knew Iris was irritated by the amount of time she still spent at the piano, but Iris was not to understand how playing endless scales and arpeggios somehow helped to wipe out of her mind all the maddening repetition of the jazz tunes she danced to every night, how the severity of the brown-and-white room cleansed the cloying sweetness of balls with pink tablecloths and balls with pale yellow ones, or two shades of blue. She never brought flowers to this room. She thought, after these few weeks, that she would never want to look at a vase of flowers again. Their scent sickened her.

She was grateful, also, for the serenity that Charles provided through those weeks, the anchor of his quiet humour. Strangely, she was also grateful for the presence of Henson, the maid whom she thought would be an intolerable intrusion on her privacy. The middle-aged woman had developed a surprising fondness for the rather aloof young woman whose personal effects were her business. It shocked Nicole at first to find Henson waiting up for her when she came back from balls in the summer dawn. She protested, and tried to stop it, until she realized that it actually gave Henson pleasure to be there, to question her about the evening, to ask her about the young men with whom she had danced or had supper. She had a curiously deep knowledge of the London social scene. 'Oh, yes, Miss, I remember Frankie Denton when he came to visit the Standishes when I was personal maid to Lady Caroline. Well, so little Lord Francis is grown up, is he? Rather good-looking isn't he, Miss? I saw a photo in *Tatler* ... I hope he's better behaved than he used to be. His poor sister, Lady Mary ... quite hopelessly plain, and so clumsy. Can't even ride. The horsy girls can so often get away with it because they can sit in a saddle. Many an unlikely match has been made on the hunting field just because a girl had a good seat . . .' And all the time she talked she would be removing and hanging up Nicole's clothes, folding the underwear, folding the stockings, even though it was all to be removed for laundering. And she would be there quite early the next morning, wearing her grey day-dress, carrying Nicole's breakfast tray, not seeming to care that she had had so few hours to sleep in between. Henson had been 'in service' as she liked to call it, most of her life. 'I was thirteen, Miss, when I went to the household of the Marquis of Bentley. I was under-nursery maid. I've never,' she added with supreme pride, 'worked as a scullery- or a kitchen-maid. Always above stairs. I've looked after the nannies of the children; I've been a parlourmaid for a time, but when the Honorable Mrs Hugh Latymer's maid was taken ill, I filled in for a while, and I've never been anything but a lady's-maid ever since. And tell me, Miss . . .' as she fixed Nicole's pillows and settled the breakfast tray with the inevitable pink rose, 'How is young Mister Hugh? You said you met him last night. Did he make it into the Foreign Office? I know he had one try at the exams and failed . . . Miss Nicole, I wish you'd try to eat something. You're going all to bone and shadows . . .'

Eat . . . it was all she ever seemed to do. Every dinner was the same, or seemed to be; smoked trout, chicken, roast beef, ice-cream done up in a dozen ways but all tasting the same. Cold salmon for supper, more chicken and ham, either strawberries or raspberries with thick cream. And in case someone might be hungry—and many of the young men who followed the débutante balls were stoking up for the next day—there was always a bacon and egg breakfast. After a few weeks the thought of food began to make Nicole feel sick. She made a fine pretence of eating it; it did not do to make anyone feel uncomfortable because they did not feel the same way. She nibbled on a piece of dry toast for breakfast, got up and did the routine exercises she had been taught at Madame Graneau's, and then went upstairs to the piano and her scales. There was a kind of sweet relief in the very discipline they imposed, the almost silence in her mind that they created.

'Nicole, what's happening to you?' Richard Fenton asked one evening after he had escorted her to a dinner party, and then on to a ball. 'You look as if you're totally detached from the whole thing. I know of a couple of men who are dying for a word from you, and you don't even know they're there, even when you're dancing with them.'

'I'm dancing with you, Rick. I know you're here.'

'Yes, but you're treating me as an old family friend. I'm not that old. And I'm not family.'

'Rick, do you mind? Couldn't we just sit this one out, and not talk? Let's make a pact not ever to talk about the band, or the supper, or any of the other things. We won't ask each other if we've been to so-and-so's dance. We pretty well know where we've been this season. It's usually the same place.'

He smiled at her and took her hand and found a place for them to sit down. He signalled a waiter for champagne, and raised the glass to her. 'Well, I suppose I should be grateful you want to sit with me and just be quiet. Do you know something, Nicole? You're getting delicious hollows in your cheeks. If you don't die of exhaustion before the season's over, you'll end up the most beautiful girl in London. How many men tell you that? Lots, I'll bet. And you don't pay any attention. You're not even interested, are you? What is it you want? Haven't you got everything?'

'I don't want anything except to please my aunt for the next few weeks. After that ...' She shrugged, 'after that, perhaps I'll please myself—only I don't know what it is I want to be pleased by.'

'Shall I do one thing that will please you?' Richard said. 'Shall I take you home early and let you get one night's real sleep?'

She smiled at him widely and realized how little in these weeks she had been really smiling. 'That's the nicest thing anyone's said to me in an age.'

'I should be offended, but I'll take it as a compliment. I'm a fool, but you might say "greater love than this ..."'

He kissed her in the taxi, and she lay for a time tiredly, contentedly in his arms. 'If I thought there was even a chance you'd fall in love with me, Nicole ... Shall I try my luck?'

She sighed. 'I like the way you kiss me, Rick. Let's leave it at that for a while. Let's leave it until all this nonsense is over. How is anyone supposed to know anything about love when what you're really worrying about is your dress and your hair, and if you've been invited to the right party? It can all wait, can't it? Surely it's possible to learn about falling in love in winter? It doesn't have to be at a ball on a summer's night.'

'Wise, cool little creature. If only you would fall in love, I bet it would be a thunderclap. And you'd be in love forever. If I can do anything about it, I'll make certain I'm around when the thunderclap happens. Why shouldn't the lightning strike for me?'

Why ... and why not? she thought. Except that no one could arrange for the thunderclap, or even know if it was going to happen. Iris didn't believe in it, nor it seemed, did many other people. They believed in people being 'suitable' for each other. Possibly they were right, most times. She felt a sudden ache of loneliness, and settled more firmly in Richard's arms. He had made a kind of reality of something unspoken in her heart, the promise that it might happen, the hope. She suddenly knew she wanted it to happen, that she could only commit herself because a passion swept her, not because it seemed a suitable thing to do. But it was, she thought, unlikely that Richard, the one who had instructed her in this, would be the one to cause the thunderclap. There would be no thunderclap with someone who was so familiar. And yet as she looked sideways at that almost too-handsome face, she knew that if the lightning should strike with Richard, if his energies could be channelled to the seriousness he affected to despise, he could be a splendid man. But she had no reforming zeal in her. She had spent the whole of her short life making herself over into the image which Anna had desired of her, and now what Iris willed on her. She had no desire, no will, no strength to start to change anyone else. Richard would remain, so far as she was concerned, as he was, frittering away his time and his talents, getting dangerously close to the age where he must change course or remain the complete dilettante, gifted, intelligent, but never really serious. The words of Professor Lermanov came back, *'You are that worst of all things, a dilettante.'*

With Richard's arms about her, comfortingly, she shivered. 'Cold?' he said.

'No—perhaps someone just walked over my grave.'

'If I had the gift of a wish just now, a fairy-godmother wish, you'd never die.'

She looked at him. 'Nor will you ever die, Rick. You'll always be the same. You'll never grow old. You'll live forever.'

Afterwards she remembered that they were young enough then, both of them, to believe that this could be true.

It was at Ascot that Richard introduced her to Gerry Agar. Later she learned from Iris that he was Sir Gerald Agar, a baronet, unmarried, and very rich. He had with him a man, almost as poetically good-looking as Richard, but younger and with the appeal of a lingering shyness about him. 'My young cousin, Brendan de Courcey,' Gerry Agar said. 'He's Irish, and if you don't want to lose your money on horses, listen to him.'

'I wasn't intending to bet,' Nicole said. 'I thought one came to Ascot just for the hats and the strawberries.'

'Dear girl,' Gerry Agar said, 'you can see my cousin turning white. Horses are the most sacred thing on earth to him, next to women. He can recite their blood lines back to Methuselah. He knows their form bang on. If you don't come to a race meeting to bet, you're just cluttering up the ground.'

'Believe me, Miss Rainard. I've never seen ... seen ...' Nicole thought he actually blushed. 'I've never seen prettier lines in my life. And I'd love to help you make a fistful of money so you can buy more delectable hats like the one you've got on.'

Gerry Agar patted him on the shoulder, 'Spoken like a true Irishman, Brendan. Go to it, man. Do help Miss Rainard with her racing form. When you're thirsty, you'll know where to find Rick and me.'

There were four days of Ascot, four days of summer weather and big hats, of champagne and heeding Brendan de Courcey's racing tips and winning money. In that short time Nicole became a part of a foursome made up of herself, Richard, Gerry Agar and Brendan de Courcey. She found herself as strongly attracted to Gerry Agar as she was to Richard. He was older than any of them, about thirty, and had a faintly cultivated air of world-weariness that made the others seem even younger. The angle at which he wore his grey topper indicated that he had not much respect for the convention of wearing it at all. When he raised his racing binoculars at inappropriate times, it always appeared that he was taking a closer look at a woman rather than a horse. He was very blond and tall and gool-looking in an English fashion; he made an absolute contrast to his dark, rather more stockily built Irish cousin. Brendan wore impeccably tailored morning dress which he somehow contrived to make appear as if it belonged to someone else. Nicole watched him often tugging at the collar of his shirt, which was not too tight, but seemed to bother him. 'Tell you the truth, Nicole,' he said on the third day, 'I'm not mad about English racing. Oh, the racing's fine, and one can't miss the Derby. But all this dressing-up. I'd like to take you to some of the country meets in Ireland. Great fun. People are there for the people as well as the horses.'

Nicole looked about her carefully, beyond the well-dressed crowd in the Royal Enclosure, down to the Paddock, beyond to the Downs where the thousands had come to bask in the sun, where the gypsy caravans were camped and touts sold the name of the winners. 'I thought people came here for the people. After all, one can hardly *see* the horses.'

Brendan shrugged. 'It's entirely different. In Ireland everyone knows everyone else.' Suddenly he touched her arm, 'You know, Nicole, it would be grand if you came over and stayed with us during the Horse Show in August. We're not far from Dublin—in Kildare. We've a few nice horses ... The Horse Show is fun.' He made an apologetic gesture. 'Perhaps a little dressed up on Ladies' Day, but really just like one big house party. The horses ...'

'Brendan,' Gerry drawled, 'is being modest. His father is reckoned to have the best stud in Ireland. And, I have to concede his point. Until you've been to a genuine country race meeting in Ireland, you've never seen racing.' He still managed to leave it in doubt as to how he regarded country race meetings. 'And don't be deceived by the modesty. Clonkilty, Brendan's father's stud, has produced a Derby winner.'

'Promise you'll come,' Brendan said.

'August is a long time off,' Nicole countered.

'I'll have my mother write you,' Brendan said firmly.

'Nothing's so exciting as the Dublin Horse Show,' Richard said, 'but Fenton Field is very relaxing in August. You just watch the crops ripen and the beef fatten, and I'll be there to amuse you ...'

'Don't you ever do any *work*, Fenton,' Gerry Agar said. 'What's all this nonsense about reading for the Bar? Everywhere I go, there you are, idling around.'

'Gerry, it's the Long Vacation. And I've never worked so hard as I am now, escorting Nicole around. I have to carry a big stick to beat off the other men.'

'I would think,' Gerry said with his drawl exaggerated, 'that Nicole was very well able to take care of herself ...'

'... Rainard. I think she's being piggish,' Nicole heard said of herself one night as she entered the crowded ladies' cloakroom at a dance. 'Three to one is a *bit* much, and all the other odd ones who go trailing around her because she seems to be so popular. Well, I can tell you, none of the girls like her—and none of the mothers, either. And if she thinks she's going to get Gerry Agar, she's mistaken. He's been around every season for the last ten years, and someone's *always* expected to announce an engagement, but somehow he always managed to wriggle out. You'll see, by next season she'll be a has-been ... After all, no one really knows anything about her ...'

Nicole closed the door of the ladies' cloakroom and went back to the dance floor, where she was immediately asked to dance by the son of the duke who had attended her coming-out party. She smiled at him, laughed at his jokes, and went into supper for the third time that evening with him. If she was going to be talked about, she might as well be talked about in the best company. Her cheeks burned, and she kept her head very high, and the duke's son said. 'You're not just p ... pretty, Nicole. In these last few weeks you've become p ... positively beautiful. I sw ... swear it.'

Iris didn't like her association with Gerry Agar. 'He has a certain *reputation*, Nicole. His name has been linked with a number of girls, and nothing comes of it. He has a way of disappearing just when everyone expects an announcement of an engagement. They say he has a flat in *Paris*.'

'A number of people have flats in Paris,' Nicole pointed out. 'Gerry's rather fond of art, and perhaps having a flat in Paris is like having a shooting box in Scotland for those who enjoy shooting.'

'I don't like you defending him. I would like you not to see him again. He's very rich, but he's not considered eligible ...'

'I don't see how I can avoid seeing him,' Nicole countered, 'unless you want me to send regrets for all the things I've been invited to for the rest of the season. Gerry's rather omnipresent.'

Iris tapped her fingers together speculatively. 'Don't encourage him. It will do you no good. There was a girl a couple of seasons ago who ... well, she ended up being packed off to visit relations in India. Gerald Agar was the cause of it.'

Nicole continued to see Gerry whenever she felt like it. He seemed to have no work to do. He had an estate in Wiltshire, which didn't appear to occupy his time. 'I've a very good steward,' he once said. 'Why should I interfere and start messing up his work?'

'You accused Rick of being idle.'

'Rick's got something in him if he'd only work.' Gerry gave a slow, self-deprecating laugh. 'Now me, I'm past it. I'm over the edge. No use trying to save me. I shall reap the harvest of all rakes. But Rick's still got a chance. If I prod him enough, if *someone* prodded him enough, he might really settle down to some work. I'll bet he'd be a howling success if he ever did make it to the Bar. The courtroom personality. He could make a jury believe black was white. But even Rick with his brains would have to buckle down a bit. They don't let you into those sort of things because they like the cut of your jaw.'

Nicole spent many afternoons with Gerry. He took her to the galleries up and down Bond Street and in St James's, where he was well known. The dealers always listened with interest to whatever comments he had to make; he had bought from many of them in the past. His particular pleasure was Oriental ceramics. 'I've a nice little collection down in Wiltshire,' he said to Nicole. 'I'd like to show it to you. But I don't suppose your aunt would let you come ...'

'I don't suppose so, either.'

'Come and have tea at my flat. No, don't look like that. I've another guest coming. Antoine Tourney. An interesting type. You might enjoy him. We have a little business to do, so you can have tea and leave. All very respectable.'

The sitting-room in Gerry's flat was dominated by a Picasso and a Matisse. 'A lucky buy,' he said. 'I really must take your education in hand, Nicole. You seem to think art stopped around 1900. But there, I'm being very severe, aren't I? You're so young yet, for all you look as if you have all the wisdom in the world. Come, play something for me.' He was drawing her towards the grand piano. 'I keep hearing you're not a bad musician. If you are, then I'll forgive you for being an ignoramus about art ...'

She played, suddenly glad that the bright smiling mask of the débutante could be dropped. She played Bach, played seriously, for a serious audience. When she stopped she turned around and found that another man had entered the room and had stood silently, listening to her.

'I congratulate you, M'selle. An excellent musician. Is it only prejudice which makes me surprised that you also are beautiful?'

'Nicole,' Gerry said, 'may I present Comte Antoine Tourney. Miss Nicole Rainard.'

They sat over tea together, but Nicole felt that she was hardly part of the gathering. Antoine Tourney was very attentive, very flattering. A man close to sixty, his manner should have been flattering to Nicole, but she found herself rejecting it without understanding why. It was one of the times she felt very young and inexperienced, not able to put a finger on what disturbed her about this man. He talked to her about Paris and was not surprised to learn that she had been a student at the Conservatoire. 'A pupil of Lermanov? Then you are indeed among the elite.'

As the tea was replaced by drinks, the Comte's talk turned more towards Gerry. 'It is happening, my friend. Violence everywhere. Spain must erupt. After Spain, what? Where? Roosevelt mouths his platitudes, our saintly politicians here and in France say what they must, believe what it pleases them to believe. But who is arming? Who is ready for the struggle? We know only one power who is actively preparing. If Churchill had his way, England already would be preparing. But she is not. There will be a great demand for arms close to the time. A demand that no one will be able to fulfil, but whoever has those arms to sell will be very, very powerful ...'

Nicole was out of her depth. She could only vaguely sense what was being talked about. 'The time? What time? What do you mean, Comte?'

He turned to her with a faint start, as if remembering that she was present. 'The time? The time, my dear M'selle, of war. War will come, you know. Must come. The men who rule the world are making certain of that—whether they mean it to happen or they are dedicated to preventing it. But while ambition

154

and hunger remain unassuaged, the desire for a war to settle it all will remain. Those who make the instruments of war will prosper——'

Nicole clattered her cup into her saucer savagely. 'Gerry, thank you for tea. Thank you for the afternoon's instruction. I'll try not to be so ignorant in future. I really will visit galleries and pay attention.' She turned to Antoine Tourney. 'How instructive it has been to meet you, Comte. How much I hope you are wrong. There can't be another war. They all promised that there would never be another war . . .'

When she had gone, Antoine Tourney looked at Gerry closely. 'Quite lovely, Agar. Very accomplished. A little young, perhaps, but intelligent enough to learn. Do I suspect, my friend, that you are at last falling just the least bit in love? Somehow I had never thought it would be a girl. I thought it would be a woman, a very experienced woman. But perhaps in this one you have found the perfect balance. Young enough to be quite entrancing; intelligent enough to learn very quickly. When she is thirty, she will be quite formidable. A very apt and able companion for you.'

Gerry crushed his cigarette into the ashtray. 'Nicole Rainard is not for discussion, Comte. Shall we come to business . . .?'

The older man bowed his head. 'My apologies. It is already beyond discussion, and therefore not my business. Now, let us come to *our* business. I have these latest figures from Krupp. Very reliable. Money invested here . . .'

They spent the next two hours discussing the figures on the sheets that the Comte had brought with him, arguing the possibilities. Both smoked considerably, but neither drank. The side of Gerry Agar which very few people knew came forward; the interests which he never declared were in evidence. Those who thought of him contemptuously as a man who did nothing except for enjoyment would have been astonished, astonished and shaken.

'The demand will be incalculable, Agar. Whatever money is at your disposal, whatever influence you have, should be directed this way. There will be rivers of money, my friend, for those who know how to tap them. There will indeed be oceans of influence. Nothing will stop that man in Germany from his own madness, and like some madnesses, it may succeed. The ones, the only ones who will gain, no matter what way it falls out, will be the ones who supply the armaments. Now, here I have a plan ... There are people you should be in contact with. When do you next go to Paris? It should be as soon as possible ...'

They ate a cold supper prepared by Gerry's manservant. And they talked until late that night.

When Antoine Tourney was leaving, his thoughts slipped back to less pressing things. 'That young woman. You might do worse. So young yet, but disciplined ...'

'I said before—Nicole Rainard is not for discussion.'

The Comte bowed. 'Good night my friend.'

II

The time came when Nicole was in total revolt against what had become a numbing ritual. She went to dress for the dinner and dance to which she was invited; while Henson brushed her hair, and the clothes lay ready for her to step into, she suddenly knew that she could not go. 'Henson, just put out some ordinary clothes, please. A light suit. I'm not going to the dinner.'

'Aren't you well, Miss Nicole?'

'Well? I'm sick of what I'm doing. Just for tonight I'm not going to have to say a polite word to anyone, not talk about Ascot or what I'm doing in August, and what plays I've seen. Just one night, Henson ...' She was almost pleading.

'Lord Francis ... what will you tell him?'

'I'll telephone I'm not well. I'll leave a message. He won't ask the details. Tomorrow I'll send a note and invite him to tea, or we'll go to a matinée, or something ... but just not tonight.'

'And Lady Gowing ... what will *she* say.'

'My aunt need never know. She's out to dinner herself tonight. If I have to, I'll tell her a polite little lie.' She suddenly burst out, 'Even horses get a rest on Sunday!'

Henson was clicking her tongue, but she did not argue any further. She knew the look of stubbornness that had come on Nicole's face, the look of determination that drove her each morning to the piano with the dark circles of last night's party still under her eyes. Sometimes she was afraid for Nicole; she feared an explosion, an explosion born of the determination to keep her promise to her aunt and the conflicting determination, the longing to belong to her own self. Henson hoped the explosion would not come, would be headed off. If it came it could be monumental, could alter the life of this girl, of whom she had become so fond, irreparably.

'This *suit*, Miss Nicole?'

'Yes, something simple. I'm going to a Promenade Concert. I expect I'll have to wait in line like everyone else. I don't have a ticket. I might not even get in. If I don't, there'll be something at the Wigmore Hall ... Just to be alone for a few hours, Henson. Not to have to talk ...'

The line of promenaders had already moved inside Queen's Hall when her taxi drew up. All the tickets would be gone, she knew. There might be one left in the stalls. She approached the ticket window when a young man spoke to her. 'Want to get in? I've got a ticket for the promenade section. I can't use it, and I can't afford to let it go. It's a bit over the price ...'

She guessed he was one of those who did that nightly—queued early, and then took a chance on re-selling the ticket at the last moment. In a depression many ways were used to make a few shillings. 'Yes,' she said, grabbing towards the piece of pasteboard. 'Whatever you say.'

He had seen her arrive in a taxi, had taken in the expensive simplicity of her clothes, and he named three times the price on the face of the ticket. She paid without a murmur, trying to keep her eyes off his shabby clothes, trying not to see the look that was in his eyes, the look of anger and a kind of contempt. There was very nearly hopelessness in the eyes of that man, and he was too young to be hopeless. She turned away, feeling sick and ashamed. But what was *she* to do? Uncomfortably she was reminded of Comte Antoine Tourney and his confident, easy prediction of war. Her legs were trembling as she ran up the stairs to the gallery. Why did one always think first of the Russians when one thought of revolution? They hadn't been the only ones, or the first ... Then she found herself among the standing crowd, mostly young people. She felt more at ease here. People who listened to music didn't join revolutions. But the silence had fallen on the crowd as the lights dimmed, and before she had time to glance at the programme, the opening of Tchaikovsky's 1812 Overture sounded out—the history of a war past, the premonition of war to come. The crowd remained still, but their force was there, the force of any mass of people, potent, but perhaps to be tapped and manipulated by people like Antoine Tourney, the force of thousands, of millions, like that shabby young man outside. In the heat of that packed balcony on a summer's night, Nicole shivered.

With the overture Nicole had been caught up by music and some of the tension dissipated; she had thrust away the menace of the crowd. The crowd itself shifted and moved on the promenade circle while the conductor took his bows. The piano was brought on stage and the conductor emerged again, leading out the soloist for the Mozart C Major piano concerto. Nicole experienced again the longing she had lived with for years that at some time she might be led out in this way, the ambition that had come to nothing. She found herself pressing forward for a better view, pressing and using her elbows. By ducking under the arm of someone who had momentarily turned away from his position, she managed to gain a position at the rail. She was totally absorbed in the entrance of the soloist, a young woman whom everyone said had a great future before her, particularly as a Mozart exponent. A surge of envy rose in Nicole; she leaned across the balcony, transfixed.

'I always thought you could use your elbows if you needed to. I didn't know they'd be such sharp ones.'

In the dimness she turned to look at the man who had spoken. 'Lloyd Fenton!—what are you doing here?'

'What, you think *all* the good things are reserved for Europe? We have something called the Boston Symphony——'

'Sshush!' someone whispered fiercely beside them. The soloist had finally settled the seat to her liking, had nodded to the conductor, who raised his arms. The first notes of the music fell into the hush. Nicole, who thought she could forget everything under the spell of music like this, was acutely aware of Lloyd Fenton beside her. She had never expected to see him again; she hadn't wanted to see him. Now it seemed an utterly right and natural thing that he was there, standing beside her.

In the slight pause between the movements, he leaned close to her ear and whispered, 'You're too thin, and you've grown quite extraordinarily beautiful.'

As the haunting, almost painfully evocative theme of the slow movement was spelled out, developed, receded, returned,

Nicole felt a mist of tears across her eyes. Evocative of what? Did it suggest love which she had not known, a lifetime of striving to be some other person than what she was, of yearning for something as yet unknown, perhaps unknowable? What did she know of love, she who had never felt it? In the midst of the rich simplicity of the slow movement, she felt poverty-stricken. She felt it, the yearning, the sense of deprivation, until the second that Lloyd Fenton's hand closed gently on hers as it grasped the balcony rail. Then the yearning seemed to end; she was comforted, warmed, poor no more.

When the lights came up, while the ovation greeted the soloist and conductor, she turned and looked at him directly, not removing her hand from his light grasp. 'I'm glad I found you.'

'Nicky, were you really looking?'

'Looking for something—someone. I wonder if you're what I've been looking for, or was it the music?'

'We'll find out, won't we? We'll take time to find out together.'

They talked little during the interval. They walked around, and went to the bar. Lloyd pushed his way in to shout for, and get, two ales. 'Nothing so grand as champagne, I'm afraid.'

'I've had rather enough champagne lately. And I've had rather enough of balls and moonlit gardens lately. I came here just to be quiet. This tastes good.'

'I'll take you to a place where the food tastes better. You need some food, and a bit more rest. Is the débutante life really so tough?'

'It's not a life, it's a steeplechase. I feel at the moment I'm just about holding on to the horse. I've lost the bridle, and I'm just clinging on to its mane.'

The bell was ringing to summon them back. He took her glass, and they returned to the promenade gallery. This time neither of them tried to push their way forward to the rail. They listened to the Beethoven Seventh leaning against the back wall. It seemed to Nicole that as she stood with her shoulder against Lloyd Fenton's arm, with her hand resting in his, as she listened to the familiar, beloved themes, the incredible second movement that always before had roused in her a feeling that she wasn't mature enough to understand what she heard, that the compelling majesty of the repeated crescendo of the theme was beyond her grasp and range, she suddenly experienced the dawn of understanding. In that very short time she seemed to travel a long distance. She took a deep breath and closed her eyes; she seemed, for the moment, to have given up the race, or was so far in front that the runners coming behind did not exist.

Afterwards they went to a Russian restaurant in Soho. 'Is this deliberate?' Nicole asked as they got out of the taxi.

'Deliberate?' He looked surprised. 'Why should it? Is there something wrong with it?'

'I just thought—I thought perhaps you remembered Judy saying something about my mother being Russian.'

'Does it surprise you I'd forgotten? No, they're friends here. I felt like a little home life tonight. I expect you go to many much grander places, but the change will do you good. Have you ever eaten Russian food?'

'Never.'

'Well, I can't vouch it *is* Russian. But it's different, and good. These White Russians have turned to everything to make a living since they got kicked out. Why not food ...?'

They were being greeted exuberantly by the owner. 'Alexander, this is Miss Rainard. We're both hungry.'

'To come to my house hungry is a compliment, Mr Fenton. We shall not disappoint you. First a little vodka, eh? while you look at the menu.

There was vodka and wine, and food such as Nicole had never tasted before, strange food, strangely delicious. It was a homey sort of restaurant, intimate and not expensive, where people strive to build up a business by serving good food at reasonable prices, and each diner was served as if his presence mattered. Nicole discovered that there was, however, a special relationship between Alexander Orekhov and Lloyd Fenton. 'He was ill about a year ago. We discovered at St Giles's that he had a brain tumour. It was in a pretty bad place, just touch and go whether we could operate and get away with it. But he would have died anyhow. I was Wygate's assistant then—very new to the job. It was left to me to explain to Alexander. He didn't hesitate a second, just begged us to go ahead. His wife, he said, was seven months pregnant with her first child. He had to be alive to see the child, help to raise it, provide for both of them.

160

I thought all that was a bit odd, but I found that she was his second wife. The first one had come out of Russia with him after the Revolution. They'd worked at anything they could and saved their money to open this place. Then she died, of cancer he said. He felt as if all the work had been for nothing. And then he met this young girl who had come out of Russia as a baby. She couldn't remember it at all, but the family were very Orthodox, and they lived as Russians. So Alexander found himself in love again at past fifty, and then with a child on the way. He said he couldn't die. Just like that.

'It was one of the finest pieces of work I've ever seen Wygate do. A sort of miracle when you saw the size of the tumour and where it was placed. So Alexander was out of the hospital when the baby was born. I went to the christening. I doubt if I've ever seen such an occasion. Every White Russian in London must have been there. I wish I could have understood half the things they were saying to each other. The baby was toasted with more vodka and tears than you could believe possible. Alexander worships him—little Alexis—and his mother, Sonya. We try never to get emotionally involved with our patients, not to sentimentalize them or our job. But it was one of the times I've been glad I had helped to bring off something like keeping a man alive ...'

Nicole was listening to him, and still conscious that she was shovelling food into herself as if she hadn't eaten food for days. Between mouthfuls she asked, 'And do you often go to the Proms?—by yourself?'

He shrugged. 'I go when I can. Usually on the spur of the moment, so usually alone. I went this evening because—oh, damn, I've just finished telling you we don't ever get emotionally involved with patients. But this morning a patient of Wygate's died. I shouldn't be telling you this. She died on the operating table. It was almost a routine job—if you can call any neurosurgery routine. But things just didn't go right. And then just when I thought Wygate had sort of found himself with the whole business, and she might have come through O.K., her heart gave out—or some damn thing. It depressed me, because it was unexpected. God knows, I should be used to the unexpected now. I shouldn't feel bothered when I've seen a great surgeon do his best, and fail. But ... it made a pretty black day. I went over to Queen's Hall on the off-chance of getting a ticket. I needed people around me. I fully intended to come here to Alexander's even if I hadn't met you. In some way they're convinced that I not only saved Alexander—which I didn't, because it was Wygate, but that I somehow saw that Alexis got born without a hitch. So they make me feel like part of the family. It's a nice feeling . . .'

'You have your own family. We talked about them at Fenton Field.'

'You remember that?'

'Yes, I remember. I wonder why you don't go back to them?'

He shrugged. 'Perhaps I'm having a love affair—with England. I'm not yet bored, or ready to settle down to practise in Boston. I won't be really in the bosom of the family until I'm prepared to get married and do all the kinds of things they do.' He gestured to her with his wineglass. 'Don't get me wrong. It isn't that I don't admire what I see in those marriages, the way Sam and Peter worked to try to pick up the pieces after the crash. But I know when I go back I've got to be good and ready to settle down. It just seems the time isn't right now.'

She felt that strange envy of him return. His world, which had been shaken by his family's loss of money, was still remarkably steady. There all knew where they were, and where they belonged. He knew it also. Once again, with a sense of panic, she thought of her own life in these last few months since she had agreed to Iris's terms and Iris's strategy which must lead her to a socially successful marriage, or to nothing. She was never going to be led out on to the stage of a concert hall by a famous conductor. And she knew of nothing else that she wanted. She looked at Lloyd, and his eyes on her calmed her once more. 'What are you frightened of, Nicky?'

'Just for a moment I was frightened—frightened about not finding my way. Perhaps of ending up never having done anything worthwhile. I'm all right now.' She nodded to him, 'Yes, I'm all right now.'

They were given brandy with Alexander's compliments, and invited to come upstairs to see Alexis. Nicole found another world there. There were tiny rooms on three floors above the restaurant, where the redolent odours of cooking were ever-present. But it was a world of deep serenity and peace, which was not at all touched by the sounds from the kitchen or the traffic noises in the narrow Soho street outside. They were taken to the room, bathed dimly in the light placed before an icon, where the child lay sleeping. He was golden-haired and sweet-faced like his mother. In a living-room Alexander's mother-in-law smilingly offered them tea from a bubbling samovar. She was dressed in black, and in a style of years ago. Nicole sensed that in spirit this woman had never left Russia behind. Like Lloyd Fenton, she knew where she belonged, but she was exiled from that place forever. Her security lay in the lamps before the icons, and the sleeping child, in the happiness in Alexander's face as he watched his young wife. They drank tea and talked of inconsequential things. The clatter from the kitchen stopped as the restaurant closed. It was growing late, and Nicole let her eyelids close as she never would have if she had been at one of the usual parties of that summer.

'I'll take you home, Nicky,' Lloyd said.

'But you will bring her back again,' Sonya said. 'Some after-noon, perhaps—when Alexis is awake?'

'I will make little cakes,' her mother said. 'It will be like all the things your family have told you about the time in Russia . . .' Lloyd had told them that Nicole's mother had been Russian; it was inconceivable to them that Nicole knew nothing about how life had been lived there.

'I'll see you again, Nicky,' Lloyd said as the taxi drew into Elgin Square. 'Remember we said we'd give it a try? I'm often tied up at the hospital, but even doctors get time off. I'd like to spend it with you.'

It seemed so coolly said, but yet in the context of Lloyd Fen-ton's background, it was a declaration of intention. They seemed committed to searching out each other, to trying to dis-cover whether it had been the music they had listened to to-gether, or if indeed the reaction had been a real changing of chemistry within both of them.

He leaned down and kissed her swiftly, with only the lightest embrace. It was like the gentle comfort of his hand on her as they had listened to the Mozart. 'You'll go to sleep now,' he said. 'Sleep a long time. You need it. I'll be in touch.'

Henson was waiting. 'You're almost as late as you ever are, Miss Nicole,' she started scoldingly. 'I thought for once you'd have an early—— Why, Miss Nicole, has something happened?'

'Why do you say that?'

'I'm sorry, Miss. None of my business, I'm sure.'

'I'm so full of food, Henson,' Nicole said, as she kicked off her shoes. 'You wouldn't believe how much I ate ...'

'I'm relieved to hear it, Miss. I've been beginning to wonder if you'd survive until the end of the season ...'

Nicole hardly heard the rest of the talk. She was drowsily relaxed as she prepared for bed; when Henson was gone and the light was out, she thought of that light kiss and an embrace which had hardly existed. Slight things on which to build. But enough.

Henson brought her breakfast at the usual time the next morning. Nicole ate it with more relish than she had shown for weeks, ate all of it. Then she put the tray on the floor beside the bed, and instead of getting up and starting the routine of exercises before she had her bath, she slid down between the sheets again. When Henson came to collect the tray she was deeply asleep. The woman looked at the suddenly vulnerable face, with the faint shadows of fatigue; it was seldom she saw Nicole's face unguarded. Then Henson reached down and gently drew the blanket about the bare white shoulders, and noiselessly went and drew the curtains to block out the light. She left the room with the quietness of a shadow, and gave instructions that Miss Nicole's room was not to be entered for cleaning until much later. Everyone was to be as quiet as possible. 'At last the child's getting some sleep,' she told the head parlourmaid.

'Well,' the woman answered dourly, 'at least *we'll* be spared one morning of those bloody scales!'

III

It amounted to a few weeks in July. That was all there was of it. Afterwards it seemed to Nicole that the time had been much longer because it had been so intensely lived. The sensation that she had suddenly stopped running remained, so that events seemed to flow past her. In her memory it was a bright and shining time, golden days of mid-summer when it didn't rain once, and she fell in love.

It hadn't happened as Richard said it might, as a kind of thunderclap, but it was there, the feeling that everything was changed. She did not even try to think about the future, not to fix it or determine it, or to make a plan for it. It was simply

164

enough that she had fallen in love with Lloyd Fenton and that the future would settle itself.

She knew she must have done other things besides seeing him every moment he was free from the hospital. There was Wimbledon during those weeks, and Test cricket at Lord's. She thought she must have gone to those things with Richard, or Brendan or Gerry Agar—or it might have been with Lord Freddie or the duke's son, who had assumed little identity except that he was called Harry. She knew she did these things, and went to parties and Covent Garden—the engagement book was full. What was not written down she did not have to remind herself of. There were quick, lunch-time meetings with Lloyd at an Italian restaurant near the hospital. After Wimbledon or Lord's, and before her dinner engagement, there was often a swift, marvellous hour to meet for a drink at the Ritz. They chose the Ritz because they felt they were alone in its vast spaces. She never remembered much about what they said, or if they talked much at all. They went one afternoon to a harpsichord recital at Wigmore Hall. They visited Alexander Orekhov again, had tea and cakes with his mother-in-law, admired the baby. Some mornings she got up very early and they walked in Hyde Park while the strengthening sun slanted down between the trees, and the mist hung briefly in shreds over the Serpentine, and then vanished before the coming heat of the day. They walked hand in hand, and sometimes they stopped and kissed each other. Nicole felt the warmth of the kisses like some drug that crept through her, some totally new sensation, that made her look back on her former existence as if it had been a state of deprivation, of hunger which was now miraculously assuaged. She was no longer alone.

During those weeks she hardly went near the piano, and when she did it was to play the things that suited her mood, the bittersweet nocturnes of Chopin, the most romantic works of Schumann. This was no time for Bach. The household at Elgin Square noted the change, and each had his own interpretation. 'Glad to see you eating so well, Miss Nicole,' Henson said. 'You've quite lost that peaky look.' Except for the mornings she met Lloyd, she slept late, and Iris saw this. 'Much more sensible,' she said. 'I really never thought that looking as if one were wasting away was very attractive.' Iris knew nothing about the meetings with Lloyd Fenton. Nicole doubted if she would have forbidden them, but she would have regarded them as a waste of time. Impecunious doctors were not on her list of eligible men.

Charles saw but remarked only to himself the kind of radiance that shone so newly from Nicole's face. He heard her laugh about small things, actually heard her sing as she came down the stairs one morning. 'I hope he's right,' he thought to himself. 'God, I hope he's right for her, whoever he is. I hope he loves her the way she loves him.' Charles was not a religious man, but he heard himself muttering the odd half-prayer, half-threat. 'She'd better not be hurt. Better *not!*' He was ready to fight anything or anyone that threatened to shatter that look on Nicole's face.

Iris thought she had discovered the reason for Nicole's new light-heartedness, the easy gaiety, which was so much at odds with the seriousness that Iris deplored when she received a note from the Duchess of Milburn asking that Nicole be included in the house party she was arranging at their Scottish estate for the opening of the grouse-shooting season. 'There will be a number of young people about Harry's age,' the note read. Harry was her elder son, and the Duke's heir.

Nicole was not in the house when the letter arrived. Uncharacteristically, Iris rushed at once to Charles to tell him the news. 'But, Charles,' she protested when he didn't seem unduly impressed, 'Lord Blanchard is the most eligible man in England.'

'What—your horse-faced Harry? Just like his father—a real idiot! Just as well he's going to be a duke. He wouldn't be any use at holding down a job. Besides, Iris, I rather thought the Prince of Wales was regarded as the most eligible man in England.'

She stormed out in disgust, going at once to accept the Duchess's invitation. Charles shook his head. He hoped it was not—he did not believe it could be—Harry Blanchard who had caused that new, wonderful look on Nicole's face. If it had been sheer social ambition which drove Nicole, he knew her well enough to know that she would be more deadly serious than before, calmly having marked and stalked her quarry. She was too intelligent to have fallen head over heels in love with that useless, if amiable, young man. He wished Iris had waited to consult Nicole before sending her acceptance. It wasn't really

fair the way the girl was being pushed around. Then he reflected that Nicole had resisted all of Iris's pushing until she had
been ready herself to yield.

With Nicole herself Iris's triumphant announcement of the
invitation hardly registered. She would be in Scotland for a few
days around the twelfth of August. They would be days away
from Lloyd. That was all she thought. But for some reason Iris
seemed to take this final crowner to the season as some kind of
prize Nicole had won, and as such it was a legitimate part of the
bargain she had made with her niece. Nicole thought that when
she returned from Scotland, having done everything her aunt
could possibly expect of her, she would then tell her about
Lloyd Fenton. Surely by then, she and Lloyd would have begun
to make their plans. She understood well enough why neither
of them wanted to push those plans. There had to be a time of
loving that was without bonds, a time to savour the sweetness
of giving without actual gifts, the time of secrecy that belonged
to them alone. Once they told the first person, they would be
locked in the mechanics of engagement and wedding plans,
plans of where to live, and how to love. So she did not worry
that both of them held off for these last precious days of freedom. She did not worry about the fact that Lloyd Fenton had so
far not even asked her to marry him. It was, for her, just an
understood fact.

Only twice in those weeks did Lloyd accompany her as her
invited partner to a dinner and a dance. And each time, before
one o'clock, he delivered her into the arms of Brendan de
Courcey and Richard. 'Take care of her, will you, Rick?' he
said casually.

'You have to be mad, man. Half of London wants to take care
of Nicole ...'

Lloyd smiled, and Nicole was delighted to see just the faintest
air of proprietorship there. 'We start operating at eight o'clock
sharp at St Giles's, Rick. The unfortunate patient who gets an
unsteady hand hovering over him isn't going to be very impressed by the dashing young doctor who danced the whole
night through ... S'long, Nicky. See you ...'

'Damn cheek,' Brendan said. 'Don't know why you put up
with him, Nicole. Now if I——'

'But you wouldn't, young Bren,' Gerry Agar said. 'When
anyone wears his heart so obviously on his sleeve, a girl could

be forgiven for thinking it might have been there an awfully long time and available. Now, Nicole, shall we dance?'

He ignored the crushed look his younger cousin wore. Brendan would have to learn some time not to be such a kid.

Gerry took her to the summer exhibition at the Royal Academy. He walked the halls wordlessly for half an hour, letting her look, and himself watching her being looked at. 'Well, it's clear that next year you'll have your portrait hanging here by the latest dull painter the Academicians approve of. They always like fashionable subjects. It insures a lot of attention from the public who don't know any better.'

'And you're implying I should know better, Gerry? How do I learn?'

'Only by looking, dear girl. Only by looking. Shall we begin?'

He led her out of the Academy and found a taxi in Piccadilly. 'The Tate Gallery, please,' he said to the driver. 'It might be fun to show you my own little collection, Nicole. Of course, it's down in the country. You'd have to come there ...'

'Some time soon, Gerry. Perhaps Rick and——'

'Aren't you tired of the mob yet, Nicole?'

'Gerry, I haven't got used to "the mob" as you choose to call it. Remember, I'm just literally out of school—as ancient as I am for a schoolgirl.'

'Yes, I do keep forgetting. You seem older. Or perhaps it's myself who's older. I have the itch to teach you. That's a sure sign of age.'

'Gerry, your family—you never talk about any family.'

'There isn't any, dear girl. None that count. I've one sister, whom I never see. She was the deb of the year ten years ago, just when things were beginning to hot up into the jazz period. She was supposed to be frightfully daring and modern. In fact, she was—is—a dead bore. Not a brain in her head. Happily she married an equally brainless Royal Navy chap, who will probably end up an admiral if we get a war. They think I'm completely decadent and they never come near the place in Wiltshire. She got a handsome share of money from my father's will, and I think she's really praying I won't ever get married so one of her stream of strapping sons will get the title and the estate. That would please her.' He sighed exaggeratedly. 'Ah, families ...' The cab drew up before the Tate Gallery.

There was an exhibition of paintings bewilderingly modern and strange to Nicole's eyes. Some of the names she knew—Picasso, Modigliani. Others were quite new, although they seemed old and loved friends to Gerry. Soutine, Survage, Miro, Leger, Kokoschka, Klee. She stared at them silently, and finally shook her head. 'You'll think me as much a bore as your sister. I don't understand half of them. I really don't think I've gone beyond Renoir.'

'Not a bad place to pick up,' he said. 'Let's go and have a drink. The Ritz?'

'No, not the Ritz,' she said quickly.

He raised his eyebrows. 'Oh, I wonder why not? Well, never mind. The Savoy, then?'

She had champagne, and he had a dry martini. He sipped it appreciatively, quickly looking round the crowd that was beginning to gather for drinks. 'The Americans know a thing or two. Yes—quite a lot. More than how to make a good martini. I hope our rulers wake up in time and don't feel too grand to ask for a little of their expertise in a few areas. Sorry, Nicole—you don't like that subject. Well, now, I think that Lloyd Fenton is going to be one of those very expert Americans. Probably is already. They have a way of applying themselves. There's no on else I can think of who would walk out on you at a dance, and strangely enough, still leave you smiling. Yes, very strange. He's either very sure of himself, or he knows he hasn't a hope. I wonder which it is. Is it true what they're saying about you and young Blanchard?'

Her gaze, which had been wandering around the room, snapped back to him. '*What* about me and Harry? *What* are they saying?'

'That you're all set to announce your engagement.'

She slammed down her glass, and when the liquid spilled, she licked her fingers like a child. 'I've never heard of such rubbish. I hardly know Harry Blanchard.'

'You're seen with him constantly. You're going to stay with the Milburns in Scotland—so they say.'

'A few days.' She let her first anger give way to amusement. 'Oh, all this talk. Gossip writers have to have something to write about. If it isn't there, they invent it. *You* know that, Gerry.'

'I should. I seem to have been the victim of the same thing

myself several times. So it isn't Blanchard. You don't plan to become a duchess.'

She plunged, 'I'm going to marry Lloyd Fenton. And *that* is not for repetition, Gerry. We're not talking about it yet.'

'Fenton? You're sure of that, Nicole? You're not just trying on the idea to see if it fits?'

She shook her head. 'I don't know how to say it, Gerry. I don't really think I've ever believed in people being in love before. I've never believed how it changes everything ...' He watched her expression, which had so often been cool and wary, always in control, slowly melt into the radiance of an almost shy smile. The creature before him was transformed, and he experienced a swift surge of envy of the man who had made that happen. 'I'm so happy, Gerry. I've never felt like this before. It's so marvellous I almost don't trust it. I expect it all to vanish. But people like Lloyd don't vanish. He's ... he's so much like a rock. He's a real New Englander, and for the first time in my life, I want to be frail and clinging. I'll do anything he wants me to do—go anywhere, live anywhere. Anything just so that I can be with him. As soon as this nonsense of a season is over, we'll make our plans. Gerry—I'm so happy. I hope you're happy for me.'

He held his glass up to her, and his face carefully masked the disappointment that surged through him. The smile he gave her was as urbane and inscrutable as ever. 'Of course, dear girl, I'm happy for you. It's just bloody marvellous to see someone happy. Here's to you, Nicole. Happiness, dear girl.'

And as they finished their drinks, Gerry Agar kept up a flow of talk, and in his mind he revised some plans which had begun to form over the last weeks. He put aside the thought that Nicole would ever come to Wiltshire except as the wife of another man. He put away the picture—he admitted now that he had spent some time adding details to that picture—of showing her the place in Wiltshire as if it were to be her own home. He was never going to witness the flowering of this dark, grave beauty sitting opposite him as mistress of that house, his pupil, his wife and his lover. He had wanted to teach her so much, and he still believed she would infinitely have repaid the teaching. Like Nicole, he had himself never believed people actually fell in love. If the sudden ache of disappointment inside him was any guide, he had been dangerously close to a state which

170

he had not thought existed. Perhaps he was already over the line. If that was so, he would have to pull himself back somehow, and no one would ever know he had crossed it.

'Well, dear girl, if you're looking for a witness at short notice, remember me. I've a feeling that Fenton isn't the sort who'll sit still for a big, fashionable wedding. There's the place in Wiltshire for a honeymoon if you want it. There's never anyone there ...' On the surface he had already begun to reshape the picture of Nicole in Wiltshire. And while he approved the cool command he had of himself, he was astonished to find that he was experiencing something amazingly like a sensation of pain.

He raised his glass again, and it was a sort of leave-taking, although Nicole would not recognize it as such. 'Good luck, dear girl. Good luck!'

The next day Gerry Agar presented himself, by appointment, at a house exactly like its neighbours in Grosvenor Terrace, near Victoria. A brass plate gave it the identification of a firm of specialist optical lens importers. He was, after a short wait, admitted to the office of a man he had never met before, but whose underlings had been busy, over the past year, trying to recruit the interest and services of Sir Gerald Agar.

The two men talked for over an hour. 'Your way of life will be seen to change as little as possible. It's fortunate you've established yourself in Paris, and the pattern of travelling on whim. Very useful cover. The race track and the art dealer ... Yes, very good. Very few could suspect ...'

Gerry finished the sentence. 'That Agar was capable of anything remotely ... well, shall be say, unselfish?'

The other man nodded. 'Use that word if you like. This is not pleasant or easy business. None of us may like what we have to seem to be to the rest of the world. But you're needed. You've already penetrated, through Comte Antoine Tourney, exactly the world we want to know better. *He* knows you as a man who's serious about making money, if very few other people do. Go further into it. Get us figures. We want to know the flow of armaments. The quantities. From where to where. Get yourself invited to Germany. The Nazi party likes to show off their successes. Continue just as you've been doing. Go to parties. Give parties. Just keep edging nearer to the sources. Now these ...'

They talked for almost an hour more, intense, concentrated talk of which Gerry was allowed to make no notes. 'All you will appear to be interested in is the money side of it—and a little reflected power, should they win ...'

As Gerry prepared to leave, the man asked one more question. 'You're not married. Is there any chance you'll be getting married in the near future? Wives can be security risks. Of course, she would know nothing ...'

'No chance,' Gerry said briefly, and finally.

Thereafter the briefing sessions were carried on at different times and at different places. Gerry never saw the man in the house in Grosvenor Terrace again.

Two nights later Lloyd Fenton walked into the Travellers' Club at about ten o'clock. He had left the hospital late; there had been an amount of paper work to catch up on, and reports from Pathology to consider and digest. He knew Nicole was at the theatre and it was useless ringing the house in Elgin Square in the hope of finding her at home. Sometimes, in these last few weeks, he had cursed his job. It would be all right when they were married, but being tied to the uncertain hours of a hospital job made the conventional courting of the season's most sought-after débutante nearly impossible. To Lloyd it was merely that—a convention. He was certain in his own mind of what was going to happen. It didn't seem to matter at this point that they had never even begun to make any plans. He was prepared to see these last weeks of the season that Nicole went through with an indulgent eye. It was a once-and-forever situation. It was amusing to see her go through the paces, and still know that she was prepared to get up very early to walk in Hyde Park with him. As he ordered a drink and thought of her, he was conscious of weariness, but not that his weariness was leading him towards the beginning of a mistake.

The voice came from behind him. 'Mind if I sit down, Fenton? Can't stand drinking by myself, and all these old fogies here look as if they made their last journey about 1900. Travellers' Club! All you need to have done is travelled to the other side of Pall Mall.'

Lloyd dragged up the name to match the young face out of the many he had seen attached to Nicole, hovering over her. But this one didn't have even the maturity of Richard, much less the urbanity of Gerry Agar. 'Oh—de Courcey. Certainly. Sit down.' He gestured to the seat opposite him. 'You seem rather down-in-the-mouth. Somehow I don't see you among all these old fogies at this time in the evening. Shouldn't you be out somewhere whooping it up?'

'Killing time until I take the train to Holyhead,' Brendan answered.

'Holyhead?'

'Yes, the place where you connect with the night boat for Dublin. I'm going home.'

'You don't look too happy about it. I thought all Irishmen yearned for the old sod again.'

'It's all right,' Brendan answered without enthusiasm. 'Usually I'm pleased to go back. Generally I just stay for the Derby and Ascot, and head for home. This year—well, this year I've stayed longer. Outstayed myself, in fact.' Glumly he signalled one of the club servants for another drink for them both.

'Outstayed?'

'Should have been back a month ago, at least. I've got two horses entered in the Dublin Horse Show. I'm supposed to ride both of them. And instead of being there training them, I've left it to other people. I've let everything go overboard ...' He seemed to take his drink in a few gulps. 'And damn all it's done for me either. I don't give a damn about Wimbledon and Lord's and Henley, and this year I've done the lot. Bloody fool. I ought to know when I'm outclassed. Bloody waste of time, it's been. I'm not in condition to ride a carthorse, much less a show-jumper. And she hasn't registered I've been here. She certainly won't notice that I've gone. She didn't even hear me the first time when I asked her to marry me ...'

'This ... this lady ...' Lloyd indicated that Brendan's glass should be refilled, though his own was almost untouched.

'This lady ... well, you know her. She's a good friend of Rick's, and Gerry Agar. But not even they've got a chance. She's going to marry that fool Harry Blanchard. Damn man doesn't know one end of a horse from the other.'

'You're talking about Nicole Rainard?'

'Who else? Damn little minx has set everybody by the ears. Tell you it hurts a man when a girl doesn't even *hear* his proposal. For God's sake, it can't be that she's in *love* with Blanchard. Well ... I don't know what makes women tick. Can

173

it matter so much to be a marchioness? When you look at Nicole you can't believe she'd have the same damn, stupid, dreary ambitions as other girls. I feel such a bloody fool——'

Lloyd cut in. 'Who says she's going to marry Blanchard? There hasn't been an announcement.'

'Everyone's tipping it, including the gossip columns. Oh, what does it matter?—even if she's not going to marry Blanchard, she certainly isn't going to marry *me*. And that's all that matters to me. Look, let's have another—got to get my train then . . .'

'Let's get moving now,' Lloyd said. 'I'll see you off.'

Brendan looked surprised. 'You will? Great. I hate getting on that bloody train by myself. You know, I thought when I went back this time, Nicole would be coming too. Bloody fool . . .'

He continued in the same vein all the way to Euston. The porter took his luggage; they went through the barrier and found his first-class compartment. As the bags were stowed, Lloyd watched the stream of people towards the third-class carriages, the shabbily dressed people with suitcases tied with string, and brown-paper bundles. They spoke with soft Irish accents, as if this train were some outpost of their green shore. The faces looked weary. Lloyd reflected that as bad as the depression was in England, to a tiny agricultural country struggling out of a civil war, it must be infinitely worse. The sight of these exiles, on the first stage of their return home, depressed him.

To his own surprise he heard himself say, 'Listen, Brendan, we've fifteen minutes before the train. Let's go and get a drink.'

Brendan accepted the offer eagerly. 'Great. Hate to drink alone. This damn train journey's not something to face without something to help you sleep it away . . .'

In the brightly lit station buffet they faced each other across a marble-topped table. Brendan raised his scotch. 'Here's to all the calculating little girls. May their calculations turn out right.'

'What will you do now?'

'Now? I'll tell you what I'm going to do. First I have to try to get back in shape. No drinking. Early to bed. Up at five to take the first stables. I probably won't be in the shape to do justice to the horses by the time of the Show, so I'll have someone else ride them, and that will be penance enough. And then, once the Show is over, I'm going to ask Caroline Leggett to marry me. Both families have been hoping I'd do it for the last three years. She's dead right for me. She'll keep me in order, and make a damn good wife. Great rider. Marvellous seat. In fact, it's been Caro who's been schooling the horses for me while I've been over here making a fool of myself. I'm going to ask her to ride them in the Show. She'll know what that means We'll just slide into marriage so easily hardly anyone will notice. After all, the Leggetts have lived next door for a couple of generations. Yes, that's what I'll do now.'

Lloyd found himself ordering another drink. He understood hardly any better than Brendan what was happening to him. 'Just one more to see you on the train. You've seven minutes . . .'

Brendan didn't pause. 'Yes, it'll be all right with Caro and me. Just grand. But look, man . . . tell me, there should be something a bit more than that, shouldn't there? I mean, when you think about a girl, you want to catch fire a bit, don't you?' Then he shook his head. 'I'm a bit drunk, but I know the answer to that one. If you catch fire, you have to get burned, don't you?'

He stood up. 'All right. It's on the train, and back to Ireland . . .' He was strangely silent as they made their way back to the platform. In the act of thrusting his hand out to shake Lloyd's, he paused. His eyes, which had taken on a slight glaze, seemed to sharpen. He was consciously watching the people who passed, listening to the things they said. 'You know, I've a feeling I won't be back in England much any more. I've never felt quite comfortable in this country, even though they sent me to school here. I think I've learned an awful lot this summer. It all began to seem pretty foolish in the end, and I'm . . . well, I'm sort of ashamed when I come back to this place and see the people on their way home. I'm riding in first class, and they're in third. It's rather like the way it seems to be in Ireland, as if we've been living off their backs for too long. We're what they call Anglo-Irish, Fenton, and some of the best friends Ireland has ever had have come from our lot. But we're left-overs from the time when England ruled the roost, and gave the orders. We still own a lot of the land, and it's beginning not to seem right to me.' He shrugged. 'Does it sound as if I've taken a long time to wake up to a few realities? So—I'll admit it. I wanted life to be nice and easy. Not to bother my head with problems. Don't know why

I'm saying all this to you. After all *your* lot kicked the English out a long time ago, and never looked back.'

A kind of wan smile flickered across his face. 'I might actually get serious about something, and all because a girl turned me down.' Now he took Lloyd's hand. 'Thanks for coming. Damn decent of you. You should come to Ireland, you know. I'd like to show you some parts of it. No, I don't suppose you will. Nobody much comes to Ireland. That's part of the trouble. Poor, bloody little country that everyone's forgotten about. They should remember ... *I* should remember——'

The whistles started to blow. He slapped his hat on his head, and opened the carriage door. Through the open window he shook Lloyd's hand again. 'Thanks for coming,' he said again. 'Bet you never thought you'd be seeing a man on his way back to trying to make something of his life. Maybe you'll hear about me sometime. Maybe I'll breed a Derby winner. Maybe I'll go into politics and start talking for Ireland ... I might surprise you someday, Fenton. I might surprise that silly little girl I lost my head over ...'

The train began to move slowly. The tweed hat was waved. Lloyd stood with the people who remained, and as he walked towards the exit, he heard their voices again; he saw one or two who wept. Were they thinking of home which lay somewhere at the end of the journey of that departing train? some place Lloyd imagined was full of small white cottages, and mist-shrouded hills, green like a jewel? A stranger's view of Ireland, of course—the pretty view which did not show the wretchedness of that lean, hungry country. Perhaps Brendan de Courcey was right—it was a little country everyone had forgotten about.

On the other side of London Gerry Agar was taking the boat-train to Paris. As usual he had told no one but his manservant that he was going. His manservant had wired to the Paris apartment to have it prepared for Sir Gerald's arrival. As usual, Gerry did not say when he would be back.

IV

It had to come, of course, the quarrel. But Nicole still watched Lloyd hurrying down the steps of the Albert Memorial, where they had sat in the morning sun, with a feeling of stunned disbelief. The lovely dream couldn't end so rudely. She expected him to stop, turn, and come back towards her, but he kept on, never once looking back, and finally he was lost as he reached the Alexandra Gate and turned out of the park.

They had met, as they often had before, for breakfast at the Hyde Park Hotel, at a time when Iris believed Nicole was still in bed. She remembered that Lloyd had been rather silent during the meal. He'd been out late the night before, he said. It was his day off. Could she spend it with him?

Her face clouded, and then lightened again. 'Most of it—at least until three o'clock this afternoon. Aunt Iris discovered I hadn't any clothes suitable for Scotland. The dressmaker is doing her a great favour by rushing them through. I don't dare miss a fitting.'

He had merely grunted at that, and signalled the waiter for his bill. Then they walked along the Park, occasionally stopping to watch the riders on Rotten Row, feeling the stream of traffic well as the city's day got into its stride. It began to grow warm. Nicole turned her face up to it. 'I can't have enough of it. I can remember my mother always used to make me wear a hat when we were in Maine. Everyone else was so tanned.' She stopped.

'Yes, Nicky, go on,' he prompted. 'I like to hear about when you were a kid. You don't talk much about it. It almost seems to me that you've put the whole American part of your life into a box and marked it "closed". Yes, tell me more about what you did when you were a kid.'

She felt the familiar twist of fear in her. One day she would have to tell him, but not just yet. Not yet. She knew that she would finally have to tell him, but it would not be until they began to make their plans. And she didn't want the plans made just yet. Why couldn't he leave the past alone for just a little longer? All she needed was a few more weeks of this delicious sense of floating free, of enjoying just to wake in the morning because it was another day of edging quietly closer to Lloyd Fenton.

So she smiled at him and hardly noticed that he answered with almost a frown. She skipped up the steps of the Albert Memorial, which they always made such fun of, and turned her head and laughed back at him. 'Dull—too dull, Lloyd. I was a kid in a convent, very prim and proper. Then I was a very hard-working student in Paris. I suspect I was—always have been—a bit of a prig. And now suddenly I'm having fun and loving it. I don't feel one bit guilty about enjoying myself every minute I can. Come on, Lloyd, I'll race you once around the whole glorious edifice to "Dearest Albert". You don't look in very good shape. They say doctors get flabby . . .'

But he was beside her, pulling her down to sit on the steps. 'No. I want to hear about the kid in the sun hat. Didn't you have *any* fun then? Didn't you let small boys fall in love with you? Weren't you ever kissed under that sun bonnet? How did you behave when you got away from those good ladies, the nuns of St Columba's?'

Involuntarily she shivered, even there in the sun. 'No— there's nothing to tell. Honestly, Lloyd. I can't remember any small boys being about. Certainly none of them kissed me. And away from the nuns, I was with Anna—I was with my mother. We were together all the time.' She shook her head. 'No—I can't remember any small boys at all.' Impossible to tell him about those long silent walks along the country roads, along the beaches of Maine, with Anna, the sense of unease hanging between them like a visible thing. How to tell him about Mrs Whalen's guest house, full of carefully preserved furniture and genteel guests? Impossible. Could she ever feel sure enough of him to tell him about Brooklyn and Mrs Burnley's? tell him about Anna keeping her away from there for the very fear of some of the small and not-small boys about, the sequestered summers at Columba's? In her heart she was pleading with him not to push her too hard just yet.

'So, no small boys in your life, Nicky? Eh? You must be the only pretty little girl in the world who didn't have any beaux. What about Paris? Full of charming Frenchmen. Weren't you ever followed around the galleries by young admirers? You can't tell me that there wasn't a single male student at the Conservatoire?'

She turned a startled face to him. 'Lloyd, what's the *matter* with you. You sound so . . . so harsh!' Her voice rose in anger. 'Yes, I am telling you the truth. The girls who went to Madame Graneau's were supposed to be returned intact to their loving parents. Nice, marriageable girls, with no unsavoury stories hanging around them. We were chaperoned every minute of the time. During the holidays Uncle Charles went everywhere with me, and I was too busy to notice . . .'

'To notice that men were watching you?' he said. 'Then, Nicky, you must be the fastest learner in the world. For some-one who stepped unskilled into the arena just a few months ago, you've notched up more kills than most women do in a lifetime.'

'Lloyd, what *is* the matter? What's got into you?'

'Perhaps I don't like to see kids hurt by people who walk over them without even noticing.'

She said coldly, 'Will you explain yourself? I'm tired of this riddle.'

'I mean young Brendan de Courcey crying into his drink, and going off home to marry someone he doesn't love because a heartless little bitch——'

'You had *better* explain yourself. What has Brendan de Courcey got to do with . . . with . . .'

'With you, Nicole. I suppose I should have seen you in the role of a flirt. I suppose, really, the idea amused me, until I'd seen someone hurt by it. You could have let him down more gently, or just not encouraged him at all. I suppose you enjoy having Richard on a string too. And did Gerry Agar ever actually get around to asking you to marry him? It doesn't matter. None of them have succeeded. I hear now you've got Blanchard on the hook. Is this just a flirtation, or is it for real? Brendan seemed to think it was for real. He seemed pretty disappointed that you were going to fall for the simple, obvious fact of one day being a duchess. Is it as simple as that?'

'Harry Blanchard hasn't said a word to me about marrying him. And he won't.'

'But are you going to Scotland to stay with his parents?'

'Yes,' she answered defensively, 'I'm going. It's only for a few days. Lloyd, don't *look* like that! It's only to please Aunt Iris.'

His hand clamped down on her wrist with a grip that hurt. 'I'm beginning to believe that you never did anything in your life to please anyone but yourself. I suppose I've been as deceived as everyone else—that rather wistful air. At times you almost seemed like a waif, the kid who never had any fun. It made every man within sight want to fall over himself to make you happy, to coax a smile from you.' He turned away from her slightly, still holding her wrist; he threw back his head as if he were laughing at himself. 'God, I ought to know better. By the time you've qualified as a doctor, you should be some sort of student of human nature. You should know a thing or two. But I see I'm no different from anyone else.'

She shook her arm in his hand angrily. 'Look at me, will you? Do I have to take all this just because I've turned down Brendan de Courcey's proposal? And as for Richard and Gerry—neither of them ever asked me. Nor has anyone else, for that matter. You're angry with me because I'm not marrying Bren. You must be crazy!'

'I'm angry with you because you didn't even *hear* him asking.'

'Perhaps I didn't because I was waiting for *you* to ask me! Go on, ask me! Just ask me!'

'I'm not going to—not just now. But I could. I probably will if I'm given a chance. If I ever have more than an hour with you. I'll tell you what, Nicole. I've a proposition—not a proposal. I'll ask you to marry me, we'll start talking about getting married, if we can get some time together. *Real* time together. I've got leave due from St Giles's. With a little dickering around I can arrange it for next week. A week, Nicole. We could go to Fenton Field. I know the Fentons would have us, gladly. You'd be nicely chaperoned. We can just spend our time ... well, just talking. Damn it, Nicky, we've got to have time to find out if this thing is on or not. At my age, having resisted quite a few pressures to marry, I don't just think it will work out beautifully because of love's young dream. Can you stick me for a lifetime? Can I stick you?'

'That——' she choked. 'That must be the most unromantic proposal on record!'

'It's not a proposal. I told you that. And I'm not a romantic guy. I might love you, cherish you, want to be everything to you, do anything for you, but I doubt if I'll ever have any romantic illusions about you. Well, will you do it? Will you come to Fenton Field?'

Very slowly she said, 'I can't. Next week I have to go to Scotland.'

It seemed to her that his face turned white with fury. He loosened his grip on her wrist with an abruptness that seemed as if he wanted to fling her away from him.

'Scotland! Then you're still going through with that! God, what is it with you! Do you think you can play the whole field and then have me still running round like a fool after you? If you don't intend to marry Blanchard, why are you leading him around by the nose? Is it just for the *fun* of turning him down? Or are you really thinking in that scheming little head that you'd rather like to be a duchess, but unfortunately Blanchard hasn't actually asked you yet? Like Richard—and Gerry Agar. Like Lloyd Fenton. No one's actually asked you.'

'Now that you mention it—no one has. So I'm asking you if you'll kindly ask me to marry you.'

'You'll come to Fenton Field then?'

'No—I'm going to Scotland. But I'd like to go knowing you've asked me to marry you. That's what I *want*.'

'You mean you want to marry me, or do you just want to have some insurance in case Blanchard doesn't come through?'

'That's an absolutely outrageous thing to say!'

'Then in God's name, why don't you be straight about it! If we ever are going to get married, it's time you took it seriously. How am I to believe you're taking it seriously when you're dashing off to Scotland so you can watch some other poor guy go through the hoops——'

'Lloyd, stop it! I can't take any more.' Her voice was shaking and she couldn't control it. 'I'm not going to Scotland for myself. I've promised Aunt Iris. I *promised* her this one season. She expects me to go through with it all and going to Scotland is the last thing. She can't *make* me marry Harry Blanchard or anyone else. But we made—we made a sort of bargain. I would do what she wanted just this one season. After that—well, after that there's a sort of understanding that I can please myself. She's done her best. I've done my best. It won't be her fault if I don't become a duchess. But it will be *my* choice. You have to understand——'

'I don't understand. I don't understand one bit of it. It's the most cold-blooded arrangement I've ever heard of. You must be a monster. Or your aunt is. Maybe both of you are. You know you're talking a load of rubbish. This is some never-never land you're talking about. This isn't the real thing at all ... People with any *real* sense don't make bargains like that.'

'You don't understand,' she said helplessly. And her voice dropped away. What she hadn't done, and couldn't now do in the face of his anger and bewilderment, was to tell him about Anna. That the bargain had been made as much to repay Anna as to please Iris. Back there, in New York, when Anna had written that letter, she had expected much of Nicole, she had expected what the background and position Iris and Charles Gowing could supply, and Nicole's intelligence and hard work could achieve. She too would have demanded that the bargain be carried out fully. Iris had played her part. Nicole must do the same. She shivered in a sort of fear, not of displeasing Iris, but of betraying Anna, of feeling, from wherever in America she had made her home, the disappointment, the near-anger because the sacrifice she had made, that unnatural demand of a sick old man she had agreed to and lived with, were to be thrown away. She would have expected the full season from Nicole. As much as Iris, she would want that marriage to a duke's son that everyone predicted. Nicole knew she herself could not go so far. The bargain had been for a season, not for life. In the end Anna and Iris would have had to accept that.

She turned to Lloyd. 'Please wait for me. Please ask me to marry you. I'll explain it all, very soon. You see, you *don't* understand . . .'

He got to his feet. 'I don't understand. I never will. And I am *not* asking you to marry me. You hear that? I'm *not* asking you to marry me.'

And then he started down the steps, and she had sat and watched him. And as she sat, with anguish and anger growing inside her, the last of innocence seemed to leave her. There was, after all, no such thing as love. It was all the fairy-tale Lloyd Fenton had said it was. You could only believe in love for a few weeks, and then it was gone, and such things as suitability and convenience took over. He had said it himself, 'I don't think it will all work out beautifully because of love's young dream.' Well, she'd had her dream, and it had come and gone very quickly. She checked the tears which threatened. She never cried. Anna had been very sure that Nicole would never cry. Nicole would go on and do all the things that were expected of her, and she would never cry.

But even as she told herself these things, as she reminded herself of all the discipline of Anna's life, the work, the courage of that last action which she had expected Nicole to live up to, still the last of the girl left in Nicole couldn't quite believe it. She still expected Lloyd to stop, turn and come back towards her. But he didn't.

After fifteen minutes she stopped trembling and gathered herself together. At the Alexandra Gate she found a cab and directed it to Elgin Square. Once there she went to the music room and played scales until lunch-time. The household heard them and took note. And at lunch, as she picked her way through the food set before her, the food she now had no appetite for, responding mechanically to questions from Iris, Charles saw with regret that her face had assumed once again that grave, guarded look, and he wondered what had happened in this last month that was now so suddenly ended.

V

The clippings were coming now quite regularly to the Post Office box which Anne Maynard had rented under an assumed name in Santa Ana. She had made arrangements for the service after seeing an advertisement in the *Wall Street Journal*. She had been afraid that the London magazines she subscribed to would not catch every item about Nicole, so the clipping service had been the answer. The gossip columns gave her the snippets of news she craved and were less discreet than the glossy magazines. It was weeks after each event before she received news of it, but her hunger for them fed upon itself. She saw informal photographs of Nicole—Nicole at Henley, Nicole at Ascot. It was long after August before she received the first rumours of a possible engagement to the duke's heir. When she read that, she had drawn in her breath sharply, and she had known how great had been the pain and resentment she had nursed all these years. Now her impatience to learn more consumed her. The mails were so slow, and she did not want to appear at the Post Office in Santa Ana more than once a week. She worked longer hours, worked at Frank Hayward's office, worked in the vegetable garden at her house, studied the financial reports that had become her consuming interest, and still Nicole hung always in the back of her mind. She found herself more impatient with each day; it was like those dreadful serials they were showing at the movies, always the question left unanswered until next week. And then she grew ashamed of her own ambition, and in a contradictory move, she allowed herself to buy a silver samovar when the contents of a house in Pasadena were auctioned. It bore the crest of some noble Russian family unknown to her. It was as if she were offering an apology to the background she had denied by polishing it and placing it prominently in her living-room.

The next day, as if to return herself to her senses, she took a plunge and bought her first shares in a largely unknown company called International Business Machines. The depression continued, seemingly not much relieved by Roosevelt's moves to bring work to the people. America seemed just to stagger along, still gripped by poverty and fear of worse poverty to come. People hoarded their savings, and no one but the very daring, or the very rich, bought shares. It seemed the height of folly for a woman stretched as thin as she was financially, with mortgages on small properties spread all over Los Angeles, to risk still more. And yet the sense of risk-taking was about all now that gave her pleasure—only that and the acres at Desert Hot Springs, her old car, her dog, and the growing pile of clippings about Nicole.

CHAPTER 5

I

Alice, Duchess of Milburn, was not unapproving of her elder
son's choice of wife. She had expected a different reaction, and
her own feelings surprised her. But she had had two days to
study Nicole Rainard, and she was beginning to understand
why she had been the surprise débutante of the season, and,
against all tradition, she had been its greatest success. To start
with, she was not English. The Duchess dismissed the fact that
her father was English; the inheritance did not show. There
was something decidedly foreign about the girl, her looks, her
deportment, the way she spoke, almost as if English had been
taught to her. The Duchess had observed her at various gather-
ings in London; they had been introduced twice, and she had
thought little about it. Now that Harry had insisted on her
coming to Carrickcraig, the Duchess had prepared to show a
far greater interest. Each year for the last four years Harry had
invited some girl or other to come to the opening of the shooting season here, and each time the Duchess had either managed
to persuade him that the girl was not right, or the girl herself
had decided that Harry was not right. The fact that two girls had
refused to marry her son did not entirely surprise the Duchess;
if she'd been a young girl, she might not have married him
herself. Though she could remember that his father had been
very little different. But she had married to become a duchess,
and a duchess she was. The two girls who had refused Harry
had been of a different breed, and now the times were different.
The two girls she had persuaded him not to propose to at all
had been too much of his own kind. Between them they would
have bred children with even longer faces, more staring blue
eyes, taller, more ungainly bodies. She rather liked this small,
neat dark girl who would bring a new kind of inheritance to

Harry's children. The Duchess was, in fact, bored with her elder son. All her love had gone to the younger child, handsome, clever, adaptable. He could, as the younger son, have a great career in politics, or wherever else he decided to launch himself. But the immutable fact was that Harry was the elder and the heir to the title as well as the estates. The Duchess sighed. Nature didn't always arrange things as well as it might.

When she knew that Harry was serious, she had, as before, gone seriously into the background of the girl concerned. She was American, of Russian background. The Duchess knew about St Columba's and about Fairfax & Osborne. She believed that both parents were dead. The American background didn't daunt the Duchess. Her own grandmother had been American and had brought the family a fortune and an infusion of new blood. This girl, Nicole Rainard, was not nearly as rich as the Duchess's grandmother had been, but the Milburns were so rich, additional money didn't matter. The function of this girl would be to bear children, and a great name. The Duchess was beginning to believe she might do both very well.

She had come impeccably dressed. That much might have been expected of Iris Gowing, who had money and sense enough to assure that. She had come with her maid, who was obviously devoted to her—the Duchess set some store by what servants thought of their mistresses. She had behaved with beautiful grace and manners; the Duchess had not missed the fact that she liked to talk with the older men of the house party, and, equally, they liked to talk to her. She could, in time, develop into a brilliant hostess, a boon for poor Harry, who tried his best, but had never, so far as the Duchess knew, said anything interesting in his life. There was just enough unpredictability in the match to give it a chance of an unexpected success. After Harry having brought along four other prospective brides, the Duchess was more than ready to take a gamble on the unknown quantity in this girl who talked little but listened well, was rather frighteningly professional at the piano, and who could make older men smile at her. She might, in later years, lead poor Harry a bit of a dance, but it would be better than dying of boredom. Yes, all things considered, the Duchess decided that she approved.

It was Henson, of course, who summed up the situation with all the authority of the servants' hall. 'You're being a great success, Miss Nicole,' she said. '*Everyone* noticed that old Lord Hawkings spent all his time yesterday at lunch with you—and everyone knows that he detests silly girls. Lord Hawkings, of course, is a very close friend of His Majesty and Queen Mary. Quite a powerful man in the Lords. And as for Lord Blanchard's brother, Lord Peter, well, they do say he'd like, just for once, to be in his brother's shoes. But of course he'd *never* cut in ...'

'You're all so sure, aren't you, Henson? I've no intention——'

Henson clicked her tongue but smiled at the same time. 'Well, we'll see, Miss Nicole, we'll see, won't we? How did you enjoy the shoot, Miss?'

'I hated the shoot. The birds didn't have a chance! And I was terrified one of the bearers was going to be shot. They call this sport?'

'Well, never mind, Miss Nicole. You looked very well in your tweeds. And there's a new member of the party today, I hear. Lord Ashleigh.' As always, Henson knew exactly where everyone fitted in the social scene, who was related to whom. 'You won't have met him before. He broke a leg just before the season opened, and he's been in the country recuperating all this time. He's Manstone's only son. Only child, actually. Lord Manstone's wife was the Honourable Cynthia Barrington. Poor thing was killed in a motoring accident—in France, I believe it was—when Lord Ashleigh was only a baby. Manstone's never married again. A charming young man, Lord Ashleigh is. I remember him when he came to visit the Hetheringtons. He was about fourteen then—still at school. Lovely manners, he had, and very good-looking.' Henson talked on happily as she laid out Nicole's clothes for tea, commenting on the gossip which filtered with amazing rapidity through the servants' hall, who had said what, who had worn what, what jewels were being worn. Henson was in high good humour. Her mistress was going to marry the elder son of a duke, and therefore would be a marchioness, and one day, a duchess. Henson's own position in any household wherever they travelled, would, among the servants, equal the social position of her mistress. The prospect made Henson very content.

It was with less contentment that Nicole went with the other women in shooting brakes to meet the men on the moors at lunch-time. She had known no moment of contentment since Lloyd Fenton had walked away from her, down the steps of the Albert Memorial. Through the days that followed, before she had travelled north to Carrickcraig, she had waited, waited by the minute and by the hour, she thought, for some word from Lloyd. It didn't seem possible that he had meant what he said, that he truly had given her an ultimatum, and it had expired all in those few minutes while they talked. As she twisted, almost helplessly, in the grip of pride and hurt, the days had gone by, her bags were packed, and she was due to go. At the last minute, unbelieving still, she had tried to reach Lloyd by telephone at St Giles's. He was on leave, they said. She tried his flat and got no reply. Finally, from Euston Station, she had telephoned Fenton Field. She listened to Judy's surprised voice, telling her that they had heard nothing from Lloyd and weren't expecting him. 'But he could show up—he has before. Why don't you come down? It's been a long time since we've seen you. Of course we hear about you from Rick—but that's rather different.'

'I can't, Judy—not for a week or so. I'm on my way to Scotland.' There was a prolonged pause. 'Judy, are you still there? Can I come down when I get back from Scotland?'

Judy's voice took on a shade of coldness. 'Well, yes—of course. But I expect you'll be rather busy when you get back from Scotland.' And Nicole knew that at Fenton Field they also had been reading the gossip columns. 'Judy, I—I want to explain ...'

Henson was rapping on the glass of the telephone booth. 'Miss, the train leaves in three minutes!'

She had, of course, taken the train. She had, in most situations, done what was expected of her. She had gone through the ritual of observing the men out shooting, meeting them at a prearranged place where lunch was served with a magnificent simplicity which depended on many servants, and a marquee ready should the Highland day turn showery. She concealed her disgust with the orgy of bird slaughter itself, and her boredom with most of the people around her. The nineteenth-century baronial splendour of Carrickcraig oppressed her. She found herself drawn more and more to the company, during these lunches, of the elderly and witty Lord Hawkings, and she didn't really mind being asked to play the piano in the evenings in the drawing-rom. But she did it all mechanically, thinking, through her hurt and anger, that somehow when she returned to London, she would again see Lloyd Fenton. The promises would have been kept. It was a vision of freedom which beckoned. She now accepted the fact that within the next few days Harry Blanchard was going to propose to her, and she dreaded the moment. She had been a fool to come, to be pushed into accepting this invitation; she would now appear to be that callous little flirt that Lloyd had labelled her, and poor Harry's face would show hurt and disappointment, and perhaps more. She had never meant anything to go this far. For the first time she began to feel that her life was out of control; she could no longer order and direct it as she chose. She was bewildered and unhappy, and covered it all with complete success; she heard herself laugh at the jokes that were told, she made herself pleasant to the older women and did not try to outshine the younger ones, and she was miserably aware that the eyes of the whole house party were on her because they presumed that she would be, very soon, the Marchioness of Blanchard.

Perhaps because his was a new face to the house party, someone who didn't appear to be observing every movement in the light of Harry's infatuation, she felt comfortable, almost happy, with David Ashleigh when he introduced himself at the lunch party on the day he arrived at Carrickcraig. 'I'm David Ashleigh, and you're Miss Rainard. Can I get you some cold chicken?—I'm sure you don't want any *more* grouse.' He laughed as he said it, and limped away.

They sat together during lunch, Harry hurrying to them from time to time, between intervals of being polite to his parents' older guests. They drank hock, and talked. 'I've missed the whole season, but it doesn't matter,' David Ashleigh said. 'The best is now ... worth breaking a leg just to see you here for the first time ...' His gesture indicated the moors about them, the heather which had come into purple bloom, the clouds scudding across the sky. He looked into her face. 'It's not true, is it, that you're going to marry Harry? Twelve thousand acres of shooting in Scotland is nice, but you wouldn't *marry* someone for that, would you?'

'You're impertinent,' she said, and her sense of depression

grew worse, because even this young man, newly arrived, seemed to have the same idea as the rest of the party. What had she done? and what was she to do?

'I'm spoiled,' he admitted. 'My mother died when I was very small, and my granny has spoiled me thoroughly. I haven't any brothers or sisters to keep me in my place, and a father who seems afraid to interfere with Granny's spoiling. So I say all kinds of impertinent things—such as, you shouldn't marry Harry Blanchard, you should marry me!'

'Now you're outrageous!' But she laughed because it was such a relief that someone was speaking to her as if any other choice was open.

'Just as long as you know,' he said. 'I warn you ... I mean it. If I could just get you to Lynmara ...'

'Lynmara ...' she repeated the name, and he talked on, inconsequential things, charmingly put. He was young and beautiful and golden. He smiled a great deal, and his eyes crinkled, so that the smile seemed genuine, someone whom no trouble seemed to have touched, the golden youth.

And why hadn't she remembered, when Henson had talked during one of those endless sessions of changing clothes that a house party seemed to involve? She had been too engrossed in her own problems, and Henson's gossip was like water running, a sound one grew accustomed to, and sometimes did not even hear. But the words came back—'Lord Ashleigh. He's Manstone's only son. Lynmara ...' And then there was the memory, frozen in time, of Anna's words that night in the softly subdued office of a man called Lucky Nolan. 'He was twenty years old and unmarried. He was John Ashleigh, thirteenth earl of Manstone. I called him Johnny, and I fell very much in love with him ...' With growing coldness and dismay she remembered the word 'Lynmara' on Anna's lips. 'I suppose if I'd been English I might have known about Lynmara, might have heard it was one of the show-places of the country ... What I can't forgive him for was letting it happen at all. He should never have asked me to marry him. But he was young ... The young can be so unintentionally cruel. Johnny just failed to see past those couple of weeks when we were in love.'

And now John Ashleigh's son sat beside her, filling her wine glass, talking, laughing, charming, impudent ... as she imagined his father once had been with Anna. Involuntarily she shivered, and the concern was immediately in his face. 'I say ... you're cold. Stupid things, these shoots, aren't they? Everyone getting frozen, and pretending to love it. I'll see if any of the others would like to go back to the house ... you need a brandy and a chair by the fire. And I'll hold your hands and make them warm ...'

Nicole learned afterwards that David Ashleigh was an excellent shot, and only the weakness of his leg kept him from the long, tiring day on the moors. But for the next two days he scarcely seemed to move from Nicole's side, and Nicole was aware of Harry's unhappy, bewildered face, and Henson's disapproving comments. 'Really, it's not at all what I would have expected of Lord Ashleigh. He used to be such a *well*-mannered boy. Not at all fair on poor Lord Blanchard ...'

No, not fair, Nicole thought. The golden boy with his good looks, and laughter and charm was hardly fair on any other young man around him. But she was strangely grateful for his presence. He felt like a younger, less sophisticated version of Gerry Agar, someone for her to trust, almost to lean on. But she still did not talk to him of Lloyd Fenton. That was an unhappiness she kept close to herself, and she was surprised that David Ashleigh could sense it.

'Something's wrong, Nicole. Every so often your face seems to cloud over, and I wish I could ...'

'Could what, David?' she said absently, incautiously.

'Could take it between my hands and kiss it, and take that look away. Yes, I know Blanchard wouldn't like to hear me say that, and everyone here thinks I'm behaving in the worst possible taste, but I don't give a damn. If I thought for one second that you'd ... oh, hell, why did we have to meet here, so late?'

She silenced him by leaving his side and going to talk to Lord Hawkings. By this time he felt like an old friend, and she risked a question. 'Lord Hawkings, can I ask you a question?' She rushed on as he inclined his head. 'Are there things in your life you regret very much doing? I mean ... you seem so wise now, so sure. Are there things you regret? ... big things ...?'

He pierced the end of a cigar, having asked her permission to smoke it. 'Child, the things I regret are not the things I've done, but the things I didn't do. I regret the chances I didn't take. It's only when you reach my age that you regret having played for safety. To live is to take chances ...'

After that Nicole asked the Duchess if she could make a telephone call to London. The Duchess called one of the footmen to show her to the Duke's study. 'By all means, my dear. I expect you want to call your aunt.' Nicole nodded, and hoped it didn't constitute too great a lie. It was an abuse of hospitality, she knew, but she was already here under false pretences. She spent the next hour in the study trying to reach Lloyd Fenton.

At St Giles's hospital they kept her ten minutes on the switchboard before finding out that Mr Fenton was no longer on duty. Once again she waited until the connection was made to the flat that Lloyd shared with Carl Zimmerman. She had met Carl Zimmerman a few times when she and Lloyd had lunched at the Italian restaurant near St Giles's; Zimmerman was a refugee from Nazi Germany, and would be, Lloyd said, one of the finest plastic surgeons in the world in a few years. She recognized the heavily accented voice at once when the telephone was answered.

'Carl?—this is Nicole. Nicole Rainard. You remember?'

'I remember.' His tone was neither friendly nor unfriendly, merely neutral.

'Is Lloyd there? Could I speak to him?'

'He isn't here. I expect him back—who knows when? He comes—he goes. One does not ask. We merely share the flat, and even that for not long more.'

'Carl?—what do you mean. Not for long? He's going somewhere?'

She could almost see the shrug of his heavy shoulders, the mild look of neutrality behind the heavy glasses. Carl was neutral to everyone and everything in England, his place of refuge, but not his home.

'When a man resigns his position, it usually means he is going someplace. He will leave the hospital in a few weeks.'

'*Resigned?* But why? Where is he going?'

'I am not quite sure that he knows himself. But if I were to guess, I would say he is going back to Boston. But I do not guess. It is better to let friends make up their own minds without advice.'

'*Boston!*' The line between this distant Scottish castle and London seemed to grow very faint, or was it a kind of ringing in her own ears 'Boston . . . You mean he's going home?'

'Home? Yes . . . I would say Boston is home to Lloyd Fenton.

But where is home anymore once one has made a break from it? Sometimes I think he's as much a rootless one as I am. I think ...' The voice drifted away into nothing. Frantically Nicole jiggled the receiver. 'Operator ... *operator*, please don't cut us off ...'

'I'm very sorry ... the line was disconnected. Shall I try again?'

'Please,' Nicole now seemed to be begging. *'Please.'*

In another ten minutes she was again speaking to Carl Zimmerman. 'Please, Carl ... please, when he comes in will you ask him to ring me. The number is ...'

'I may be in bed.' So calmly said.

'Please wait for him. Please wait until midnight, at least. I'm asking a favour. I'm *begging* you, Carl. If he comes in before midnight, he's to ring me here. Will you take the number? And if it's later than that, he can ring me any time after seven. He's to insist on speaking to me. There may be a delay. There are a lot of people in the house, but tell him he must insist on the butler bringing me to the phone. I'll wait until after midnight. I'll be awake at seven. Will you, Carl?'

'I am taking it all down,' the voice answered calmly. 'Whether I am in bed or not, he will have a note. What more can I do?'

'Thank you,' she breathed. 'Thank you, Carl. You will say it's urgent won't you? Very urgent.'

'I will say it is urgent,' he answered as if he were speaking to a child. 'Good night.'

And after that there was only the long silence on the line between London and the Highlands, a silence of heartbreak and uncertainty to Nicole. She sat there numbed, with the receiver still in her hand, her face close to the mouthpiece. The operator's voice came through. 'Have you completed the call, madam? Is there another number you want?

'No—no, I've finished, thank you.' She replaced the receiver. Finished. Resigned.

She went and sat before the log fire in the great carved fireplace, bending towards its warmth as if towards succour. What spirit she had ever had seemed momentarily among the fine grey ashes that settled as each part of it died. It was there that Harry Blanchard found her, came to her side, and asked her to marry him. She turned stricken, contrite eyes upon him. 'I'm so sorry, Harry. I can't.'

'Can't ...' For an instant his brow wrinkled in puzzlement and dismay. 'You can't ... Pi—Pity ... It seemed su—such a good thing. Everyone tho—thought it was such a good thing.'

'I'm so sorry, Harry,' she repeated. 'It's my fault. I didn't know ... no, that's not true. I just didn't think. I was so selfish. I just let it all float along. I never should have done that. I never should have done that to you, Harry. You're so kind ... And I've been ...' She turned her head away from the hypnotic draw of the flames. 'And I've been a selfish little girl. Forgive me, Harry. Can you forgive me? I just didn't see ... I didn't see what was happening. There's so much I still don't understand.'

He shook his head. 'You mu—mustn't get upset. My f—fault. My fault, entirely.'

And then she turned, and it seemed for the first time she actually saw that bland, good-natured, unintelligent face. Then she leaned and kissed him. 'I could never possibly deserve anyone as nice as you are, Harry.'

He flushed and started back from that kiss. 'No—you mu—mustn't say that. My f—fault. Entirely.'

She looked at him closely. 'I must go in the morning, Harry. I couldn't possibly stay here now. You understand?'

'Yes ... yes, of course. I'll speak to my mother.'

As he was leaving the room, he turned back. 'You're in lo—love with someone else, aren't you, Nicole?'

She answered him as honestly as she could. 'I'm not sure I know what love is, Harry. But if I understand it, I'm in love ... yes, I'm in love.'

'Ashleigh? Is it Ashleigh?'

For a moment she stared at him, bewildered. 'Ashleigh? You don't mean David Ashleigh? How could I be in love with him? I only just met him. No—no, it isn't David Ashleigh.'

He nodded. 'I thought it was someone else—someone you knew before you came here.'

Her nod answered him. 'I've only known him a little while. I never wanted to fall in love with someone like him. But still— it almost seems that I've known him all my life.'

His determined smile at her had more spirit and understanding than she had ever expected of Harry.

'G—good luck, then.' And he closed the door. Once again Anna's words came back, 'The young can be so unintentionally cruel ...' As she had been to Harry.

She waited, dressed, in her room until long after midnight, but no summons came to the phone. She had dismissed Henson, and the vigil was long and cold. The fire sank in the hearth, and the wood was exhausted. Finally she gave up, undressed and crept into bed, and the hot-water bottle had grown tepid. Still she lay awake, straining to hear through the long stone passages of that great house the lonely sound of the telephone ringing. But she heard nothing. She fell asleep as dawn came to the Highland sky, and dreamt an exhausted dream of Lloyd Fenton who walked away from her, never once turning his head, and Iris and the Duchess of Milburn who stood before her in his place holding a long string of pearls which suddenly broke, and the pearls scattered and were lost. She woke to the sound of Henson drawing back the curtains from the windows, the morning tray of tea beside the bed. 'A lovely bright day, Miss Nicole. The gentlemen will enjoy the shooting. Shall I lay out your green tweed, Miss? You've never worn it before.'

Nicole struggled to sit up, rubbing sleep from her thickened, puffy eyelids. The bedside clock pointed to eight. 'Has there been a telephone call for me, Henson?'

'Gracious, no, Miss. Whoever would be telephoning as early as this?' She was pouring the tea, and Nicole sipped the hot liquid gratefully.

'We'll have to pack, Henson. We'll be leaving today. I'll have to speak to the butler about times of trains, and things ...'

Henson's face was at first stricken, and then outraged. 'We are *leaving*, Miss? *Whatever* have you done?'

'I've done the right thing, Henson—and if I hadn't been such a stupid little fool, poor Harry wouldn't be in this mess, and neither would I.'

Unexpectedly the Duchess delayed her own departure for the shooting party on the moors to be at hand when Nicole's bags were brought down to the car. She was waiting in the hall when Nicole herself descended the stairs. She came at once and offered her hand. 'I'm sorry it didn't work out.' Astonished, Nicole realized she actually meant those words. 'I thought you would accept him ... oh, I know, you're much more intelligent than Harry, and no doubt in time you would have become very bored. But I thought you were ambitious. A little scheming, perhaps. But I was prepared to accept that. You would have been an excellent wife, I'm sure. I suspect you'll make a very good mother, though you're not the obvious type. Now that I know this much more about you, I'm even sorrier it didn't work out. You mustn't worry about Harry. He'll be upset for a while, but things don't touch him very deeply. He'll recover. He has before. Now his brother, Lord Peter . . . he's different. He might have interested you very much if Harry hadn't been in the way. Peter will go very far. He will have a very interesting life.' She gave a dry little laugh. 'Things don't always work out the way we think they should, do they . . .?'

Nicole drove to the station, staring at Henson's back, rigid with disapproval, and thinking that while she would never regret not having married Harry Blanchard, she might just have missed having the best mother-in-law any girl could hope for.

At the station she saw David Ashleigh, his luggage piled about him, fishing rods in hand, looking towards her as if he had expected her arrival. 'You're bound for London too? Marvellous! I was dreading a dull journey. What fun! Did they telephone for sleeper reservations for you from Edinburgh?'

'What are *you* doing here?'

He looked innocent. 'Me? Oh—the leg has been bothering me a bit. Thought I ought to get the London chap to look at it. I expect it's nothing—maybe just the Highland damp.' He smiled at her, and she doubted that his leg was troubling him in the least.

'I'm sorry. Such a shame to have to cut your stay short.'

He cocked an eyebrow. 'And aren't you leaving before time?'

He shook his head as she frowned at him. 'No use, you know. It was all round the breakfast table this morning, and by to-morrow everyone in London will know it. I wonder why you turned him down? Of course, I have my own opinions about that, but I'd like very much to hear yours.'

'Keep your own opinions,' Nicole snapped at him, her temper fraying under his teasing, and Henson's frigid stare. '*My* opinions are my own business. They're not for discussion.'

He bowed his head slightly. 'Sorry. Properly put in my place. But I'm glad. I just can't see you married to old Harry.'

'I really don't care what you think, David.'

He smiled. 'You can't make me angry, you know. Even if you are implying I have atrocious manners. It really matters quite a lot to me what you think. And I'll show you. Well, here's the train. We'll be together until Edinburgh, at least. And would it be going beyond the bounds of propriety if I asked if we can't dine together at the Caledonian before the train leaves for London? Surely nothing wrong with that, is there? A chance meeting. Two acquaintances travelling south happen to be on the same train ...' The local train had come to a stop, and he was establishing her in a first-class compartment, while Henson and his valet gave directions to the porter about placing the luggage. 'I hope you don't think you're going to read a newspaper,' he said. 'We've got from here to Edinburgh to talk, and I don't intend to miss a minute of it.'

It was then she became certain that he had left Carrickcraig when he had learned that morning that she also was leaving.

Nicole dined with David at the Royal Caledonian while they waited for the departure of the night sleeper train for London. She would have enjoyed the dinner, the occasion, the charming presence of this charming, golden young man if she hadn't been nagged with anxiety about Lloyd Fenton. In desperation she had asked the hotel switchboard to put through a call to his flat, and a waiter came to summon her as she and David finished coffee. 'Will you excuse me?' she said. She didn't know why she felt it necessary to add, 'A call to my aunt ...'

He stood and smiled. 'I'll see that the baggage is all there—and collect your Henson, and all that. See you in the lobby ...'

There had been too many lies, she thought, as she went to the booth to take the call. Why lie to people like David Ashleigh? Why say anything? Had it all begun with the lies she had told as a child at St Columba's, the lies about living in Brooklyn, the lies that were told simply by saying nothing? Was that why she grew nervous at the thought of Lloyd Fenton, and the time when she would have to tell him the total truth, the truth that Anna and Iris said she must not tell? She picked up the receiver. 'Lloyd,' she said, unable to control the quaver in her voice.

'Carl Zimmerman here.' The heavy Germanic tone was bored, as if she had interrupted a more exciting activity, probably his medical reading.

'Is Lloyd there? Could I speak to him?'

'Fenton is not here.'

'Then—could I leave a message?' She clung to the receiver and fought back tears. How did she get through to this man her desperation. 'Or is he at the hospital?'

'He is not at the hospital. A message you can leave. But already I have given the message.'

'But he didn't telephone. I waited ... last night ... all this morning.'

She could almost see his heavy shrug. 'To telephone or not is Fenton's business. Your message I have given him.'

'But this is another message. I've left Carric ... the place I was at. I'm taking the night sleeper to London. It gets into London at ...' Frantically she searched for the schedule. 'It gets into London at seven-thirty tomorrow morning. Euston Station. Seven-thirty.'

'You wish me to tell him this? Why not telephone when you arrive?'

'Because ... because I want him to meet me at Euston in the morning. *Meet* me. Euston Station. Seven-thirty. The night train from Edinburgh.'

'All this I have already written,' came the bored reply. 'The message he will have.'

'And something else—please, wait a minute. Will you also tell him that I am not going to marry Harry Blanchard.'

'You are not going to marry ... ?'

'Harry Blanchard. B.L.A.N ...'

He copied it word for word. *'Miss Rainard is not going to marry Harry Blanchard.'*

She began to shake with fury and frustration. 'Oh—for God's sake, can't you make it sound a bit better than that!'

'What do you want of me? That I should write a love story?'

'No!' she shouted at him. 'You wouldn't be able to!' And she crashed down the receiver. She spent several minutes more in the booth. When she emerged the traces of the tears which had started were gone, and the smile of greeting to David Ashleigh was fixed back on her face.

'Lady Gowing would not approve, Miss,' was what Henson said as she stowed the small bag with Nicole's needs for the night in the sleeper. 'Young Lord Ashleigh ...'

'Young Lord Ashleigh is a chance traveller on the same train ... in a different coach.' Nicole snapped at her. *'You,* Henson, are travelling in the next compartment, instead of sitting up all night in the third-class coach. I will keep my door locked. I'm quite safe. Perhaps unfortunately. I suspect Lord Ashleigh is a gentleman.'

'Nevertheless, Miss Nicole, I won't get a wink ...'

'That will be your fault, Henson. Not mine. Be thankful we're not in Russia. Otherwise you'd have to sleep lying across my door all night ...'

Now why had she said that? What on earth did she care about what they did, or had done, at one time, in Russia?

Whether or not Henson slept, Nicole herself slept very little as the train rushed through the night. She seemed to hear every click of the connection of the rails, seemed to roll in her bunk with every curve. She thought of Lloyd Fenton and the coming confrontation. Henson needn't have worried. There was no discreet tap on the door from David Ashleigh. However eager he may have been, he wasn't crude. She had the whole wakeful night to think of Lloyd, and for some reason she didn't quite understand, she was afraid.

And he wasn't on the platform when the train shunted slowly into the platform at Euston the next morning.

Henson was supervising the unloading of Nicole's luggage and David Ashleigh's valet was doing the same farther along the train. 'Hallo—did you sleep at all? Horrible things, trains, aren't they? I never seem to close my eyes.' And David Ashleigh looked at her with wide-awake blue eyes that she suspected had not missed any sleep. He was freshly shaven and immaculate, rather different from the way she felt, as if the ancient soot of the Great Northern was deeply engrained in all her pores. 'You look rather tired,' he said, his voice dropping into a lower tone. 'You certainly don't look as if you'd just had a week of bracing Highland air. You should be going straight down to the country, not holing yourself up in London.' His face brightened, as if he had had a sudden idea, but she knew it wasn't sudden. 'Tell you what? Instead of going back to your aunt's, why don't you just give her a ring and tell her you're coming down to Lynmara with me? Do you a world of good to be in the country for a while. No house party, or any of that stuff. Just very quiet. Granny will be delighted to see you—and my father, of course. Do say you'll come ...'

She looked at him, that fresh young face, heard the beguiling words, the smiling entreaty that had behind it the quiet assurance that the hearer would never be able to reject his plea. He was a darling, golden boy, and life had dealt with him easily. And here he was, inviting her to the place of her mother's ultimate humiliation with the confident words ... 'Granny will be delighted to see you ...' A kind of rage and longing stirred in her.

'I have a telephone call to make.'

'Yes, of course. Your aunt. I'll help you find a telephone. Have you any money ... coins?'

She wasn't used to public telephone booths, and the paraphernalia of putting in the coins and waiting for the operator. She was conscious of David Ashleigh's presence outside, of his polite distance away from the booth, but also that her face, if he cared to look, was visible. But he didn't look. Eventually she did everything the printed instructions told her, and she was connected with Lloyd's flat. The remembered New England voice answered.

'Lloyd, it's Nicole! Did you get my messages?'

'Yes, Carl has written me bulletins.'

'But you didn't come to Euston.'

'Obviously not, since I'm still here.'

'Lloyd, why—why not?'

'Because I have more to do with my time than chasing about after silly little girls.'

'But Lloyd—didn't he *tell* you? I'm not going to marry Harry Blanchard.'

'*That* was spelled out in very plain words. It makes absolutely no difference. I still don't go chasing about after little girls who not only are silly, but also spoiled. I must have been out of my mind. Midsummer madness. I suppose it was a good lesson for me. I'm not immune from the infection any more than the next guy is. I'll try to steer clear of the sources of the infection in future.'

'Lloyd! You're not being fair. I haven't had a chance to explain. You've never given me a chance. Lloyd ... I love you. Do you hear? Do you *hear* that! I love you. That has to mean something to you. A few weeks ago it did.'

'A few weeks can be a long time in any man's life, and even if you do think you love me, it really doesn't matter a damn. If

I ever thought I loved you, that doesn't matter a damn either. I've been in love before, I suppose I will again. The way I see it, there's a hell of a long step between being in love and getting married. I thought I wanted to marry you. The few weeks in between, which you don't seem to think is so important, was just long enough to make me open my eyes. If you hadn't gone to Scotland, I could have gone on believing that we could marry and make a go of it—that you'd be able to accept the sort of life I have to live, and been glad to live it with me. I——'

'I *will* live it with you, Lloyd. Every part of it—however you want it. *That's* what I had to say to you. I've kept my promise to Aunt Iris. It's all finished now. I can do what I want.'

'You don't really expect me to believe that, Nicole! You went to Scotland because you wanted to. What went wrong, I wonder? Didn't Blanchard finally come around to asking you to marry him? Did you have to salve your pride now by pretending you never meant to marry him? If you never meant to marry him, then you did a rotten and cruel thing to that guy. And if you didn't know what you were going to, then you're stupid—which was something I didn't think you were. You're a shallow and silly little girl, and I've been even more stupid than you for ever imagining that we could have made a go of it.'

She blazed with anger and shame. 'You arrogant, pompous idiot! Here I've come back to say I'm free of everything now, and I want to marry you. And all you can say is that we've both been stupid, but you're even more stupid than I. Well, that isn't good enough! If you want to apologize, well, I'll accept it. I have a lot of things to tell you, but only after an apology. I'd do a lot of things for you, Lloyd Fenton, but I can't just let you walk over me.'

'Apology—nothing! I've no intention of walking over you because I don't intend to see you again. It's finished, Nicole. Can't you understand that? You're not really so stupid.'

'Finished?—why? Just because I went to Scotland? You're more than arrogant and pompous, you're selfish as well.'

'It was what going to Scotland implied that made the difference. Call me anything you like. It may be the truth. In that case we're both lucky to be out of it. Marriages that don't work out are a waste of time and energy. I have neither to waste. I've spent a summer chasing around after a silly little girl, and I should have known better. Let's not waste any more time, shall we? Perhaps you can now telephone Blanchard and tell him you've reconsidered. You may yet be a duchess, Nicole. As far as I'm concerned, he's welcome to you, but I feel sorry for the poor guy. Goodbye.'

Unbelievingly she listened to the dial tone after he had hung up the receiver. With trembling, furious fingers she jiggled the hook in a hopeless attempt to recall him. Then she found more coins and dialled the number again. It rang and rang, ten, twenty, thirty times. She counted all of them. He wasn't going to answer. Her fury overcame the sickness she felt inside her. This high-minded Boston aristocrat, who never had scruples because he had faced no problems of moral importance, had dared to lecture her without knowing the whole story. Well, she was well rid of him. He would never have understood about Anna—about herself, the reason for the silence, the bargaining with Iris. To hell with him, she thought. In another minute she was dialling the number of Elgin Square. Briskly she gave the butler a message for Iris when she came down to breakfast. Then she rang off, waited long enough so that the angry spots of colour should have faded from her face, then she stepped out of the telephone booth and went smilingly to join David Ashleigh. 'Yes, I think I would love to accept that invitation to Lynmara.'

III

At the gate-house a man swept off his cap and called, 'Good morning, Lord Ashleigh. Didn't expect to see you so soon ...' And stared at Nicole in frank and open curiosity. The drive wound on between beeches and oaks, wound on for several miles before they saw the house. The house was more than she had expected. It was beautiful enough, in the moment of seeing its golden stone warm in the summer sun, to make her gasp. It would be, she guessed, of the high- and late-Elizabethan renaissance, perfectly symmetrical as they approached its south fore-court, its end wings coming forward to form the classic H design of the period. The sun glinted on its thousands of window panes, on the fresh green of the ivy which girt it. Its chimneys stood above a lacy frieze of stone. She caught a glimpse of walks below stone terraces, clipped yew and boxwood which led the gaze farther on and on until it caught the distant glint of a river. There was a deeply shaded portico where the car stopped, and the butler greeted David with the words, 'Good morning, my lord. Lady Manstone is in the Long Room. She is expecting you.'

There was a great hall and a carved staircase which split in two and led to a gallery. David took her hand in his and raced up the stairs, his limp seeming to disappear in his eagerness. Nicole had only a swift and fleeting impression of the ornate carving of the gallery rail itself, the many pictures that hung on the staircase, the faded banners that recalled regiments and battles of far-off wars. The gallery led them back to the front of the house, and opened out into a huge stretch of open space, where the midday light poured in, gleaming on the polished floor, picking out the detail of the moulded ceiling, throwing up the colour of the glowing alabaster mantels of the two fireplaces they had to pass before approaching the third, and last. A thin, elderly woman sat there in a carved chair covered with gold brocade. Her slender hands were clasped about the silver top of a cane. She wore a very plain high-necked brown dress, severely elegant. The bright blue eyes which gazed steadily at Nicole wore no film of age; they shone as hard as jewels. Even on this day in August a fire burned in the grate. She leaned a little towards its warmth, but those bright eyes were fixed relentlessly on Nicole. The two women looked at each other for a second before David's voice broke through.

'Granny, this is Nicole Rainard. And even if she doesn't know it, this is the girl I'm going to marry.'

The old woman seemed not to blink an eyelash; she extended her thin hand, as if this was any ordinary occasion, and Nicole any ordinary guest. 'Welcome.' The hand was cold, but the grasp was firm. Nicole was flushed from the run up the stairs, she was conscious of the grime of the long train journeys, and yet she was totally at ease. Her eyes met those bright blue ones steadily.

'How do you do, Lady Manstone? I'm afraid David's statement is a trifle ... premature, shall we say?'

The woman leaned closer, her hand fumbling for the pince-nez which hung from a gold chain. When it was in place, she scrutinized Nicole for several seconds in silence. 'But we've met before, surely?' she said. 'Where was it, I wonder?'

'No—Lady Manstone, we're never met. I should have remembered.'

The pince-nez came off. 'You're right, I'm sure. It is one of the penalties of age that one remembers the wrong things, or forgets the important ones ...'

'Oh, Granny you've seen her picture in all the magazines and newspapers this season. *That's* why you think you've met her.'

'No doubt ... no doubt. Well, please sit down, Miss Rainard. It was a pleasant surprise when David telephoned me that he was coming down this morning. I've been spoiled this summer, having him here for so long—selfish, no doubt, since it meant a broken leg for him. Now will you have some sherry before you go to your room? Lunch isn't for an hour yet ... Sweet or dry?'

The sun shone in the cut crystal decanters, turning the wine to gold and golden red, gleamed off the silver tray with the glasses and the pale, thin biscuits.

'Dry, please, Lady Manstone.'

'Yes ...' she poured and Nicole noticed that her hand trembled slightly. 'For myself, I start with sweet, then go to dry. Many years ago I was in Jerez in Spain where the sherry comes from. *There* they always start with an *oloroso* first, then go to a *fino*. "It cradles the stomach" they say—and they all live to great old age. How wonderful it was in Jerez and Seville at that time ... the wine and the horses. It was a wonderful time to be young ... Ah, here comes my son. He always tries to join me at this time each day. We have what the Spanish call a "copita" together—a little cup.'

Nicole turned slightly and watched the advance, down the long sunlit space, of the man her mother had called 'Johnny'.

That evening Nicole played the piano in the Great Saloon of Lynmara, a room all golden and crimson, with three Van Dykes', a magnificent Turner, a Constable and some lesser paintings on the wall, a room whose carpet had been woven in Belgium to fit its great space and whose ceiling James Thornhill had painted and Grinling Gibbons had laid his hand to the cornices, a room whose mirrors reflected the others' silver-gilt frames, and the silver-gilt sconces shone softly back upon themselves. A room of beauty as well as magnificence, Nicole conceded. And she could too well imagine Anna's paralysing fright when she, in her turn, had sat here.

204

David and his grandmother walked on the terrace outside. 'Leave the windows open,' the old woman had said, 'I like to hear the piano. You are very gifted.' So the old woman and the golden young man walked on the terrace below the windows open to the summer night, with the scent of stock and lavender growing stronger as the dusk came down. The last of the sun was caught on a high point of the downs, the river at the end of the long descent of formal gardens had turned dark and silvery. And Nicole played the Chopin nocturnes, and watched, across the piano, each turn of the old woman and the golden-haired young man on the terrace. His head was bent close to hers. They were deep in conversation. The sound of the old woman's stick punctuated the music.

And as the shadows gathered in the corners of the great room, she saw in one of the mirrors John Ashleigh's cigarette glow from the far corner where he had placed himself. She saw, as if from a vast distance, her own reflection, white gown and Iris's pearls, hair brushed and coiled into a shining chignon by Henson. No rings were on her fingers, but David Ashleigh would shortly put one there. She was all the polished perfection that Anna had never been able to achieve in the presence of the old woman she had hated and feared; but Nicole, watching the reflection fade and grow dim as the light also went, knew that she would never be as beautiful as that young girl of a generation ago.

She paused at the end of a nocturne, feeling suddenly cold as if a breeze had blown too sharply up from the river. Then, closing the book of nocturnes, her hands strayed deliberately to their own melody, the notes indelible on her memory. At first it seemed a silvery trickle, the sounds almost tentative. 'Für Elise' ... the first piece that Anna had ever played alone for her Johnny, the girl behind the palms at that London party of long ago.

'Für Elise' ... did he remember, that formidably handsome man seated in the dusk behind her? Did he ever think of it, ever think of the time when he had been carelessly in love, had carelessly wounded and hurt, and nearly destroyed? Nicole's fingers stayed with the haunting little rhythm, hoping that she would wake and shake him from the vast, cruel carelessness. She was playing too against her own hurt and pain of that morning, the rejection of the love she had offered Lloyd Fenton, the carelessness that she also had shown. She had thought love could be taken up for a time, and set aside, and taken up again, and Lloyd Fenton had taught her that it could not be. Not all things were forgiven in love, as he had not forgiven her. So she was alone, and desperately lonely in this enormous emptiness left after her only love had gone. It was stupid, this feeling of aloneness, but it was there. At her age she should have been in and out of love half a dozen times. And she had loved only once, and now that love had gone. She knew that she would marry David Ashleigh; she wished she loved him, but she did not. She had waited too long for Lloyd Fenton, and he had come and gone as quickly as the summer.

She was thinking of herself then, Anna almost forgotten, the fingering of 'Für Elise' automatic, when John Ashleigh's hand was laid fiercely on her bare shoulder. Looking up she could see in the mirror now only the whiteness of his shirt-front and the shimmering white of her dress.

'Stop it! Stop that god-damn thing!'

She kept on. 'Don't you like it, Lord Manstone?'

He brushed aside the taunting question. 'In God's name, who *are* you? Has she sent you? Has she?'

The darkness was almost complete. She took her hands off the keys. His own hand fell away from her shoulder. She looked up at him, face pale in the dusk, the golden hair turning silver, as handsome as she had believed her mother's love would be.

'You remember her then? Anna Tenishevna? She was—*is*—of course, my mother. No, she isn't dead, as David believes. No, she didn't send me. She didn't send me *here*. She sent me to learn to become English, in a way she never could be. I'll tell it all to you some day. And some day she'll know that I have come back to the place where you brought her. You brought her here, and then you let her go. You did nothing to stop her going, offered her no comfort in that misery. Now you, Lord Manstone, are going to see your only child married to her only child. Strange how these things happen ...'

'You god-damned heartless little bitch! I don't know how you've managed it, but you've done it.'

'Yes, I've done it—and yet I really didn't do it. I didn't lie in wait for David. As I said, things happen. David and I fell in the way of each other. If things had gone as I planned I would be marrying another man—no, *not* Harry Blanchard. But the man I wanted to marry wouldn't have me. And in his place, suddenly, was your golden, handsome, charming son. What girl wouldn't marry him? I'll make him a very good wife, you know.'

'But why—*why*?'

'Why?' She half turned from him and struck an A on the piano. 'It really needs tuning ...' She turned back. 'Why—because that is how it happened. When I tell you—some time when I tell you about Anna, and how we lived in New York, about how seriously she was hurt, you might, you just might begin to understand why I have come here. It has happened very quickly. If David had not fallen in love very quickly, it would never have happened. I couldn't *make* it happen. I had almost forgotten your existence—although I'm sure my mother hasn't. I wouldn't have done anything about the situation. Revenge is so melodramatic, isn't it? But the man I loved turned me down—and there was David. I didn't know until this morning that David wanted to marry me. And now I know I will marry *him*. And I will do it with complete foreknowledge. I will live in this house. I will be its mistress. In time if I can ever find my mother, she will come here to visit. That is, if she consents to, which I really doubt. I will do all the things which you invited her to do when you asked her to marry you—the things she was never permitted to do. The things you, and your mother, never let her do. Do you understand now? I have nothing to lose ... so I will take your David, and I will be mistress here.'

In the darkness she saw the silver-gilt head shake. 'No, you won't. It's very simple. I shall tell him. I shall tell him about Anna and myself. I shall say anything humiliating about myself that it may be necessary to say. Tell him I was crude, and cruel and mistaken. A coward. I don't mind telling him those things. Until today I would have minded very much. No man relishes being stripped naked before his son. But I'll do it. I'll do anything so long as it prevents him marrying you. He has all his life before him ... I won't see it ruined by an ambitious little schemer.'

'You're quite wrong, Lord Manstone,' she cut in. 'Quite wrong. Tell David anything you like. The truth is bad enough. Will he respect your judgement any more? I really do think he has fallen in love with me in a very old-fashioned way. He'll marry me, come hell or high water—come whatever you may throw at him. After all, it wasn't *I* who invited him to stay with the Milburns. *I* didn't encourage him. When he first met me, he was quite sure I was going to marry Harry Blanchard. If you start making absurd accusations against me, you will only drive him to stubbornness. Being the heavy father isn't going to make your case, Lord Manstone. In the end, you didn't marry my mother. I sense, I *believe*, David will, no matter what you say, marry me.'

'I'll prevent it. He's still under age.'

'He won't always be under age. I'll wait. I can afford to. I'm not like my mother. I won't be driven out. I won't be frightened away. It is you, Lord Manstone, who will be driven away. Do you really want to lose your only child? I believe I can make that happen. I will, if you force it on me.'

'I never believed anyone so young could be so cold-blooded.'

'You were young—and cold-blooded. I tried to excuse it— *she* tried to excuse it. Youth and ignorance. But *you* shouldn't have been so ignorant. You should have known how she would be treated by that cruel old woman outside ...' Nicole tossed her head in the direction of the open windows. 'You exposed Anna to it all needlessly. You changed her for the rest of her life. You changed *my* life.'

She turned from the dark mirror image to face him directly. 'You know, perhaps it is rather fanciful of me to think it, but there's a sort of inevitability about this. Perhaps I'm more Russian than I quite understand. I have a sense that this was meant to be—that I was meant to be here in this place. As if I were taking *her* place for her. It's as if a wheel has come full circle, yet none of us did anything to set it in motion. It started, by itself, all those years ago, when she was here. How will it finish, I wonder ...?'

'It will finish *now*. I won't let it happen.'

She sighed and turned back to the piano. 'You just can't admit that you're beaten. Time and circumstances have overtaken you, Lord Manstone. In our wildest imaginings none of us would have thought of *this* happening. Can't you see it that way?—see it, and accept it?'

'I'll never accept it. I'll do my damnedest to stop it.'

She shook her head. 'You'll be very foolish if you do. You love your son, don't you, Lord Manstone? Don't force him to choose. Don't hurt him. It isn't necessary. I'll be very good to

David. I think I can be a good mother to our children. I have a lot of strength and energy to give if I have a purpose for giving them. David ... and David's children will have all of them. No ...' She shook her head. 'No, I *will* not retreat wounded and hurt, as she was. She tried to make sure that whatever happened in my life, I would be trained, and ready. I am ready. This has happened. Accept it. Accept it now. Gracefully. You must accept it in the end.'

The tapping stick sounded on the paved walk of the terrace. 'Why has the music stopped?' the old woman's voice cried to them. 'I was enjoying it.'

'It has grown dark, Lady Manstone.'

'Dark? Then why don't you have some light?'

She heard a movement behind her. In a second the sconces all round the room had been lighted; a small standard lamp beside the piano was switched on.

She stared at the blanched and twisted face of the man who had confronted her across the piano. So like David's face, but without its youth, and the splendour of its freshness. 'And now, Lord Manstone, shall we have some more music?'

And she began on the simple, infinitely subtle shadings of a Mozart sonata.

She was aware that the tapping had ceased on the terrace outside. In a short time one of the great double doors to the Saloon opened, and David and his grandmother came into the room. Glancing up from the music, she looked at David's face, and then, very quickly, towards Manstone. His gaze was directed towards his son with such a look of yearning that she almost was persuaded that he could risk as much as he had said he would. She thought of Anna, in this same room, and she was determined to risk as much.

She heard David's voice. 'Have you ever seen anything so lovely, Granny? Haven't I been lucky to find her?'

She didn't hear the Countess's reply.

CHAPTER 6

I

How long was it, Nicole wondered, from the innocence of May, with the hawthorn in blossom in the hedgerows of Fenton Field, the time when she and everything about her had seemed young and carefree, to this swift dying of the summer at Lynmara? Much longer than the very few weeks that had actually passed. She had travelled much farther in time, and the days of innocence would never come back.

She stayed on at Lynmara, and it might have been possible to fall in love with David Ashleigh if she had never loved Lloyd Fenton. The days continued warm and dry, but there was a feeling of the ending of the season in the twilights that shortened, in the sound of the machinery which was already gathering the barley, the steady golden ripening of the wheat. The grass down by the river where David and she took picnics was burned and brittle. They drank chilled dry wine from the Rhine, and David said, 'How soon can we be married?'

'Soon—very soon. As soon as summer's over.'

'Does that make a difference?'

She nodded. 'I'd just like to have the last of the summer before any of the fuss begins.' She turned to him sharply. 'David, please let's not let them make a big fuss of the wedding. I'd like it very simple ...'

He looked at her wonderingly, grateful. 'You really mean it? I thought all girls wanted——'

She silenced him by putting a finger over his lips. 'Ssh ... I'm not all girls. I'll never be like any of the girls you've ever known. But it doesn't matter, does it? Does it matter, David? Sometimes I wonder what the Countess—and your father think of me. A stranger dropping out of the blue.'

'Granny dotes on you—because I do. I told you she's spoiled

me. She's happy because I am. My father likes you. I'm sure of that. I see him watching you so much. Perhaps he wonders how I managed to get you.'

She silenced him once more. 'Let's never wonder about how we managed to find each other, David. It happened.' She said the words that made him happy, and hated the lie. She watched him as he lay back in the dry yellow grass, hands behind his head, watched his smile reveal the perfect teeth. He was the golden, perfect boy, and she was cheating him. And yet how did she deny him the thing he thought he had when it was already gone, had been given, thoughtlessly, mindlessly, to Lloyd Fenton? If David did not miss it now, he never would. She vowed she would never let him miss it.

'I suppose I'll have to go back to Oxford. It'll be strange, being up at Oxford, and married. I wonder if they allow that for an undergraduate? We'll have to rent a house somewhere. Damn—I hadn't thought. I'll have to eat in college so many nights a week. What will you do?'

She said it promptly. 'Practise the piano, and have babies.'

The laughter broke from him. 'How marvellous! How absolutely incredibly marvellous! How Granny will love the babies. She's always wanted dozens around the place. It will make a difference to my father too. He seems so damn lonely at times. But babies ... Nicole, you won't mind missing all the things ... the parties and all the rest?'

She gave a long look back to the great house at the top of the graduated steps of the formal garden, the house whose beauty had won her as no other thing before. 'This house needs children.'

What she had not expected was the way she came to feel for Lynmara itself. The house seemed to reach out and possess her, like something living. A relationship grew between her and it, a personal thing that she believed had nothing to do with the feeling about Anna which had brought her here. She had not expected to love it, and yet she did, helplessly. As she walked its rooms, she felt in her being that she had done so before, that it lived in her memory like some dream which on awakening is only half-remembered. There was a sense of familiarity about it, as if she might have known it in some other time that existed before she was born.

They planned their wedding in the chapel of Lynmara. It was a small building with a square Norman tower, set some distance from the house itself in a grove of yew trees. The pieces of stained glass that remained from the thirteenth century were primitive and startlingly beautiful. It was now seldom used, and smelled of damp stone. 'We must be married here,' Nicole said when David showed it to her. 'I couldn't bear to be married any other place ...' But where would she have been married if Lloyd Fenton had asked her? She put the thought firmly aside. She must always remember that Lloyd Fenton had refused to ask her.

'What?' Lord Manstone said, when David announced their decision. 'You're surely not going to give up a fashionable London wedding?'

Nicole shrugged. 'We have so little time to get ready, and David has to get up to Oxford ...' She didn't want him to sense how moved she had been by the sight of the chapel, nor to know the kind of emotional hold Lynmara had already taken on her. She was afraid to give him any bargaining strength, and loving —loving a man or a place—made one vulnerable. Let him find out later, if he ever cared to do so, how she felt about Lynmara.

Daily she walked its great rooms until they were like friends to her. There were the obvious things to admire—the hammer-beam roof of the Great Hall which was said to be one of the finest in England, the collection of Turners and Constables that would have made any house notable, the splendour of the Saloon, and the more delicate beauty of the Green Room which had Fragonard panels and Louis XIV furniture. There was the clock room with its one hundred and twenty-three clocks, the map room, because some dead earl had been a member of the Royal Society and backed scientific expeditions to fabled places. The library had a ceiling thought to have been executed by one of Tiepolo's sons from a cartoon by the master himself. There was a sense of a family having lived in, and used, this house for a very long time. She studied the faces in the family portraits. At times, in some generations, there had been numerous children. She wondered what had happened to them all. In the Victorian period there was a portrait of the old Countess when she had been young, by Sargent. Her only son was at her side. An almost identically posed portrait of David and his mother existed—both of them blonde and beautiful, but the face of

Cynthia Barrington told Nicole almost nothing of her personality. A strange stillness seemed to have fallen on the Ashleighs with the advent of these two women, each with an only child, a son. It seemed to Nicole that the rooms had become too quiet because there had been too few children. There was a static quality about them, as if life had stopped and only existence continued. They almost seemed to be waiting for something to happen.

She longed then to fill them with children, to hear them laugh and quarrel, to collect butterflies and birds' eggs, to take the beautifully bound books from the library shelves and actually read them. The clocks ticked away in the clock room, and it seemed that no one had listened to them for a long time.

Iris and Charles came down for a hurried visit. 'I think it's absolutely *monstrous*,' Iris said to Nicole as soon as they were in private. 'You have turned down Lord Blanchard, and created a scandal by that. Now you are rushing headlong into a marriage with someone you scarcely know. Can you imagine what's being said in London? Of course everyone knows you met David Ashleigh at Carrickcraig. You both left there at the same time. You came straight down here together. It really isn't *decent* ...'

'I don't care,' Nicole said. 'It's right. It's perfectly all right. Please, *please*, Aunt Iris, let's not even discuss Harry Blanchard. I never could have married him. Aren't you pleased about David ... ?'

'I didn't say I was displeased,' Iris snapped back at her. 'It's just the way the thing's been done. Why can't you have an ordinary engagement, like any other girl? Why can't you wait to be married until next year, until David has finished at Oxford? I'd have plenty of time to arrange——'

'I've always thought,' Nicole said in a dreamy fashion that she knew must infuriate Iris, 'that the absolutely ideal wedding would be simply to get up one morning, put on a pretty dress, pick up a bunch of flowers, and stroll along to some lovely, simple, homey place like the chapel here, and just get married— a few friends about, nothing else.'

'You are wilful, stubborn, headstrong—and at times, I believe, stupid. You could have a wedding any girl would remember for the rest of her life ...'

'I'm going to have that.'

'—instead of which you've got your name in all the papers for the wrong reasons. It's a scandal—an absolute scandal!'

'Well, then, don't you think it's about time we put a perfectly respectable notice in *The Times* that David and I are engaged? And you can invite a few carefully selected photographers down to witness *the* wedding of the year—the simplest, the quietest, the most perfectly beautiful wedding of the year. Don't you think Lynmara is a perfectly beautiful place? I must ask David why it's called that. It's an odd name for an English house ...'

Iris would not be deflected. 'The *bride*'s family is supposed to arrange the wedding. How can I feel free to invite all the people I'd like to invite when this isn't my own home?'

'But it will be *my* home. I want to be married here. It pleases David and the Countess that I want to be married here. And in any case, there'll only be a dozen or so people here—apart from the estate workers, who'll all be invited. Oh, it'll be a delicious wedding. You'll have every newspaper and magazine in London angling to be asked, not just putting it on the list like all the other old weddings ...'

'If you insist on marrying in such haste, you must know what people will say. What they're already saying. That you *have* to get married. And a wedding down here in the country ... as if you've something to hide.'

'You mean they'll say I'm pregnant? I wish I were. But David's rather too much the gentleman for that. Besides, when we're going to be married so soon, one almost feels one *should* wait. That's why the wedding will be special, too. We might even spend our honeymoon here at Lynmara. After all, we have to get up to Oxford so soon after ...'

Iris looked at her, her face twisted with fury and frustration. 'You are the most ungrateful, selfish——'

'I know, Aunt Iris. But since I can't possibly please everybody, I'll have to try to please myself. What would make you happy, wouldn't suit me at all. Now, I've kept my promise, haven't I? I did the season in all the proper style. I showed myself everywhere I was invited—even to Carrickcraig, which was a mistake. Now, honestly, Aunt Iris, if there'd been no Harry Blanchard, if I'd simply said at the end of the season that

I was going to marry David, you'd have been quite pleased, wouldn't you?'

'There is nothing wrong with marrying David Ashleigh,' Iris said tightly. 'It's the *way* you're doing it.'

'And he's only going to be an earl, not a duke,' Nicole added softly. But even she could hear the malice in her tone. What she did not say, could not say, was that filling that promise to Iris had cost her Lloyd Fenton. And then she quickly dismissed that thought because there was not, had never been, any guarantee that Lloyd Fenton would have married her, if there had been no visit to Scotland, no Harry Blanchard. And because of that, there was David and Lynmara ... always Lynmara.

'Are you perfectly certain, Nicole?' Charles asked her. 'Perfectly certain? I mean ... it seems a good marriage, and David is such a ... well, I suppose most girls would love to marry him. But it's such a short time. Can you be sure?'

Nicole and Charles walked on the terrace of the North Front of Lynmara, a side that had been much altered and extended during the first half of the eighteenth century, the great age of English country houses. Nicole liked it less than the other parts of the house, which seemed truer, more personal, warmer in style. But there it was, grandiose, as that period had been, with a terrace and formal walled gardens which took the upper level of the gentle slope on which the house was built. The afternoon sun was warm, and the perfume of the roses came to them, along with the dry smell of threshed barley from the fields beyond the great park.

'What's certain, Uncle Charles?' She slipped her hand through his arm as they walked. 'You can know a person all your life and end in a mess. Would it help at all if I waited, as Aunt Iris wants me to, until next summer, and had a very grand wedding, with half London there? David and I would see each other a few times in between. Sometimes, when the magic is going, one should just go along with it. It's like ... it's like when the mackerel are running. You're either there for the catch, or you're not. It doesn't come again.'

He looked down at her, frowning. 'I wish you didn't sound so *old*, Nicole. But then, I thought that the first time I spoke with you.' He sighed. 'Well, you seem to know what you're doing, which is more than one can say for most young people who get married. And having turned down the heir to the richest dukedom in the kingdom, no one could ever say you did it for the title or the money . . .'

'Or the house?' Nicole added. 'Wouldn't some girls do it for the house, Uncle Charles? It's a marvellous house. The park, the woods, the river, the downs. You feel as if you've got the whole thing gathered here—the whole of England. A precious bit of England put together in one place, by one family . . .'

He said dryly, 'I didn't know England meant so much to you.'

'I didn't either. Until now.'

And how or why she did it, she never knew—how she remembered the words so well, why she felt the need to say them —but she heard herself repeating the words spoken by Richard that last afternoon in the orchard at Fenton Field, the world of a long time ago, when she had believed herself innocent and happy.

'. . . Gives somewhere back the thoughts by England given;
Her sights and sounds; dreams happy as her day;
And laughter, learnt of friends; and gentleness,
In hearts at peace, under an English heaven.'

Most of all at Lynmara she loved the Long Room. Here the quiet was something she almost could touch, and she fancied that if she stood still enough, she might hear the rustle of the silk gowns of the generations of Ashleigh women who had taken their exercise walking here during bad weather. She listened to the sound of the stiff silk of her own gown moving as she walked the Long Room alone that same evening before dinner. She had dressed early so that she could come here, to pace gently this length of shining floor and dark oak panelling, where the portraits of the Ashleighs looked down on her. At the end she paused at the west window where the sun still gave warmth, her eye traced the path lined with beeches which wound to the dark grove where the tower of the chapel raised its blunt height. She smiled to herself, and turned again.

He was approaching her in the same unhurried way as he had that first morning when she had sat drinking sherry with the Countess—Lord Manstone, the man her mother had called 'Johnny'.

'All alone?' he said. She was aware that until this moment, since the first evening, he had avoided being alone with her, even avoided her gaze, when he could. But she was also aware that he had watched her, had weighed her in cold judgement, her words, everything she did. He could not be charmed, so she had offered him none. She had not smiled at him, or attempted to appease him. He would never be a friend. Something in her hoped that he would turn out to be a worthy enemy.

'Alone?' she countered. 'No ... I don't think so. There are the ancestors, Lord Manstone.'

'Yes, the ancestors. Shall we look at them?' They began to pace back down the length of the gallery, the girl in a dress of ice-blue silk, the man in a red velvet jacket.

'Gainsborough,' he said, and then added, in a low tone. 'You're still determined to marry David?'

'Kneller,' she nodded towards the next one, the portrait of a plump-necked lady in green. '*David* is determined to marry *me*. Did you take my mother on this tour, Lord Manstone? Wasn't it a bit too much for her?'

'Suppose we leave Anna out of this.'

'How can we? She'll always be here—in my mind she'll be here.' They paced back and forth, back and forth. The pictures came and went by rote ... Reynolds, Raeburn, a Stubbs. She talked softly; in a very soft tone she told him about Brooklyn, softly she told him about Lucky Nolan, about her grandfather's will. 'Does it sound sordid? On the surface it does, and yet you look beneath, and you see that Anna did everything she did because she never wanted me to feel afraid or uneasy in a place like this. For me she built a great façade of lies. You caused that —you and your mother.'

'Then why must you compound the wrong by marrying David? Aren't *you* building another façade of lies? To start a marriage that way ... it won't work.'

'I will *see* that it works.' She stopped short. 'You don't understand, do you? I told you I lost the man I wanted to marry. So that kind of love is gone—for me, it's gone for ever. What am I to do with my life? It seems that to devote it to David, to David's children, is as good a thing as any. God—I might even bring some life into this house! Think of it ...'

'I am thinking of it. I grow cold with horror at what you are attempting to do. To marry a man *knowing* you don't love him

217

... And he is hopelessly in love with you. What can the end of it be ...?'

She sighed. 'Please, let's stop it. David wants to marry me. *Wants* to. Your mother has accepted me. I say *accepted*. I don't know if she likes what she sees, but she has accepted the situation. Does she suspect, do you think? Do I look very much like Anna? But she is certain of one thing. David is in love with me. Is she thinking, do you suppose, that she interfered with your life, and she has doubts about interfering with her grandson's? Perhaps she even thinks it might have been better if she hadn't interfered? Was your marriage successful, Lord Manstone?—or was it just socially suitable? Does you mother have doubts this time, do you think? Is she afraid of what she might do ... or has age mellowed her?'

She was shaken into silence. She found surprisingly hard hands on her shoulders. 'My marriage is not for discussion. Not now, or ever. You have no right. You may be taking over everything else, but there are a few things you may not have. Take anything you want, but leave my affairs alone. Take David, if you must. But by God, you'd better make a success of it. You'd better make him the sort of wife he has the right to expect. I'll be watching you—oh yes, I'll be watching you, you bloody little bitch. Of all the rotten luck—that David should find *you*!'

'Luck? ...' She pulled free of his hands. 'No ... luck, good or bad, has nothing to do with this. I told you it all has the feeling, for me at any rate, that it was inevitable. Something that was meant to be. I believe it more strongly. I have the feeling that I was *meant* to be here.'

'Rubbish!' he said. 'You're too young to be a fatalist.'

'Too young? I feel as if I've never been young. There's never been time, in my life, to be young. Perhaps now, here ... at Lynmara ...'

She stopped. His face showed—what? Hatred—no, not that. His fear for David didn't leave room for that. Fear and pain mingled there, the aloofness suddenly wiped out. For the first time she thought of him as human, someone who could be hurt. She saw him even as someone who could love, and be loved. She began, for the first time, to understand that passion of more than twenty years ago, the time that Anna had called him 'Johnny' and had loved him.

David stood and watched them as they stood beneath the Kneller portrait of the lady in green. He saw them turned to each other in deep conversation. He admired what he saw, the girl in her ice-blue dress, the hair sensuously dark against that white skin, his father standing tall above her, the red jacket complimenting his fair good looks. He was happy at what he saw, these two people he loved drawing close together.

He could not, however, hear what they said to each other. Nor could he see the intensity of the grip with which his father took Nicole's arm as they became aware of his presence.

'There you are. I've been looking for you ...'

Since Nicole's back was to the light in the west window he could not see the way she suppressed the cry of pain as Manstone's fingers tightened on her arm. He did not hear the words his father murmured, 'You'd better do well by him. You'd just *better*. If you don't, I'll find some way—*some* way to be rid of you.'

II

The engagement was announced in *The Times* and the Press began telephoning Lynmara and asking for interviews and photographing sessions. Iris was uneasily suspicious of Nicole's ready acceptance of all this, her efforts to please those who came, to co-operate. She and David were photographed for the *Tatler* and *Country Life*, photographed in the Great Saloon of Lynmara, photographed with the dogs of Lynmara, the golden and black labradors, on the terrace. There were photographs of them at the foot of the great staircase and in the Long Room. The papers which had made the most of the expected engagement to Lord Blanchard in their gossip columns, were happy to speculate in ambiguous terms on the new twist of events. Iris's lips twisted sourly at the picture of Nicole, smiling with deceptive sweetness at the camera, holding David's arm on the steps of the tiny Norman chapel in the yew grove. '*Romance of the year. Couple to wed in family chapel ...*'

'I've never known her to welcome this sort of attention before,' she said to Charles. 'Now she's positively inviting it. And to think it could have been Lord Blanchard.'

'Iris, it could never have been Harry Blanchard, and be glad of it. As for the publicity ... well, I wouldn't complain. Maybe it just means the girl is happy, and wants everyone to know it. Only natural, after all.'

'Well, she's doing exactly as *she* wants, after all. All this nonsense about a simple wedding ... It's more trouble, *far* more trouble to arrange here than in London. Every time I try to plan something, I find I have to ask that old glacier, Lady Manstone, if it's all right. The bride's *family*, after all! Pruned down guest lists, and all the rest of it. So inconvenient, here in the country. I've had to book out the entire Swan hotel in Feathersham, and the whole of the Rose and Crown, and the Black——' she rustled papers irritably in her hands—'the Black Bull or whatever ridiculous name it's called, in Hawkinge. And even that will only accommodate *your* family, Charles. Heaven knows what we shall do with all the others we should invite. I could, of course, book a special train from Waterloo, but then how shall we accommodate them all in that stupid little chapel? I try to discuss the reception with Lady Manstone.' She flung her hands wide to indicate the whole of the house about her. 'Heaven knows, this place is big enough to accommodate *three* wedding receptions. But she won't have this moved, and she won't have that moved. She's afraid of damage to the pictures. She's afraid of too many people crowding into the Long Room and bringing down the ceiling in the Saloon. Oh, it's impossible. And all this to plan in about three weeks, and Nicole's clothes as well. Impossible!'

'I'm sure you'll manage, Iris. You always have done so splendidly before.'

Charles said it automatically. He knew Iris would manage. He was staring at the photo of Nicole and David in the *Tatler*, and wondering, despite the smiling loveliness of her face, what had happened to that kind of radiance he had glimpsed so briefly for a few weeks during the season and now had gone again.

Nicole was more than patient with photographers and the lady journalists who asked her what seemed to be silly questions. She wanted every photograph, every paragraph they were willing to give her. She was certain that somewhere, at some time, Anna would see one or other of these tiny items of trivia which attached to the engagement of the season's most talked-of débutante to an extremely eligible, handsome young man. She spun out the facts which were not facts, just to make the paragraphs. She was endlessly patient with the photographers, posing where they wished her, changing her clothes as many times as they suggested. She soothed David's impatience with this invasion. 'It'll soon be over. Completely. The whole thing. In a few weeks we'll be rid of them for ever, David. Isn't that better than a nice, properly long engagement, and you and I losing our tempers over guest lists and all that rubbish? In a few weeks we'll be married, and then it'll be no one's business but ours . . .' And he had smiled at her, and settled, with a sigh, to do what she asked him. She was so right. Get it all over with quickly. How few girls would have given up a big London wedding, with months of planning, the grand trip abroad for a honeymoon . . . So he agreed patiently to the next request.

'David, just one last thing. You know *Country Life* is rushing through an article on Lynmara to come out next month for the wedding . . .'

'To my certain knowledge that will be the third article *Country Life* has done on Lynmara in the last ten years . . .'

'Well, they're asking, as a special favour, if Lady Manstone and your father will pose with us—and Aunt Iris and Charles —in the Long Room. Do you think your grandmother . . .'

He patted her hand. 'Granny loathes photographs, but she knows the next few weeks belong to you. So I'll see that she does exactly what they want.'

'Your father too?'

'If Granny says yes, then Father will fall in with it. Granny still rules the roost here. I wonder . . . Nicole, I wonder how you'll get along with Granny when you both live here? She won't give up gracefully. My mother lived such a short time. She never really did take over the reins from Granny. And yet she's old now, and a young woman as mistress of this house would be a good thing . . . don't you think?' His gaze on her had the look of pleading. 'She's a stubborn old lady, Nicole. But I think she respects you . . .'

'We'll get along, David. I can be very accommodating when I need to. So long as I let her know that she has a lot to teach me . . . I think she might enjoy teaching me.'

He smiled with relief. 'My clever girl. I might have known you'd find a way around it. So long as Granny thinks she's running things . . .'

'I'll see that she does, so long as it's necessary. And your father ...'

'It will be best of all for my father. God knows, but I don't know, what he's done with himself all these years. Of course it's ridiculous that he's never married again. He *should* have married. It's been so damn lonely for him. After I went away to prep school, there was hardly ever anyone in the house except at holiday times. He certainly put himself out during the holidays to see that I got a good time. I was allowed to invite half the school if I wanted to. At one time we had enough boys and their sisters staying here to get up a scratch cricket team against the village children. Of course the village beat the pants off us, probably because we had three girls on the team. At Christmas I can remember having little Indian rajahs and Arab sheiks staying here because there wasn't time for them to get back home. Anybody at all could come to Lynmara if it would make me happy. But I never knew what it was like when I wasn't here. He's hardly ever used the London house. He hardly ever left here, Nicole ...' He looked at her again with that half-pleading expression. 'It's absurd to suppose there haven't been women in his life. One can't have expected him to live like a monk all these years. But we've never known anything about them. At least *I* haven't. Granny may have, but she never says. Having you here will make a great difference for him, I'm sure. And if there are children ...'

'There *will* be children, David.'

While she rubbed cold cream on her face that night, Iris commented, through the half-open door of the dressing-room, to Charles, 'I can't imagine why he hasn't married. It's such an *odd* household, Charles. They live so quietly. That house in Belgrave Square shut up most of the time ... It isn't lack of money. It costs fortunes to maintain this place ... but then, Cynthia Barrington had *millions*. Her father was in railways, I remember. And in steel. There was some connection with Krupp, I think, though I don't suppose they talk about that. I seem to remember her father was involved in the Congo. *That* must have made a couple of fortunes for him. Her father was made a baron, but Cynthia was the only child, so the title died out.' Iris's inexhaustible memory refreshed itself. 'I'm almost certain *she* died before her father did, so I wonder how the money was left ... There must have been a *lot* of money, Charles.'

'I would think, my dear, that they need a lot,' came Charles's voice, rather absently, from the dressing-room. 'Just keeping the roof repaired here would need a tidy bit.' He came to close the door. 'Good night, my dear. Don't worry about it all. I know you'll manage splendidly.'

'Oh! ...' she said to the closed door. 'A lot *you* know about managing.'

III

Iris finally found her way around her frustration at Nicole's wedding plans by giving a pre-wedding reception dinner-dance at the Savoy. 'There isn't time to arrange it at Mowbray,' she said, 'and the big room at the Savoy will hold *everyone* we want to ask.' The invitations were printed and rushed out within a week, Iris using the list she had prepared for Nicole's coming-out dance, and adding to it. Then she flung herself into an orgy of planning the details of the reception, the decorations, the flowers; she hounded and bullied London's top dressmakers into keeping their workrooms open late at night to produce Nicole's trousseau.

'But Aunt Iris,' Nicole protested. 'I don't *need* a thing! Everything was new at the beginning of the season.'

'Nonsense,' Iris retorted. 'If you imagine you're going to be married and present yourself as a bride in the things you've been seen in all season then you've been mistaken in me. The Manstones will have nothing to complain about in the way you are turned out.' There was an edginess about the way she spoke of the Manstones. Was she, Nicole wondered, just faintly uncomfortable in the presence of John Manstone?—did she sense some sort of agreement between him and his mother not to hinder David's marriage in any fashion? Or was it that, in her disappointment that Nicole was not marrying Lord Blanchard, she had set out to make the best of a second-best situation, and show the Manstones how beautifully, how efficiently she could produce this part of her niece's marriage celebrations? Was she declaring her contempt for the 'nice small wedding' at the chapel at Lynmara, telling them that they were too casual about what should have been the wedding of the year? Iris was going, Nicole decided, to make certain that no one would ever accuse her of marrying her niece off 'on the cheap' just because it was going to be the sort of 'country-bumpkin' wedding people like Iris despised. Iris's recollection of the stinginess of her mill-owner father, the rather shabby little wedding he had given his only daughter, was a very long one. The bitterness of that memory was to be erased for all time in the sheer extravagance of what she would give her niece.

The Manstone house in Belgrave Square was reopened; Iris didn't know whether to be pleased or sorry that Lady Manstone would be present at the reception for a few hours; it would, of course, set the seal of approval on her grandson's marriage to Nicole, but Iris was aware of a reluctance to share the limelight with this frail but dominant figure. Of Lord Manstone Iris was even less sure. He was an enigma to her, as he was to other people, an outstandingly handsome man who belonged to several London clubs, and seemed to appear in none of them, who was a sportsman and a rider, but preferred rough shooting alone with one keeper on his estate and did not join the shooting parties in Yorkshire or Scotland, who at one time had won prizes for show-jumping, but never went hunting. He seemed to live an aloof, even lonely life. There were seldom guests at Lynmara, Iris had heard, except those his son invited. It had not taken Iris many hours of the few days she had spent in that house to decide that behind the façade of deliberate, quiet calm, Manstone's feeling for his only child was passionate and deep. It seemed to go hand in hand with his feeling for his home. With these two things only, Iris thought, could this man be reached. In her heart she did not envy Nicole's future living between the pride and possessiveness that the Countess and her son could not help but betray. She would need consummate tact and patience to weld the diverse elements of her own nature into the timeless rhythm which the years had established at Lynmara. Iris wondered if Nicole would begin to establish her own customs, gradually institute change. Then she shrugged, and stopped wondering, and went back to her lists. Nicole could have married Harry Blanchard and had an adoring and completely malleable husband, as well as parents-in-law who would have welcomed her openly and made her life easy and pleasant. If she had chosen to marry into this rather distant and difficult family, it was her own affair. If she was not happy, she could blame only herself.

The evening of the dinner-dance arrived. Nicole and David were to be married three days later. 'I still think it's *ridiculous* having the bride already in her future husband's home before the marriage,' Iris protested again as they drove to the Savoy. 'This business of the two of you strolling hand in hand along the path to the chapel. Nonsense—and suppose it rains?'

'Then we'll run, and carry an umbrella.'

Everyone had come that evening. Nicole seemed to see the whole of her one season revolve before her eyes. It was September, and most people had come back to town. This was the first big party after the August break, and they came eagerly. They came because Iris Gowing gave splendid parties, and because they wanted to look once again at that extraordinary American girl who had appeared out of nowhere and upset all the accepted ideas of how débutantes should conduct themselves. It wasn't that she had done anything wrong; it was that she had done it differently. 'It isn't as if she's even pretty,' one disappointed mother said to her son and daughter as they waited for their turn to pass along the receiving line. 'It's really *too* much. She's thrown over the most eligible man in England, and just gone and picked up probably the next one down the line. These *Americans*—no sense of what's right.'

'I think she's delicious,' her son murmured.

'*You* would! Why she's even had Gerry Agar in tow, and you know what *that* means.'

'I wouldn't mind having Gerry Agar for a while,' her daughter said plaintively.

'You, Miss,' her mother hissed, 'don't know what's good for you. For God's sake, *smile*, can't you. Sparkle a little. Do you want people to think you're envious?'

'Well, it just so happens I am ...' Their names were announced, and they moved forward. 'Thin as a rake, she is,' the mother whispered when they were past. 'And pale. Can't imagine what anyone sees in her. I wonder if she's pregnant? All this rush to get married ... Well, I don't envy her coping with Manstone's mother. Looks a regular old Tartar, doesn't she?'

'I envy her David Ashleigh,' her daughter sighed, and then giggled. 'And after all, it's Nicole Rainard who's a Tartar. She's supposed to be half-Russian or something funny like that, isn't she? Funny the Ashleighs letting their precious heir marry a *Russian*.'

'The Milburns were willing for *their* heir to marry her,' her mother snapped back. 'I tell you, things are going to pot. When I was a girl, no one would have spoken to her.'

'Well,' said the son, eyeing the packed room, 'things certainly have changed.'

The line of faces had become almost a blur for Nicole. She was smiling, as people smiled at her; she listened as congratulations were offered to David, as greetings were extended to Lord Manstone, 'Well, old man—good to see you out of your shell. It must be years ...' The Countess insisted on remaining standing until the last of the guests had been announced, leaning on her gold-topped stick, wearing an old-fashioned gown of grey chiffon. She wore the Manstone sapphires, and a tiara. 'Good show the old girl puts on,' Nicole heard someone say, rather too loudly. 'She's been out of circulation so long one tends to forget that she is one of the Haversley daughters. Formidable lot, *they* all were ...' Iris was splendid in pink silk, which did little for her sallow complexion, and Nicole had again insisted on white. 'I don't know why you do it,' Iris had protested. 'Every dress looks the same.'

'That's the idea. No one will notice when I stop having new ones.'

Gerry Agar had been invited, but sent regrets from Paris. And there was Richard in the line, suddenly facing Nicole. 'Can I claim a kiss?' he said to David. 'You've really pulled it off. Do take care of this girl, won't you?'

And as David smiled and nodded, not quite sure who Richard was, Richard bent close to Nicole and kissed her on the cheek. 'Beautiful. You're beautiful. But I hope now you'll settle down and start to eat, before you vanish. I wish I were David. Be happy, Nicole ... he really is a golden youth, isn't he?'

For some reason Nicole's eyes suddenly misted with tears. She was remembering that last afternoon at Fenton Field, the afternoon they had sat in the orchard, and talked about the future, the future she had then been so certain would be all beautiful and peaceful and serene. She had not then known about falling in love; she had never dreamed that rejection of love could be this hell of pain and confusion. She had not known David existed, and that he and Lynmara were to be her future. She was at the instant aware why he had seemed so familiar to her the day he had limped towards her on the moors of Carrickcraig. He bore a startling resemblance to the pictured face of the young poet, Rupert Brooke, whose book had lain face-down on the grass that day at Fenton Field, the book that Richard had read from, the book that spoke of war, and the hope of the end of all war, the romantic illusion that had died. In the heat of that crowded room she suddenly shivered.

'Nicole!——' It was Judy's voice, a voice that belonged back in Paris, in the early mornings when they both had risen to work at the things that had absorbed them, the shared companion-ship of the trek around Europe, the generosity of welcome that had flowed from Fenton Field. 'Look, who's come! You re-member Gavin McLeod, don't you?' Judy's face was radiant. She pulled Gavin forward as if he were some prize she had won. 'It took a lot of persuasion to get him here tonight.'

Gavin's hand was briefly in hers. 'I hope you'll be very happy,' he said automatically. Nicole remembered that he had thought her frivolous, and his opinion didn't seem to have changed. But his features, which she had thought over-serious, had seemed to relax a little. He looked at her, and at the big room and the crowd with an air of tolerance; he could put up with it for one night, he seemed to indicate.

Nicole caught Judy's hand as she made to move along. 'Judy, you're coming over to Lynmara for the wedding, aren't you? It's going to be tiny, but I couldn't bear it if you weren't there. You haven't replied to the invitation ...'

'Of course I'm coming. Wouldn't miss it. I expect the reply's just got lost in all the others.'

'There aren't many others, Judy. It's going to be quite small ... David and I wanted it like that.'

Judy beamed at her. 'I don't know why, but that makes it sound right. I was so afraid it was going to be that Blanchard chap. Poor thing. ... he can't help it, I suppose. But David ... next to Rick, I think he's the best. Rick's heart-broken ...' She pulled a wry face. 'As usual, I expect he didn't try hard enough.'

Nicole was suddenly conscious that time was slipping from her, the past was giving way to what would be her future. Judy represented the best of her past, and she now wore a special radiance that Nicole wished she had for herself. She said on impulse, 'Judy, come and see me tomorrow afternoon? It's been so long since we talked ...'

'Tomorrow?' Judy was surprised. 'But won't you be awfully busy? All the last-minute things ...?'

'With Aunt Iris there are no last-minute things. I shall have nothing to do. Come about four ... Will you? Please?'

Judy nodded, then the next person in line took Nicole's hand. It was a girl she remembered having met and re-met at various functions all through the season, a handsome, forth-right girl whose voice had always been the loudest in the ladies' cloak room. 'I say—you do move fast, don't you? Well, they say the race is to the swift. In that case—congratulations. You won!' And her laughter boomed out.

The food was good, the two bands played non-stop, the good wishes were all about Nicole. 'Splendid first party of the season,' someone said. Some of Iris's frustration melted in the face of everyone's evident approval. The *Tatler* was there to the end, taking pictures. And watching the Countess making her de-parture with her son, Nicole thought of Anna. 'Strange how things turn out,' she murmured as she danced with David.

'What ...?'

'Oh, nothing. Just saying it's turned out rather well—the evening, I mean.'

His arm tightened about her. 'It's just the beginning.'

Lord Manstone returned to the party after he had escorted his mother back to Belgrave Square. Nicole accepted readily when he asked her to dance. He danced beautifully. 'I'm out of practice,' he said.

'It doesn't feel that way. Did you dance often with Anna?'

He nodded to an acquaintance as they passed. 'Hallo, there! Yes—David's a lucky man, isn't he?' She thought he was trying to avoid answering her question, but he looked down at her directly. 'Yes—I danced often with Anna. She moved so beauti-fully. She was more graceful than you, you know. Now ... do we agree to stop these teasing questions? Will we for ever be talking about Anna? Can we never leave it alone?'

'Perhaps I shall, in time. But on *this* night, I can't help it. I've been thinking of almost nothing else. I wish she were here. Have *you* been thinking of her?'

He nodded, and his smile, which had seemed fixed in place for the whole evening, vanished. 'Tonight—and all these last weeks. If you meant to break up whatever gloss I've managed to put on the memory of how badly I behaved, then you've succeeded. Until you came, I've managed to persuade myself that everything went well with Anna—she was so strong in her way. Stronger than I ever was. If your father had lived, it would have gone the right way. But then, if other things hadn't happened ... It makes no sense. You told me about her job, and about that ...' It seemed an effort for him to go on. His step faltered, and he was out of rhythm with the music. 'You told me about that man, Lucky Nolan ...'

Suddenly Nicole found herself roused in defence of the man she had thought she despised. 'Don't be insulting about Lucky Nolan. He did better than you. He was good to Anna. And very fond of her. He was good to me, but I was a stupid little prig who couldn't see it that way.'

He shook his head. 'And neither of us can do anything to change the past. I hope you won't go on taunting me about Anna. Life won't be tolerable. You must know by now that my only happiness is centred in David. If he is happy, then I am. If you make him happy, then I will ...'

What had he almost said?—she didn't know. A new twist entered her feelings about him. Could she possibly pity this man? She shut the thought off abruptly. Beware pity. So she asked the next question sharply, tugging at his hand to emphasize it. 'What do you think of me—now? Now that we know each other?'

'You?' He looked puzzled, as if she, as an identity, hardly entered his mind. 'You?—I don't know whether you're a curse or a godsend. If you do all the things you've said you will then ten years from now I might agree with what a lot of people are saying tonight—that David is a lucky man.'

She halted abruptly. 'Then let's drink to that, you and I. Let's drink to promises. Promises kept—not broken.' She beckoned to a waiter who held a tray of filled champagne glasses. Nicole took one for each of them. 'Lord Manstone—here's to promises. And absent friends. Here's to Anna. Here's to the things that didn't happen, and the things that are going to happen. You and I are the only ones who know the full story.'

She raised her glass to him, 'Look, the whole room thinks we're having a nice, cosy little toast together. How beautifully they get on together, people will say. Well ... people never know, do they? Here's to Anna.'

His lips murmured the name after her, but the sound of the

band drowned it out. 'Anna ...'

As she drank another name rose, was silenced, and demanded to be said within her. Lloyd ...

They put aside the glasses and danced again, smiling, smiling for the room, not for each other.

IV

It was raining the next afternoon when Judy came to Elgin Square. A few yellowed leaves from the square garden swished along the pavement in a wind that had in it a feel of autumn. Nicole led Judy upstairs to the little music room. She had carried a tea-tray up there, and Wilks would bring boiling water; she had spent the whole afternoon there, relentlessly playing scales. The whole frantic pre-wedding rush now seemed suddenly to be over; after the party at the Savoy, there was little to do except pack, and tomorrow to go down to Lynmara. It was strangely quiet. David had gone to Oxford to make last-minute arrangements with his tutors and about the house they were renting. Iris was still wrestling with the logistics of getting all of Charles's family into the right rooms at the right hotels. The bustle of activity would be at Lynmara now, preparing for the guests invited to stay, preparing for the party that would be given for the tenants. But that was all far removed from Iris's sphere. It needed only the delivery of a few more dress boxes to Elgin Square, and there would be nothing more to attend to. Last night Nicole had worn the most splendid of Charles's and Iris's wedding gifts, a diamond and sapphire brooch which complemented the diamond and sapphire ring David had given her. 'Something blue,' Iris had said with uncharacteristic sentimentality. Nicole had removed the ring, as she always did, when she had sat down to practise at the piano. It lay there still, beside the keyboard, when Judy entered.

'Just imagine leaving it off,' Judy said, turning the great stone, with its circle of diamonds, watching the light refracted back from its heart. 'I couldn't think of leaving mine off. I even wear it to bed.'

Nicole spun around from the tea-tray. '*Yours* ... Judy? Are you engaged?'

The same radiance that had lighted Judy's face the night before showed again. 'Didn't you guess? How do you think I dragged Gavin to a party like that? I can't pretend that social life is likely to be easy with my brooding Scot, but whatever it is, I'll like it. I'm still amazed that he even noticed I existed. When he went back to Cambridge I had to invent all kinds of excuses to get him back to Fenton Field, or to get myself in the neighbourhood of Cambridge, and just sort of ... drop in. At last he woke up. Of course he'll be one of those brilliant dons who have silly wives, but I think I'll be a good wife, Nicole ... I think I will.'

Nicole had her arms around her. Although their friendship had been close, they had never been demonstrative with each other. It was a rare break in the pattern. 'Oh Judy ... I'm so happy for you. If it's what you want, then it's bound to turn out beautifully. And if Gavin has finally woken up, then he *knows*. And he'll make a good husband—yes, he *will*. He's one of those ... those *unshakeable* sorts.'

Judy laughed. 'You know, I'm not really worried about anything. I think it will work out. Of course we're going to be poor as church mice. Research fellows don't get paid very much. And we'll have children. Isn't it a blessing I took up cookery, and I can sew a bit? I'll have to give dinner parties, and sort of help push Gavin along in college politics. He's too engrossed in his work to see that he needs a bit of help ...' And while she was talking, she was twisting the tiny single diamond she wore on her left hand, and Nicole was acutely aware that David's great sapphire seemed vulgar and splashy, as last night's party had been; Judy's small diamond represented a hope realized, while to her the cold blue gem was some sort of consolation prize for what she had not been able to win from the man she had fallen in love with. 'I'm so happy for you,' she said again, and just managed not to say 'I envy you.'

But something of the unspoken words must have shown in her face. She turned away to pour tea, but Judy persisted. 'Nicole ... perhaps I ought not to say it ... but I wish you seemed happier yourself. This ...' she indicated the music room '... was the last place I expected to find you today. If *I* were getting married in two days—we'll have to wait until next spring, at earliest ... find a house, all that sort of thing—well, if I were being married in two days' time I think I'd be off my head with excitement.' She touched the open music on the piano. 'Czerny studies ... on the eve of your wedding?'

Nicole kept on with what she was doing. She didn't meet Judy's eyes directly. She passed the teacup to Judy, who perched on the edge of the piano stool. Then she nibbled at a piece of watercress which decorated the sandwiches. The sight of the food on the tray almost made her sick. Automatically she passed the plate to Judy, who ate hungrily.

'Well, Judy ... it's different. You know me. I'm not the sort to go off my head. About anything.'

'Then you *should* be—about getting married! David seems happy. He seems just as you'd expect a young man to be at this time. I think he cares a great deal about you—and he's so nicely unconceited for someone so good-looking. But you ... Nicole, what *is* it? Sometimes last night you looked as if you'd stopped feeling anything, were going through some sort of part you'd learned.'

'Just tired,' Nicole answered shortly. 'It'll be such a relief when it's all over. When it's finished and ...'

'Done with?' The shock showed in Judy's face. 'My God, Nicole, getting married is just the beginning! You sound as if it were something you had to make yourself get through. Like some sort of sentence ... an execution. Nicole, you can't ...? What *is* wrong? You're so much on edge. You're just like Lloyd. He's as touchy——'

'Lloyd!' Nicole, neat and precise in her movements always, tilted the cup until the tea splashed down on her skirt; the spoon slid sideways and clattered to the floor. With shaking hands she righted the cup and set it on the tray. 'What about Lloyd?'

'What about him? He's leaving. I went around to the flat this morning and found him packing. None of us knew he was going. He's leaving on the *Ocean Queen* tonight. We've been trying to get in touch with him—all the family have. He just resigned from the hospital and took himself off to some place in Cornwall. That man ... what's his name?—Zimmerman?—didn't know where. Mother's written and hasn't had a reply. I wanted to see him. Naturally I wanted to tell him about Gavin. And so I just phoned this morning and said I was coming round. And found him packing.'

Nicole no longer attempted to control her trembling. 'What was he like? What did he say?'

'Nothing much. He was busy. He kept on packing while I

was there. Just throwing books into boxes to be shipped on afterwards. All right, I'll tell you the truth. He was in a foul mood. Oh, he said all the right things about Gavin and myself, but I could see it had hardly registered. It isn't like Lloyd at all. We've been like his family, and then all of a sudden he isn't with us any more. He never even told us he'd resigned. He didn't say anything about going off to Cornwall. Every other time he's spent at least a few days of every holiday at Fenton Field. And now this going off back to Boston and not saying a word. Oh, he *said* he'd just got on the ship because of a cancellation, and would have phoned Mother, but I don't believe it. Something's happened to Lloyd. And I think it's to do with you.'

'*Me?* How do you know? Did he say?' Nicole leaned forward and caught at Judy's arm. 'What did he say?'

Judy licked her lips. 'He wouldn't have said anything if I hadn't seen the photographs.'

'What photographs?'

'Of you—all the things that have been appearing in the magazines. All the things about the engagement to David. The photos of you both in the *Tatler*. All that kind of thing. Not at all the sort of stuff that Lloyd would ever bother with. I never saw him even open that kind of magazine. But there it all was—as if he'd been saving it all. And it was lying in the waste-basket. I asked him what it meant.'

'What did he say? Judy—did he say——?'

'He just said one thing. And that was all I could get out of him. He just said "I'm suddenly in a hurry because I've decided I'd rather not be in England when Nicole is married. I don't think I can stand the sight of the newspapers." '

'He said *that*—and threw out my pictures! Judy—he must have said something else! Something about me——'

'Nothing. I couldn't get him to talk about anything. He just packed, and made it clear that I was in the way. I think, if he could, he would have taken back what he said about your getting married. But I'd seen the stuff in the waste-basket.' Judy put her cup down on the tray. 'Nicole—*what* happened between you and Lloyd? None of us knew . . . knew anything.'

'Neither did we.' Nicole stood up, walked around the piano, stood facing Judy who had swivelled on the seat to follow her. Her voice, which had held a note of frenzy, was back to a dull control. 'I suspect neither of us knew—but I knew far less than he. I played around with what I didn't understand. I played around with both our lives, and thought it could all come out just as I had planned it. All very neatly. I should know by now that life isn't very often neat and tidy. We can all make terrible messes of it. Lloyd tried to tell me. I didn't believe him, then. I couldn't. It didn't seem possible that I could have him, and lose him, within a month. And we'd never even been to bed together.'

'Nicole——'

'Oh, I'm not supposed to talk about that? Well, what does it matter? The truth is I love him—I do love him—very much. At least, I think I love him. I don't know anything else. Makes you wonder about how ignorant we are—how they bring us up. You see, I had him, and I lost him. And so I took David. Dear David—very sweet, very trusting. He'll never know that I couldn't fall in love with him because I was in love with another man. With luck, in time, I expect I shall come to love him. But falling in love would have been easier to begin a marriage with. He'll never have that. And I'm sorry I have to cheat him so.'

'Nicole—you *can't* do this. You can't marry David Ashleigh feeling the way you do.'

'How else shall I ever feel? I expect the first time you fall in love you think it can never happen again. Most older people would say that wasn't true. But all I know is what I am now— what I feel *now*. I'm in love with Lloyd Fenton, and so I can't be in love with David.'

Judy swung her leg from the edge of the piano stool. She shook her head, as if rejecting several things she might have said. 'I take it back. Of course you must marry David. He loves you—you will make a very good wife for him. In time—as you say—in time, you'll probably love him. He wouldn't be a hard person to love. You'll have to forget about Lloyd, though. If you keep thinking of him, if you go on the way you are now, you're just going to be miserable. And you'll make David miserable. I don't think he's a fool. He's sure to sense that things aren't right. At this moment I suppose he's thinking what we're all thinking—that you're exhausted. There's been all this Blanchard business, and an engagement and a marriage all within a few weeks. But if you go on looking as if your mind is somewhere else, you'll make him very unhappy. So forget Lloyd. Obviously it didn't work. Whatever you thought you had, it wasn't there, or you wouldn't have given up so easily. The two of you—how strange. I never really thought of you together, but now I see it's really possible. Both Americans, understanding the same sort of things. Both more serious than the usual run. He's so mad about his work, and you, in your way, about yours. I wonder what did go wrong? No . . . better not to dwell on that. Let it go, Nicole. It was one of those things.'

Nicole flashed back at her. 'Suddenly I don't think I want to just let it go. What you've told me changes things. I think—I *think* there's just a chance that he loves me as much as I love him. He misses me in the same way. Oh, Judy, it's been so *empty* since I've lost him. The days are filled, and yet I'm wandering all alone. There hasn't been anything—no, not *anything* that's been able to drive him out of my mind. And now you tell me he's going. He doesn't want even to be in the country when I marry David. My pictures have been saved, and now they're in the waste-basket. Well, I'm going to give it another try. It's that damn, stubborn Yankee pride. He just won't lift the telephone. Well, I'm not waiting anymore. I'm going to him . . .'

'You've probably missed him. He was taking the boat train from Victoria. I think he said about four-thirty. It's almost that now.'

Nicole's look of exhausted apathy dropped from her face, 'Judy, *quickly*. Have you got any money with you? Give it to me. I can just make it in time. Come down into the Square with me. We can each go to one end. Whoever sees a taxi first, grab it. Quickly . . . oh, God, quickly.'

'Nicole . . . !'

'Judy, *please*. I can't stop to argue. *Quickly* . . .'

She made Judy's refusal impossible by snatching up her coat and purse from the chair. 'I'm taking them, whether you come or not.' She flung open the door and began to run down the stairs.

Judy followed. 'Now why on earth did I have to open my mouth . . .?' Nicole never heard. She was already two flights below.

Victoria Station had that dank smell of steam and soot trapped under the roofs of the platforms, and of wet as people shook out umbrellas. Some might have been startled by the sight of a young dark-haired girl dressed only in a blouse and skirt, dodging her way through the beginning of the rush-hour crowds. Another girl, blonde and pretty, followed, calling after her. But mostly they took no notice. Notoriously, railway stations were places where dramas occurred, even if it was only the small drama of missing a train.

Nicole cannoned into a porter. "Ere, watch it!'

She grabbed his coat sleeve. 'The boat train for the *Ocean Queen*? Which platform?'

'Seven. If you took yer time ye'd see it chalked on the board in the ticket hall ...' He glanced up quickly at the big clock overhead. 'Bit late, ain't y' ...? Never goner catch it now ...' He had thought he might have felt some satisfaction in telling her she was going to miss it; he didn't like being grabbed and having questions hurled at him, but when he saw her stricken face, he relented. "Ere, quick—there's seven over there. You'll need a platform ticket if you're not travelling ...' She didn't look as if she was travelling. But she was gone, racing in the direction of his pointing arm. The blonde girl following her changed direction. They both came to the barrier of platform seven just as the ticket collector was starting to slide it closed.

'You ladies travelling?'

'No—just here to see someone off,' Judy panted.

'Sorry, too late. You'll have to buy a platform ticket from the machine.'

'Then we're travelling,' Nicole said. 'We're travelling to Southampton. We can pay on the train, can't we?'

'Yes——' the man conceded. 'Be sure you *do* pay.' Nicole was past him, and running down the terrible, horrible length of the train. The clock pointed to two minutes to departure.

People were bundled in raincoats. The last goodbyes were being said. Every man standing on the platform looked alike, hats pulled down, collars up. And why would Lloyd be standing on the platform?—unless there was someone to see him off? His could be any one of the hundreds of faces already lost behind newspapers and magazines, already settled for the journey. 'Lloyd!—Lloyd!' She didn't know she cried it aloud. As she ran, one of those raincoated, hatted figures turned.

'Nicole!'

236

She didn't know whether his arms opened to receive her, but she was there, and he was not able to deny her embrace. 'Lloyd —don't go! Please, don't go! Or take me with you ... at least as far as Southampton. I've got so much to tell you. If you don't understand by the time we get to Southampton—if you don't see that you've *got* to take me all the way with you, then I'll get on the train and come back.'

He looked down at her, ignoring the porter who was trying to urge him into the compartment, the whistle blown piercingly in their ears. 'You're sure, Nicky?'

'Sure. Completely. And whatever happens—whether you take me with you or not, I'm not going to marry David Ashleigh the day after tomorrow. I can't marry him, Lloyd. I love you.'

'Board. We're leaving, sir. Please get on board.'

Lloyd took her arm. 'No, I'm not going.'

A dawning light spread on Nicole's face. She never cried, so it had to be rain that dripped from the platform on to her cheeks.

'Your luggage, sir?—there isn't time to get it off.'

'Leave it. We'll find a way of sorting it out. Or it can just travel all by itself to Boston ... Come on, Nicky. You're shivering.'

The last doors were banged, and the train began to move. Neither of them took any notice of the carriages sliding past them. They were not part of the crowd that waved until the travellers were out of sight. They started towards the barrier. Judy was waiting for them there. 'I saw you found each other,' she said. 'I just thought I'd wait ...'

'And there's the matter of two platform tickets,' the ticket inspector said. 'And yours, sir?' Lloyd produced his train ticket. 'You were supposed to be on that train,' the man said, outraged.

'A lot of things were supposed to happen,' Lloyd said, 'Perhaps some of them will, now.' Irritably, the inspector made change out of the pound that Lloyd offered for the platform tickets.

'You can get a refund on this ticket by returning it to the Station Master's office. It's valid for one month,' he snapped.

'We might have used it by then, and bought another,' Lloyd answered.

Judy left them, and they sat alone in the station buffet for the next two hours, alternately drinking strong, dark tea, and brandy. Lloyd ordered toasted crumpets for Nicole, who protested that she couldn't eat anything, and then cleaned the plate and asked for more. She wore Lloyd's raincoat; she had stopped shivering long ago.

As she ate and drank, she talked, 'I have to go right back to the beginning. That's the only way I can tell it. Right back to the time when you said I should have been kissed by small boys, and I told you I never was. *That* was the truth. There was a whole lot I left out and that's where the lies were. I'd better begin with my mother, Anna ...'

The rush hour came and was about finished, and still they sat; still Nicole talked. Lloyd kept pouring tea, and signalling the waiter for more brandy.

At last the man interrupted, 'Will you be wanting dinner, sir? If so, I'll just lay the table ...'

'No, just two more brandies ... and some cheese and biscuits.'

'Cheese and biscuits, sir? As a starter?' The man was shocked. 'What about a few oysters instead, sir? Lovely month for oysters.'

'Cheese,' Lloyd said. He had an urgent need to put food into Nicole, a need that he recognized as one of the oldest, least complex symptoms of love. Looking over their brief history together, it seemed to him that he had spent a good deal of time urging Nicole to eat. God knew, at this moment, he thought, she looked as if she needed food. The face, which he had always considered on the fine balance between delicacy and asceticism, seemed to have gone over the edge. She seemed to flame with a kind of transparent beauty which threatened to burn itself out.

'Why—*why* didn't you tell me all this sooner? I would have understood. I would have understood about your aunt—about a sort of promise you made your mother. Though I think sticking to that sort of promise, the kind that a kid is often forced to give, is sheer madness. But you didn't trust me enough to tell me. God damn it, Nicky, that's no basis for marriage.'

'I know. I know it now. But, Lloyd—you don't understand how *hard* it seemed. I just couldn't get my tongue around it. All the sort of things that stood in my way when I was growing up were all there still. I've never been able to talk to anyone like this in my life. Don't you *understand*! You're the kind of person Anna was trying, in her own way, to push me towards. *You're* the sort of man she was hoping I'd meet if she could just get me through college—with Lucky Nolan paying the bills. I was ashamed. I knew I'd have to tell you, but I thought just a few weeks ... I wanted to go on playing the game just a bit longer. Perhaps ... yes, probably I was afraid you might just walk away from me. The background was so phoney, so painted.'

'But suppose you had married Blanchard, or married Ashleigh. Would you ever have told *them*?'

'Well—I suppose I knew that you were the *only* person I could have told it all to. That's why I've been getting so desperate as the wedding got nearer. I didn't want to deceive anyone—especially someone like David. But you—you know what America's like. You've been in places like Brooklyn. You *know*. That sort doesn't. It was first an honest and fairly ordinary ambition my mother had for me, though she was going to fairly extraordinary lengths to achieve it. And then that old man in Yorkshire made that hateful will, and my mother agreed to the conditions. You see, I don't think she ever got over this English thing. She suddenly saw a chance, a hope, that I'd be able to do what she'd never been able even to try. I'd have a chance to do it in *England*. If she hadn't agreed to the terms of the will, she'd have had to go on with Lucky Nolan, with him paying all the bills, trying to hide him away from any friends I made. And she knew I hated Lucky Nolan. At least I thought I did. I was such a snob. I took everything his money would buy me, and I looked down on him. She knew that. So she just took herself out of my life—pushed me over here and into Iris's arms. She wasn't really to know that Iris had ambitions of her own.' She laughed suddenly, rather hysterically. 'Between them, what these women have made of me. And I agreed. *That* was what I wasn't quite able to tell you.'

He watched the tears streaming down her face, she who never cried. 'You were pretty young, Nicky. And you must have been about the loneliest kid in the world.' He was thinking of the child left at school during the summer, the silent walks with Anna during the two vacation weeks each year, the weeks during which the piano practice was never allowed to lapse; he could feel Nicole's shock as she had seen Lucky Nolan that one and only time. He marvelled at the extent and intensity of the bitterness that Anna Rainard had carried through her life that its effects could still be so startlingly visible in the face of the girl seated opposite him. And yet he was forced to a reluctant admiration for this unknown woman. She had lived her life in a tight discipline, and had brought her daughter up the same way. When the chance, and the change, had come, they had both been ready.

'It's time you had some company, Nicky—really close company. Like a husband. Like an ordinary husband, not one who puts you into a house with miles of corridors and old enemies for company. Oh, I don't doubt that Ashleigh would have tried to give you company. But he's pretty young, too. He couldn't help the place where he put you. God knows, *he* wouldn't have known that he was just some sort of a grand pattern that had been worked out. He'd never know that you were there because your mother had been more or less kicked out ... I'd say Manstone's a pretty poor sort. He should never have let it happen ... not first with your mother, or now with you. Whatever he did, he should have stopped it.'

Nicole brushed her hand across her cheeks. 'It *wasn't* planned. I'd hardly thought about Lord Manstone—not as a person, until David sort of fell into my path. Even then I did nothing about it. I didn't try to make him fall in love with me. That morning I wanted you to come to Euston——'

He passed his handkerchief across to her and groaned faintly, 'All right. I know I made a stupid mistake. But how could I guess all this was behind it? You always seemed faintly mysterious to me, but I assumed you were the ordinary middle-class New York kid who found herself mixing in pretty high society, and was smart enough to keep her mouth shut, and play the part beautifully. I couldn't have known that what I thought of as your ambition was an ambition you'd inherited, some sort of crazy promise you'd set yourself to keep.'

'That morning at Euston, that was when I decided to let David Ashleigh fall in love with me, to go along with the whole thing. Perhaps I even had the hope that I'd fall in love with him too, and forget all about you. I won't say it wasn't some sort of consolation to be able to ram it home to Lord Manstone whose daughter I was. I would have loved to tell the same thing to the Countess, and watch her squirm. But that wouldn't have been fair to David. So ... I just let happen what happened. It all seemed so extraordinary. I didn't *plan* it—I swear that, Lloyd. It came my way. It seemed something that was fated. I'd lost you, but because of that I was free to go ahead and give my mother the greatest gift of all. I even had the faint hope, the thought, that one day she might even come to Lynmara, though I don't suppose she would have agreed to that—not so long as Manstone was alive. But it seemed as if I'd been set on a course, and there was no turning ...'

'My God, you're far more Russian than anyone would ever suspect. You thought it was all some part of the inevitable turn of the wheel of fortune. There you were, about to become mistress of the house they'd virtually thrown your mother out of. Everything I've ever read about Russians convinces me they're obsessed by fatalism. What is to be, will be——'

She smiled, and the last of the tears were gone. 'I'm afraid I said something like that to Lord Manstone. I actually believed it. If Judy hadn't come this afternoon and told me about the photos, and what you'd said—*that* broke through the idea that it was all fated.'

'Well, you see, some other things are fated too. Now, don't you think we'd better start doing something to untangle this mess? Look, I'll get the bill and then start to do some telephoning. You'd better get yourself into the ladies and wash your face. We'll start with Manstone. If he's at home, we'll go there. And so much the better if Sir Charles can be there also. It'll save a double explanation, and save you having to face your aunt to-night.'

'And us?—what happens to us?'

'We'll get married just as soon as we can get a licence. In the meantime, we'll go to Fenton Field.'

The growing happiness registered on her face made him a little sick to watch, sick at the thought of what he had failed to comprehend, of what he had almost missed. He was a doctor, and doctors were supposed to be perceptive of things like that. He felt humbled and ashamed because his own blindness had almost cost him the chance of his whole lifetime. Never before had he felt the tenderness he felt for this girl, never before the need to protect and cherish, to banish the memory, even the thought of loneliness. He felt as if something incredibly beautiful, but infinitely fragile, had been placed in his hands. She had trusted his love enough to break the silence that had closed over her whole life, the shell of bitterness and discipline and a kind of fear. If he could cause this trust, this love she offered him, to grow and flower, he might, some day, call himself a successful man.

The effort to control his emotion made him almost brusque when he spoke to her. 'Better go and wash your face. Here's some money for the attendant.' Signalling the waiter for the bill, he suddenly turned back to her, 'God, you're going to need some looking after, aren't you?'

In the cab on the way to Belgrave Square, Lloyd held Nicole close to him in the beginning of the protectiveness that he was at last coming to know she desperately needed. He knew he faced the task of trying to take her back to being a child, to learning to trust, and building all over again, until she became a whole woman.

It was of that past he was thinking when he said, 'We'll have to try to find your mother. There are ways . . .'

'She won't like that.'

'How do you know? Perhaps she's been waiting . . .'

'No—she'd never go around the terms of the will. If she wants to see me, she'll be in touch with the New York attorneys when I'm twenty-one. She's always known that. That miserable old man up in Yorkshire, my grandfather, must have calculated that I'd be completely alien to her by then. I suppose he could have made it a condition that she *never* saw me again, but perhaps he didn't dare be quite such a monster. If there was going to be a break between us, it would have happened before I was twenty-one. He seemed to know everything there was to know about us both, so he probably knew we weren't at all close. After all, how could we be? We hardly ever saw one another . . .'

'But you've done all this, and you've sounded as if you've done it for her.'

'In a way, I have. Don't you think *I* felt humiliated by that story too? Don't you think I haven't wanted to smash that arrogant old woman's confidence, because she did it to Anna? Don't you think I despise Manstone because he was so weak, so cruelly thoughtless? But no—we mustn't push to get in touch with Anna, to find her. She's a very private person. She'll find out about me, I'm quite sure of it. Why do you think I encouraged all these bits in magazines and newspapers? I knew that she'd be watching—she'd be watching for something. In the last resort, she'd look up Burke's Peerage. I knew from time to time she's done it before. She knew all about whom Manstone married, and about there being only one child. I thought the present I would give her was my marriage to David. But I'll find a way to let her know that *this* is a much better present. The best of all. Until I'm twenty-one, that promise still binds me. If I try to see her before that, I may shatter something she's been building up. For all I know, there may be some provision about her having to return the money if we are in contact. Lloyd, you say your family lost money during the crash, but honestly, you don't really know what it's like not to have any money at all. You think you're all poor now ... love, that's one thing I could teach you something about. No, leave things as they are. On my twenty-first birthday I'll be in the office of Fairfax & Osborne. If they have no address for her, *then* we'll start looking ...' She jerked forward as the taxi came to a stop. 'Oh, we're here.' In sudden panic she held him tightly. 'Oh, God, *what* am I going to say?'

'Just you be quiet, and I'll talk.'

She relaxed into the almost unbelievable luxury of realizing that she would never be alone again.

V

John Manstone and Charles were waiting in the library of the house in Belgrave Square. Although the room was sombrely immaculate, a fire burning brightly, it still had a feeling of deadness, of disuse.

John Manstone was standing, smoking, near the fire. Charles sat in a leather chair facing him, a drink in his hand. They both turned expectantly as the door opened. 'Miss Rainard and Dr Fenton, my lord.'

Manstone gestured them to chairs. Nicole seated herself as close to Charles as she could. Lloyd, refusing a drink, remained standing. He leaned back against the desk, seemingly quite at ease. For the first time it occurred to Nicole that she was seeing him in some sort of professional light. He was ready to tell a story, give a verdict, a prognosis, to fend off questions if that was necessary.

He talked quietly, and for quite a long time. Manstone let him go on, uninterrupted. Nicole began to grow more nervous from the very lack of argument.

As Lloyd came to the end of it, right down to the last things they had said to each other in the station buffet, Manstone tossed his cigarette end into the fire, and immediately lighted another. 'If this were a Shakespearian comedy, there'd also be someone for David to be paired off with, once we got the ill-matched lovers sorted out. But it doesn't go that way. For a time he'll be very hurt. He won't ever understand why this has happened. Unlike you two, he can't, not for a while, go marching off into the sunset holding hands with someone. Well, London's been having quite a lot of chatter about Blanchard. Now there'll be the same sort of talk about David. Only this time you almost went right up to the wire. You almost married him. And *that* would have turned the comedy into a tragedy. Thank God you didn't do it.'

Charles's eyebrows shot up. 'You're being generous . . .'

'Generous—not a bit of it!' Manstone snapped. 'I never wanted this marriage, but I saw no way to stop it. David really is, as we say, head-over-heels. Nothing on God's earth I could have said would have made him change his mind, once he was convinced that Nicole really did love him. Now he'll know otherwise.'

Nicole spoke softly, as if she hardly dared to take the role of spokesman from Lloyd. 'You *could* have told him about Anna. You threatened to. You said you would humiliate yourself in any way if it would stop this marriage.'

'Once I said that, I knew the reverse was true. Telling him the story of Anna would have driven him more firmly than ever into your arms—should I say arms, or clutches?' Nicole could not prevent herself from wincing at the word.

It brought a growl of protest from Charles. 'I say, Manstone, that's——'

'All right, all right,' he conceded wearily. 'I shouldn't use such harsh terms. She's still a young girl. Why should I expect wisdom, as well as brains? I suppose it was the sheer instinct of decency and survival which drove her to Fenton today. That's something I can be thankful for. I've experienced a loveless marriage, and I don't want to see it repeated for my only child. I realized, once I'd made my threat to tell David the whole story, that he would react like a young man in love. In short, he would never believe that it was a contrived situation in which Nicole did not return his love, but that it was the perfect example of justice being done, but a generation later. The young can be very idealistic. He would think of the wronged mother, and he would champion the daughter all the more. No, on consideration, I had to admit that I was helpless. Whatever action came, could come only from Nicole. Now it's come, and even though David will be severely hurt, I'm glad it's come.'

Now he gave his attention wholly to Nicole. 'Don't think I haven't studied you. I've done little else. And I saw no prospect of the marriage working out. You're the sort who has to be passionately dedicated to something ... or someone. Whatever chance an ordinary girl would have had of making a go of it, there would have been very little for you. Without an intense involvement, the source of that rather surprising strength you display would, I think, have dried up. I didn't think you could ever feel that passion for David, and without it, you'd have either burned up, or sought it elsewhere.'

'I think you're wrong.' Nicole held up her hand. 'No—let me speak. I admit I didn't have that feeling for David, otherwise I'd never be here with Lloyd this minute. I could have had it for Lynmara. Yes—for Lynmara I could have had it. But when it came down to it, what I feel for Lloyd was greater.'

He stared at her steadily for almost a minute. For the first time, she thought, she was seeing his features without that guarded, wary look that had characterized them since the moment they had met. He looked tired, but in a normal fashion, not as if some terrible tension knotted him, so that everything he did and said seemed false. Then he looked to the others. He held out his hand towards Charles's glass. 'I'll give you a refill. No—let me. I'm having one myself.' To Nicole he said, 'Shall I get you a drink? I'd like you to stay a few minutes longer. There's something I'd like to say to all of you.'

They were seated then, Lloyd and Nicole on a sofa together, Charles and Manstone in opposite chairs. Manstone sipped his drink and seemed to consider how he would choose his words.

'Interesting—what you just said,' he nodded towards Nicole. 'About Lynmara. That Lynmara could have become your passion, and might even have been the rock of a good marriage to

245

David. You might have been right about that. I didn't think of it myself—but then, I really had no idea about what went on in your head. But Lynmara ... yes, I might believe that. I could believe it because Lynmara is—was—my passion. Whatever I felt for Anna—your mother—was second to what I felt for Lynmara. Everything was second to Lynmara. A man shouldn't love a plot of earth, a pile of stones as I love it, but there it is. There are probably things in all of us that can't be rationally explained.'

Lloyd stirred restively. 'I appreciate that, Lord Manstone, but I don't see ...'

The older man held up his hand. 'Wait ... just a few minutes. I won't try to apologize at this late date for what I did to Anna, but now at least I can tell the truth. I think I would have married her, in spite of whatever opposition my mother put up. Anna was not only a very beautiful woman, but extremely in-intelligent. She would have learned our ways very quickly, as she would have learned much better English. She'd already shown great courage in the way she'd handled her life. She could have come to terms with our system, our peculiarities. I used to think what children we'd have. That mixture of Russian and English'—again he nodded towards Nicole—'as you are. The prospect excited me. I wanted very badly to see a horde of little Tartars rushing about Lynmara. The house so badly needed life in it ...'

'Then why in God's name didn't you do it?' The words burst from Nicole.

'Because if I had, there would have been no Lynmara for them—for me, for Anna, for anyone. The real trump card against my marriage to Anna which my mother played then was money. She told me, quite bluntly, that there was no money. *There was no money.* My father had died only a few months before I met Anna, and they were still trying to straighten out the estate, untangle his affairs. I didn't pay much attention to it. I just assumed the money was still there. I remember a really miserable and frightening morning when my mother summoned the accountants and our solicitor, and had them go through the figures for me. It was impossible to disbelieve them. My mother had only recently found out herself. She hadn't painted the picture worse than it was. My father had gambled excessively, had plunged on the stock market, and lost, had pursued every wild scheme a man could think of to try to recoup, to pull himself out of the mess. Every way he turned, he lost. He'd virtually killed himself with worry and drink, and even more speculation—and this on top of a heart disease. He'd mortgaged our lands to the point where the interest on that and his other debts was eating up the whole income. The lands couldn't support the house. When my mother was sure I'd really grasped the figures, she told the accountants and the solicitor to go, and then she told me what I had to do.

'I let Anna go, as I knew I must. And I married Cynthia Barrington as soon as possible. Cynthia was never deceived about our financial position, nor was her father. He insisted on a very thorough investigation to our affairs, which was pretty humiliating. And he insisted on a very careful marriage contract. Cynthia was his only child, and she'd been brought up like a little princess. He had great ambitions for her, and he was a multimillionaire. Perhaps he hoped for a far better match for Cynthia, but there was one awkward fact which he couldn't get around. Cynthia had fallen in love with me. I'm ashamed to say that I used that fact as a bargaining counter without in any way returning her love. I just saw the Barrington money as the way out of our troubles. Her father quibbled a little, but his was a very new baronetcy, and people were still a bit snobbish in those days about money made in trade. God knows, he was in every sort of trade you could think of. Well, in the end he bought me, and Lynmara, and the title for Cynthia, just as he'd always bought every other thing she had ever wanted. He tied everything up in trusts. There was a trust for the children of the marriage long before we were married. There was a trust which to this day provides an income for me—*and* I take it. There was a trust to provide for the upkeep of Lynmara. The mortgages and the debts were paid off on our marriage day. There was even a trust to give my mother an income. How she hated swallowing *that*! By the time we were married, we—my mother and I—knew that we had been bought in every way. Lynmara didn't belong to us any more, but to Barrington and all his trusts. He didn't become a millionaire by being a fool. He had no intention of handing over a fortune to the husband of his only child just to see it gambled away, if I turned out like my father. I could do what I liked with my bit, but I couldn't touch the rest of it.'

He shrugged, and took a long time over resuming. 'Well—many marriages are made that way. I did it because I had to keep Lynmara. I hadn't expected that the price would be quite so high. We were married in the summer of 1912—an enormous wedding which satisfied Cynthia's need for show and spectacle. The party that began with the marriage never really seemed to stop. Lynmara was always full of guests, half of whom I didn't know, or we were up in London, giving parties and going to parties. And Barrington acted like the proprietor that he was. He came to Lynmara when he pleased, used it as he pleased, even issued invitations to people we'd never heard of. And he was frankly and openly impatient for his first grandchild—and it had to be a son. The only time I ever knew him to be angry with Cynthia was when she miscarried the first time she was pregnant. She had lost his grandson, the one who would have been Viscount Ashleigh. He ordered the parties to stop, and Cynthia to have a quieter life. He was *going* to have a grandson, he said.

'It was fortunate for us all that Cynthia was pregnant by the time war broke out because I was sent to France as soon as I'd finished my training, and I didn't get any leave until I was wounded and sent home for a while. That was when I first saw my son, and I was completely hooked as Barrington himself was. It was Cynthia who was suffering. She didn't enjoy motherhood. She didn't enjoy the quietness the war years forced on her. She didn't like being left alone at Lynmara with my mother. While I was in France, she kept escaping to London, but when I came back Barrington ordered her to stay at Lynmara with me. Hoping for another grandchild, I expect.

'In her own odd, rather frenetic way, Cynthia was still in love with me. I wish I could have given her something in return, but the feeling just wasn't there. I tried to keep my side of the bargain. I gave her everything I could, but she knew by then that there was just nothing at the centre of it. She was beginning to realize what the money hadn't bought. The knowledge of this seemed to make her even more possessive—and jealous. I was very careful to give her no reason for jealousy, but I couldn't help showing how I felt about my son. And Lynmara also. It seemed she began to hate both of them, because I loved them.

'I was posted back to France, and the scene she made was

frightful. She insisted on coming to see me off, and went into a fit of hysterics at the station.' He shrugged, 'You see, there were some things which even Barrington couldn't control.

'The war ended. I came back. I longed for peace and quiet. To enjoy Lynmara and David. Cynthia would have none of it. She wanted her parties again, and so we had them. Endlessly. She also wanted me—my undivided attention. She made sure she had it. The fits of hysteria became common, and demanded a lot of time and attention. I had to give it. That was part of the bargain too.'

Nicole stirred restively. 'Look, I really don't think I want to hear any more of this. This is your business——'

He cut her off swiftly, 'Yes, you *will* hear it. You've told me Anna's side of the story. Now perhaps it's time you knew mine. Perhaps, some day, you'll see Anna again. Then she can hear about Cynthia, and the sort of marriage *I* made. I had to hear about a man called Lucky Nolan.'

Nicole slumped back in the sofa, her gesture one of resignation. 'Say what you have to.'

'I have to because you ought to know the full price I paid, how far the bargain took me. There are very few people who know. I wouldn't mind if Anna was one of them.'

He lighted another cigarette from the one he still held. 'The real horror began when Cynthia's hysterics changed into fits of withdrawal. The parties went on, but then there'd be a sort of sudden quiet. It was as if the music stopped for her. She'd draw into herself. See no one. Take her meals in her room. Those times she didn't even want to see me. When these spells came on her, she'd always go down to Lynmara, as if it were some kind of bolthole. Lynmara changed too. I'd suddenly find that she'd ordered the dust sheets put on all the rooms, the shutters closed. The place was like a tomb. I used to get David away at those times—send him and his nanny away to the seaside, or up to London—anywhere, so he wouldn't notice. Then Cynthia would come out of her spell. The dust covers were off, the rooms filled with flowers, and a whole mob of guests would descend on us again. For a while I thought it was the strain of living in a marriage which wasn't working out, and I waited for her to say she'd had enough. But she didn't want to divorce me. That would have set me free, and the trusts that Barrington had set up for Lynmara was irrevocable.

'It was Barrington himself who recognized that Cynthia's wasn't just the erratic behaviour of a spoiled child who'd never really grown up. He was in the house at one time when a party was in full swing. Ascot week, I think it was. She started giving the usual orders about closing up the rooms—while the guests were still there. Then she just drifted off, shut herself up and refused to talk. She refused to talk to anyone—not to me or Barrington. That infuriated him—and frightened him. We both were frightened when she complained of the noise, the voices. And the house was empty. They were talking about her, she said—always talking.

'Barrington ordered her to stay in her room. I don't suppose she heard him, but she stayed. He brought two doctors down from London. They stayed almost a week observing her, trying to get her to talk, to react in some way. But she did nothing but complain about the voices. When she could be got to talk, she would fantasize, but so often her speech was incoherent. Then she would retreat, become, well ... inaccessible. They diagnosed schizophrenia.

'Barrington reacted violently. At first he accused the doctors of not knowing their business. Then he overreacted by deciding to send Cynthia away. No one was to know that she was ill. Of course I was to go with her. We travelled under a different name. It was the beginning of the trek round the clinics. It seemed to me that we'd been to a hundred of them, all over Europe, by the time we—or Barrington—finally gave up. He would hear of a doctor here or there, and off we would go. Paris, Zurich, Vienna. Always accompanied by nurses, of course. Always staying at out-of-the-way places, where we'd be unlikely to meet anyone we knew. Barrington gave the orders. We moved on when he told us to. The story was that we were simply travelling ... just travelling. The truth was that he was terrified that people might get to know the nature of Cynthia's illness. He didn't want the stigma of that sort of illness—not for himself, but above all, not for his grandson. Periodically he'd join us himself, just to see how she was. She was always worse. There were hallucinations. Delusions of persecution. She thought, once, that I was trying to kill her, and so she, in her turn, tried to kill me. There always were nurses at hand, so that didn't succeed. The doctors didn't know much about schizophrenia then—still don't. They tried this drug and that, shock treatment, anything and everything. In the end they said it was better if she were confined. Permanently. She was so far gone in dementia, they saw no realistic hope of a cure. Perhaps Barrington even aided them in that decision. He wanted it one way or the other. He couldn't let us go on "travelling" for ever.'

He went and filled his glass again. Nicole slipped her hand into Lloyd's. Manstone came back to face them. By now they knew they must hear it all. It wasn't, Nicole realized, just because at some time this story might be retold to Anna. The man before them had the desperate need to speak.

'I wish I come out of this whole affair with just something to my credit. But there isn't anything. I let Barrington do as he wanted. I was used by then, I suppose, to taking his orders. And probably I was tired. I knew I was longing for a sight of my son—and of Lynmara. You see, Barrington refused to let his daughter come back to England. He refused to allow her to be put into a nursing home here. He was quite sure that her real identity would be discovered. He was probably right in that. She'd had her picture everywhere—the fairy princess, with a mountain of gold to command.

'So I left her in one of those beautiful little valleys in Austria, in a beautiful clinic that was like a private house. Everything so quiet, so peaceful. The gardens a delight—the walks in the woods so good for the patients, under careful watch, of course. They couldn't have made it more beautiful, but it was a house of the dead. None of the attendants wore a uniform. It had no appearance of being a hospital. And yet you could always tell who were the patients and who were their keepers. And you also knew that once one of these patients had reached that beautiful valley with its little lake, the mountains, the beautiful house, it was very unlikely they would ever leave it. I think of it as the most dreadful place I've ever seen.

'Barrington set up even more trusts. We were in the never-never land where a person is neither alive nor dead. He had arranged for the newspapers to get hold of an item that Cynthia had been killed in a motor accident on the Continent. To Barrington she was already dead, but she could not be buried. What mattered to him was that David was protected. He should not grow up, go to school, with the story of a demented mother hanging over him. Barrington was ruthless for what he believed

—and I can't say, to this day, he was wrong. I've been back, a number of times, to that beautiful valley. I see Cynthia only at a distance. She doesn't recognize me. They don't encourage me to come. If she recognized me, it might disturb her—might disturb the calm. And the Barrington solicitors go to make their personal checks from time to time. She is well cared for —and she is dead . . .'

Charles shook his head in protest. 'Barrington has been dead for years.'

'Yes, Barrington has been dead for years, but his trusts still go on. Once he determined that his daughter was incurable, he set his solicitors to work on even more interlocking, and obscure trusts. David was to be protected, whatever happened. He and his children were to have the Barrington money, and Lynmara. And I—of course I was tied for ever to the woman who existed in that beautiful little valley. No mention of her name must ever come out in the English press. Cynthia, his daughter, was dead. David, his grandson, must grow up exactly as Barrington decided. It must have been a great shock to Barrington when they told him that he was dying, and he wouldn't be alive for ever, like God, to oversee all this. He made his will as tight as he could, but there was really no way he could protect it all. Since his daughter was not legally dead, a lot of difficulties came up. I can't pretend to understand the obscurities those solicitors went into. But I was a living husband, with a living wife. He gave as much as he could to David, but David was still a child. He had no heirs. Where was Barrington to leave his money? His only hope was David—David, and his children. Lynmara still had its own trust. I had my income. My mother had hers. And very discreetly, a trust was set up to provide for whatever Cynthia might need, as long as she lived. He couldn't do more than that without revealing the condition his daughter was in. That he wouldn't do. To be ill was one thing. To be mentally ill was quite something else. After trailing around Europe for more than a year from clinic to clinic, I was almost prepared to agree with him. Well, whatever I thought, I had no voice in his decisions. I had to say *I* didn't want her back. It would have needed a braver, a more compassionate man than I ever was. And—like him—I cared more for David than for her.'

Without asking them, he went and refilled each glass. It was a deliberate action, as if he wished to give them time to absorb what he had said.

As Nicole expected, Lloyd spoke first. 'Hereditary? Not in all cases. As with the treatment—they still don't know.'

Manstone echoed him. 'Hereditary?—well, we all take our chances, don't we? What are the chances of producing an idiot —or a genius? You don't think, do you, that I was going to shadow David's whole life by making him afraid to have children? He has as good a chance as anyone. They told me that. Now you two are going out to take your chances. Well, that's the way it always has been.'

Nicole swallowed nervously at her drink. She had had too much drink. She couldn't remember how many brandies she had had at the station. Too many.

'What will you tell David? Do you want me to wait for him to come, and tell him myself?'

He shook his head. 'No—there's really nothing to tell him, except that you changed your mind. For another man. Well— don't look like that! What else can you expect? You said you didn't plan it. If you—if you and Dr Fenton hadn't got your-selves mixed up, hadn't lost each other, David wouldn't be involved. I'll just have to tell him the truth. You wanted to marry someone else, and now you're going to. I'll just have to try to make him see that it was better it happened now than later.'

'But Anna ... you're not going to tell him about Anna?'

'Look, girl,' he said harshly, 'you can't have everything! You said yourself you didn't do this because of Anna. Now have the guts to stick to that. Whatever David may think of you, you'll just have to live with that. Why drag in all of this? What has Anna——'

She struggled out of the depths of the sofa, her face flaming. 'If Anna has had nothing to do with it, then why have you told us about your wife? *Why?* Only because you think that some day I'll see Anna. I'll be able to tell *your* side of the story. We all want to make our side of it look nice. All right—then tell David I've gone off to marry someone else. That's true. The rest isn't relevant. It doesn't matter. I just wish ... I wish David didn't have to think so badly of me.'

Manstone took the glass from her shaking hand. 'That's what will happen. He'll think badly of you. Other people will think badly of you.' Then he looked from her to Lloyd. 'But you say you're going for something better. Then for God's sake, have the strength to stick by it! All that I've told you had only one purpose. Don't trade yourself in for other people's opinion of you. Do what you can ... what you will. Have the courage to believe in it. In the end, there's no one but yourselves ...'

They went to the door. Lloyd turned back to Charles. 'We're going to Fenton Field. We'll expect you, Sir Charles. There are certain formalities, since you're Nicole's guardian, and she's under age ...'

Charles nodded. 'I'll be there.' Manstone had turned back to the fire, tossing a cigarette butt into the flames.

They let themselves out, and found a cruising taxi in Belgrave Square.

VI

Later that night Iris sat, tight-faced, wordless, while Charles tried to tell what had happened. At the end she said, 'Why? I don't understand why!'

'She loves him ...' Charles answered, helpless to explain any more.

'Love! The little fool doesn't know there's no such thing. And for that she's thrown away ...' For a moment her fury threatened to choke her. 'I'll never forgive her,' she said finally. 'And she need never expect it. She'll have made me the laughing stock of London. By tomorrow they'll be laughing ...'

Charles tried. 'My dear, if only you could realize how worthwhile you are yourself. All the things you do ... People will never laugh at you, Iris.'

She gestured to indicate her contempt for such naïvety. 'A lot you know about *people*, Charles ...'

And then she went to her desk to draft the notice which she later telephoned to *The Times*. '*The marriage will not now take place ...*'

Very early the next morning she called in the packers and began the enormous task of sending back the wedding presents which threatened to swamp the house in Elgin Square. She was at her desk, working on the lists, when Charles came to tell her that he was going down to Fenton Field. 'She will need permission to marry, as she's under age. As her guardian ...'

Iris did not raise her head. 'Do as you please. I have no further interest in that girl.'

VII

They were married three days later by special licence at Stoke-ley, the village near to Fenton Field. Nicole had read none of the newspapers in that time, nor cared to. She had written one brief note to her aunt, and ended by telling her where she would find David's ring, which was to be returned. She also wrote to David, a letter almost as brief as to Iris. There was no way to write it all down.

She gave to Charles the pearls and earrings, the diamond and sapphire brooch which had been Iris's presents to her. She shook her head when he suggested that she might keep them. 'No—I can't take any of that with me. There's only one thing I'd like you to send. Would you have them pack my music ... ?' She gave him the address of Lloyd's brother in Boston. 'That's just until we find a place of our own ...' She added, a little wistfully, 'You *will* come and see us, Uncle Charles? You won't let Aunt Iris ... ?'

'I'll come,' he said, and meant it. He had, in these few days of waiting for them at Fenton Field, seen that quality of luminous happiness return to her face, the kind of radiance which he had glimpsed so briefly, and which transformed her. He knew the kind of trouble she had caused; he felt very deeply for the hurt which David Ashleigh would suffer; he knew the kind of humiliation which Iris would have to endure. But when he looked at Nicole's face, he was grateful that an equal knowledge of these things had not turned her back from what she was now doing. Charles knew that his own life with Iris was going to be hellish for as long into the future as he could see, for she would find no compensation for the fulfilment of pride and ambition which Nicole's marriage to either David Ashleigh or Harry Blanchard would have given her. Through Nicole, a new life had opened for Iris. It might have been possible for her, one day, to mellow in the light of what she had accomplished through her niece. Now the door to that life had closed, and he didn't doubt that an already bitter woman would become more bitter still. Nicole had come, and gone. Charles grieved at his own loss, but looked at her face once more, and knew that he should not grieve.

Nicole and Lloyd shopped for a few pieces of essential clothing in Brighton. She was married in Margaret Fenton's wedding dress and veil—the dress had to be shortened a little, and a few tucks taken in it. 'We'll let it down again when Judy needs it,' Margaret said. She and Charles signed the register as witnesses. Judy was there, and Richard, and Ross and Andrew Fenton. To everyone's surprise, Gavin McLeod came down from Cambridge. For the first time he looked on Nicole with approval. 'Only sensible thing I've ever known you to do,' he said bluntly.

Charles drove them to Southampton and waited on the dockside until the liner sailed. Nicole and Lloyd stood on the deck in the rain, the dog, MacGinty, which they were taking with them, at their side, until the mist obscured that tweed-coated and hatted figure. 'I'll miss Uncle Charles,' she said. 'Next to you, I love him more than ...'

Lloyd's hand closed over hers, her hand which wore the gold wedding band, and a very simple diamond ring, bought also in Brighton. 'As long as I come first, you can love anyone you like.'

Nicole smiled, and fingered the new golden band. Then she put her hand to her neck, and felt for the slender golden chain, the chain with the little upturned horseshoe in its centre. It was the first time she had worn it since the day she had dutifully put it on when Anna had handed it to her. It, and the golden band, and the single diamond, were the only jewellery she owned. To herself she recited the little legend engraved on the inside of the horseshoe. *Good luck. Lucky.*

They arrived in Boston to the wondering, bemused welcome from the Fenton family, and the first chill of the fall, the first gold and scarlet in the trees of this graceful but hard city, this centre of New England, which had nurtured and carved and chiselled men like the Fentons since they had fled from the old England she also had left behind her. There was a characteristically reserved welcoming dinner at the house on Beacon Hill. The reserve did not frighten or worry Nicole. It was to be expected of New Englanders. She felt she had come home. Though she had come to the symbols of wealth which had almost vanished, she knew she would never again stare at a notice on a beach which said 'Private' and feel shut out. She held Lloyd's hand, and she was afraid of nothing, not of the elderly aunts who asked questions about her family, nor of the old gentlemen who seemed to be waiting for the return of a better day. The depression was all about them, and she and Lloyd, by the standards of Boston wealth, were poor. She thought of Anna, and wished desperately, that somehow she could know of these hours of splendour in an impoverished house on Beacon Hill.

A cable reached them at the house on Beacon Hill. Nicole never knew how the address had been obtained, but the method was typically efficient. *'Damn good show.'* It was signed: *Gerry Agar*.

VIII

The news came to Anna in painful dribbles. She read about Lord Blanchard, the heir to the Duke of Milburn. She saw photographs of Nicole with him. Then there was nothing. Weeks passed before the next mail from Europe came in. This time there was nothing printed in the fashionable magazines, but there was a burst of speculation in the newspaper columns. Nicole Rainard was a guest at Lynmara, having just left the Scottish estate of the Milburns. Since it was still summer and the passenger liners on the Atlantic were still plentiful, the next clippings came more rapidly. She saw the multiple coverage of her daughter's engagement to Lord Ashleigh, the heir to the Earl of Manstone.

The day those cuttings came she telephoned Frank Hayward and said she was taking a few days off. He mentally shrugged. 'So ... O.K. Business is slack. When is it ever any different? So, take a few days off ...'

She went with Mike in the old Ford out into the desert. She sat too late among the rocks and pools of the oasis, until the chill of the desert night hit her, and Mike's nudging nose reminded her that neither of them had eaten. The desert stars were cold above her and she was shivering as she fed him from the cans she carried in the car. Then she went to the cluster of cabins where she always stayed, booked in, and went along the road to a hamburger stand. She pretended she kept a great discipline about feeding Mike, but she bought him a hamburger there also. Then she went back to the cabin, went to bed, and for the first time in many years, she wept. She couldn't have said exactly why she wept, but the pictures of Nicole had been less than right. There was a falseness about them that disturbed her. Never before had she seen Nicole look at the camera as if she were trying to get beyond it to reach someone else. Nicole was not absorbed in the handsome young man beside her, but in the impression she was creating. For a very long time she had studied that picture of the Countess, John Ashleigh and his son, David, and Nicole in the Great Saloon of Lynmara. There was an expression on Nicole's face that troubled Anna. She stood there, in the room which had seen her, Anna's, humiliation, and she was both triumphant and defiant. Anna remembered the night at Lucky Nolan's when she had told Nicole about John Manstone, and now she wept with regret. She had tried to remove herself from Nicole's life, and in leaving this deadly seed, she had failed. It was a kind of torment then, to lie alone in that bed, to feel the stillness and silence of the desert about her, and for once, Mike's untiring efforts to comfort her, to lick her hand, to try and get on to the bed beside her, were of little help. As she had wept so little in these past years, so she had felt little need for human comfort. But this once, her own self and this animal comfort would not do. She learned that she was not quite self-sufficient. At last she slept, and when she woke it was already hot in the last days of a desert autumn.

The next time she went to the Post Office box in Santa Ana there was the notice from *The Times*: *The marriage will not now take place* ...

In the same clutch of press clippings was the news that Nicole Rainard had that day married an American doctor, Lloyd Fenton, of Boston, Massachusetts. They sailed for Boston immediately after the wedding. It had been a quiet ceremony in the village of Stokeley in Sussex.

She drove along the road, and at the first hamburger stand she and Mike ate ravenously and in a kind of rapture of relief. 'She's going to be all right,' she said to the dog as she fed him chunks of the bread and meat. *'All right.'*

The next day Anna, as if in celebration, went to a Ford dealer on Wilshire and asked about a second-hand car. She wanted to trade in the old one for a slightly newer model. The salesman looked doubtfully at the old one, tried it out on the road, and shrugged, 'I can't allow you much on it—it's pretty well had it. Now, if you were to trade it in for a brand new one, I could maybe sharpen my pencil quite a lot, and give you a real good deal.'

Anna shook her head. 'I can't afford a new one. It's as simple as that.'

The salesman nodded. It was the usual situation. Most people couldn't afford new cars in these times. The boss, he thought, took crazy risks stocking so many new cars and rather expensive models, on the hope that he would make sales to members of the thriving movie industry—which seemed to be the only industry which could be said to be thriving. 'O.K.——' he said. 'I'll talk to the boss. He'll give you what he can, and we'll fix you up with the best used job we've got, for what you can pay.'

The boss was a man in navy grease-stained overalls, whose hands looked as if they daily lived in contact with the engines of the cars he sold. He grinned at Anna from under thick straight dark brows and a shock of greying black hair. 'Well, the old one's pretty well had it,' he said. 'But I think I can sweeten her up a bit, and maybe some kid getting his first car will take it as a bargain. Now let's see what we can fix you up with in place of the old jalopy ...'

He toured the lines of his stock of used cars, going from one to the other, selecting at last three which he insisted Anna take out on the road before making her choice. He said little to influence her in the selection, but nodded gravely when she finally made it. 'That's the one I would have picked for you, but I wanted you to feel you'd made the decision. Listen, Mrs ... Mrs ...'

'Maynard.'

'Mrs Maynard, my opinion is the carburettor needs a bit of work done on it. No extra charge. Just give me till tomorrow, and I'll have her all sweetened up. How about if I put on a new muffler? Only cost a few dollars, and I won't charge for labour. I do it myself in any case.' He grinned at her again. 'The boss always works hardest in these outfits ...'

She paid the deposit, and went back to the old Ford. They made arrangements about what time she was to pick up the other one the next day. 'Listen, Mrs Maynard, don't ever let anything go on it, will you? I can see you've tried to take care of this job, but they've only got so many miles in them. But if there's anything wrong, you bring her back to me. Bring her in for regular servicing, and I'll promise to keep her running sweet and pretty for quite a while yet ...'

As she got into the Ford, Anna paused, and then said to him, 'Why do you take so much trouble, Mr ...?'

'Name's Mike. Just ask for Mike.'

'Mike ... why do you take so much trouble? My business is worth what? ... a very few dollars to you.'

He shrugged, and grinned again, and looked almost embarrassed, 'Well, I figure it this way. Some day, perhaps, you're going to want a brand new car. You'll come to Mike's. Someday, I aim to be the biggest Ford dealer in L.A. This is a city made for automobiles.' He looked, for just a second past her, to his lines of used cars, and to the three expensive new models sheltered in his small showroom. There was something almost wistful in his expression. 'You know, Mrs Maynard, to some people an automobile is a beautiful thing. Lovely to listen to her running sweet and clean. I like to work with automobiles. So you have any trouble, any trouble at all, you come back here and I'll put her right. Just ask for Mike ...'

'Mike,' she repeated. 'That's the name of my dog.'

He tore his eyes away from the contemplation of his stock, to the dog seated beside her in the old Ford. 'You look nice and safe and cosy with him beside you. The way a lady should. S'long, Mrs Maynard. See you tomorrow.'

In the rear-view mirror she watched his diminishing figure as he once again surveyed his line of cars waiting for the customers he visualized in the future. She hoped he'd get them. When he had talked of automobiles, for a second his face had flickered with the passion of a monomania. His speech had been the ordinary speech of every American, but overlaid with a faint remnant of an accent—French, perhaps, but no, not really she decided. It was heavier than that. The brave pennants fluttered in the breeze. MIKE'S NEW AND USED CARS. Then she turned into the darkening streets of the city. And she had an odd feeling that she had met him before, or was it just that she recognized someone who had the same feeling as she had for this place? He thought of it in terms of automobiles to traverse its endless miles of almost rural sprawl. She saw it in terms of real estate, in terms of sunshine and climate to be sold to people who fled the winters of the East and mid-West. These were lean times for people like herself and this Mike to dream grandiose dreams, but she felt warmed and comforted by a rare sense of companionship.

The next day he had the car ready at the agreed time, the old bodywork as shining as hands could make it. He smiled as he listened to the engine when she turned on the ignition. 'Hear that? Sweet as sugar ... sweet as sugar.' And he passed a grimy hand over his chin, transferring some grease to it, and grinning at her with the pleasure she might have expected if he had just sold one of the showroom models. Whatever else he loved, this Mike loved automobiles.

'Goodbye, Mrs Maynard. Take care now.'

'Goodbye ... Mike.'

The post office box at Santa Ana yielded only one clipping on Anna's next visit. It was an item from a gossip column of a London paper giving the information, tinged with a little malice towards the girl who had shaken the London social scene that season, that the former Nicole Rainard, now Mrs Lloyd Fenton, had left England for Boston with her husband, who was about to take up practice there. Lady Gowing had not been available for comment on any of her niece's proposed future plans.

Anna then wrote and closed the account she had had with the London press clipping service. From the telephone book she selected a firm of Santa Ana attorneys, one with whom she had never done business, and giving the post office box as her address, asked them to write to a New York clipping service and take out a subscription for clippings dealing with Dr and Mrs Lloyd Fenton, or Nicole Fenton, and that they should concentrate on the papers of Boston, Massachusetts. She paid in cash for the services of the attorneys, and they in turn paid the clipping service with their own cheque. They didn't ask questions of the woman for whom they performed this routine service. The world was full of such people, those who wanted to remain hidden, but wanted information. They would have been ready, if she had requested it, to recommend the services of a private investigator, but apparently that was not required.

She asked them to let her know, through the post office address, when the subscription expired. She would renew it regularly, she said.

Thereafter she received at Santa Ana sealed envelopes from the New York clipping service, resealed in the envelopes of the attorneys. Each year she renewed the subscription, paying in cash, and paid the few dollars extra charge they made for postage and handling. They never learned any more about the woman with the post office box, and she did nothing to make them curious.

Part 3

Lynmara

CHAPTER 1

February 28th, 1939

I

My dear Nicole. Tomorrow is your twenty-fourth birthday, and I send you . . . Charles Gowing paused in his writing. What did he really send her that she didn't know she had in abundance? London that evening was shrouded in fog, and as always some of its choking, sulphureous mass had seeped in at windows and doors, an acrid, unmistakable smell. It had been dark since three o'clock. The fire that burned in the grate did little to lighten Charles's mood. He looked for a long time at the photograph in the silver frame which was the only one on the desk in this room which Iris had fashioned into a bedroom-study for him in the year that Nicole had spent her one brief summer flaming brilliantly on the London social scene, and then disappearing into what, if anyone now thought of her at all, was thought of as obscurity. He looked long and closely at the features he so often studied, the once too-delicate features which now were more slightly rounded, at the smile that was not forced or coy, but natural, as a happy woman smiles. He looked at the two young children—one seated beside her, one on the lap, her arms closely about him. An ordinary enough picture, but to Charles, one infinitely precious. It didn't matter that Lloyd Fenton himself was not in the picture; not only had he fathered these sturdy, good-looking boys, but it was he who was responsible for the air of calm serenity, for the naturalness of the smile that Nicole wore. If Charles sometimes cursed Lloyd Fenton for having taken her away from England, much more often he was profoundly grateful to him for what he had fashioned of this young woman whom Charles loved so much.

Charles had not grown used, over the years, to missing Nicole's actual presence. The loneliness he had expected to experience on that day he had seen the liner slip off into the mist of Southampton had actually been worse than he feared, sometimes a physical ache, rather like that which afflicted his wounded leg, and, like it, did not go away. He had busied himself as best he could, but even the pleasure of an occasional weekend at Dencote was now not his. He had rented the lodge soon after Nicole had left when he discovered that he really could not bear its emptiness when there was no hope that she would join him. These were the times he acknowledged his jealousy of Lloyd Fenton, as jealous as he would have been of any man Nicole might have married. But the renting of Dencote had had a more practical side. He found he needed even the little it brought in so that he might have extra money for the gifts he wanted to shower on Nicole's children, and in his frustration, could not. He found himself, almost from the beginning, practising little economies—going less often to his clubs to save the expenses of drinks and meals, taking an extra year out of a suit until Iris protested that it had begun to look shabby, taking a bus or the underground when before he would have used a taxi. He stored up the money saved as a small child with a money-box, and his reward had been three visits to Boston, and Nicole's joyful welcome. For nothing in the world would he have accepted help from Iris to pay for these journeys—but then, none had ever been offered.

Each time he had announced he was going, she had merely shrugged and asked what period of time he would be away. Never once did she mention Nicole's name. In the years since Nicole had left, Iris, oddly, without seeming to try, had achieved the height of an ambition Charles had always known was present, but which, through years of striving, had still evaded her. With Nicole's departure, Iris had seemed to relinquish the approach to the world she had so desired to be recognized in. With this she had grown bolder, more daring, more ready to take risks. Charles had to acknowledge that it seemed ridiculous that a woman dedicated to charitable fundraising would be thought to take risks, but Iris, in her anger and bitterness over Nicole, had finally shaken off any timidity. She didn't any longer care that people might mention her Yorkshire mill-owning father, that they might say her money was in city blocks and steel mills, rather than in shooting moors and country acres. With Nicole's going, she had seen all that swept away, and she then had nothing to lose. The result was that she had become one of the most prominent women in London. She very loosely involved herself in politics, but only when the presence of a great name would help one of her charities. Three permanent secretaries now inhabited the library, and Lady Gowing's was a name to be courted for the list of any charitable venture. It was a pity, Charles thought, that her success didn't seem to give her more satisfaction. As night after night he attended charity balls and functions with her, he wished that just once her face might have relaxed into the smile of triumph which she had earned. But she never did relax. He had sat with her through ballet and opera and concert and after-dinner entertainment, and he knew that she was mentally planning the activities of the next day, how to focus her soliciting letters more accurately, how to snare a bigger and ever bigger name as guest speaker, or comedian, or whatever was needed, for her next dinner. She seemed never to rest; she seemed never to tire. Charles himself, at times, felt very tired.

At these times the great refreshment had been to look at the photographs of Nicole, from which he had made an album, to re-read her letters, to summarize in his mind what the pictures conveyed—that, and to plan the next journey to Boston.

'You must come in the fall,' she had written the first year of her marriage. 'You can't even imagine what the colours are like here.' He had sold some of his few remaining shares, found an inexpensive, slow steamer that would land him in Boston, and had gone. She had greeted him, laughing and with her eyes bright with tears, hugging him with a fierce strength, and she hadn't needed to tell him she was pregnant. 'When I knew you really were coming, I thought I'd surprise you ...'

'If I'd known I might have cancelled ... Shouldn't you be resting? ... and all that.'

'What nonsense. My doctor says I'm as healthy as a horse. Everything's going beautifully.'

He had gone back to the rambling frame house, in a modestly affluent street in Cambridge, and had never before realized that Nicole lived almost on the campus of Harvard College. 'I always thought it was out in the woods somewhere,' he confessed.

'That,' she said, 'was back in the time when Paul Revere took his ride. Oh, but we'll go to all the places. Concord ...

Walden Pond. I remember you like Thoreau ...'

It had been very American, in a special way. She gave dinner parties to introduce him to all the Fentons, and others to introduce him to the medical people that were Lloyd's world. In between, they had driven together to all the places she had promised, and he had witnessed the splendour of a New England fall. And he had witnessed the shared happiness of two people who loved each other almost to the exclusion of everyone else. He was pleased in what he found in Lloyd Fenton, a steadiness which had a balancing effect on Nicole's intensity. Sometimes he watched her as she in turn watched Lloyd, and he saw again the radiance he had once so briefly glimpsed in London. He welcomed what he witnessed between them, and yet he was somewhat afraid of it. Was it possible to love too much? He feared a little for Nicole should anything flounder, and yet who, once having seen the full expression of such a love as she appeared to have for Lloyd, would have wanted to deny it to her? She had experienced what few people had experienced, and that, whatever happened, could never be taken from her. It pleased him to see that Lloyd Fenton seemed to realize this. Without appearing to coddle Nicole, he tried to protect her, and yet to draw her out into a world that was not wholly centred in himself. It seemed to Charles an eminently sensible, tender approach, and he felt a new respect for this quiet, but rather tough-minded man.

The Fenton family, he had noticed, had played its own part in drawing Nicole into the centre of its life, and therefore the life of Boston. She had arrived, new to the city, and unknown to them. In a family fashion, they had closed ranks around Lloyd, and treated his bride gently, but still had given her an eagle-eyed scrutiny. Most of them liked what they saw, some reserved judgement. Then inevitably, shortly after Lloyd and Nicole arrived, the stories had followed them across the Atlantic. The knowledge of her jilting a young man called Lord Ashleigh two days before her wedding did not help her, until they could see for themselves that she did not live except through Lloyd Fenton, and were, in a back-handed fashion, complimented that her choice should have been this man whose family was part of the history of the city. Then, people who had been visiting England that summer returned and told the stories of an expected engagement to the elder son of a duke. The young girl who had turned down both a marquis and a viscount became an object for speculation, especially since it was known that the only money Lloyd Fenton had was what he earned from medicine, and a very small income which was all that was left of the family fortune. Boston society began to feel protective of Nicole, especially when it was conceded that she could not possibly have put on such a show of being in love if that were not the truth. Unexpected offers to help finance the mortgage of the house in Cambridge came to Lloyd, which he accepted. They were asked to dinner parties which might have taken a young married couple years to achieve. Charles even found out that the thing that really swayed the most proper dowagers of Boston, who he saw had made rather a pet of Nicole, was her ability at the piano. For years all these ladies had religiously attended the Friday afternoon concerts of the Boston Symphony. They recognized and respected a professional standard when they heard it. They even, tactfully, some of them, asked Nicole if she would consent to give piano lessons to their grandchildren. The word went through Boston society. Lloyd Fenton's young bride, who seemed to have come out of nowhere, had been presented at the Court of St James, her Engish was of the standard rarely heard, even in Boston, and lacking its hard vowels, her manners were impeccable, except when someone else's demands crossed the wishes of her husband, and then she was a tigress in not allowing one to conflict with the other. Boston society decided that Nicole Fenton would more than suit them. They admitted her.

Charles, seeing her through that October of the brilliant flaming leaves which drifted before his face, and rustled beneath his feet, the month when Nicole's pregnancy advanced until she moved clumsily, knew that Nicole herself did not care whether Boston accepted her or not. What she did care for was that Lloyd should have not been hurt by his marriage. He had not been, and her satisfaction lay there. She continued to play her scales, the sonatas, the etudes, the ballads and waltzes and nocturnes, and laughed with Charles that her swelling belly was pushing her too far from the piano. On Thursday nights she played with an amateur chamber music group who met for the simple and complex pleasure of making music together. She wept a little when she saw Charles off at the end of his visit, but he knew there was no real sadness in her. She had so much to return to when she left the dock. And he was returning to the brisk efficiency of the house in Elgin Square which was organized to accommodate Iris's activities, and to the November fogs of London.

The child was due about Christmas. Before that, Charles, through means he didn't altogether approve but which his determination drove him to, raised some extra money. He did it by a combination of putting Dencote even further into debt, and by implying to his bank manager that naturally his wife would see him through any contingency. This part was not the truth, but not everything was known to bank managers. All they knew was that Iris Gowing was a rich woman, and these lean years had, by sound investment, made her richer. So Charles made his plans, and the letter came back from Nicole.

'I opened the door one morning, and there was Henson! She had even found her way to the house without telephoning, and had paid off the cab. She was there, bag and baggage, and she simply said, "Well, Miss Nicole, I've never been a nanny before, but I've worked in nurseries, and I know how things should be done. You can trust Baby with me." Uncle Charles, dear, you shouldn't have done it, but it's *nice* to have her to lean on. I'm afraid I shall be such a fool with a young baby ...' Charles had sought Henson out in her present employment with the Honourable Mrs Robert Maitland, tempted her with the thought of being with Nicole again, paid her passage, and guaranteed three years' salary, paid quarterly. By that time, he knew, Nicole would have control of her own money, and Henson would either be a fixed object in the Fenton household, or she would have long before returned to England. As he sat there on that last day of February writing his letter, Henson was still with the Fentons, the second son was almost two years old, and Henson continued to write her rather laborious letters to Sir Charles, detailing each stage of both children's growth and progress, the older one now being referred to as Master Daniel, and the younger had taken the name of Baby.

But Charles didn't really need the reports, though he savoured each detail as much as Henson liked to write it. He was like a man who suddenly had grandchildren, when he had expected none, and it grieved him that Iris refused to share this peculiar pleasure with him. He wished she knew what she was missing. He had even, tentatively, rather diffidently, suggested she accompany him on his second visit to Boston, in the summer of 1936, when Nicole was twenty-one. Iris had stared at him and he had watched her lips tighten. 'I thought I made it perfectly clear to you, Charles, that what becomes of that girl is a matter of complete indifference to me. I do not wish to discuss it further.'

So he had gone and spent the summer mostly with Nicole, the children and Henson at the small, rather shabby beach house out on Cape Cod, a house whose redwood shingles the salt and weather had faded to marvellous, silvery hue. The house was one of a cluster of houses that belonged to the Fenton family, some grander and kept in better trim, others with slightly sagging porches and old basket-work chairs. It was a good reflection for Charles on how each member of the family had come out of the 1929 crash, or how their wives' fortunes had fared. But beyond everything else, they were a family, visiting back and forth, enjoying both companionship and small feuds, the children learning the rough and tumble of a life lived among a swarming mass of cousins, children whose names Charles never did entirely sort out. Lloyd visited at weekends, and was grateful for Charles's presence as company for Nicole. To Charles the life had a beguiling simplicity. He read, sitting on the porch, walked the deserted beaches and sand dunes with Nicole. At one memorable time she managed to tell him what it had been like when she had walked the beaches of Maine with Anna, and how fiercely she had envied the privacy and privilege of the rich. Most of the Fentons were no longer rich, but they enjoyed the privileges that went with being long-established; they had bought empty acres of beach and dune-land when it had been cheap. There were few, in those depression years, who would have offered them anything for it now. Nicole, Charles could see, gloried in the isolation of the Cape. She walked on Fenton land, on Fenton beaches, and she never got over the seeming miracle of it.

She talked to him frankly about money. When she had reached twenty-one, she had come into control of what had been left to her by the Yorkshire mill-owner. It had been skilfully invested, and the capital had grown. 'We don't touch that,' she said. 'We want to spruce up the Cambridge house a bit, and then of course we're saving for the boys' educations. We'll want them to go to Groton and Harvard, like Lloyd—and I expect there'll be more kids ...' She spoke with the confidence of one who had borne her children with surprising ease, considering the slightness of her frame, and looked forward to more births. 'We'll probably have to buy a larger house in Cambridge. We'd like to stay there. It's nice being near the campus ...' Lloyd's practice as a neuro-surgeon was growing steadily, and he lectured at Harvard. So she made her plans with a wonderful sureness that she had at last found her proper place, and that life could only grow richer and fuller, friendships deepen, family matters more absorbing. She wanted nothing else. 'If I don't watch out, Uncle Charles,' she had said one day as they walked the beach in the early morning, 'I'll become fat and complacent and, I suppose, even dowdy!'

And Charles, looking at her, knowing that she wore her simple, rather inexpensive clothes with some undeniable chic which might have been learned in Paris, but was decidedly not Bostonian, had simply laughed.

That summer, when they had so much time together, when he had walked as he hadn't done for years, his face tanned by the sun and salt wind, and sailed with those Fentons still affluent enough to have boats, when even his bad leg had seemed to strengthen from the hard exercise of the sand dunes, and the stingingly-cold rush of the water as they walked the tide's edge, that summer Nicole had told him more things about her mother. 'The day I turned twenty-one Lloyd telephoned Fairfax & Osborne,' she had said. 'We hoped they might be holding a letter from Anna, that some message had been sent, but there was nothing. I honestly—Uncle Charles, I have to say it this way because I'm finished with all those lies and cover-ups, all that sort of thing that nearly let me miss having Lloyd—well, honestly I didn't know whether to be sorry or relieved. I didn't want to think she'd vanished for ever, and yet I didn't know how I'd feel about trying to get to know her. Anna was—well, she was a formidable sort of woman. There's no woman I've ever encountered who had so much self-discipline, such control over herself. I tried to remember exactly what it was like when we used to have those holidays together. Was it just because I was a kid and didn't understand her, that I felt slightly afraid?—well, not afraid

272

of *her*, but afraid of letting her down in some way. She was—is—a very special woman. I don't think I could ever measure up to her, or what she wanted me to be. Well, there was no message from her, Osborne & Fairfax had no address, but a week after my twenty-first birthday, the watch arrived——'

She had brought it with her to the Cape because she had meant to tell Charles this, had wanted to share it with him. 'There was a note in Anna's handwriting.' She held the slim gold pocket-watch with fob and chain reverently. 'We had the best jeweller in Boston examine it. He said it came from the workshops of Fabergé—the gold and enamel-work is typical. And look here, the inscription ... I had it translated ...' It was engraved within the lid in Russian characters. 'It says "To my dear friend Nicholas Mikhailovitch Tenishev in gratitude. Mikhail Ovrensky. 1907." That would have been the year my grandfather left Russia. Just imagine Prince Ovrensky giving him *this* when he was already bankrupt! It's ...' she closed the lid gently. 'It's very *Russian* somehow, isn't it? Making such a grand gesture. Making my grandfather a friend when he was only the music and French teacher.'

'I think we have a lot yet to learn about the Russians,' Charles said, attempting not to show her how much moved he had been by the sight of this obviously treasured object. 'What was in the note?' he asked.

'Almost nothing.' She recited it, its sparse, bare wording. '*It was your grandfather's. I would like your son to have it. I am glad you have returned to America. I hope you are happy. Love. Anna.*' Nicole had raised eyes that shone with tears to Charles. 'That was all. Not another word. Of course she had not been able to send it when Dan was born—that would have been breaking the agreement she made. But it came so soon after my birthday, and to the exact address, that we sensed that she knew everything about us. It sent Lloyd nearly wild that he couldn't trace her. The first money we spent from the income was on trying to find her. The watch had been posted in Chicago, at one of the central post offices. The agency pointed out that Chicago is one of the easiest cities in America to reach from anywhere. All sorts of railroads go there. She could have come from the South, the East or West Coasts, or she could just be living in Chicago itself. Well, they didn't find her. We advertised. The agency made up a list of every important paper in the States. I remembered that she always took the *Wall Street Journal* and we ran an ad every day for three months. They even got the list of mail subscribers but that didn't help much. We would have had to check up every one of them, and even then, still might not find her. You wouldn't think it was possible for someone just to disappear—especially someone who must have kept a pretty close check on me, however she did it. But we couldn't find her. Obviously she intended that we shouldn't find her. Since then, there's been nothing— nothing at all.'

And there had been no word from Anna Rainard in the years that followed. Charles, looking once again at Nicole's happily serene face, almost hoped there would not be. She was doing so well, this beloved girl of his, that he didn't want her life upset by the appearance from the past of a mother of whom she was half-afraid. He respected Lloyd's continued efforts to find Anna Rainard, not to attempt to drop her behind the screen of anonymity which Iris's father's will had erected, but still he hoped the efforts wouldn't be successful. Charles knew as much and as little about Russians as most Englishmen. He feared for the calm smile on Nicole's face if this unknown woman, of fearsome discipline and will, should reappear.

In 1938 he had visited Boston once again, spent as before most of the summer at the Cape with Nicole. This time he had been prodded by Lloyd's urging. 'She talks to you best of all, Sir Charles,' Lloyd had written. 'It's good for her to have a special friend. And the boys are growing up. They're a bit of a handful. I think it would be good for them to have a bit of military discipline out on the Cape this summer ...' Kind of him, Charles thought, to find reasons for his presence ... kind, and somehow typical, because there was an element of practicality in what he wrote. So Charles had gone, and the summer weeks had slipped into months, and the beginning of the New England autumn was on them before he took the steamer again from Boston. He felt vaguely ashamed of staying so long. But he couldn't drag himself away. He realized that never in his life before had he lived in such close proximity to people who were completely happy with each other. What a rare thing this marriage was—almost unique in his experience. He did not worry any more lest something should happen to cause it to flounder. By now he felt comfortably sure that nothing would ever drive a wedge between them. He had witnessed their small disagreements, and witnessed the way they resolved them. He thought that sometimes Nicole was too compliant, too ready to give in to Lloyd—but then Lloyd had never, so far as he could see, guided her badly, or wilfully acted to hurt or wound her. Nicole, in her marriage, had blossomed to a new kind of beauty, and Lloyd, Charles saw, made it clear by look and touch and gesture, that he couldn't have enough of her.

He returned to London and wished very much that he could have told Iris some of this. But he was not invited to talk, and he doubted, in any case, that she would have understood.

The only thing wrong with those visits was that he was lonelier than ever when he returned. But still, this must never be hinted at to Nicole. He looked again at the picture and went back to his letter '... *and I send you my dearest love and every possible wish that there will be many, and even happier returns of this day* ...' He paused again and thought of the Cambridge house, across the river from Boston. At this time of year the snow would be piled high on its old lawns, the walk and driveway would be shovelled clean. Perhaps guests were coming that evening for dinner—or perhaps Nicole and Lloyd were going to one of his brothers' houses for a celebration. The Fentons were a close lot, given to observing family occasions. The house that Sam lived in on Beacon Hill was still the gathering place for his brothers and his sister, regarded by them almost as belonging to them all because they had banded together to preserve it. It was part of Boston's history, that house, and Charles had noticed that those who helped Sam with its upkeep seemed to feel no jealousy about him being the one actually to inhabit it. It just happened that he was the oldest, and it had become his task and his responsibility to keep it as it had been in his father's time, and his grandfather's and great-grandfather's. Charles had learned that Americans could be just as conscious of their family background as any Englishman of long lineage; England had little to teach the Bostonians in that respect.

There was one other gift that the Fentons had given to Charles. It was the gift of the friendship he had formed with the Fentons of Fenton Field. It had begun during those few days when Lloyd and Nicole had waited to be married. Their calmness, their lack of fuss in the face of the storm that had broken in the gossip columns of the newspapers, the reporters who had appeared at their door and had been politely, firmly turned away, had aroused Charles's admiration and respect. Margaret Fenton's instinct for the feel of a lonely man had caused her to invite him to visit later, and she had pressed the invitation so that he was convinced that it was genuine. Since then he had visited several times a year, sharing to a degree the events of their lives. He had attended Judy's wedding to Gavin McLeod, he was godfather to one of Allan and Joan's sons, and to Judy's first child. Richard had finally married a totally unexpected girl, a shy, quiet girl, someone who had lived near by all her life, someone almost plain by comparison to the good looks of her husband. Charles guessed that Richard had once been in love with Nicole, and he had expected some girl quite as exotic in background to replace her. On the surface the marriage appeared to have worked. Richard had steadied as much as his temperament would ever allow him. He had been admitted to practice at the Bar and was making progress there, having that kind of presence which, allied to brains, makes an impact in the courtroom. During the week he lived in a flat in Middle Temple. On weekends he returned to his wife, Celia, at Potters, the place he had bought next to Fenton Field, and which his father and brother farmed for him. He continued to fly his own small aircraft. But for all the seeming placidity of his life, Charles sensed a certain restlessness which would never be assuaged, and he was not surprised one evening entering a restaurant with a party of Iris's guests to see Richard with an unknown young woman seated inconspicuously. Charles had been careful not to notice him.

Ross had followed Richard and Gavin McLeod to Cambridge, and was doing brilliantly in science. The English Fenton family seemed as close-knit as their American cousins, and instilled in Charles that same vague sense of longing. His life at Elgin Square as a puppet-host whose strings were pulled to Iris's bidding seemed to grow more useless and empty. He thought of rebellion—and knew he was too old for it. He had sold out, and with the millions of unemployed about him, he knew his rebellion would be futile. So he gave his services to a tiny centre in the East End that tried to care for homeless, jobless men, and he tried himself to be grateful for the warmth

276

and comfort of Elgin Square. He found poverty sordid and demeaning, and he knew he would not have the strength to stand it long. It was difficult, with the medals he had won and which were worn each Armistice Day, to admit that he was a coward, but he did that. And more and more the young woman in the photograph became the core of his life. He looked at it now and smiled wistfully, and wondered how soon he could decently visit again.

And still, as he looked at the calendar, he wondered if he would ever again make that journey. He had heard Chamberlain's 'peace in our time' speech, and he did not believe it was possible. A man called Hitler had arisen, and the shadow grew sharper and shorter.

II

A light snow had fallen that day, and a hard freeze on top of it had turned to a thin ice. Lloyd drove with the care and the swift skill that seemed inborn in every New Englander. They had lived with hard winters for a long time. On the way home he and Nicole had talked amiably about the dinner party given for Nicole on the eve of her birthday. Twenty-four of the family had been there. 'I wonder did Sam and Ginny make up the number for my birthday, or was that just how many the table would seat?' Nicole said idly. It didn't really matter. It had been a fine evening, the talk argumentative, the wine mellow as these New England aristocrats liked it. Everyone had gone off with a sense of satisfaction, and a renewed belief in the family unity.

They slid once or twice on the ice, but Lloyd corrected mechanically and without fuss or hurry; he waited though until they had turned into their own short driveway before he began to focus his thoughts on what he wanted to say to Nicole. The headbeams of the car briefly swept the front of the house. At the sight of it Nicole touched his arm. 'It really looks like home, doesn't it? Look, there's the light in Henson's room. You could bet, couldn't you, that she'd wait until she heard us come in? She's so terrified of wooden houses and what she calls "these monstrous furnaces, m'am." I don't think it's ever occurred to her to wonder how else we keep so warm all winter. That's something that firmly belongs in Jenkins's department. But if there wasn't hot bath water for Baby, we'd know all about it. How *English* she still is, Lloyd. So firmly a nanny...'

He slipped the car into the garage with a niceness of judgement that allowed for the ice. Nicole went out on her side, and through a door into the kitchen, which gave off the warm subdued smell of cooking, and the comfort of reassurance that everything in the silent household was ticking over as it should. She knew that above, Henson would have heard their arrival and have settled down to sleep; that tomorrow morning, early, would bring the arrival of Jenkins, the gardener and handyman, to tend the furnace and take out the rubbish; that Nan, the Negro cook, would serve an English breakfast for everyone; that Ellen, the daily cleaning woman, would put the house to rights. It had become such a smooth, well-ordered world. Nicole smiled softly as she went to poke up and add wood to the dying fire in the library. The old dog, MacGinty, lay there, and he indicated his pleasure at their return by briefly thumping his tail and falling back into a snoring sleep. And Lloyd was bringing two glasses of very old brandy, saved for special occasions. He put one into her hand as they stood before the fire.

'Here's to the return of all the good things, Nicky ...' They sipped, and then he bent and kissed her, not in a light salutation, but deeply, and she felt her lips open against his. There were many good things. Because she had never been absolutely sure that life was meant to be this way, a thought flickered at the back of her mind that perhaps it was all too good. Then she put the thought aside, or rather Lloyd did it for her. She didn't think of it any more as he kissed her.

'Would you like a summer in England, Nicky?' he said casually after they had sipped the brandy again.

'A summer in England? Could we manage it? Could we afford it? What about——'

He sank down into one of the long shabby chintz-covered chairs that made the place look so much like an English house. 'A letter today. They'd like me to do a few lectures at Cambridge. I've ... I've been in correspondence with Wygate—you remember him, my senior consultant at St Giles's? Well, we've been trying a new technique over here that he'd rather like demonstrated. I'm to do a couple of lectures with slides, and then, if the appropriate case turns up at St Giles's, actually to operate. Naturally, I'd be there to learn what I could myself ...'

'*You're* going to demonstrate to Wygate!' Nicole turned her head sharply away from the fire to look at him. 'You know, Lloyd, I'm so snug and complacent these days, I hardly ever bother to think about what you're doing professionally. I have people tell me what a genius I'm married to, and I always smile and say I always knew it. But I just don't *realize* ... Could we really go? Could the practice afford it? What about the classes at Harvard ...?'

'Well, Nicky, with a surgeon, if you can't get one man, you just take another. The practice could stand it as far as being away a few months. And they could reschedule the last lectures at Harvard so that I could make the last weeks of term at Cambridge ... After all, they like their men to have overseas experience ... overseas honours, I suppose you might call it.'

The brandy moved wildly in her glass as she waved it. 'Let's go ...' And then her face clouded. 'But how? Where do we stay? I can hardly trail the kids up to Cambridge and keep them quiet in a hotel ... and then back to London ... They're not old enough to do any sight-seeing.'

'Fenton Field,' he said. 'Aunt Margaret's just waiting for us all. You can park the kids there with Henson, and come with me to Cambridge and London. A chance to see Judy ... and Sir Charles ... and ... and everyone ...' he finished lamely.

She sighed. 'No, I suppose Aunt Iris *wouldn't* see me. But, if I were actually in London, who knows how she might change? She might want to see the boys ...'

'She might. Her grand-nephews ...' Lloyd himself didn't believe Iris Gowing's rigid attitude would change in the least, but he would never say so to Nicole. Leave the hope as long as Nicole wanted to keep it. She was leaning towards him.

'Shall I write to Aunt Margaret then, and ask if that would be all right? A whole summer ... is it asking too much? But I'd *love* to go.' He thought she looked like an Italian Renaissance painting in her gown of red velvet, the garnets he had given her for her birthday gleaming darkly in the firelight, her hair coiled about her head; she was beautiful now, he thought, and she would be beautiful when she was sixty. She now possessed a degree of confidence and charm that had been missing in the rather waif-like beauty of the young girl he had married. She was adding anxiously, 'But it'll cost an awful lot, won't it, for us all to go ...?'

'Nicky ... Nicky ...' He laughed and shook his head. 'You know things aren't all that tough with me. I'm not doing too badly. And you ... you're *rich* by most people's standards. Relax. You're getting to be too much of a proper Bostonian, afraid even to spend the interest on the income.'

She laughed also. 'I know ... I know.' Her eyes went lovingly over the big shabby room with its books and worn carpet. 'But perhaps I've always been that way. I never did like show ... Aunt Iris's sort of show. I keep thinking about what the boys will need in the future——'

'Stop thinking of them, Nicky. There'll be plenty. They're not going to be coddled. They'll get an education. The best there is. And then they'll be thrown out into the world to find their own way. The Fentons have always done that. And kids of yours are always going to be tough, even if they weren't Fentons as well.'

She nodded. 'I suppose I grew up frightened of money ... frightened of spending it. It was Anna, of course. To her it made all the difference. It was so hard to come by, so when it was spent, you thought about how you spent it. There always had to be value for money. I tried very hard to give her value ... give her a return.' Her voice tightened. 'Lloyd, do you suppose she *knows*? The way the watch came here ... I'd like to show her this house. I'd love her to see her grandchildren. I'd like her to meet the Fentons. Yes ... I think she'd consider all this value for money. If only I could be sure she *knew* ...'

'I have a feeling she does. Someone like your mother ... so thorough ... efficient. I'll bet she knows more than you'd believe. I'll bet she knows which charities you've begun to work for. I'll bet she knows about the chamber music group. She'd like things like that. That was what she meant you to do. But, damn it, Nicky, it makes me mad as hell that *I* haven't met her. A woman like that ... she'd be more than a match for any of the *grande dames* of Boston, and to do them justice, I'll bet the old girls would recognize it too. You know something, Nicky? Sometimes when I pass a really striking-looking woman—the way I imagine your mother looks—I have the oddest sensation that maybe that's Anna. I have the feeling that maybe she's even been here and seen this house, seen you come and go, seen the kids. It's a kind of creepy sensation. And yet I'd never dare go and take a strange woman by the arm and say "Are you Anna Rainard?" You know, Nicky, I'd be awfully *satisfied* if I could meet your mother. She must be one hell of a woman.'

The smile that quietly touched Nicole's lips was a gesture of gratitude. Only this man, this beloved man, could have so embraced her mother, made her a part of this family. Because he loved her, Nicole, he managed to reach out to Anna, that distant figure. He made her mother admirable as well as strong. For an instant she thought she saw Anna through Lloyd's eyes, and dimly another personality emerged. She was not only the mother whom Nicole had respected and obeyed, but transformed almost into a person of heroic proportions. In those seconds Nicole's half-fear of her mother began to alter; she perceived strength, but not dominance. She breathed deeply, and her sense of what she had inherited was right and good.

Slowly she got to her feet. 'Perhaps one day we will meet her, Lloyd. We'll keep on trying ... Well, now, since it's my birthday, then I'm going to propose a toast. Just between us two. To Anna ... to absent friends ...'

He rose and came to stand beside her. 'To Anna ... to absent friends.' He bent and kissed her. 'And to present lovers ...'

Afterwards, Henson, half-dozing, heard the laughter on the stairs, the stifled laughter, as if between children. And then quite distinctly she heard Dr Fenton's voice. 'You know ... you're getting far too big and heavy for me to carry you to bed any more ...'

Henson knew she hadn't been meant to hear, but she heard most things. She nodded a kind of agreement, stretched in the warmth of her bed, and turned over and went to sleep.

III

The West Coast of America is three hours in time behind the East Coast, so it was late afternoon in Los Angeles when Nicole and Lloyd were sitting down to dinner with the Fentons, and Anna was driving towards MIKE'S NEW AND USED CARS on Wilshire Boulevard. She was very conscious that it was the eve of Nicole's birthday. Occasionally she had been tempted to lift the telephone and place a call to that house in Cambridge,

Massachusetts. But she never did. Sending the watch to her oldest grandchild had been her sole gesture. She had not been able to bear the thought that it might, if she died, pass into the hands of a stranger. There would be one man in Boston, her grandson, who would carry a watch inscribed in Russian characters. Anna found contentment in the thought.

She drove towards Mike's with an unusual sense of gaiety. As she recognized it, she shrugged and said to herself, 'Why not?' It surely was still an exciting event to go and buy the first new car of one's life. Since she had bought the first used Ford from Mike's, she had had two others. Both of them had been old, and both of them had stood their usage as well as anyone could ask of them. Whenever there had been difficulties, she had taken the car back to Mike's, and they had managed to find a spare part, a replacement, and the car would go smoothly along until the next bit wore out. They had come to recognize her at Mike's and they always said, 'Could you just wait, Mrs Maynard, until the Boss has a minute? He'd sure like to take care of it himself. Nobody in L.A.'s got the ear for an engine he has ...'

The years during which she had put so much mileage on the old Fords had not been easy ones, but their challenge had stimulated her. At the time Nicole had been settling into the house in Cambridge on the other side of the continent, Anna had been forced to take full charge of Frank Hayward's business. She could still remember that frightening day when she had returned to the little office, after taking a client to see a house in Hollywood, to find Frank Hayward slumped face down on his desk, his uneven breathing hard and gasping. He had looked at her from the agony of a coronary attack, and had not been able to speak. She had dialled swiftly, and the ambulance came ten minutes later. He had survived that night while Anna sat with his wife in the waiting-room at the hospital, but he had never returned to the office. Every day Anna would telephone his wife, and then, when he was stronger, she spoke to Frank himself to give details of the day's business, if there had been any. Every week she went to the Hayward's house in Westwood and took the money—what was left of it after the expenses of the business had been paid, and her own salary deducted. Frank Hayward insisted that she take commission on all sales. 'Hell, Anne, if it weren't for you, there'd *be* no business ... When I'm better ...' But he never did get better, and one morning a weeping Mrs Hayward had telephoned the news that he was dead.

Afterwards, when the funeral was over, Anna had gone to Mrs Hayward, offered a down-payment on the small building from which Frank had run his business, and offered a share in the proceeds of the business itself for the goodwill. This last, she knew, was not a sensible business gesture, but Frank Hayward had taught her much, and had been a base on which to build. Mrs Hayward surprised her by refusing. 'I can't take any money for the goodwill of the business, Mrs Maynard. Frank was right when he said there wouldn't have been any business these last two years if you hadn't carried it. You've earned whatever you can make of it. I'd be glad to have the building taken off my hands, though. Glad of the money, though Frank left a good insurance policy ... He used to joke he was richer dead than alive.' She had shrugged bleakly. 'I'd rather have him alive.' They settled the details swiftly between them. Mrs Hayward shook her head, wonderingly. 'I don't know how you'll manage these payments. It's a lot for a woman to take on by herself ... Well, good luck.'

Anna had kept Frank Hayward's name on the door of the office because she judged that people preferred to do business with a man, hired a young girl to answer the telephone, and set out to do business for herself. Sometimes a month would pass without a single sale, and then there would be a small rash of them. She drove all over Los Angeles, watching for the sort of properties that clients asked for, persuading people that they might turn a profit by selling. She learned the macabre business of watching death notices, and getting in touch with the relatives to see if the house would now be for sale. She made herself known among the executives of the movie industry, watching for those who were taking big increases in salary, and finding a more expensive house for them before they knew they wanted it. Hers was the name very often mentioned by the same executives when a newcomer arrived from the East to take a position, and began to look about for somewhere to live. She concentrated with a single-mindedness which some people thought unattractive and unfeminine. But they did business with her because she seemed to know exactly what sort of property they required, and she didn't waste their time by

283

urging them to view what wasn't right for them. She was at the office early in the morning, and she stayed after it closed. This was when she did her paperwork, kept the account books, did the routine chores of the office. The regular office hours she kept free to be able to respond immediately to any enquiry, to show a client a property at a moment's notice. She had long ago learned that in the real estate business any delay could be the death of a sale. She had developed a sixth sense about the moment when a client had come almost to regard the desired property as his, and the moment when the seller might be ready to lower the price just the amount that would close the deal. She kept the small wooden office building painted and trim, its interior immaculate, kept its window-boxes planted with ivy and geraniums. Its walls were lined with filing cabinets and very large-scale maps of Los Angeles. She could show a client exactly where the house she wanted him to view was located in relation to whatever else was important to him in the city; she knew the people at various banks who might be helpful with mortgage money; she even knew the names of reliable furniture moving companies.

There were less opportunities now for the long drives to the desert. Saturday was a good day for people to view houses, and she held herself available. Sunday had to be used to catch up on reading—the *Wall Street Journal*, the stock market reports. Her heart had ached over the advertisement, run for three months after Nicole's twenty-first birthday, asking Anna Rainard to contact her. She had long ago decided that she would stay out of Nicole's life, and the decision had been final. She no more wanted to become involved in the life of the Boston ruling families than she wanted to return to what she had found so humiliating among the English. She liked her life as it was, she liked her work, and her independence. She didn't want to know what had happened between Nicole and David Ashleigh, or perhaps even more, she did not want to know what might have taken place between Nicole and John Manstone. The past was very much the past. Her daughter was a stranger, though a fascinating stranger. Anna wanted it left that way. She had achieved a kind of peace. She was almost forty-seven.

Although she had maintained her silence, she had, to a large degree, satisfied her curiosity. A small clipping from a Boston paper had told her that Dr Lloyd Fenton was to address a conference of neurologists and neurosurgeons in Los Angeles. That had been in the fall of last year. The conference had been held at the Roosevelt Hotel. Anna had booked in there for two nights, giving an address in San Francisco. It hadn't been difficult to slip into the ballroom where the lectures were held because it was assumed that no one but medical people would have the faintest interest in the rather obscure topics lectured on and discussed. She had seen her son-in-law, Lloyd Fenton, before she had seen Nicole. He was older than she had expected, perhaps ten years older than Nicole, but among the medical fraternity he was still a very young man. She thought his manner, as he had delivered his lecture, gave perfect recognition of his place in that world. Quiet, but confident, deferring to work done by predecessors even when he was disagreeing with their findings, or explaining advances on them. He was a striking-looking man, rather than handsome, with features so distinct that he stood out from the other men on the platform. Later, with the lecture over, she had watched the doctors stream out, and among the few women, she had seen Nicole. She stood at Lloyd's side as he talked with a small group which had gathered about him, and Anna saw the same transformation of the face which had so impressed Charles Gowing. The young woman who stood there, her face upturned towards her husband's as he talked, was a woman wholly and utterly possessed by the love that was plain for everyone to see. She had about her a bright, glowing quality which had never been present in the schoolgirl Anna remembered. From behind the dark glasses, which with the large-brimmed hat was Anna's camouflage should Nicole chance to see her, she studied the scene until the room began to empty. She waited in the lobby to see them walk through. They went in the direction of the swimming pool. Anna followed and found herself a table far enough away from them that she could not overhear their conversation, but equally its distance lent protection from a chance look from Nicole. But Nicole sat sideways to her, and most of her attention was given to the two small dark-haired boys who were already waiting there, in the charge of a nurse—a nurse who had to be English if one could judge by the severity of the grey, white-collared dress she wore, the grey felt hat pulled firmly down on the severely dressed hair. Two other doctors had come to the lunch table with them, so there was no reason why Nicole's attention should wander. Anna ordered herself a drink, and took a long time sipping it and looking over the menu at the small group, before ordering a hamburger salad. She noticed Nicole had the same thing. Nicole's attention seemed equally divided between helping the nurse with the children, and listening to what passed between the doctors. The younger child had to be held in Nicole's lap, the older was just old enough to keep the nurse busy. They were healthy-looking, rather beautiful little boys, Anna thought. She was surprised to find that it was rather difficult to swallow the food against the lump which had so unexpectedly risen in her throat. She was also surprised to find that she had no desire to go over, to hold and kiss these children who were her grandchildren. She was just content that they were there, they existed, they were loved. Their very presence here was proof of that. They were not children who would be left behind with nurses and servants. Nicole, she thought, had developed a stronger maternal streak than she would ever have believed possible in that tight-faced schoolgirl who had made no friends. But noticing how Nicole seemed to follow every word and gesture of Lloyd's, she decided that the father, in this case, would always come first. As Anna sat over her cooling coffee, the group finished lunch, the children were taken away by the nurse and Nicole, the baby asleep in Nicole's arms; the three doctors drifted back to the conference rooms.

That night Anna sat in the lobby, a newspaper as her shield, until Nicole and Lloyd emerged from the elevator. They were dressed for the formal dinner of the conference. Unexpectedly, Anna felt a sudden, enormous pride in them, both of them. She had no more than that one glimpse, but it satisfied her deeply. That decision taken long ago on the Staten Island ferry was vindicated. She had not allowed the sense of hurt or anger against that dying man in Yorkshire to stand in the way of the development of this young woman. She wanted no more reward than what she witnessed at that moment, and she wanted no thanks.

The next morning she left the hotel early. She didn't know how much longer the Fentons were staying, but she would not risk Nicole's discovery of her. Even in Los Angeles one could not spend a week sitting around a hotel in dark glasses and a face-shielding hat. The deep joyous barking of Mike and the grin from the Japanese gardener welcomed her back to the house in Laurel Canyon. She surveyed her little world with a sense of fulfilment and pleasure. There was no need to wonder any more about Nicole. Now she knew. She could concentrate on what was at hand. It didn't occur to her, even after seeing the closeness between Nicole and Lloyd, to feel a sense of loneliness for herself. Long ago she had learned the peculiar strength of self-sufficiency; loneliness was a useless luxury she could never afford to indulge. After that one sight of Nicole and her grandchildren, she had settled back into her life of work and application to the things that interested her, and she had been conscious of missing nothing.

Apart from the successes which came her way in the selling of houses, she had tasted one major success, and the pleasure of it, and the profit from it added to her sense of excitement in going this evening to pick up the first new car of her life. One of the early purchases she had made soon after coming to Los Angeles had been a parcel of fifteen acres out at Culver City. She had done this after careful study of the area, noting the railway line that ran there, and after she had had her first tour of the Warner Brothers and Metro-Goldwyn-Mayer Studios in downtown Hollywood. Films were what had put Los Angeles on the map; they poured out of the major studios and still were not enough to satisfy the hunger of the huge audience around the world, the people demanding this new medium of escape from the drabness of the depression years. Anna had noted the big sound stages of the studios, and had then realized that the real shooting of the endless Westerns the public craved was actually done on location, out on the arid hills that thrust through the sprawl of the city. From dealing so often with executives from the film companies, she heard bits of gossip, heard it from the people in the real estate business itself. When she bought the fifteen acres at Culver City, she did it with no sure knowledge that it would ever pay off, but it had been so cheap that she knew, in time, it would yield some return. It had been what the people of California called 'bean fields', acreage worked by the industrious Japanese. Soon after she bought, MGM began to construct permanent stage settings on what they called their 'back-lot'. For a long time no one had needed her bean fields except the Japanese who worked the adjoining land, and who rented it from her for a small payment. Then MGM had wanted to expand as the volume of movies became greater. It hadn't been too difficult to persuade the Japanese to move their gardens a few miles farther away, but Mrs Anne Maynard was not a Japanese, and she wouldn't budge. She felt the pressure once or twice when the banks, prodded by the film-makers, had tried to foreclose the mortgage they held on one of her other properties, but it had always been possible, in one way or another, to increase a mortgage with another bank, and raise the money to buy her way out. Finally, with a shrug, the film men had offered her twenty thousand dollars. She had accepted it without revealing either her sense of relief or excitement. It had been touch and go, and several times her nerve had almost broken as she realized how thinly spread was her small reserve of capital. No one could go on juggling mortgages for ever. But she had held out, and won, and her sense of triumph was something she could almost not contain. To her this money had a kind of sweetness that she had never associated with the money which had come from the will of the Yorkshire mill-owner. This was her own, earned by her own forethought, patience and willingness to take a risk. The money itself, she realized then, was not very important to her; its importance lay in the fact that it provided her with more capital with which to take more risks. The seed of the long-term gambler had been growing in Anna almost without her being aware of it. Money was something to be used, not hoarded. Because she read the newspaper carefully, because she sensed what would happen in Europe, and through the world, when a maniacal Hitler could no longer be restrained, because she believed that, despite the policy of isolationism which America officially espoused, she would eventually have to go to war, Anna began to invest some of the newly won money in small properties close to the great Naval Base at San Diego down the coast from Los Angeles. They were cheap little wooden houses, some were stores; the rents they yielded were small. But if the Naval Base was suddenly forced to operate at full capacity, the industries it required to service it, the people who would find themselves needing to live near it, would send the value of her purchases skyrocketing. It did not shock Anna that she was gambling on the fact that war would come. There was a kind of fatalism she faintly realized as being a Russian trait which told her that war would come, no matter what was said in the Senate of the United States. The last war had never really been finished.

288

With these decisions taken, she permitted herself to relax a little. She had a coat of paint put on the little house in Laurel Canyon, and she went to confer with Mike about ordering a new Ford car, for the first time, a *new* Ford. She had gone to Mike, and he had treated her order with the respect he would have given to the most expensive model that Detroit turned out. When asked about her choice of colour, she had automatically said 'black', and Mike's nose had wrinkled slightly in disapproval. 'Mrs Maynard, aren't you tired of all those black cars you've had?—After all, they're only old painted-over jobs. Now with the *new* one, you can have almost any colour you want. For a lady like you I see a . . . a . . .' He had hesitated, closing his eyes as if he were seeing some sort of vision. 'For a lady like you I see a blue—their sapphire colour, with dark-blue upholstery.' He had opened his eyes and smiled at her. 'It costs just the same as black and besides . . . it *looks* like you. Red's too flashy. That yellow-coloured one, that's for kids. And the white one's for movie people. Yes, the sapphire is the one for you. I think I know a dealer over in Santa Monica who might have one in that colour. I could have it brought over tomorrow. If you don't like it . . . well, we could always find you something different. It might have a few extras on it, but nothing that would run you into any big money. You don't want an expensive job, do you, Mrs Maynard? No—I wouldn't have thought so. Just something nice and easy to drive around in that won't start to rattle after ten thousand miles . . .' While he talked he had been dialling a number, and then he spoke rapidly. He nodded to her across the phone. 'Have it for you tomorrow, Mrs Maynard. Can you leave it till late in the afternoon? I'll drive it back myself. I don't want to trust one of the kids with a new car . . .'

'You make it sound like . . .' She couldn't think of a car grand enough for the concern he was showing.

'Like a Rolls-Royce or a Daimler?' he said. 'When a person buys a new car, it *is* a Rolls.' Then he shook his head. 'But I don't give a damn about Rolls, or any of that sort of thing. America's being built on Fords, and I'm going all the way with them. America lives on wheels, Mrs Maynard, and I aim to sell quite a few of them . . .'

The sapphire-blue Ford was waiting outside the showroom. The location as well as the size of MIKE's NEW AND USED

CARS had altered since the first time she had gone there. It had moved several blocks farther along Wilshire to a lot about twice the size of the first one. The showroom was large and plate-glassed, and its shining floor reflected the polish on the new cars. There was a new workshop for repairs, the two salesmen wore neat jackets and ties, the two mechanics wore navy overalls with 'MIKE'S' in scarlet across their backs. Only the boss seemed unchanged. Anna wondered if he ever bought a new pair of overalls. With a kind of pride that Anna would have thought belonged to a younger man, he displayed the new car to her. 'You have to road-test it, Mrs Maynard. Can I come along?' He had carefully draped a cloth over the passenger seat so that his overalls would not soil the new upholstery, and had held open the door to the driver's seat for her. 'She's still a bit stiff in the gears, but if you break her in real nice and gently, she'll work like a good horse for you. Cars are a bit like horses . . . Feed them, treat them well, they'll give it all back to you in service . . .' He had talked more as they drove, mixing his metaphors between cars and horses in a crazy fashion, obviously loving both of them. She wanted to ask him when he had come to know horses, but she was too busy concentrating on sliding in the gears with a smoothness that would win his approval. He suddenly stopped talking and sat silent for a time. Then he spoke, 'You're a real sweet driver, you know that, Mrs Maynard? Aren't too many women drive like you do. Not too many men either, come to think of it. Everyone seems to go for snatching and grabbing at the gears, and jamming on the brakes. Americans have a word I thought was kinda funny when I first came here, until I understood what they meant by it. You're a class driver, Mrs Maynard. Yes, ma'am . . . a class driver. Well, I guess you've got the feel of her now. Do you still want to buy her?'

'Yes, Mike,' she said happily. The unexpected compliment had pleased her to a degree she hadn't thought possible. In the darkness she smiled to herself and swung the car back towards Wilshire and Mike's lot. They didn't talk on the way back, and she was conscious suddenly of how little she knew about this man with whom she had now done business for years. She didn't know if he had a wife and children, or a dog, or where he lived; he had talked to her about the inside and the outside of cars, and now he talked about horses. In the dimness she saw his hand go without fear to stroke the head of Mike, her dog, who, with no regard for the new upholstery, had placed himself on the back seat. The lights of MIKE'S appeared on Wilshire, and she turned smoothly into the parking area.

'We'll go and sign things up,' she said.

She was paying cash, so it was an easy transaction, but it took time to fill up the guarantee form, and make out the insurance certificate. While Mike did this, she made out her cheque, and then she sat and watched him as he swiftly filled out the blank spaces on the form. He had become more grizzled in these few years, but his hair still sprang back from his forehead full and thick. Long hours in the drying Californian sun showed in the seams of his deeply tanned neck and face, the lines beneath his eyes. His eyes, she noticed for the first time, were an intensely dark brown, close to black. And yet he hadn't the features of any of the Italians she came across. She realized that this was the first time she had ever sat down with him in the neat office off the showroom. Always before, when she had bought a car, or come to pay for some repair, once Mike had seen the car was in proper working order, she had been dealt with by one of the salesmen, as if Mike's time away from one of his beloved engines was too precious to be spent at a desk. But now the place was closed, the salesmen gone, only the lights blazed in the showroom to tempt those who might pass in the darkness. She watched the big, work-seamed hands, with the grease embedded almost beyond cleaning, as they worked with the pen. But he did make efforts to clean his nails. After the careful, clearly readable script in which he filled in the details, he signed his name with a swift flourish, and then stamped his name and the address of the dealership from a red rubber stamp. He turned it around and passed it across to her. 'There you are, Mrs Maynard ... if you'll just sign there, where I've put the cross ...'

She never signed anything without reading it all, and she was about to explain this, and ask his patience when her eyes went to his almost illegible signature, and the name stamped clearly beneath. Michael Ovrensky ... *Ovrensky*. She felt a swift coldness in her whole body, and she shivered. Beside her the dog was aware of it, and put his head on her knee.

'Ovrensky?' she said. 'Your name is Ovrensky?'

'Sure ... why——?' Then he stopped. 'Something the matter,

Mrs Maynard? You don't look well.'

'You come from Russia?'

He nodded. 'From ...'

She whispered the name 'Beryozovaya Polyana. A place called Beryozovaya Polyana. Quite close to Tula. Your father was Prince Michael Ovrensky.'

He nodded slowly. 'Yes ...'

Her voice sank even lower so that he had to lean across the desk to hear her words. 'Mikhail ... *Mikhail Mikhailovitch*. It is I ... Anna Nikolayevna Tenishevna. You remember my father, Nicholas Tenishev? ... and my mother, Katerina Andreyevna? ... speaking French with you, teaching your sisters the piano ... you remember?'

He got to his feet. 'Anna Nikolayevna ... we cried when you left ... I remember we cried. And Papa's estates were all gone, and even some of the ponies sold. *Anna Nikolayevna ...*'

They laughed and wept and embraced as they had done when they were children. The words tumbled out. Some half-forgotten Russian words came to lips that had not used them for so many years. The unsigned contract and the unsigned cheque lay on Mike's desk forgotten as they went out into the parking lot. Anna trembled so much that she crashed the gears of the new Ford sickeningly so many times on that drive up to the house in Laurel Canyon, with the lights of Mike's car following steadily behind.

They were still sitting by the fire in the small wooden house when the dawn spiked the eastern ridge of the canyon. They had drunk vodka and wine, and eaten steak, but eating had been a mechanical thing, something each had done while the other talked. The ageing dog lay between them, his paws and head on the hearthstones, and occasionally looked at Anna as if he wondered why, after all these years of quietness and near solitude, this outsider should have caused the excitement, the talk, the occasional tears that still came to her eyes. The dog was bewildered by the tears because the voice was the one Anna used when she was her happiest, so often the voice reserved for him alone. And yet he did not resent the stranger. The dog sensed Anna's contentment along with her excitement; a strange peace had come to the house along with this unending babble of voices, jumbled with odd sounds he had never heard before. So while they sat and toasted each other and other people whose names the dog did not know, and filled the glasses again and again, the dog dozed. He was dozing when they fell into exhausted silence as the first day of March dawned.

There had been much to tell. It came in a disorganized fashion, trying to fill the gap of the years. 'Andrey died at the front before the Bolsheviks took over. Vasily was at Tsarskoe Selo guarding the Tsarina when the Tsar abdicated ... afterward he was killed in the fighting. Alexis must have gone the same way. We never knew. I was the youngest ... you remember I was the youngest, Anna Nikolayevna?' The whole of the great surge of the Russian Revolution was encompassed in these brief personal histories.

'I remember. You are two years younger than I, Mikhail ...'

'I fought a little, scared to death all the time. It was a bitter time. We were all so hungry. And then word came to me that my father had died, and I found my way back to Beryozovaya Polyana. They had burned the house. My mother and Olga and Marya were still there, living in a hut, and starving by inches. Tatiana Fedorovna had a few jewels left, enough, when they were pawned, to get us to Paris. I had a dozen jobs in Paris, and the girls tried to do dressmaking. Nothing was very successful. I borrowed money from Dmitry Alexandrovitch for a passage for us all to America. I felt if we could get here, that working would have some point. But my mother ... she wouldn't leave. Paris was full of Russian *émigrés*, all borrowing off one another. She spoke French but no English. She was frightened of America. She clung to Paris because of all the old friends there. It was like some suburb of St Petersburg. In the end I went alone. Olga married—married quite well. Into a Bordeaux wine family. Marya finally opened her own dress shop ... very chic, expensive, she said. It failed. She and my mother lived on what I sent from New York. And then my mother died. No real illness ... just pining for things as they used to be. Marya became a housekeeper to an old man in Brussels. Eventually she married him, and died before he did. They weren't good transplants, the women of our family, Anna. They didn't take to foreign soil. Now you ...'

By this time he knew her story. She had broken the silence that had not been breached since the night she had talked to Nicole in Lucky Nolan's. Every stage of the journey from the

Conservatoire in Paris, every part of the agony of her love for John Manstone, the humiliation of her leaving England, the meeting with the young Stephen, Nicole's father, had been told. Without faltering she told him about Lucky Nolan, and she told him what she did when the will of Stephen Rainard's father had laid its strictures on her. From the place where she kept it locked in her desk, she brought out the old photo of Nicole from the *Tatler*, and the latest, published in a Boston newspaper, of Mrs Lloyd Fenton on the committee of a fund-raising dinner for the pension fund of the members of the Boston Symphony. She told him about the desert acres, and the hard work at the little white-painted building that still bore Frank Hayward's name.

'Aren't you lonely?' he said.

'Never ...' And then she stopped. 'I've never been lonely until I walked into this house with you, Mikhail Mikhailo-vitch ...'

She knew now about the wife who had divorced him. 'I suppose I bored her, Anna. I was always working ... working late at night to fix cars. There wasn't much money in the beginning. I didn't understand Americans. She looked pretty to me ... pretty and blonde. She was always playing the radio. She once had a part in the movies ... that was before the talkies came in. She never forgot it. She used to say if she hadn't married me she would have been a famous star. From the moment our little girl was born, *she* was going to be a movie star. By the time she could walk, she was learning to dance. It ... it sickened me. I just fixed cars. More and more I fixed cars. Machines were something I could understand. Machines and horses. I had a job for a year on a cattle ranch in Montana, and then I went ... this was before I was married, you understand? ... I went to Nevada, and then to Salinas. I learned about machinery. I love machinery, Anna. It's hard to say. I love it the way I love horses. I was commissioned in a cavalry regiment, Anna Niko-layevna. It's very different, but it interests me the same way. But Americans don't know about horses. They've forgotten. Auto-mobiles interest Americans. I don't remember any machines at Beryozovaya Polyana. There were so many workers. Who needed machines? Well——' He stopped to fill their glasses once more. He stopped to walk around the room, touching the shelves of books in Russian, the two icons, the samovar. 'So she

—my wife—found a man in the movie industry. I don't know what he promised her—how could I know? I didn't promise her anything. But our little girl ... she'll grow up one of those little kewpie dolls—maybe she'll look like Shirley Temple. I don't understand ... I remember the children in Russia. They were probably hungry, and I didn't notice it. It's all past now. Now they say no one in Russia is hungry. I wonder how that can be if there are still people hungry in America. Do you understand that, Anna Nikolayevna?

'No—I have never understood that, Mikhail.' She didn't want to talk about reading the *Wall Street Journal* because all of her reading of it had never made her understand this simple fact.

'So——' Mikhail gestured. 'So now she is married to the man who works with the movies. Maybe my little daughter will be a movie star. I hope not. She is very pretty, my little daughter, but I hardly ever see her. Her mother doesn't like my greasy hands ...' He spread them before her, and then shrugged.

Suddenly she reached out with a gesture she had thought long dead, something that perhaps died back there when they had all said their tearful farewells at Beryozovaya Polyana. She took his work-hardened, grease-stained hands in hers. Her own had always been perfectly kept, kept soft and pliant for the piano, which she now never played. The hands fitted together. 'You always have had beautiful hands, Mikhail Mikhailovitch. Clever, useful, skilful hands ... Beautiful hands ...'

Two weeks later Prince Mikhail Mikhailovitch Ovrensky and Anna Nikolayevna Tenishevna were married in a civil ceremony, and later, because suddenly it seemed to matter to them both, they were married according to the rites of the Russian Orthodox Church.

CHAPTER 2

I

Nicole wondered if all her most abiding impressions of England were somehow to be of times in the afternoon, times of mellow sun, and flowers, and the sound of birds. She remembered Elgin Square in the afternoons, she remembered the bitter-sweet afternoon in May when they had all sat in the orchard at Fenton Field, and had seemed so impossibly young and innocent; she remembered the languorous afternoons of that August at Lynmara, the afternoons when she had learned to love the house, and wished she could have loved David Ashleigh also. This was yet another afternoon, and they were again at Fenton Field, with the rays of the September afternoon sun already seeming to hold in them the hint of autumn. They were all here, the same people, and a few others. But they sat, not in the orchard, but in the drawing-room. There was little conversation among them, and when they did talk, the talk was of war.

She looked around the familiar faces, only slightly altered by the years that had passed. There was Judy and Gavin, Gavin half-scowling, or seeming to, and Judy smiling still. There was Richard, restless, leaving his chair often to pace the room, and always followed by the gaze of his wife, Celia, as if she did not quite trust his presence, as if he might leave at any time. Nicole found herself sorry for this almost plain little mouse of a girl that Richard had married; she was so much in love, and Richard seemed so incredibly indifferent to the fact. Joan, Allan's wife was there; she was seated at a secretaire copying recipes from a tattered book into a new, well-bound one. She looked around at Margaret Fenton, her mother-in-law. 'I wonder how severe the rationing will be? I mean, is it any use writing up something that starts "Take nine eggs ..."?'

Margaret raised her head from the big garden book she was studying. Nicole recognized it as Margaret's own personal record of all that had been done and planted at Fenton Field since she had come there as a bride. She removed her glasses and shook her head; there was a close rapport between herself and Allan's wife that was missing in her relationship with Celia. Perhaps Celia's own nervous impression of a sense of impermanence was responsible, her own shrinking into the background. Margaret said, 'Impossible to say, isn't it ...? I mean, if we've suddenly got to start to feed ourselves. We don't produce enough food for ourselves in England, that's certain. I was just trying to calculate where would be the best place for the new vegetable garden. The south lawn I expect ... luckily I ordered the wire and stakes long ago. But we'll have to start digging at once, or nothing will go in this autumn ...'

'The south lawn!' Nicole said. 'You *can't* dig up the south lawn, Aunt Margaret!'

Gavin chuckled as if he enjoyed her naïvety. 'What—you're thinking of that old English joke about what it takes to make a good lawn? A bit of seed and four hundred years of rolling it? Well, we'll be digging up quite a few lawns, Nicole, before we're through.'

Nicole looked at him with distaste. He seemed almost to be amused by the situation, as if he took some macabre satisfaction in being able to say 'I told you so,' though he had never actually said it. He had prophesied war long ago; he had disturbed that peaceful afternoon of her memory by his disquieting forecast, but then so had Richard, in a dramatic and practical way. That, Nicole remembered, was the afternoon he had announced he was learning to fly. He had been a member of the Air Force Reserve for the last two years. He was ready, and it almost seemed that he *wanted* to get started, and his wife's eyes were terrible to look at.

Finally Nicole looked at Lloyd and found no comfort there. His expression was unreadable; he seemed lost in a world of his own thoughts, and she felt excluded, shut out. Nicole felt her sense of irritation and grievance rise as she stared at him and he did not respond. Oh, God, she thought, what was the matter with him? Why were they still here, at this side of the Atlantic, when they should now be settled back into the house in Boston, Lloyd picking up the threads of his practice, getting his lecture schedule for the fall settled? The fall semester was about to begin at Harvard, and still they lingered over here, seeing out the end of an English summer.

Nicole was coldly conscious that they might be seeing out the end of a world that might never be refashioned again. Last year Austria had been annexed almost overnight; the Sudetenland had been handed over to Hitler at Munich, and he had proceeded to take the rest of Czechoslovakia. And now Poland had been invaded, and England was tied to her by treaty. A feeling of frustration and anger grew in Nicole as she stared at her unseeing husband. These were all matters which did not concern them. They were Americans; they belonged in America. And yet he dragged out this visit, even to postponing their sailing, which had been planned for last week. What in God's name, she wondered, was he waiting for? If war was declared, they could just as well know of it, and know of it in more safety, if they were already back in Boston. What was so special about *England* that he had to be here when her fiddling government was finally shamed and forced and pushed into a declaration of war? And when would that be? She looked at the date on the copy of *The Times* which lay across the arm of her chair. 2 September. They should have landed in Boston yesterday.

Upstairs her boys, Dan and Timmy, shared the nursery with Judy and Gavin's children, Alistair and Fiona, jointly watched over by Henson and Judy's nanny, Tomlin. Henson had been another source of irritation to Nicole in these past days, her constant querying of when they were going back, her talk of the war, her fears for the children. Nicole had given her answers, said they were booked for the end of September, which wasn't quite true. They were on a waiting list for the end of September. Suddenly, everyone needed to get back to America, and still they tarried here. And Lloyd seemed like a man in a fitful daze. At the moment it would have been a relief for Nicole to go and physically shake him.

Instead the relief from the tension which had built in the room came from Wilks announcing that tea was served. They all moved towards the dining-room. Nicole thought bitterly that on any other day as fine and sunny as this, they could have had tea in the garden and the sense of gentler times restored and renewed, but now no one wanted to be separated from the wireless set. Andrew and Allan and Ross were already waiting for them. They had spent the afternoon on a tour of Fenton Field and Potters, ostensibly to try to determine just how long they had before the harvest of the barley, but Nicole had the notion that they had been looking at their ancient acres in much the same way that Margaret had been replanning her garden, and Andrew must have been wondering which, if any, of his sons would be left with him to carry it all through. Ross had just put in his full training with the Territorials. All summer long he had spent crawling about in the wet heather of Scotland, and learning how to manœuvre a tank, and sight its guns. He had come back hard and bone-thin, and the fresh youthful-ness that had seemed to Nicole his greatest attraction had died in those weeks. Ross had come out of Cambridge with a bril-liant First in Physics, and Gavin was still his idol. He was going on to post-graduate work there, he said, but he always said it as if a question mark lingered in his mind. They were all marking time. Judy and Gavin had arrived unexpectedly at Fenton Field, giving as their reason that they wanted to spend the last few days of Nicole and Lloyd's visit with them there. The house had been crowded with children, for Allan and Joan had three, and they came over daily to play with their cousins, and another nanny settled into a good gossip session in the nursery, or out in the garden. But the sailing date had come and gone, and Judy and Gavin also lingered, and no one said anything. The Fentons had always been a close-knit family, and they drew closer in those days. Promptly at five o'clock, when they were in the middle of tea, Ross went and turned on the wireless as if he expected an emergency news bulletin. There was none. The Cabinet was in session. No ultimatum had yet been sent. 'A bloody disgrace,' Gavin said. 'They should have signed a pact with Russia instead of Poland. Now there's Russia and Germany holding hands, ready to carve up Poland, and we've got an ally who's already beaten but just hasn't lain down yet. Those dithering idiots ...'

And in Warsaw, they were told, the Warsaw radio continued to play the first notes of the Chopin Revolutionary Etude, over and over and over, indicating to the country and the world that they still held control. Long ago Nicole had become sickened by the sound of it, the monotonous, dreadful sound and its implied threat. In those days she came close to hating Chopin.

She passed the scones and cream to Lloyd, and he took them and managed to thank her and still evade her eyes. And heartbreakingly she remembered how, that afternoon in the orchard long ago after Richard had read to them Rupert Brooke's poem 'The Soldier', Lloyd had lightly dispelled the mood of sombreness that had fallen on them by quoting from another Brooke poem:

> ... stands the church clock at ten to three?
> And is there honey still for tea?

Now Nicole looked closely once more at her husband's face, saw its expression of abstraction as if he wrestled with something he could not communicate even to her. She realized that he had contributed nothing to the conversation all afternoon. He might well have been completely alone as he had sat among that group. He was waiting, as they all waited, but it seemed to her that his vigil held an element that was missing in all the others. The question that hovered over their future would be decided for them, and they would be committed, one way or the other, simply because they were English. But she and Lloyd were still free. No commitment would be made for them. But if they were free to go, they were also free to stay. The thought hit Nicole like a sudden touch of death. No—he could not be so mad, he *could* not be. But she knew this was what she had been refusing to recognize during these weeks in which they had lingered at Fenton Field. And her irritation and anger died because it gave way to the much stronger emotion of fear.

She sat silently through the rest of tea, and when it was over, she went upstairs to get a jacket against the growing chill at the end of this September day, slipping down the backstairs, around by the kitchen garden, and found her favourite place at Fenton Field, the edge of the orchard which gave the best view of the house, the lawns, the ancient trees. She sat with her back against the apple tree around which they had gathered that afternoon she remembered best of all here, and gave herself up to the thoughts of the summer just past.

It has almost, Nicole thought, been the honeymoon she and Lloyd had never had. Margaret Fenton had gladly taken the children, and Henson had happily settled into the nurseries at

Fenton Field which had been for so long unused. Lloyd had insisted on engaging a young girl temporarily to help with the extra work having Henson and the children would cause. 'Just like the old days,' Henson had purred happily. 'Nannies always had nursery maids ... and it will do Master Dan and Baby so much good to hear *proper* English spoken.' So Nicole and Lloyd had been free, once the two lectures he had agreed to give at Cambridge before the end of term were finished. For Nicole it was a time of delicious idleness, a time of lying in bed late in the mornings at their hotel, of wandering through the colleges and along the Backs, of attending Evensong at King's College. Lloyd had been invited often to dine at High Table, and she was often at Judy's house, and they, between them, filled in the details of the missing years. She helped Judy put Alistair and Fiona to bed, and marvelled at the efficiency of the way Judy ran her household—delicious food, thriftily prepared, a choice of inexpensive but good wines, the little dressmaking room in the attic from which Judy's distinctively chic clothes came. 'I was damned if I was going to turn into a frumpy don's wife,' Judy said. 'I just *had* to become professional. I never stop blessing Mother and Father for scraping up the money to send me to Madame Graneau's. I miss the horses, though. But in a year or two Gavin will be able to afford a pony for the children, and that'll be fun ...' They were happy evenings, and Nicole was always reluctant to leave when Lloyd came to take her back to the hotel. Often Gavin had returned from dining at his own college, and he urged Lloyd to stay. Nicole had discovered that Gavin's secret passion was for a rare Highland malt whisky, and a case of it had been her and Lloyd's present to the McLeods. Gavin sipped it contentedly with Lloyd by the fire as the clock slipped past midnight and the talk flowed on. There was often talk of war. It startled Nicole to learn how closely Lloyd had followed the events of the past years. Between them, he and Gavin had thrashed out the whole tragedy of the Spanish Civil War and Hitler's rehearsal and trial of his new planes and weapons. They talked of the regime in Italy. Lloyd's talk even turned to Japan, and Gavin was silent, eager to listen. It had been the only dark shadow on that perfect summer for Nicole, the knowledge that Lloyd had many thoughts he had not wanted to share with her, frightening thoughts, the vague threat to the secure little world she had built up around her. Almost then, she was glad when the time at Cambridge ended, and they moved on to London, where Lloyd was almost daily at St Giles's. The talk of medical men was something Nicole was used to. Their problems were always so immediate, they had little time for speculation on what had happened in Spain or Austria last year, and even less to conjecture about what might happen to their own lives next year.

The period in London was another revelation for Nicole. Almost daily she was with Charles, and they went to the places they had visited when he had taken her around that first summer before Madame Graneau's. This time, though, she was more considerate of Charles's leg, and there were many rests on park benches, or the cloisters of the Abbey. She was surprised at Charles's insistence on visiting all these places, the Tower, Hampton Court, Greenwich. It almost seemed to her that by the intensity with which he gazed at these loved and beautiful buildings, these milestones in the whole progress of English history, he was like a man saying farewell. She began to fear that he was ill, an illness that had nothing to do with his bad leg. But she discovered the source of this nostalgic turning back to the past when they stood before the poppy-lined Tomb of the Unknown Warrior in Westminster Abbey. There Charles read the inscription on the black marble silently until he came to the last lines *They laid him among Kings because he hath done good towards God and towards his house.* This he said almost under his breath, and then, more loudly, 'One should almost turn now and pray that there won't be another one to lay here for the next time around.'

'Uncle Charles, *you* don't really believe there's going to be a war? I've heard so much talk in Cambridge, and it sickens me ...'

He had looked down at her small white face which suddenly had become peaked with anxiety. 'No,' he lied, 'I really don't think so. Just an old soldier's talk, my dear. We're always rambling on ... Tell you what. I'll get the car and we'll go and have lunch on the river somewhere ... Marlow, maybe. We'll sit out in the sun and watch the swans go by.' They had done that, and found much to talk and laugh about, and all the time she had known he had lied.

One of the most joyful encounters of that time in London had been at the Tate Gallery. Nicole had the afternoon to herself, had intended to do some shopping, and at the last minute had, on impulse, directed the taxi to the Tate Gallery. She had wandered its halls realizing that now she saw what she had been unable to see five years ago. The process of education had been subtle and insidious, visiting exhibitions at Havard and at the Boston galleries, flicking through and somehow learning from the art magazines to which Lloyd subscribed, or which had been loaned by some other member of the family; the Fentons were thrifty about magazine subscriptions, and saw that what they did subscribe to was circulated widely among the family. So the paintings Nicole saw now had an air of familiarity about them that had been totally lacking on that visit years ago. It seemed hardly a startling thing, then, when the hand fell lightly on her arm, and she turned to look into the face of Gerry Agar.

'Glad to see you made it all by yourself this time.'

'*Gerry!*' Without thought she put her arms about his neck. 'Oh, I've been ringing your flat, and all your butler will say is ...'

'Yes, I know ... Sir Gerald is abroad, and we do not know when to expect him home.'

'Are you always so mysterious?'

'Saves a lot of boring explanations, dear girl—and saves me from a lot of boring parties. Old Gerry is no longer the Deb's delight. Even the saddest of mothers with daughters longest on the shelf have given up on me.'

'You're not married?'

'No one will have me, dear girl. I've tried ...'

'You haven't tried ... You were always the most attractive man I knew.'

'Was I? Funny you married Fenton then, wasn't it? Or did I get so absent-minded I forgot to ask you myself?'

She laughed. 'Never serious, are you?'

'Never—too much trouble. Have you had enough of looking this afternoon? What about the Savoy? That was where we went last time after the Tate. Do you remember ...?'

'I don't think you're at all absent-minded. And I bored you to death talking about Lloyd.'

'Then come and bore me some more, dear girl. I'm longing for all my old chums to see me with the girl who turned into the most ravishing woman in London ...' He talked in the same vein, lightly, flippantly, all the way to the Savoy. Then when their drinks came, he settled himself back in his chair. 'Now—tell me about Boston and this man you've married, and your kids, and all the rest of it.'

She shrugged. 'What can there be to tell? I'm just a suburban matron, Gerry ... looking after Lloyd, the house, the boys. Trying to practise every day, and not always succeeding. Trying to learn a bit ... being sorry I didn't finally get to Radcliffe. But in Boston having been at the Paris Conservatoire *almost* makes up for not having a college degree. It would be better if I had both. The Fentons are a rather formidably intelligent lot. They have libraries that they use, and the older ones have some good pictures. There have been some Fenton bequests to Boston galleries which some of the family rather wish they had back now. One of the uncles collected a few Renoirs. Some of the family haven't forgiven him for leaving them to a gallery instead of inside the family. The younger ones would like to splash out a little—Matisse, Modigliani, Picasso ... your sort of thing, Gerry. But none of them have any spare money. But they *talk* about them ...'

'So you were in the Tate today. Doing what?'

She laughed. 'Why else would I be there except to enjoy myself? Perhaps I learned a little ... One always can.'

He questioned her further about the life she had; she found herself talking about the winters of concerts and music, the summers walking the sand dunes of the Cape, the life lived among the Fentons, the exchanges of books and magazines, the borrowing of tennis rackets and sailing boats. 'They know I'm useless at sport, so they leave me alone on that,' she said. 'There's a family joke that's grown up about my reluctance to prance around a tennis court, or get on a horse. "She has to take care of her hands, you know." But still, they respect that fact that I *have* to have the piano. I've made friends with the very oldest of the clan—Great-Uncle Pete. He has a house about a mile away on the Cape. I go over there every day to practise. He keeps the Bechstein tuned for me. He likes to sit outside on the porch and listen. He pretends to read the *Wall Street Journal*, but I notice he never turns a page. The family thinks it's a very odd friendship because he's always quarrelling with all the rest of them. *I* like him.'

Gerry nodded. 'I rather like the sound of all your Fentons.'

Nicole suddenly pressed him. 'Why don't you come over,

Gerry? Uncle Charles has—three times. He seems to like it. Look—why don't you come to dinner tonight? It's just Lloyd and myself and Uncle Charles. Of course you must know that Aunt Iris won't see me . . .'

He shook his head, and she was aware of a sense of withdrawal. 'Would have loved to do that, dear girl, but I'm off to Paris tonight. Got a few things to see to . . .' She had the sense that the Paris visit had been decided upon just at that moment; Gerry had been an attentive and flattering listener to her recital of the life she lived in Boston and among the Fentons, but when she had tried to draw him into it, he had pulled back. She didn't know why.

As they left the American Bar of the Savoy she knew that several people stared at them. Gerry acknowledged the curt nod of one man wearing a military uniform, who, after giving that greeting, rather ostentatiously turned his back. 'A cousin of mine,' Gerry said briefly. 'We always were a devoted family.'

That night at dinner she related the meeting to Lloyd and Charles, told them about the visit to the Savoy, her invitation to Gerry to join them for dinner. She saw that Charles looked rather uncomfortable. 'Perhaps it's just as well he couldn't come, my dear.'

'Why ever not? What's wrong with Gerry? Oh, I know—all that nonsense about him playing ducks and drakes with a few dreary debs. But surely *that* can't matter anymore?'

'It isn't that. There's been . . . well, there are some rather odd stories about Gerald Agar. He's keeping rather strange company—for an Englishman. Always showing up in Berlin. They say he advises Goering about his art collection. There's even a story that he's visited Berchtesgaden, but I couldn't really be sure of that.'

'You mean,' Lloyd said, 'that he hob-nobs with the Nazis?'

'More or less. Can't say what makes him do it. A man like that—plenty for him here in England. Of course, he's no fool where money's concerned. I've heard rumours that he's into armaments in a very big way. And South African gold mining.' Charles looked uncomfortable. 'Well—I've never understood how these fellows make money. I just wouldn't like to think it was made at the expense of this country . . .'

Suddenly Nicole was aware of the curious glances that had

come their way when they had sat in the Savoy, and Gerry's quick excuse to avoid having dinner with them. The glances that had then seemed merely curious, now seemed hostile. She ate the rest of her meal in silence, and knew that Gerry had wanted no embarrassment for her, but had been unable to resist that one swift return to the summer of five years ago. But one never did go back, and they both knew it; it was only make-believe for a few hours. She knew then that Gerry would never make that visit to Boston. She had a sad and unreasoning intuition that she would never see him again.

Gerry Agar did not go to Paris that night. He remained alone in his flat, having given his manservant instructions that he was to tell any telephone caller that he was not at home. Not that there were any but a few expected callers these days. Many people tended to look the other way when they saw Gerald Agar—especially since Munich, and since one photograph had appeared in a London paper of him witnessing a Nürnberg rally. He ate his meal alone, and afterwards sat listening to a Beethoven string quartet on records, smoking a cigar, sipping his brandy and staring around the room at the pictures he had gathered there. He thought of the luminous beauty of the young woman he had been with this afternoon; he remembered her as he had seen her first, her expression thoughtful and withdrawn as she had gazed at the pictures in the gallery. He wished he might have walked those Cape dunes with her, might have sat with the old man on the porch and listened to her play the piano. But he knew he never would.

Then he went to his safe and removed some papers which had recently come into his possession. He memorized their contents carefully, thoroughly, translated them into the code they had taught him. Then he burned the papers, and flushed the ashes down the toilet.

The next morning he visited his solicitor and made a codicil to his will. When that was done, he walked out into the sunshine and wondered what he would do with the rest of the day before he took the night train to Paris. He decided to go racing. It was more interesting being cut by people who once had been his friends on a race course than in the street. Made it more pointed. He was aware that he took an almost masochistic pleasure in the way he was now regarded by some people. And there was always the added fillip of gambling with what was, for the race course, rather large sums of money.

One other episode had disturbed those summer weeks in London for Nicole, but this time she did not speak to Lloyd about it. It happened one morning when she had arranged to meet him at St Giles's, and she strolled on the Embankment and into Parliament Square, wandering about enjoying the flowers in the window-boxes of Whitehall, making a half-smiling, half-reverent salute to the statue of Abraham Lincoln who sat morosely viewing the House of Commons. The city was sparkling and fresh that morning after a night of rain; she stood and looked with eyes that had become more appreciative at the whole scene—the great looming tower of Big Ben, the ancient splendour of Westminster Hall, the great buttresses of the Abbey seen through the moving tracery of the plane trees. She strolled and looked, and then her eyes fell on a man who sat on one of the benches, a man whose body seemed slumped down into itself, and his gaze was riveted on the House of Commons.

'Brendan!' she said. 'Bren——'

He turned, and she knew at once that she had not only spoken his correct name, but that he recognized her. Then his features seemed to freeze into a stare of dismissal. They were the features of Brendan de Courcey, but features too much aged for the five years that had passed since she had seen him; his face seemed sunken and thin. He had lost the look of young enthusiasm which had made his striking good looks so appealing. The eyes he turned on her were hard and suspicious.

'Brendan de Courcey?' In face of his refusal to respond, she had to use his full name.

He rose from the bench. He seemed to her strangely dressed. His raincoat was soiled, his tweeds rumpled; it was a long time since his shoes had been cleaned. He stood and looked at her for a second or two, then lightly touched the brim of the pork-pie hat which had partly obscured his face. 'Your mistake, Madam. Good day.' And then he was striding off, and with hardly a look at the oncoming traffic, dashed across the road to the corner of Whitehall. Nicole stared after him in utter disbelief. It *had* been Brendan, and he had sat, staring with a seriousness that had been quite uncharacteristic of him, at a group of buildings in the heart of London. It certainly had been Brendan, but this man had nothing to do with the eager boy who had chanted the racing form, and the blood lineage of the horses at Ascot as if it had been a holy litany. Even if he had reason to dislike her, why did he deny his identity? It was something she found quite impossible to talk to Lloyd about. It had been too disturbing; there had been something about this man which had frightened her, and she didn't want to be told by Lloyd that she had simply made a mistake. She crossed Westminster Bridge then and walked along the Embankment to St Giles's, puzzled, haunted by the air of desperate intensity which had hung over the man she had addressed as Brendan de Courcey.

At lunch she drank more wine than usual to drive out the dankness of the feeling that had touched her. Lloyd had brought Carl Zimmerman to lunch. They went to the same Italian restaurant she and Lloyd had met at during that brief and shining month when they had fallen in love. Carl Zimmerman kissed her hand with heavy and clumsy gallantry; in his movements he had always reminded her of some shambling animal, and yet in these five years, Lloyd told her, Zimmerman had become a consultant at St Giles's, and in a few years he would be a senior consultant. He was now, certainly, one of the finest plastic surgeons in England.

'You see, Miss Nicole Rainard,' he said, his accent as thick as it had been all that time ago, his manner quite as maddeningly calm, 'I did deliver all those messages. And now you are Mrs Lloyd Fenton. It is good, isn't it, when the messages finally reach the right place?'

They had laughed, and relived the earlier time, and for those hours at least, Nicole had forgotten about the encounter with the man who had worn the look that she now had begun to think of as the look of a fanatic, the sunken eyes too bright, the gaze that only saw one object. But why had he sat there, bundled in a raincoat, on a bright summer's day, staring at those monuments of England's Establishment?

But she did speak to Richard about that encounter with Brendan de Courcey one weekend they spent at Fenton Field.

'Bren? You ran into him? I thought he didn't come to England any more.'

She described the circumstances of the meeting, Brendan's non-recognition of her. 'But I *know* it was Bren. He looked up when I spoke his name. He'd changed, but not so much that I couldn't recognize him.'

Richard frowned. 'Damned if I know. He certainly isn't seen about in any of the places he used to be. Doesn't even come over to the Derby any more, though his father's entered a horse every year. I wonder . . .'

'What?'

'Well, I saw an item in *The Times*. Nothing sensational. One of those shindigs that started up at Speaker's Corner in Hyde Park. Some IRA chap sounding off about Ireland's ills and Partition and all the rest of it. Some people in the crowd didn't like it, and a fight started. About six men were charged for disturbing the peace, one for hitting a policeman. The item just said that a Mr Brendan de Courcey went bail for the four IRA men. It never occurred to me that it was *our* Bren. I hope to God he hasn't got twisted up in Irish politics in the wrong way. Doesn't seem to me to be the type who'd do it the usual way—you know, run for Parliament, or that sort of thing. Doesn't seem to me the type who'd be sitting on a bench in Parliament Square. You know, just sitting . . . He got married, I heard. He's got a couple of kids, I think.'

'I meant to ask Gerry about him, but there was so much else to talk about . . .'

'Gerry Agar . . . now *there's* another odd sort. He's hardly ever seen in London any more. But I wouldn't suppose *he'd* have any IRA sympathies. That lot's a bit too grubby for him. Gerry's in the money business, and the IRA isn't exactly a fashionable outfit. Funny . . . we've all split up, haven't we?'

'What do you mean?'

'Remember that year you were at Ascot—the year you came out? We were quite a foursome, weren't we? And all winning loads of money on Bren's tips. Funny, I've never been to Ascot since that year. Don't even have a bet on the Derby these days.'

'Well, we all get a little more staid, don't we? I mean we settle down. Lloyd and I . . .'

'Lloyd and you are different. Yours isn't like most marriages. And don't ask me why. I don't know.'

'But, Rick, everything's all right with you, isn't it? I mean

Celia ... ? You're doing so well in law.'

'Celia's a good sort. The law ... well, the law is beginning to bore me stiff. It's too damn slow. I'm great if I can get cracking in something that really interests me, but I'm beginning to wonder if that's what the law needs. Most of all it seems to need patience, due process, and all that. You know I've never been patient. I want things fast ... *fast*. I want some excitement. If I'd had any head for money, I would have gone into the city. At least you can gamble there. Even horse races are too slow for me now. The only thing I really want is flying ... and the tougher things get the better I like it. Did I tell you I made a trip out to the Persian Gulf last year?—solo all the way. Celia wouldn't come. She doesn't like flying. *You* would have come, wouldn't you?'

'It really doesn't matter what I would have done, Rick,' she said quietly. 'That's not the point.'

He had turned away and gone and poured himself another drink. 'No, it's not the point. You're right. We've all gone our own ways now. Times like that year at Ascot, that isn't for any of us any more ...'

The rest of the summer she and Lloyd had toured about. Lloyd rented a car, and they had gone to his favourite places in Cornwall. They had explored the valleys of the Lake District and had driven on up past the Border into Scotland. From Oban they had taken the little steamers that ply out to the Western Isles. They had picnicked and drunk malt whisky and wine, and had made love. They had had days of sunshine, and days when the rain and strong winds drove them back to the fireside. Nicole didn't remember that they talked very seriously. It was a period of peace, as well as love. Sometimes, she thought, it was as if they were together and alone for the first time. But there was more than that. Lloyd's hand would touch hers, and she would look at him, and there was not only the strength of their first love, but the firm rock of these five years. Anything that had troubled her during that summer was gone, not spoken of, unimportant. She had Lloyd, completely with her and for herself alone. She had that, and the comfortable thought that when this idyllic period together was over, they were going back to Fenton Field to gather up their two sons and return to the waiting house in Boston. In those weeks she felt like a vessel filled to its brim. It was a rich, mellow, and heady liquid. She felt far older than her years because she had given the whole of her love, and had it returned.

Only one thing Lloyd did in those weeks puzzled her. He insisted on buying presents for each one of the English Fentons —even though they had brought presents with them from Boston—presents of mohair lap robes woven in the Isles, heavy hand-knitted sweaters, caps and scarves. Even Gavin McLeod had been included, and Nicole had protested at this. 'Don't you think that's a bit much? You know how touchy Gavin is. He doesn't like taking presents. And can you really imagine Andrew wearing a knitted tam-o'-shanter? All these rugs, Lloyd, you'd think another Ice Age was on the way ...'

But he had insisted, and she hadn't wanted to argue further. They had packed the back seat of the car with all the wrapped bundles, and turned south and headed for England and Fenton Field. They were to sail the last week in August.

II

Lloyd found her sitting in the orchard and while he said, 'Getting a bit chilly out here,' he still dropped down to the grass beside her. She made no answer. She was afraid to speak in case putting into words what she feared would turn it into reality. She hoped he would not speak either. If the blessed silence could just continue long enough, they would be out, and gone from here. But after postponing a sailing, and a week of listening to the bulletins from Poland, she knew that it was already too late. Events would overtake them.

He didn't try to lead up to it gently. Even though she had known it was coming, it still was shocking when it was actually spoken. 'I'm going to stay, Nicky. You know that, don't you?'

'You're going to stay ...' It was no question, just a restatement of what he had said. 'Why are you going to stay, Lloyd?'

'Damned if I know. I can't put it into words. Just the conviction that half of what I am was shaped by this country. It's going to be rough, Nicky, and I can help.'

She turned on him in fury. 'You're going to stay! Just like that! Some addle-pated sense of misplaced patriotism for a country that isn't even your own——'

'I've never cared for the word patriotism,' he said quietly.

311

'It's too narrow. It says this country rather than that country.'

'Well, if you don't care for one country more than another, then why don't you take it all the way and go to Germany. *They* might need you there.'

'Oh, Nicky, for God's sake! You'll have to try to understand.'

'I *don't* understand. Why should I? You have your own job to do, your own place to be. What's so damn marvellous about England that you have to stay here? You're saying, of course, that they *are* going to fight. That's what all the talk's been about this summer, hasn't it? Isn't that really why you wanted to come? You wanted to find out what everyone over here was thinking. You wanted to go back to what was five years ago. You can't go back, Lloyd. You've got a home, a country, a wife and two sons. You're not free.'

'I'm still free to make a choice, and I'm going to make it. Look, Nicky, you know as well as anyone does that there's going to be war with Germany, and this country's damn ill-prepared. They'll need everyone they can get. I've got special skills ... They don't have to train me. I *know* what I can do. I won't be winning any medals, but I will be saving some lives. And you know that some time—no one knows how or when— America will be in it too. I'm just coming in sooner rather than later, that's all.'

'No—you *don't* know America will come in. Who says so? What makes you so damn sure?'

'Look, Nicky,' he said wearily, 'I've thought about this thing until I'm sick of it. I'm *sure*. I can make all sorts of excuses— or apologies—to you, and I know it won't make one bit of difference. You'll never know why, and I can't put it into words. I'd feel pretty foolish if I tried. People don't make patriotic speeches these days. It isn't fashionable. If I were a lawyer or stockbroker or someone in insurance, I'd have been out of here weeks ago. I'd say I was just cluttering up the landscape because they'd have to teach me from scratch. Oh, I'll learn plenty, because we'll see casualties with injuries we've never even dreamed of. It's got to do with being a doctor. I've got something to offer here and now. You don't become a doctor, Nicky, to make money or to have an easy time. To start with, it isn't even easy to become one. The grind sort of gets into your bones when you're doing those years of training. You never expect ease from then on. You don't become a doctor to have it easy. England gave me something when I was sort of drifting. I might have stayed on here for ever if it hadn't been for you. When I finally knew that you wanted to marry me, going back home seemed an even better idea than the sort of flight I'd been thinking of then.' He paused, and then started again slowly, 'Nicky, I've never tried to say this to you. There was so much else. When you told me that time about New York, about your mother and your grandfather's will, and I knew that you'd run from Blanchard, and were prepared to run from a marriage to Ashleigh just two days before it was to have taken place ... Well, after that, Nicky, I knew Boston was the only place for us. You needed an anchor. You needed a family. You needed to be away from England and away from the gossip. If we'd stayed here at that time, our marriage wouldn't have had much of a chance because everyone would have been scrutinizing it too hard—trying to see if you'd regretted opting for a doctor without two pennies after——'

'Oh, for God's sake, Lloyd! None of that ever mattered ...'

He went on as if she hadn't spoken. 'I had only one thing to offer you. That was a sense of family, of belonging. I knew they'd look you over in their Bostonian way, and I knew they'd take you in. Some would love you, some would be envious of you, and some would just accept you as someone who'd joined the ranks. The Fentons. That's what I had to offer. And it's been a wonder every day of my life since then to look at you and see you expand and open up, like some sort of plant that someone had brought in out of the rough weather. So leaving England did that for me—for us. But England is some kind of drug for me. I'm addicted. *And* I know I'll be of some use—more than some use. I've got highly specialized skills, Nicky. They don't come easily, and they're not easily found. So I'm giving them back.'

'England didn't give you those skills! You became a doctor in a place called Boston, Massachusetts, Remember that? Your training was paid for by Boston Fentons. So if you've got such very special skills, why aren't you giving them to your own country? If you're so certain that the United States is going to come into the war, why aren't you offering your very special skills to the Americans? They'll need them too. Charity begins at home, Lloyd.'

313

'I will—of course I will. The moment the States is in it, I'll transfer. The Army or Navy will have any doctor who offers. There won't be any trouble. I've made enquiries about that.'

'Oh, have you? You've got it all planned then. You've always had it planned. And you never talked to me about it. Never!'

'Why should I worry you? There was always the possibility that Chamberlain would go for appeasement again. I didn't see the sense of volunteering for an army that Hitler could simply order to lay down its arms. But it's been clear for quite some time that no matter how they tried to stave it off, either England would fight or become a minor dependency of Germany. And if England fought, you could bet that the Empire would. And eventually America would. Like it or not, there'd be some way of pushing her into war. And I planned to change then. I'd come back to you and the kids. We could have some time together. But there'll be more than one Boston Fenton joining up——'

Nicole felt the warm flush of rage. 'What do you *mean*! You'd come *back* to me and the kids. Are you really so cracked you think I'd leave England if you're determined to stay here? You can't be *that* mad! If you stay, I do too, and so do the boys!'

'Nicky, you *can't* stay. It's going to be bloody awful here, as well as bloody dangerous. There's going to be civilian bombing. This little corner of England's only a few minutes' flying time from the coast of France. You've got to go on that ship at the end of the month. I can't risk you and the kids, Nicky. I *can't*!'

'You'll just have to. If that's your choice, then I have the right to a choice too. I married Lloyd Fenton. I intend to stay as close to him as circumstances permit. I intend to stay here. Those very special skills you talk about ... well, neurosurgeons aren't thick on the ground. They're not going to post you to some isolated little place in the Highlands. I'm going to stay where I can see you every minute of every day I can. I'm selfish, Lloyd, I always have been. I mean to keep you. If you think you're sending me back to Boston to spend all my days with two little boys instead of the man I married, then you're mistaken. I'll stay here at Fenton Field.'

'You can't! You'd be in the way! Extra mouths to feed ... Trouble for the whole family.'

'Why didn't you think of that before? I don't care what trouble I am. I'm not leaving you behind here. Oh—I don't doubt I could do my bit. There'll be plenty for women to do. After all,' she added with bitterness, 'isn't Aunt Margaret going to dig up the south lawn? Surely any fool can grow vegetables? Who knows, I might even learn to drive a tractor.'

'Nicky, you're being foolish. You can't——'

'Don't you say *can't* to me! Don't you dare use that word! *I* can't say it to you. You're not even listening. If you can stay, then so can I. And I'll stay and think it's all a damn shame and a waste—a stupid waste! *You* talk of being foolish. Well, I'll leave you to write the letters to your brothers and sister in Boston. You can write the letters to the uncles and aunts. Try to explain to *them* why you're staying—why the boys and I are staying too. See what they think of their fine, level-headed brother. A man of such eminent good sense—who's suddenly gone mad. And what for?—for England! England? I *hate* England!'

She was on her feet and running, running across that smooth green turf that would shortly be ploughed up, running towards the house that she had once thought the utter perfection of all houses laid like a jewel in its English setting. She brushed aside the angry, outraged tears that sprang to her eyes. Damn the Fentons! Damn England! And damn the impossible, inescapable love she felt for the man who had brought her back here.

III

Late that night they listened to the news bulletin which announced that the British Government had sent an ultimatum to Germany which would expire at 9 a.m. the next morning. When it was announced the next day that the Prime Minister would speak to the nation, all of the Fentons gathered at that time. Richard and Celia had come over from Potters; Joan and Allan had come also. Gavin pretended to read the newspaper while he waited; Judy was knitting. Nicole noticed that Margaret just stood by the window gazing at the south lawn. Whatever talk started between them died swiftly. There was nothing to do but wait. During this waiting period there was a sound of a car in the drive. Wilks hurriedly showed in Sir

Charles Gowing. Nicole went swiftly to his side, and Margaret came forward to give him her hand. No one seemed surprised to see him there at that time; no one questioned his presence. All over the country friends were coming together to hear this message. It was spoken at last in Chamberlain's dry, thin voice, the tones of a man who has seen the death of his own honour, and the beginning of physical death. '... my painful duty to declare that a state of war now exists between Great Britain and Germany ...'

'That's it!' Richard said when the speech was ended. It was like a cry of exaltation.

Both Margaret and Celia looked at him with eyes that reflected horror and hurt. And Nicole looked across the group towards Lloyd, and for him alone her lips soundlessly framed the words 'I'm staying.'

Gavin, whom everyone knew was not given to sentiment, surprised them by bringing out a bottle of the malt whisky which Nicole and Lloyd had given to him. It occurred to Nicole that he had been very much prepared for this moment when he had come down from Cambridge. He poured the whisky and passed it around. No one refused.

'Victory,' he said.

'Peace,' Margaret countered.

They drank it, and Gavin said to Andrew, 'If you don't mind, sir, I'll put the rest of the case in your cellar. We'll drink again when it's all over.'

To Nicole it tasted both bitter and fiery, as if it were a taste of the years to come.

CHAPTER 3

I

The dispersal of the Fentons began from that day. Afterwards
Nicole grew angry once more at the speed with which Lloyd
seemed to disappear from her life. The arrangements had all
been made. He knew exactly whom he should go to, and he
appeared three weeks later at Fenton Field in the uniform of
the Royal Army Medical Corps. He had a few days' leave, and
would go back to training camp for only a few weeks more. 'I
suppose I have to learn a bit more about just being in the
Army,' he said. After that he would be posted to a special
neuro-surgical unit being set up at a military hospital near
Maidstone, in Kent. 'Of course we'll be doing other things
there. I'll assist in general surgery, and when my kind of thing
comes along, I'll be leading the team.' Nicole accepted him
back and tried to still the bitter and scalding words of reproach
which threatened. It was done now. There was no sense in
driving Lloyd from her while she turned into a scold and a
shrew. But her sense of resentment was real and deep, and
when the leave was over, she viewed the present and the future
with a distaste and fear that went with her through the days,
and allowed her little rest at night.

There seemed a thousand small annoyances. People were in
a hurry. Ration books were new things to learn to juggle with.
There was an issue of gas masks, and instructions about how
to construct air raid shelters. Surprising people appeared in
uniform. Ross was already settled with his regiment near
Lincoln; Allan was on an officer's training course in Wiltshire.
Richard had his place, as though it had been carefully prepared, in a fighter squadron of the Royal Air Force. Gavin
had also made his plans, or they had been made for him. He
had been swiftly inducted into something that was described

as Intelligence, but was really a research group wearing uniforms. Judy closed the house in Cambridge and moved with the children back to Fenton Field. 'I'll be of more use here,' she said. Her nanny, Tomlin, who had had one year in nurse's training, went back to Bart's Hospital as a trainee nurse again. Mrs Fenton told her she could come to Fenton Field whenever she had leave; she had no family of her own. That left Henson in charge of Dan and Timmy, and Judy's Alistair and Fiona. She did not keep her feelings to herself. Her complaints were vocal and loud. 'We shouldn't *be* here, Miss Nicole. When I think of that lovely house back in Boston ... and these children here exposed to this risk. Why, we might all be *killed* ...'

'We might, Henson, we might,' Nicole agreed wearily because she was tired of trying to explain Lloyd's decision, and refused even to discuss her own reasons for staying. Henson had surprised her though, in the strength of her desire to return to America. 'Things were nice there, Miss Nicole. So comfortable. Things aren't going to be very comfortable here. I don't see why we can't go back where we belong.'

This most English of Englishwomen had suffered a sea change during her years away. Suddenly everything she had ever complained about in America was changed. She could only see that she was in an old and draughty house, that the nurseries lacked the facilities of those in Boston, that the help had vanished from the kitchen, that the days of careless abundance were over. The Boston house glowed brighter in her memory. 'Oh, it was always so warm in that house, Miss Nicole,' she said, as the days of autumn grew colder, and only a thin trickle of heat was allowed into the radiators at Fenton Field. 'And now Mrs Fenton says that they really can't spare the coal to get the hot water to the nursery bathroom. Everyone's to use the *same* bathroom. Well—it isn't what I expected.'

'It isn't what any of us expected,' Nicole admitted. 'But there's really nothing to stop you going, Henson. I'm sure there's some way of getting you a passage back. I know Dr Fenton's sister would love to have you look after her children, and help out.'

Henson had looked at her in astonishment. 'You really don't think I'd leave *you*, Miss Nicole. What I can't understand is why we don't *all* go back. Plenty of people *are* ...'

Nicole didn't know either, but she dared not voice her complaints as Henson did. But Henson stopped talking of a new sailing date as the news came that during that September German U-boats had sunk 26 British merchant ships. The dullness of the first months of the war wore on Nicole's nerves as no kind of action would have. It all seemed so pointless to be going through this exercise in preparing for a fight which did not come. The south lawn was indeed ploughed up, and she helped plant the vegetables. She hated the sight of the stark posts and wire to keep out the rabbits. She hated most things, she admitted to herself. There was the boredom of learning first-aid, of studying to pass the St John Ambulance test. She felt so much less effective than Margaret and Judy, clumsy and muddling, where they were efficient. Joan was running her own house now with no help at all, and without complaint. She was also, as Margaret was, getting rooms ready for evacuee children from London which they had been told to expect. '*More* trouble,' Henson said darkly. 'There's just no knowing what sort of children they'll send to us. Dirty hands and no table manners, I expect.' Nicole silently agreed with her, but dragged out every cot bed and extra mattress from the loaded attics of Fenton Field, tried to find blankets for them all, and stifled the desire to wonder aloud if it was all of any use.

'I'm so frightened,' Celia whispered to her one day as they stacked dishes and carried them into the kitchen for washing. Celia had offered Potters to the Red Cross, and it had been accepted. It was being prepared as a convalescent centre for the wounded that were expected. But it was empty at the moment, staffed by a skeleton team. There were, as yet, no wounded.

'Frightened of what?'

'Of Richard's being killed.' She said it in a dull voice, as if she had long ago accepted the fact. 'I don't know that I can just spend the war here at Fenton Field, just waiting. I've been thinking of joining the WAAF. Daddy says there's lots to do, and perhaps I should have a go. He's at Biggin Hill. There was where I met Richard ... Daddy said Richard was a brilliant pilot. I remember the day we met ...' Nicole then remembered what she had forgotten, that Celia's father was Air Vice-Marshal Hastings.

So Celia went off to training camp. On her first leave back she wore her uniform with a sharp authority that she had lacked before. 'It's pretty grim, really,' she confessed to Nicole. 'I hate being stuck into those big barracks with hundreds of other girls. No place to wash properly, no place for clothes, or any of that sort of thing. Some of the girls are pretty awful too. I'll never be much good at whatever they decide to do with me, but I *have* to do something. I mean Richard would despise me ... If I just wait out the war for him, I really doubt he'll come back to me.'

'*Celia!*'

'It's true,' she said. 'He's so free now. Plenty of women available. The sort of women he admires. *Doing* things. I have to try. And yet I have the feeling that it's no use. He's either going to get killed, or he's not coming back to me.'

'That's absurd! Why do you imagine such things? Any rate, at this moment there seems to be no chance of *anyone* fighting —in the air or anywhere else. The French are just sitting on the Maginot Line, and a few British battalions are in trenches in France and they're doing *nothing*.'

Celia looked at her and shook her head. 'It's no use pretending even to yourself, Nicole. That's what's got us into all this trouble. Since September Germany and Russia have neatly parcelled up Poland between them, and Russia's having a nice bit of Finland. When they've got it all straightened out, do you think they won't turn their attention to *us*?'

Nicole looked at her with a new respect. Even the few weeks away from Fenton Field and Richard had worked a difference. Nicole was reminded once again that Celia was the daughter of an Air Vice-Marshal. But the very calmness of Celia's acceptance of the storm to come in all their lives, and her own personal anguish, shook Nicole almost as no other event up to that time had done. 'I'm not trying to scaremonger,' Celia added, perhaps seeing the fear reflected in Nicole's face. 'I'm just telling you not to be surprised ...'

Richard came home for Christmas, but it was Celia who could not get leave. Lloyd came on Christmas Eve; Ross was still in Lincoln, and Allan had no hope of leave. He telephoned Joan and his mother with Christmas messages, and then had a discussion with his father about the crops they were to plant in the late winter. There were still enough toys left in the shops that year to make a normal Christmas for the children. Andrew sacrificed a spruce tree from the small plantation of conifers they had on a patch of poor land at Potters. The same decorations which had served the Fentons since they had been children came out. Nicole and Lloyd helped trim the tree, watched and listened as Margaret and Andrew served hot punch to the carolers who came each year to Fenton Field to sing. This year there were a number in uniform, and all the others seemed either too old or too young for uniforms. A house like Fenton Field, with its laid-down cellar, and its well-stocked pantry of summer fruits, its own cured hams, could still put on a spread for the carolers, and Margaret insisted, over Judy's objections, that they do. 'If *we* don't keep things up, who will? As long as there's a spare half-pound of sugar, I won't hoard. When the time comes, we may all have to do without.'

Charles came for the carol singing on Christmas Eve, and afterwards went straight back to London. 'I must be with Iris,' he said. 'Though she's so busy now, we hardly glimpse each other. But still, it's Christmas . . .' Charles was back in uniform, and looked happier for it. 'I fiddle papers on a desk,' he said. 'About all the use I am to them is that I *do* know Army Regulations. When they can't spare anyone more important, I go and inspect anti-aircraft installations and all that sort of thing. All supposed to do with morale, but all these boys know I'm a pretty worn-out old war-horse. It isn't easy to face them and know that we really never finished the last war. And know *they* know it. Iris is marvellous, of course. She's become a very big-wig in the Red-Cross. And she's volunteered as an air-raid warden for the area just around Elgin Square. Heaven knows how she'll find time for everything. All the secretaries have gone. Most of the staff has gone. She's bullied and coached Adams until he's passed the St John Ambulance test. *He*'s a warden too. We're having a mixed bag of young soldiers and airmen for Christmas dinner, and Iris is helping to cook it. We may all be laid up with acute indigestion this time tomorrow, but Iris will have done her bit. Well . . . must be going. Don't know when I'll be able to get down in future . . . Petrol's getting so short . . .'

They saw him off, and went back and mingled with the rest of the family. But when the others had gone up to bed, leaving them by the fire near the Christmas tree, Lloyd leaned over and touched Nicole's knee.

'Hey—feeling it a bit rough? Sorry—it just can't be helped. Sorry you and the kids are still here, Nicky, and yet—so glad, so glad, my darling ...' And then he gave her the little velvet box. It contained a single spray of gold, with a leaf of diamonds, and a rose-bud in rubies.

'I never promised you roses,' he said. 'But at this moment jewellery isn't rationed.'

'Nor is my love,' she answered. 'You fool—you silly, wonderful fool. Did you think I needed jewellery?'

'No, but perhaps I need to give it to you. Nicky, at times when I think that you might be hurt ... or the boys——'

'Shut up!' she said fiercely, simultaneously hugging him and trying to pin on the brooch, and pricking her finger so that the blood smeared the tiny diamonds. 'I won't get hurt. Nor will the boys. Nor you. I'm lucky, Lloyd. I've got a special sort of luck. It's going to take us right through this ... you'll see.'

She went to the mirror to see how the brooch looked against her grey sweater. She fingered it and smiled back at Lloyd's reflection behind her. But the fingers with which she touched the glowing rose-bud were hard and cracked from housework and the vegetable garden; her supply of hand cream had run out, and she hadn't had an hour at the piano in the last month.

II

That winter they waited for what everyone said must come—bombardment from the air. And yet nothing happened. At Fenton Field Andrew moved the map which until Christmas he had had on the wall of the small room he used as a farm office, into the kitchen. The whole of Europe was spread there before them, and they traced the boundaries of places whose names they had never before thought about—Estonia, Lithuania, Latvia. There, in the room that had now become the hub of the whole house, they learned about ice-free ports, and Sweden's iron ore, about the Karelian Peninsula and Russians learning to fight on skis as their stubborn Finnish enemy did, holding the Russians for what seemed an unendurable length of time that frozen winter. There was now no question at Fenton Field that the family was invading Wilks's territory by taking over the kitchen. It was a huge, bright room, old-fashioned enough to have retained a solid-fuel burning stove when the modern electric ranges had been introduced. It was to this place they all gathered, whoever was there, and Wilks was part of the family in a new way. Even Henson overcame her horror at this erosion of social barriers. The kitchen was warm, there was no help to be had, and it made more sense for the family to gather around the big, scrubbed table, to eat at whatever hours were convenient to their activities, instead of the old fixed times. Wilk's silver pantry was locked, and the key put away in Margaret's desk. The dining-room was unused and often dusty, as was the drawing-room. The sitting-room of the family became the small room that they had once called the library or the study—a room easier to heat than the others, and closer to the kitchen. It was an untidy, much-used room, littered with sewing, newspapers. children's toys. There was a radio there and in the kitchen, and neither room was ever uninhabited, and certainly not at the hours of the news bulletins. Fenton Field became noisy with the cries and tussles of the six evacuee children who arrived and then drifted away as their mothers decided that, after all, there was going to be no bombing. Henson sighed with relief, and more than once wanted to complain that even with the evacuees gone, four young children were too much for her to look after. But people had developed a way of clamping their mouths shut when such things threatened to come out. On the surface it was still a serene and well-enough run house, and underneath the tension grew.

Andrew and Wilks joined the Local Defence Volunteers which afterwards they came to call the Home Guard. They were gone three nights a week, drilling and making plans, or accepting them, about what they should do in the event of an invasion. Andrew taught Wilks how to use a gun, and handed out the two that had belonged to Allan to other members of his group. They were lucky that, being country people, they actually had guns. Most men in the towns, they learned, were still drilling with broom handles. 'It all seems so useless,' Andrew said wearily to Margaret one night as they sat late over cocoa in the kitchen when he returned from a meeting. 'We're all running around bumping into each other in the dark. There's not enough ammunition to hold up a German troop for three minutes. There isn't a one of us there under sixty, except that Turner boy who's so shortsighted he can't see his hand in front of him. Oh—we got a new recruit. About forty. He's head of some business firm near London. Making parachutes, I think. The heads of businesses usually don't get called up. Oh, hell, I'd better go to bed. The damn milking time comes around so quickly. You know, I still wonder at myself—I used to think what a good thing it was to be a farmer. A good, useful, healthy, outdoor life. And now that I have to do half the bloody chores myself, I'm already wondering how I'll be able to drag myself through this war. And I don't think it'll be short. The Ministry of Labour says I might be able to have the Harkins chap next week. He's been turned down by the Medical Board. It'd be a great help.' He gulped down the rest of his cocoa; it had become cold, but one didn't waste anything any more. 'I don't know,' he admitted, as he pushed back his chair and got to his feet, 'what I'd do without Judy and Joan and Nicole. Well, Judy and Joan we might have expected to pitch in—after all, they've been around a farm all of their lives. But Nicole—now she really surprised me . . . Good night, dear. Don't be too late up . . .' He was yawning as he went off.

Nicole knew that she continued to surprise everyone, but she didn't surprise herself. They had expected her to be useless, and she determined that she would not be. She had also determined that they would not know what an effort it was. She got up for the early milking, and pretended, as she gulped down the cup of hot tea in the kitchen, that it was like the early rising at Madame Graneau's, when she would go then to the piano, and Judy to the stables. But now she went to what to her was a smelly barn, overheated by the concentration of the animal bodies. She washed the udders of each cow as Andrew prepared to milk them, and when each in the line was done, she took her own place at the milking stool. It seemed to her a stupid way to do this job, but milking machines were things only dimly heard of from America, so they would just sit there and gently squeeze with infinite patience, with the chance of getting a good kick if she somehow got out of rhythm, or did the wrong thing. 'Wouldn't have expected you to be so good at it,' the young hired boy, Ben, said. Nicole knew she would be good at it; that was why she had volunteered for the task. Musicians were supposed to know what to do with their hands. It meant that, morning and evening, seven days a week, she was chained to the dairy herd. After the milking there was breakfast. After that she mucked out the stables of the three horses they had left—heavy

324

plough horses, held over from a former era, and now expected to be put back to service when there was no petrol for the tractors. Andrew had kept them as a hobby, to display them at shows. Now they were a substantial asset. The riding horses had gone. Nicole had seen Judy's face in the days after the stables had suddenly emptied, and did not dare ask where they had gone.

After mucking out the stables and spreading clean hay, she boiled up the pig swill and took it to the pens. She was dismayed to find that she became fond of the large, intelligent beasts who came eagerly to the sight of her carrying the buckets. She often stayed a few minutes after they had emptied the troughs to scratch the backs of a few of her favourites with a long stick. She liked the grunts and snorts of pleasure. 'Just don't ask me to be around the day they're slaughtered,' she said to Andrew.

After the pigs she saw her children for the first time in the day. She washed their clothes while they played about her. That there were four of them bothered her; there were too many for her to give much attention to her own two. But Henson had to have some relief, some time to sit in the kitchen over a strong mug of tea. The rest of the day passed in a muddle of haphazard chores. She filled in wherever she was needed. Weeding the vegetable garden, or peeling potatoes. Then it was time for the evening milking. It came early in the short winter days. After that there were the children again, all to be bathed and put to bed. For convenience they had put all four of them in the same room. Henson slept next door, with the door open to hear the least whimper. Nicole doubted that she would have wakened at such a slight sound. She fell into the big double bed in the room Margaret had allotted to her and Lloyd on all their visits, and while its emptiness was like a void, she was too tired to remain awake long to ponder it. The worst times were the very early hours of the morning. With her first fatigue gone, she would wake with a sense that something was happening. She thought she heard the sound of aircraft, but there were no aircraft. Then the emptiness of the bed assailed her, and sleep was hard to come by. The harsh clatter of the alarm clock seemed to wake her just when sleep had come again. It was a winter of hard days, bright and sharp with frost, of aching bones, and exhausted, yet fitful sleep. Lloyd had leave too seldom to make the emptiness less empty.

Margaret, noting the hollows of her cheeks had said, 'Nicole,

325

don't you think perhaps you're overdoing it? I mean, surely there's *someone* we can get to help. You're such a little thing. Not terribly strong.'

'Nonsense, Aunt Margaret. I'm strong as a horse. Don't you know musicians *have* to be strong? How do you think I managed to thump that piano so hard?' She shrugged to dismiss the suggestion. 'And besides, what else would I do? I can't cook. I'd ruin the food, and we can't afford that. I'm not very good at organizing things—not like you in the WVS and the Red Cross. Judy's great on a tractor, and she can make a soup out of two bare bones and a carrot. I've only got a little brute labour to offer. And besides—the cows and the pigs seem to like me ... That's something ...'

'I've noticed,' Margaret said, 'that the hens are all laying very well. I suppose it's all nonsense, but the old country people used to say that getting them to lay was mostly to do with the person who was looking after them. I wonder ...'

'Well,' Nicole said ruefully, 'I *do* admit to singing to them. I get desperate when the eggs start to fall off, and so I sing all the time I'm feeding them, and when I'm hunting for the eggs. Silly creatures ... they seem to like it.'

'I believe they do. Not even Judy is better with the horses. Mr Carbury was saying the other day he never saw anyone take to medicating animals so well so quickly.'

Carbury was the elderly, overworked vet who, once he had diagnosed a complaint, often had to leave it to the farmer to follow through on the treatment, since he was the only vet in the district. Nicole made a point of being there whenever he came, watching how he ran his hands over a beast, learning his techniques of patience with the restless, fretful animal. 'I only do what he tells me—and if he knew how frightened I am ... But I bribe the horses, you know ... those lumps of sugar you've been saving. I must say I never imagined myself taking a horse's temperature or pouring some stuff down a cow's throat ...'

'I wouldn't have believed it,' Andrew said to Margaret once as the dawn was striking the kitchen window, and Nicole had gone off to bed to get an hour's sleep before the milking. 'She's been out there half the night heaving and hauling with me to get that calf born. Carbury couldn't come ... I've always thought she was pretty, but just a little spoiled, and definitely soft. The way Lloyd shielded her from everything, you'd have thought she'd be utterly useless. You have to respect someone who turns to and learns the way she has. You'd almost think she liked it, but I suspect it's quite the other way. All I am sure of—she's damn useful.'

Nicole did, in fact, hate it all. She hated the cold of the mornings when she left her bed, she hated the sight of the string of cows waiting to be washed. She often felt sick at the smell and sight of the pig swill she boiled up, the endless task of cleaning out the stables. It was true that she did sing to the hens, but from a sense of desperation; they were getting good feed, feed that often had to come by ships that were being hunted by German U-boats, and it would be her fault if they didn't give a return of eggs. She hated the whole endless, grinding routine of it, the sense that she was no longer a woman but a machine which produced labour. She hardly looked in a mirror these days, not wanting to see her too-thin face, the hair that was often lank and falling in wisps about her face. It was enough to look at her hands, chapped and rough. It seemed an unbelievable span of time since she had lain and soaked in a hot bath, used perfume, had the energy and leisure to brush her hair. She seemed only vaguely to remember an impossible, fairy-tale time when Henson had drawn her bath, added bath salts, laid out her clothes. Henson who had folded silk stockings and lace-trimmed underwear. The Henson she knew now darned children's socks, and dried their sweaters and underwear before the kitchen stove. To herself, Nicole always seemed to smell of cow dung.

When any of the men were coming on leave, she noticed how they all made a greater effort. Hair was shampooed, and they helped each other set it; the last of the bath salts were carefully portioned out. Sometimes Richard or Lloyd would arrive without notice, and Nicole could see the puzzled glances at the women they had always considered so trim and smart. Nicole in heavy corduroy pants she had inherited from Ben, who had grown out of them, and the sweater bought in Scotland, streaked with dirt, was a new sight to Lloyd. Also new to him was the alarm which clattered in the morning, and as he sleepily stretched to draw her close to him, to hear her voice, 'Not now, stupid . . . It's milking time.' And then, with her clothes on she would bend to kiss him. 'Remember all the mornings you used to leave the house at seven because you were going to operate at eight? Well ... now you've got a working wife ...'

And at times she would lean her head against the warm, gently heaving side of the cow, and the tears of longing and despair would rise, and were choked back. She longed for the times of ease and pleasure and love once again. She longer for clean, warm rooms and delicately cooked food. Most of all she longed to lie in bed when Lloyd was there. But the inexorable rhythm of farm life went on, and she could not stop it, nor turn away from it. Wearily she studied the big map in the kitchen, and wondered how long it would go on.

Only Richard, Lloyd and Gavin now came to Fenton Field on leave. Allan and Ross were in France. All winter the small British Expeditionary Force had dug themselves into their trenches, and the French Army had lived comfortably on the Maginot Line, while Hitler had been busy consolidating his position in Poland, and conquering Norway. Denmark he had taken in a day. In Britain they put up with the inconveniences of war, the shortages, the black-out, the drilling, and they grew bored and restless. They had gone into a war to help a Polish ally for whom, in the end, they had never been able to fire a shot. The months wore on and the situation seemed totally unreal. The country was arming and marching and drilling, and nothing happened. Nicole saw the green quicken in the pastures and along the hedgerows, saw the grain begin to sprout like a tender fuzz on the fields, and she began to experience an illogical hope. She wrote to her sister-in-law in Boston, Liz. 'Don't rent the house just yet. I've a feeling it's a stalemate. Perhaps there'll be an armistice ... Perhaps they'll come to terms ...' She didn't discuss this half-born hope with Lloyd. She nursed it to herself during those gentle days of April, and told herself that soon, soon they would go home. There would be hot water and hand cream, and she would go back to practising the piano, reading books and playing with her children. She would go back to being a wife who didn't have to leave her husband's bed.

The dream ended on 10 May. The Germans attacked the Netherlands and Belgium from the sky before dawn, and by daylight had captured bridges around The Hague and Rotterdam. By the end of the day the Dutch Air Force had been destroyed. Rotterdam was razed from the air. The attack on Belgium came almost at the same time. A German general named Guderian did what the French had declared impossible; he attacked through the Ardennes, and so the Maginot Line was useless. On 13 May, Guderian crossed the Meuse near Sedan, and the Germans were on French soil.

And almost unnoticed to Nicole, because there was so much else to think about, so much else to occupy her, at the end of the House of Commons debate on the fall of Norway, someone called Leo Amery said to Chamberlain, using the words of Cromwell, 'Depart, I say, and let us have done. In the name of God, go.' By the time the Germans invaded the Netherlands and Belgium, Winston Churchill was Prime Minister.

Now the thing was real, and the fear was real. At Fenton Field they stared at the kitchen map in horror as the Netherlands and Belgium were swallowed up. From the bridgeheads across the Meuse the Germans could be seen making their obvious attempt to cut the Allied Armies in two. By 16 May the Germans were moving ahead against an ill-co-ordinated defence at the rate of forty miles a day. By the 20th, German tanks had reached the sea.

With a kind of blank numbness Nicole went about the daily routine of the farm and hung over the radio for every news bulletin. The battle of France was fought all over again on the fields of Flanders. Not even the little coloured pins Andrew used on his map could sort out the confusion of each conflicting bulletin. 'It's chaos,' Andrew said, and he did not dare to look at Margaret. They had no idea where, in this muddle of orders and counter orders, of gallant but unrealistic orders to counter-attack, and the inability of the French to drag themselves out of the numbness of shock and the distaste for heroic endeavour, where either Allan or Ross's division was. The commanders themselves couldn't have said. All the Fentons could see was that the British were being pushed into a box around Dunkirk. On 26 May the British Cabinet authorized Lord Gort to evacuate it. They expected very few of the troops shut in there to reach England.

It was called Operation Dynamo, and it was being run from Dover. Dunkirk lay twenty-four miles away across the Straits. The Navy had not the ships; others of any size, standard, capability, would have to be found. Andrew received a call at Fenton

Field from a friend with whom he occasionally sailed during the summers, light-hearted expeditions they had been then, with nothing very daring attempted, and a watchful eye for bad weather. They knew themselves to be fair-weather sailors, these two ageing men; they also knew that they had to go. Andrew asked Ben if he would make up the third member of the crew. Ben had never sailed before. He agreed. Andrew drove to Dover, met up with his friend among the armada of small boats that was gathering. They received their stores, fuel, provisions and charts. They were told where to go and what to do. The Navy would give them what help it could, and so would the Air Force. And so they sailed.

It was a combination of weather and luck. It was not good weather for flying, and so the Luftwaffe was hampered in its attacks initially; when the weather for flying improved, the RAF was able to hold the Germans in check. The orderly lines of men waiting on the beaches of Dunkirk slowly dwindled as the Navy and the flotilla of small craft made the voyage again and again. Andrew began to think that never again would the ache leave his bones, and never would he be able to sleep for the horror of the wounds he saw. At first Ben was seasick, but by the second crossing he seemed to have lost both his sickness and his strangeness to the craft. It was he who cared for most of the wounded, applying the first-aid lessons he had thought so useless. The lad seemed to Andrew to grow up visibly in those few days. By 1 June the air attacks had become too fierce, and the journeys to Dunkirk could be made only at night. By 4 June the Germans were pressing irresistibly against the tiny space now held by the British, and the evacuation had to be called off. Over 330,000 men were evacuated across the dangerous twenty-four miles. The Germans had believed that none could escape. They came back without weapons, but with their lives.

Some men died on the small boat that Andrew helped to crew, and Ben was wounded. At Dover Ben went to the hospital and Andrew went back to Fenton Field. He slept for twenty-four hours, and woke to the news that Ross had been safely evacuated. None of the family then knew that he had distinguished himself for bravery on the Dunkirk beach where he had marshalled his men. There were many brave men in those days. Of Allan there was no news. Richard had been in action all during the campaign, fighting over France. He was given a few days' leave to rest. It was expected that his squadron would be sent to France to continue the fight, and would be based there. He came back to a house that was silent with apprehension over Allan, silent with exhaustion and fear. He didn't like it. Celia couldn't get leave, so he went up to London. 'Don't worry about Allan, Mother,' he said cheerfully as he left. 'He's far too sensible to get himself into any bother. See you soon . . .'

He was, thought Nicole, having all the action and the speed that his nature craved, and Fenton Field must have seemed a dreary place to him.

For Lloyd there was no leave. After an autumn and winter and spring of waiting, his medical unit had more to do than it could properly cope with. 'I'll get there some time,' he promised Nicole on the phone. 'When the serious cases are through the worst. But we'll have the backlog for quite a while. Men have got shrapnel in the damnest places. You'd wonder how some of them made it back alive.' He went on, 'You all right there, Nicky?'

'Yes—everything's all right.'

'Good—take care of yourself and the boys. See you soon.' He too was in a hurry, Nicole thought, after he had hung up. He was in the fight at last, and there was no time for anything else. She thought it might become possible to hate the men who had embraced the war so easily and so well—men like Richard and Lloyd and Ross.

That June of beautiful summer weather saw the end of fighting on the Continent for some time. Dumbly they listened to the news that Italy had declared war, now the fall of France seemed imminent, and the invasion of Britain only a matter of time and planning. The Germans swept through France and on 14 June, entered Paris. By 22 June the French had signed an armistice with Germany in the same railway carriage at Compiègne which had seen the same ceremony in 1918. Britain braced itself for bombing, and once again Fenton Field was crowded with evacuees.

'What a place to bring them,' Judy said with a trace of bitterness. 'We could be having Germans marching across the fields any day now.'

Ben came home from the hospital and helped pull down all the road signs so that the enemy might be confused as to their location. Churches were forbidden to toll their bells; that was to be the signal for invasion. Farmers sharpened pitchforks, ready for the troops that might descend from the sky. There was still no news of Allan; Nicole began to dread the arrival of Joan Fenton in the big kitchen—the moment of hope when the door opened, and then the sight of the dark gauntness of her face, the silent shake of the head, the shrug. There were still men waiting for evacuation all along the coast of France, men sent there in a last desperate effort to turn the tide of battle. Allan was with the 61st Division. They were at Brest and Bayonne, at Bordeaux and St Jean de Luz. About half a million men were evacuated from France that month. About two-thirds were British, the rest were a motley mixture of French, Polish, Czech, Canadian and Belgian. No official telegram reached Joan at the house along the road from Fenton Field. She coped with her own tasks, and her own evacuees, and no word of Allan came.

So the remnants of a great army gathered in England, and were almost without weapons. Churchill told the House of Commons, and the speech was reported on the radio, 'When Napoleon lay at Boulogne, he was told "There are bitter weeds in England." There are certainly a great many more of them since the British Expeditionary Force returned.' He went on to his climax. 'We shall go on to the end ... We shall fight on the beaches, we shall fight on the landing grounds, we shall fight in the fields and in the streets, we shall fight in the hills; we shall never surrender.'

Never surrender. Nicole went to feed the hens and the words haunted her. Never surrender. What in God's name were she and the boys and Lloyd doing in a place where the thought of bloody battle should even be possible? Surely now Lloyd would see that they had no business here. But now the way was barred. He was locked into his work here, and he would not, in his own fashion, surrender it either. And for her, there was no way out. She stared over the sweet green pastures of Fenton Field and tried to imagine it as she had seen the pictures of the battle-scarred villages and fields of western Europe. It seemed beyond imagination, and yet she knew it was a possibility. 'There are bitter weeds in England.'

How she hated all the men who had made this war—the unknown men who were only names to her, and the completely unknown men who had stood behind them, done their planning, written their ultimatums. And what was the use of hatred? It produced nothing. She might turn and hate Lloyd and Richard and Ross and Allan—even Andrew. It produced nothing. They were pawns in this, as she was—she and her children. Far better to turn to what might do some good. So she went about her business in the hen-run.

There were much fewer eggs than usual. She scrambled about in the nests, looked everywhere that the hens had ever laid before. The count was smaller. They flocked about her, those hens, as they always did. She listened to their raucous cries for a moment, and then her frustration and fear were let loose.

'Never surrender, you hear? Never! You stupid birds. Don't you know you have to lay more than ever? Don't you *know*? We're going to be invaded, and you'd better be done with your laying. Oh, why, now—*now*. You know we need the eggs? What about them—eh? What about them?'

She brandished her arms and they scuttled back from her in alarm. And then she realized that she had never spoken to them in these tones before, and it could result in a further falling-off in the laying. So she made conciliatory gestures with her hands and stood still. Gradually the agitation among the fowls died down. To her surprise she could hear her own voice, tunelessly croaking because of the tightness in her throat, into that perfect June evening, the Brahms lullaby.

'Lullaby, and good night ...' She didn't know the rest of the words so she just kept up the melody; eventually the birds settled down and seemed as if they might go peacefully to roost. 'Lullaby, and good night ...'

A strange piece of news came to Nicole shortly after the fall of Paris. Everyone now scanned the death notices in *The Times* —there were names of school friends, the brothers, sons, husbands of acquaintances scattered all over England and Scotland. One day Margaret gravely handed the paper to Nicole when she came in from the stables. 'Gerald Agar,' she said.

Nicole snatched the paper. '*Sir Gerald Agar, 7th Baronet, in Paris ...*' The notice was painfully brief. It gave him no service rank, nor the cause of death. Nicole spent an hour trying to reach Charles in his Whitehall office. 'I'll see what I can find out,' he said. 'Though what the hell Gerald Agar was doing in

Paris at that time, I can't imagine. Perhaps he was waiting for his Nazi chums.'

'I'm sorry to bother you with it, Uncle Charles—but I want to know. He can't have——'

'Don't be surprised at anything, Nicole,' Charles said curtly, and hung up.

He rang back late that night. 'Best information I've been able to dig up,' he said tersely. 'Agar wasn't in any of the services. He simply hasn't been in England since war broke out. They fished his body out of the Seine. It rather looks as if someone had taken some pretty frightful reprisal against him. You know, not all the French agreed with the Armistice. They thought they'd been sold out. I don't know where Agar fitted in, except that he was known to be living there apparently without any plan to leave before the Germans marched in. It's hardly the way an Englishman acts . . .' Charles's tone was tight with suppressed anger. He, like many, believed that Hitler would now move very swiftly to an invasion of England, and the thought of an Englishman calmly awaiting the arrival of the Germans in Paris roused him to fury. 'It's taken a bit of time for all this to be confirmed. The body had to be identified. The information came through the Red Cross in the end. Naturally the family isn't saying much. What can you say about a man whom everyone supposes was collaborating with the enemy? Did you know he'd been kicked out of his London clubs long ago? *In absentia*, of course.'

'I can't believe it,' Nicole said. 'Not Gerry. I'll *never* believe that that's the whole story.'

'Well, my dear, that's the official story now, and from what I know, it's the true one. Don't grieve for him, Nicole. There are plenty of decent men who didn't come back. Perhaps he helped in that . . .'

Nicole hung up.

The house in Grosvenor Terrace which Gerald Agar had once visited, wore a wartime look of innocence. It was sandbagged and had heavy air-raid shutters on the windows. It now wore a name-plate of the Ministry of Food, Research Division. No ration books were kept there, nor did any of the public ever make routine enquiries there about food, or how to apply for ration books, how to report lost ones. Any who did wander in were directed to the nearest branch by the commissioner. The man who had once interviewed Gerald Agar still had his office there, and in the basement were enormous steel fire-proof files. The file on Gerald Agar was removed from one, which had been active, and placed in another, which was dead storage.

The organization knew almost all the details of the death of Gerald Agar. He had died under torture by the SS, who had, by a freak chance, discovered the game he had played all these years with their high-ranking masters in Berlin. It would not have done to expose the mistakes of their masters, so it was better that a doubt should exist as to why Gerald Agar had died. Reprisals of French patriots seemed an obvious answer, so the body was dumped where it could be found, and with identification. In London there was concern for some time that the SS might have extracted information from Agar before he died, but time went by, and the next link in the chain seemed safe enough, and still covered. They breathed a little more easily, and turned to the task of recruiting more agents who might operate under the eyes of the Nazis. Gerald Agar had been valuable, but he was dead, and his value had ended.

The man who had once talked with him in that room reviewed the file for the last time, before it went into its dark storage place. Agar had been a rather special case, a case of a man who had been willing to appear to be a traitor in the eyes of his own countrymen in order to serve them. The man who had given him orders thought that that required a rather higher order of courage than the type displayed by men who won medals for gallantry in the heat of battle. Only if Agar had survived the war, and only if Germany had lost, could his reputation ever have been salvaged. And the man knew human nature well enough to know that no medal from the King after the war would ever have erased from people's minds the memory of Agar spending the war in a German-occupied country. It was still possible that it might be done, when the war was over. But to the man the war looked as if it might go on for a long time, and so Gerald Agar's file would remain hidden and highly secret. To the man's way of thinking Gerald Agar had been the only kind of patriot that mattered, the one who was willing to do the dirty and dangerous things, with little chance of recognition. But Agar had known that, had taken his risks, and finally lost. He had given his life, and his good name as well.

The Battle of Britain began in a quiet, almost unnoticed fashion. It was the strategy of the Luftwaffe to draw the squadrons of Fighter Command out over the Channel by attacking the convoys of ships passing through it. The shorter range of the German Messerschmidts made this desirable, and there was the hope that a British pilot shot down over the sea would never return to fly another plane. Early in July the attacks on Channel convoys began, and the RAF went up to intercept. The losses were heavy, more than Fighter Command could stand, but they had the advantage over the Germans of the possession of radar, in an early form. This let them keep their fighters on the ground until the last moment, conserving fuel and saving their pilots from having to seek out their enemy. To the Luftwaffe these air battles over the Channel were part of the plan to destroy Fighter Command and leave the way open for invasion. They envisaged the coasts of England across the Channel unprotected by fighter aircraft. It was a dream that drew them to destruction.

Now the skies over Fenton Field sounded almost hourly with the drone of planes, coming and going from their stations. For the family there was the added anguish of knowing that any of those planes might be piloted by Richard, who was part of Eleven Group, the group whose aerodromes covered the whole slice of south-east England from the Isle of Wight up to Suffolk. The teasing attacks on the convoys continued, and Air Marshal Sir Hugh Dowding began to protest the very presence of the merchant ships there. His strength was being wasted, he said. Eventually it was decided that the convoys would sail only at night. The Luftwaffe then turned its attention to the Royal Navy, and the news came that German troops intended for the invasion had begun massing in their newly-won French ports across the Channel.

It was then that Margaret Fenton made one of her few gloomy remarks. 'I feel as if I just stretched out my hand far enough, I could touch them. They're just such a few miles away ...'

That was also the day that Joan Fenton burst into the kitchen with the telegram form in her hand. 'He's alive! He's a prisoner—but he's alive!' Then she broke down and sobbed in hysterical relief, and Nicole went down to the cellar and, without compunction, poured half a tumbler of Gavin's precious malt whisky and made her drink it. The telegram had said that Allan had been wounded, but not seriously. It would be possible, later, to have direct contact through the Red Cross. They did not yet know where Allan was imprisoned. Nicole looked fearfully at the kitchen map. Hitler owned so much of Europe now.

The pace of the air battles stepped up. The German dive-bombers attacked the shipping, while individual battles went on between the RAF and the Luftwaffe fighter planes. Richard, whose squadron had been stood down for three days' rest, decided to come down to Fenton Field. He seemed to them all to be in quite impossibly high spirits. 'This is it! We'll beat them in the air, and they'll *never* invade. Give us just a little more time, and we'll be chasing them back across France.'

No one believed him. Nicole thought he had about him an air of euphoria, almost as if the action he was engaged in was some kind of powerful drug. He spent, in those three days, when the weather was ironically beautiful, most of his time out of doors, field glasses in hand, watching the planes that went over. Almost as if he could not bear to be away from it, he hitched a lift to Dover to watch the battles over the Channel. 'We're not doing badly,' he pronounced. 'Not badly at all.'

They did not know that Hitler had given his directive. 'The German Air Force is to overpower the English Air Force with all the forces at its command.' Goering issued a timetable for his Luftwaffe. RAF fighter defences in the south of England were to be smashed in four days, and the whole RAF must be defeated in four weeks. Then the way would be open for Hitler's Operation Eagle, the invasion of Britain.

Richard, sharing with his family in the kitchen the three bottles of gin he had managed to bring with him, talked laconically about Celia. 'Well, she's gone and done an officer-training course, and has landed herself at Stanmore, under Dowding in Fighter Command. Funny to think my little wife might be one of those cool and efficient ladies who send the signal that gets my squadron into the air. Of course, "dear Daddy" had some pull in getting her there, but she seems to be making out all right—if I'm to believe those very precise little notes she writes me. So discreet. No information given. She isn't an Air Vice-Marshal's daughter for nothing. Funny, the mouse is turning into a lion, but the lion isn't very feminine. There isn't even the mouse to come home to any more.'

Nicole blazed at him. 'If you'd paid her a little more attention, she might still be here for you to come home to.'

He looked at her with the kind of gaze that seemed to take in everything she now was that she hated—the tired, unglamorous, half-washed tender of pigs and cattle and hens and cabbages. 'Well, you've made yourself into a nice, good, quiet, little housefrau, but you don't notice Lloyd here every half-day he gets off ... Perhaps you should have done what he wanted. He would have a beautiful memory of a beautiful woman waiting for him snugly in a house in Boston. The trouble with you, Nicole, is that you've overplayed your hand. You've made him feel guilty by staying here. You've become the super-patriot, denying yourself everything, going around looking like a hag, just to let him know what he's done to you. You've made him feel guilty, and men don't like to feel that way about women—especially not their wives.'

Her nerves, which every day seemed to grow more taut, snapped. In full view of Margaret and Andrew, she reached across and slapped Richard on the cheek. The sound seemed unnaturally loud in the quiet of the kitchen.

But her anger could only be sustained for an instant; she was filled with horror at what she had done. 'I'm sorry,' she said immediately. 'I don't know what's the matter with me. I shouldn't have done that ...'

'Please forget it,' he said. 'I asked for it. It's none of my business. Listen, why don't you get a dress on and we'll go down to the local. You don't ever leave this place. That's part of the trouble.'

'I can't ... thanks, Richard.' And she turned and fled out of the kitchen and straight out to the pigsties. She no longer went even to the orchard when she wanted to be alone. It was too hard to go there, the memories were of better times, and the contrast was too painful.

The big, cheerful-faced animals came to the fence to greet her, even though she wasn't carrying the swill buckets. 'Of course he's right,' she said to them, and the grunts seemed to be agreement. 'I've turned myself into a drab martyr, showing him and everyone else what a good little girl I'm being. I should have had a few extravagant weekends in London with

Lloyd. Got to a hairdresser. I've got all the clothes I brought over last year. Why do I think I have to live in dirty pants and a sweater?' She looked at the big pink bodies crowding on the other side of the fence. 'Well—shall I do it? Shall I break out? Now that Ben's back Andrew could spare me ...' They grunted back, and that also was agreement.

But when she finally reached Lloyd by telephone at the hospital near Fighter Command base at Maidstone, he was discouraging. 'I just don't think it can be managed, Nicky. Since all this new activity started, we don't get more than a few hours to sleep even. There are pretty heavy casualties—a good few of those who bail out survive, you know, but with some pretty shocking wounds. I'm back doing just routine general surgery most of the time. Trying to save arms and legs. Occasionally we get something in the spine that I go to work on. Of course there's still a lot of the chaps who were brought in after Dunkirk ... Honestly, Nicky, things are so busy here I just can't even ask for leave, much less expect it. You understand, don't you?'

'Yes,' she said dully. 'I understand. It was just a thought. We just don't seem to have had any time to ourselves for so long ... You'll let me know when you can get away, won't you? I've just had a lecture from Richard on looking like something that came in with the cows——'

'Richard? And what damn business is it of his how you look?'

'Oh, Lloyd, don't get so het up. I deserved it, I expect. Everyone's nerves are a bit on edge. And Richard—he's wound up tight as a wire and all he wants is to get back into the air again. You'd think he *enjoyed* shooting it out up there—and being shot at.'

'Some of them do, Nicky. Some of them do,' Lloyd answered soberly. 'I don't know about these fighter pilots ... Strange lot. Some of them come to visit their buddies here. I wonder how most of them are going to come back to earth when it's over ... Well, I'd better go. Take care of yourself. Take care of the kids. I love you.'

Then he was gone, and the flush of excitement which had accompanied her thought of meeting him in London for a few days' leave died into dull disappointment. She sat beside the telephone for a while. Then she looked at her watch. It was coming up to the time for the evening milking. But before she went out she went back to the kitchen and sat with Margaret and sipped the rest of the gin she had left when she had walked out on Richard.

'No leave for Lloyd,' she said, slumping down in her chair. 'It was rottenly selfish of me to ask it. He's probably busier now than he's ever been in his life.'

'Why don't you let yourself be a bit selfish now and again, Nicole? We all need it, you know. Very few of us were born saints.'

'*You* say that, Aunt Margaret. I'm pretty certain you're one of the ones who was born nearly a saint. The trouble is, I'm terrified of people finding out how selfish I really am.' She poured herself another gin. 'So I lean over backwards so no one will notice. But Richard has seen it. He always knew me pretty well.' She looked at her watch and drained the gin. 'Time for the milking. If Richard comes in, tell him I'd love to go for a drink at the local with him, if the invitation is still on. And tell him I'll wear my nicest dress, and perfume. The warriors are at least entitled to that, aren't they?'

Margaret watched her walk across the farmyard towards the milking sheds. She was back to that dangerous degree of thinness she had possessed in those few days when she had waited here with Lloyd before her marriage. Her face now, though, was that of a woman, not a girl; it had gained strength and maturity and therefore the lines of strain were more threatening of real danger should she break. Margaret wondered how it would be possible to make her stop this compulsive routine of hard and distasteful tasks she had set herself. She must try ... she must find something else for Nicole to do, something with a little more gaiety in it, something to make her smile. Then she looked at the clock and knew in half an hour she was due at a WVS meeting. She scribbled a note for Richard and went out into the scullery to find Wilks. He was peeling potatoes, something that would have been unthinkable if there had been other help in the house. 'You'll make sure that Master Richard gets it, won't you? I must fly now ...' And she was off, on a routine just as binding as Nicole's was, and at her age, far more wearying.

Nicole bathed and dressed with care, and they walked in the summer twilight to the pub in Stokeley a mile away. The place was packed and thick with smoke; the windows sealed with black-out curtains. There were many veterans of Dunkirk there, and some, like Richard, wearing the insignia of Fighter Command. All of them had their own stories to tell. Richard was hailed by some of the regulars who knew him, and pressed for details on how the fight was going. 'Don't know,' Richard said cheerfully. 'I only know what our own chaps shoot down—and that's been a fair few. Don't worry—we'll blast them out of the sky.'

'Didn't see so many of your lot about when I was on the beach at Dunkirk,' one young soldier grumbled.

'You didn't see us because we were keeping the Stukas from dive-bombing you,' Richard answered. He appealed to the company around him. 'Look at him—back here and fit as a fiddle. Well, some people are never satisfied. I think he wanted to be *flown* home.' And the half-implied taunt was turned into a laugh.

'Well, here's someone who seems to be bagging his share. They say he got eight Jerry planes in the last ten days.' The newspaper was passed over, and Richard and Nicole bent to look at the picture and read the caption underneath. '*Squadron Leader David, Lord Ashleigh ... recommended for DFC.*'

Richard looked at her and smiled. 'You still got the better man ...'

She examined the face, somewhat blurred by the grainy newsprint. He was still the golden, beautiful young man, photographed beside his aircraft, helmet in hand. He was smiling, as if his whole life was some amusing adventure which he revelled in. It was the sort of picture which the newspapers these days were full of—the Ministry of Information propaganda picture, meant to boost morale. 'We've heard of him,' Richard said quietly. 'He's stationed at Hawkinge. Actually, that number might be less than he's actually bagged. He's the genuine article ... an absolute honest-to-God war hero, and quite becomingly modest about it. One of the beautiful boys who never gets it wrong. He'll get his DFC—*and* bar, I'll bet.'

'He looks as if he's enjoying himself.'

'I'd be looking that way if I'd brought that many down.'

'Is he married, do you know?' She had often wanted to ask, and her tongue had always stuck on the words.

'Yes—I did see something about it a few years ago. Big London wedding. Nothing at all like the one——'

'The one we were going to have. Don't be afraid to say it,

341

Richard. I *did* get the right man. I would have been cheating David if I'd married him. He looks as if he hasn't suffered.'

'Wouldn't be too sure. When you get yourself out of those farm overalls, you're still beautiful enough to make a man stop and think thoughts he perhaps shouldn't have. Oh, hell, why not? Lots of thoughts, and little action ...'

'Time, gentlemen. Time, please ...'

They were turning out the lights, hurrying to wash up the empty glasses. Nicole and Richard edged around the black-out curtain at the door and went out into the last of the twilight glow of this midsummer's evening. It was fragrant and warm as they walked along the road to Fenton Field, and overhead were the sound of bombers.

'Sounds like Jerry,' Richard said. He slipped his arm about Nicole and drew her close to him. 'You know, the thing I find hardest to imagine now is that some Stuka may actually come down on Fenton Field. They went for civilian targets in France —why not here? I always thought I'd be doing my fighting somewhere else. It's unreal when the squadron goes up, and I can actually look down and see places I know—and there's a battle going on over them. From up there it all looks so beautiful down here—like the toy farm I used to have when I was a kid. It's so easy to forget that beautiful girls boil up pig swill, and their hands ...'

'Please, Richard, not that again. I try. I'll try harder in the future. But it's just not possible not to get yourself and your hands into a mess——'

'Shut up,' he said quickly, and turned her to him and kissed her hard on the mouth. 'I was trying to apologize. You're very beautiful, Nicole. I would have been sick if I'd gone away without ...'

She tried to draw back from him, and his arms resisted. 'You're not going to act the offended lady just because I kissed you? I *used* to kiss you. You didn't mind it then.'

'You said it once yourself, Richard. We've all gone our own ways. We'll never go back to that summer when it was all such fun.'

He shrugged, and released her. 'I should know better—and yet it isn't an insult when a man wants to make love to a woman. But then you're married to Lloyd Fenton. And I never saw a woman so much married to her man. You really don't live except through him, do you, Nicole?'

She sighed. 'Life might be easier if I didn't care so much about him. But I *do* care. It's as if I've never got over being in love with him the way I was when I first knew him. We've been married nearly six years, and I still go weak at the knees when I see him after we've been away from each other. I suppose I'm terribly jealous and possessive and all the wrong things. I just can't help it.'

He paused to light a cigarette. He shouldn't have done it at this stage of darkness, but Nicole couldn't make herself say anything about it. 'And no other man will ever have you while he's there. This is war, Nicole. Things come and go quickly. Like making love . . .'

'This is war,' she repeated, 'and I hate every single second of drudgery it has brought to me. The time drags like lead every minute I'm not with him. And when I'm with him, it's gone in a flash—like making love. No, Rick, there'll be no one else . . . ever.'

CHAPTER 4

I

Afterwards, Nicole was never able to sort out in their exact order the events of those weeks of August and September when their whole world nearly came to an end. She could remember the weather on 13 August when the real attack came inland from the Channel and headed for its targets of the Fighter Command bases. It was heavy and rainy, with clouds which obscured the German bombers as they went overhead, and also obscured them from the covering of their own fighter planes, who turned back. But that was the last time they turned back. The German planes, both bombers and fighters, came from France, and even from the coast of Norway. At Fenton Field they lived, it seemed to Nicole, off the news bulletins. The reports were broken and fragmentary, and the totals of losses on both sides did not tally. They heard of the vital radar stations being attacked, but which still were kept functioning. The Fighter Command bases were bombed until it was impossible to use some of them. The wave of battle swept over the skies of Kent and Sussex, and seemed to leave Fenton Field behind, in some kind of no-man's-land of confusion and fear. They went about their tasks, as they had to, and didn't talk much. There was the farming routine to keep going somehow, the children, their own and the evacuees, to feed. 'I wonder,' she said to Judy, as the motley crew gathered around the table in the kitchen, 'why they sent evacuees *here*? We're the front line already—or has it passed us?' Margaret wrestled with the ration books, and attempted to produce filling meals. She steadfastly refused to keep back any of the farm produce for their own use. But the hens had stopped laying. 'How can they lay,' Nicole demanded, 'with all this noise going on over them?' They bickered and fought over small things because the bigger,

344

greater danger was too great to bear talking about. They didn't hold the frayed tempers, the hasty words against each other. It was taken as part of life during which they were, in a sense, under attack. Suddenly the Ministry decided to move the evacuees away. They breathed a sigh of relief at Fenton Field; they had enough young children to worry about. 'I wonder,' Judy said, 'if we couldn't get our own lot sent too? Suddenly Cornwall seems like some remote and wonderful desert island.' Anxious letters reached Nicole from Boston. 'Isn't there any way you can send the children back here?' Liz wrote. 'You know we'll take care of them. Uncle Pete says he thinks he might be able to get a passage for you all on one of the Palmer line. Mostly they go in and out of Liverpool. Not luxury but at least you'd be safe since they're an American line.' Nicole only let herself consider the prospect wistfully for a few moments, and then put it out of her head. For the time being, they were locked in here—locked in by her own stubbornness, and her refusal to leave Lloyd. And at this moment, it was too dangerous to think of sending the boys off alone. She doubted that they could, in these desperate days, be got to Liverpool to wait the hospitality of the Palmer line which the Fenton influence in Boston, and their American citizenship could give them. By the time she might safely think of sending them back to Boston, Nicole knew the question of invasion this year would have come and gone, successful or defeated. She looked at her small sons with a sense of shame. Her selfishness and possessiveness had kept them here, and they had become, in a way, a terrible weapon of guilt against Lloyd. She acknowledged that Richard had been right. She should have gone back. She should at least have sent them. Then she shrugged and went on with her work. The question was academic. If the Boston Fentons blamed her, and through her, blamed Lloyd, it must all now wait until time and events decided what would become of them. Distantly they heard the aircraft—always the aircraft, and that was the true reality of those days.

One date she remembered, Sunday 8 September, was designated as a day of prayer. They had heard reports of Hitler's address 'In England they keep asking, "Why doesn't he come? He's coming. He's coming." ' On the Saturday night teleprinters and telephones passed on to the Eastern and Southern

Commands the code word 'Cromwell'. This code word was one stage removed from the actual declaration of invasion, but in some places it was taken to mean invasion. Church bells pealed, and farmers blew up bridges. Nicole walked to the village church the next morning with Dan and Timmy, and found that she was too dry-mouthed with fear to join in the hymns. All she could think of was her argument with Lloyd a year ago on her right to remain here, among these people, trying to sing the hymns in their church while the bombers flew overhead. They knew now that the night of the 7th the first wave of bombers had hit London, and the war of the blitzkrieg was on. They didn't know until long afterwards, when the final score was reckoned up, when the true losses on both sides were tallied, when the great mistake of changing the battle plan away from bombing the airfields to bombing London was made, that the battle was already won. Exhausted pilots climbed back time and again into their aircraft which, repaired, refuelled, the long shiny bands of ammunition fed into the magazines, took off to intercept the bombers and their covering escort. But the airfields were still usable and the battle carried on. It was actually a day of deliverance on that Sunday when they prayed in all the village churches and in the great cathedrals of England.

There were no telephone communications in those weeks. No one dared to lift a receiver unless it was an emergency. Everything, it seemed to Nicole, was geared to emergency. She knew that Lloyd's hospital near Maidstone stood in the middle of several Fighter Command Bases; as the casualties from civilian bombing mounted, he must be working as long as he could stand on his feet. The news of the bombings of London grew worse. The East End was devastated; a bomb fell on Buckingham Palace. They heard, and re-heard, on the wireless the words Winston Churchill had spoken in the Commons on 20 August, speaking of the battle between the young airmen which raged over their heads. 'Never in the field of human conflict has so much been owed by so many to so few.' He had not meant it to be a rousing speech; to him it was a simple statement of fact.

By telegram the news came of Richard. Shot down, over Kent, wounded, but alive. Margaret and Celia were given special facilities to get to see him at the hospital at Hastings.

Margaret came back ashen-faced, after two days of sleeping in the lounge of one of the local hotels. Celia had gone back to Stanmore. 'He's alive,' she managed to say when she reached Fenton Field. She had been brought by car by one of the farmers who had chanced to notice her sitting in the waiting-room of the station nearest Fenton Field. 'He's got a smashed leg—and head injuries. His sight ...' She swayed and clung to the table for support. 'They think he might not be able to see again. He's ... he's out of danger.' When she collapsed on the kitchen floor, Wilks was the first to reach her, it was he who attempted to revive her. Andrew, her husband, was helpless.

The bombings of London continued. Fighter Command flew inland every day to intercept the German bombers. From the bombed and collapsed cellars of London, a spirit, almost tangible, seemed to arise. People gathered themselves up, after a night in a shelter, and, for the most part, went to work that same day. Many returned to the ruins of their homes. Many did not reach the shelters, despite the orders and injunctions of the air-raid wardens.

The telephone ringing at Fenton Field could mean only good news or bad. This time it was Charles, talking briefly from his office in Whitehall. 'Nicole, it's about your Aunt Iris. You knew she took on this extra job of being an air-raid warden for our district. Well ... last night a house at the back of us was hit by an incendiary bomb. It was full of people. You know we've been taking in everyone we can pack under the roof from the East End. Well ... your Aunt Iris ...'

'Yes ... she was an air-raid warden ...' Nicole knew that she had been much else beside, but it was typical of Iris that she should undertake this additional task. The time had to be fully filled; the extra duty always volunteered for.

'She went into the building, and brought out a young mother and her child. It wasn't until they were out safely that Iris learned that the grandmother was left inside. The building was going up very quickly. But Iris had her gas mask. She evidently thought she could still go in. The firemen hadn't reached the building, and there was no one in authority to stop her. They don't know whether she ever reached the grand-mother. The stairs came down.'

Nicole reached London by train and bus, and the journey took twelve hours. She walked from Charing Cross to Elgin

347

Square. Charles was there, in full military dress, wearing his decorations. Neighbours from Elgin Square and people from the mews houses behind came to speak to him. 'Never really knew her until these last few weeks. A real demon for getting things done.' One of the temporary evacuees from the East End said, 'A proper old sergeant-major, she was. Got our cards in order. Got one of the kids to the hospital. Got the old lady evacuated to Devon. She'll hate it there, but at least we don't have to listen to her moaning ... Oh, sorry, Sir Charles. You have your own problems. A real good lady she was. Tough as they come ...'

Other people, closer friends, said more gentle things, but none more real. Nicole went with Charles to Highgate Cemetery. The strange, rigid woman of her girlhood had turned into a heroine. 'She was very high in the Red Cross,' Charles said. 'I've had a telegram from the King.'

Nicole put her hand in his. 'I wish she had let me come to see her—just once. It would have made it easier now. I'm left feeling guilty, and yet I could never have said to her that I was wrong. I suppose in the end we all think about our own feelings, not about the person who's dead.'

'Iris,' Charles said, 'was a splendid woman. She was completely and utterly thorough. Even her death was typical. She didn't like things left undone. But she would never have understood a marriage like yours, Nicole. It would have done no good to see her. Remember that.'

She spent one night in the shuttered and sandbagged basement of Elgin Square, while the bombers came once more. It was the first time she had heard high-explosives close at hand. The sound terrified and shook her, but the real amazement was the calmness of the people. Several shared the basement with them. Charles had brought them himself from the East End, friends formed during the time he had worked with a shelter there. Adams, as air-raid warden, was in charge of them. During a lull in the bombing he went out to tour the square, mostly watching for signs of incendiaries. 'Adams,' Charles said, 'is terribly upset about Iris. He was devoted to her, you know. Yes, I know—he looks like a wooden-faced old snob, but he respected her highly after all these years of serving her. He feels partly responsible for her death. You see, she was a sort of honorary warden—she had so much else to do that she didn't have much time to get to their training sessions. Adams let her get out of his sight that night, he says. She should never have gone back into the building. And yet if she hadn't gone the first time, the mother and the child were too paralysed with fright to move ... So she saved two lives, and was on her way back to save another. Adams mourns for her, genuinely ... He's sixty-eight you know. Sometimes I look around and I almost think it's the old ones who are keeping this country going ... the old and the very young. They're kids up there in those planes.'

'And how old are you, Uncle Charles? Adams isn't the only one who grieves ...'

'Me? I'm just an old fool.' In the semi-darkness of the basement his hand sought hers. 'Try to stay safe, will you, Nicole? It would be hard on me to lose you.'

She had a lift in Charles's official car the next morning but only to the point where it did not deviate from its usual route. 'I couldn't look Aunt Margaret in the eye if I used a drop more petrol than was strictly necessary.'

Charing Cross was sandbagged and dusty from bomb damage, but functioning. Nicole changed trains three times in the journey down to Fenton Field, which had once been so easy and swift.

She found Wilks alone in the kitchen when she got back to the house. How much he and Adams fitted the pattern—an unquestioning devotion to a family and a way of life which both were determined, in their own fashion, to see survive. 'I've been reading about your aunt, Lady Gowing, Mrs Fenton. A very gallant lady.'

She sat while he made a cup of tea for her. He was as troubled as Margaret was by the tense thinness of this woman who seemed to have aged before his eyes. 'Dr Fenton telephoned,' he said.

Nicole sat upright, her fatigue vanished. 'He *telephoned*! Is there something wrong? Is he all right?'

Wilks was worried that so much of this young woman's being, her vital strength, was bound up in this one man. 'He didn't speak himself, Mrs Fenton. He'd read about Lady Gowing. But a secretary, or a nurse, or someone was trying to reach you. I expect he couldn't spare the time to come to the phone unless you were available. The bombing all along the

Thames has been pretty bad, you know. He said he'd telephone again—tonight.'

Nicole drank her tea slowly. It was very strong, and sweet. The sort of tea they had handed out in the basement the night before, hoping that the warmth and sweetness would help fend off the shock of the earth rumbling around them. It was very different from the China tea Wilks had brought out to the lawn in the thin fine china on the fine summer days of a world that seemed forever gone. She roused herself out of her own thoughts, the thoughts of Lloyd, the greedy, selfish thought that tonight he would telephone her.

'Richard,' she said. 'Is there any new word on Richard?'

Wilks sipped his own tea, and then went on with his task of stirring egg powder. It always amazed Nicole that they sent so many fresh eggs from the farm, and got back egg powder in return. 'Master Richard is improving. He's very strong. All the Fentons have good constitutions ...' Nicole looked away from the silent tears that streamed down the old man's cheeks. It was his private grief, and he would live with it. She rinsed her cup at the sink, and went upstairs to change into her pants and sweater. It was almost milking time.

II

She waited up. About two o'clock the call came, and she snatched the receiver. The voices of several operators came between. At last she heard Lloyd's voice. 'Nicky?—are you all right? You've been up to London to the funeral? I'm sorry I couldn't get there. No time off duty. But of all people your aunt would have understood that. Is Charles all right?'

She hesitated. 'He seems all right. It's all such confusion there ... Lloyd, you've heard about Rick?'

'Yes. Rotten luck. When this lets up a bit I'll get over to see him—professionally. I've talked to his doctor. Nicky ... don't let the family hope too much. The sight of one eye is gone completely. There's only a small chance of saving the other ... Does the family know that?'

'I ... I don't know they know that much. Everyone keeps hoping.'

'Then perhaps you'd better say nothing. Time enough to get used to the idea when they must. Time enough ...'

'Lloyd ... Lloyd ...' What had she been going to say? There were no words.

'Yes, my love. I know. It's rough all round. And guess who I've had as my particular patient these last five days? No—don't guess. I didn't mean that. I've got young David Ashleigh——'

'David——!'

'Yes, the young golden eagle of the skies himself. Famous air ace. The word hasn't been released to the press yet.'

'*What* word? What happened to him?'

'Nicky, he's been incredibly lucky. He got a bullet through the cheek-bone which went on up to lodge in the skull. By whatever reflexes the gods gave him, he managed to get himself out of the craft and pull the rip-cord in time. He was unconscious when they found him. I imagine he must have passed out while he was still coming down, and was lucky someone didn't shoot at him. However, he's here, and he's all right.'

'All right—what does that mean?'

'He's all right. He's alive. I've managed to extract the bullet from his skull, and so far as we can tell, the brain isn't damaged. It was five days ago, Nicky. I didn't want to tell you until I was fairly sure he was going to make it. Not just make it as a vegetable, but as a person. He's showing responses, and good reflexes. His eyes react to light—he hears sounds. The rest of his body is almost undamaged, considering that he came down in a parachute unconscious. A broken ankle, two broken ribs. Nothing, really.'

'But you said a bullet went through his cheek ...'

'Well, that's something different. If I manage to get through my part of the job and keep him and his brain alive, then the plastic surgeons are going to have to take over. That side of his face is shattered. They'll put it together, one way or the other, but they'll have to rebuild it. They'll have to find small pieces of bones from other places in his body. The cheek-bones are gone ...'

'Gone ...' she echoed the word dully. The beautiful, blond David was destroyed, the young man of poetic beauty.

'Nicky ... after I'd done my piece, taking the bullet from the skull, I watched the plastic guy get to work. God, I nearly wept, and surgeons aren't sentimental. They had to do an initial repair job, just so the dressings could be put on him.

But if only we'd had Carl Zimmerman. Hell, I've seen him handle a dozen far worse things brought in off street accidents ... The way he can pick out the splintered bones, and start to reconstruct the face even from the beginning. Young David won't be beautiful ever again, but he would have looked a damn sight nicer if Carl had had him.'

'And where is Carl? Why couldn't you have ...?'

'Carl, love, by chance of the winds of fortune, is now in an internment camp on the Isle of Man. I guess he got so preoccupied with his job that he forgot to do anything about becoming a British subject. He was still a German when war broke out. So he's in a camp on the Isle of Man. And people like young David Ashleigh have to do without him.'

'God—it isn't true!'

'True enough. Carl's fault—and our fault for letting him have the wrong nationality at the wrong time. Now if this invasion succeeds, he'll have the right nationality but the wrong religion. I wish I could think Carl is religious ...'

'Lloyd, we're wasting time. David's all right. Carl will survive. Rick lives. Charles will manage. How are *you*! How am I? Have we forgotten?'

'No, love, nothing is forgotten. No second is not relived. And we've held the telephone line for too long. Everything's O.K. I don't know how long it'll be O.K. for any of us. But Fenton Field still exists, and so does England. While that holds, I'll say it's a bargain. Good night, my darling love, good night.'

'Good night ...' There was no more to be had from him. He had violated all the codes to speak to her of the things they both held most in their hearts. Even his last words had been strangely free, uninhibited, for Lloyd. The mood of the hour held him, the fatigue, the urge to fight, the will to win, as it did every other person she had encountered in these past weeks.

'Good night, my love,' she echoed softly into the empty buzz of the dial tone.

III

The anti-aircraft batteries over Dover and Folkestone had been very active. The cloud was only scattered and light, and the big wings of the German bombers showed plainly. They had swung a little north in their passage over the coast to try to avoid the worst of the flak; the plan was then to head north-west when the Thames was sighted, to follow it, and deliver the nightly load of bombs on London. Most of the squadron followed the plan, but one of the pilots, watching his instruments nervously, saw that the flak which had shaken the craft so badly ten minutes ago had caused a leak in the fuel line. One of his port engines spluttered and died, the propellor fanned uselessly. He had to fight the rudder with his whole strength to hold the aircraft steady against the dead useless weight of the engine. Finally he signalled his squadron leader that he must break formation; he had enough fuel, he thought, to make it back to the airfield near Wissant, on the French coast. It was not his squadron's airfield, but it was the nearest. So, with the Thames glinting greyly on his starboard, he made a slow bank to head back towards the coast. He asked his navigator for his position, and the position of secondary targets. The light of the flak was all about them; behind them now lay the glow of London's dockland fires. The navigator made a hurried fix on their position; he also was nervous about the fuel steadily leaking away, the chance that a fighter would come up from under them, that bullets screaming through the fabric of the plane would set the leaking tank ablaze. There were a thousand things to worry about, and the few miles that separated them from the safety of Wissant seemed incredibly too far. On the intercom he gave the position to the bombardier. He had hoped for the Fighter Command base at Biggin Hill, but it was already behind him. They could try for the bases of Canterbury or Hawkinge, but the flak of Dover and Folkestone lay directly beyond that. So they dropped their bombs in haste, not really knowing where they were. With the load of the bombs gone, the whole crew could feel the speed of the aircraft pick up, its controls become more responsive. The bomber survived the intensified flak of the coast, and landed safely at Wissant. Even their aerial photographs did not tell them that two bombs had fallen on a hospital near Maidstone.

The break that Margaret had dreaded and feared in Nicole did not come when the telegram with the news of Lloyd's death reached Fenton Field. It did not come as the arrangements for Charles to make formal identification at Maidstone were made, nor did she weep when the coffin came finally to the village church of Stokeley. She went through the service stony-faced; she had shown no interest whatever in choosing the hymns for the service, she had refused to see the vicar for more than a few minutes, had left it to Margaret to give the background and details of Lloyd's life of which he would speak during that service. It seemed a matter of indifference to her that the vicar should speak of the sacrifice of a man drawn into a war which was not his own country's. Margaret doubted if Nicole ever heard the vicar's words when he ended. 'One might say that Lloyd Fenton gave more than any of us here, even those of our young men who have already given their lives. He did it unasked, unbidden. He did it for England, this, his second home, with a pureness of love that knew not the boundary of country or birth. England claimed him. England must acknowledge her debt.'

Charles and Andrew led Nicole towards the grave, where Lloyd was to be buried among these cousins of his, these English Fentons. Only for a moment did she seem to hesitate, to pause for a second as they moved along the wet grass. It was as if she was about to refuse these final terrible moments. She looked for a moment into Charles's face, and shook her head. But still she didn't speak. Then, visibly straightening her body, so that she seemed taller than she was, she went on to the open grave. Margaret noticed that she never looked once at the coffin, nor did her lips move at all with the words of the service. She was staring at the old beeches planted against the churchyard wall. They had a touch of gold in them, as they had had on the day she had been married here six years ago. There were too many such burials in those grim days to allow for the practised protocol of a military funeral. There was no sounding of the Last Post, mercifully no ceremonial folding of the flag. The only thing Nicole had insisted on was that Lloyd's coffin should bear the American Stars and

Stripes. 'Old Glory' she had called it. It was Charles who had received back the flag.

Nicole ignored, or did not see, the hands outstretched to her in sympathy as she left the churchyard. She had refused the car which would have taken her back to Fenton Field. She walked the mile there flanked by Charles and Andrew, and turned only vacantly when someone came from one of the cottages along the way to murmur words of condolence.

Margaret grew even more fearful when, as soon as they were back at Fenton Field, Nicole had gone to her room and changed back into the filthy corduroy pants. The weather was warm, so she wore an old, washed-out shirt which had belonged to Lloyd. People had gathered with the Fentons—distant cousins, close friends, all people who had known Lloyd during the times he had stayed at Fenton Field. They were in the drawing-room, which Wilks had insisted on putting back into use. The fire was burning brightly; tea and whisky were circulating.

When Margaret went to try to intercept Nicole she met with a blank stare. 'Don't you know it's milking time?'

V

Margaret sat at the cluttered desk in the sitting-room, ostensibly busy with the weekly task of juggling with the ration books. And yet in the past ten minutes she had thought nothing about rations, or meal-planning. She was tired. She didn't sleep very well these nights; she told herself that the sounds of the planes overhead would disturb anyone, but it was not really the planes any longer that troubled her. It was only a year since the war had begun, but already it had made terrible inroads on her family. She thought of Richard, lying still in the hospital in Hastings. She had visited him again, and been dismayed to find that he barely wanted to talk to her. The truth about his own situation was coming to him swiftly. His hatred of it was evident. He made short, sharp answers to her questions and seemed indifferent when she said she must go. Richard had seemed already to have closed into his own darkness. And Allan ... Joan was allowed to write one letter a month to the prison camp in Germany, to send an occasional package. He was well, he said; his leg wound was healing. There had been parts of his letters which the censors had struck out. And Ross. Since Dunkirk he had been recommended for an MC; he refused to talk about what action the recommendation had cited. There was a hardness now in Ross which somewhat frightened Margaret; the eager boy had gone for ever. She was not sure she liked the hard-eyed, thin man who had replaced him. He had his own impatience, and an anger that came to the surface too often. His last leave had been an uncomfortable time. 'We were sold out,' he said. 'Here we are, with Hitler about to invade, and we've hardly got a tank in the whole country. Everything left behind there in France. We've been sold out by a bunch of foolish old men who refused to see what was coming . . .' The bitterness seemed to embrace them, his parents, because they were the generation who had refused to act. He was enthusiastic about the new job which had been given to Gavin. Gavin had been sent to a research establishment somewhere in Wales which was so top secret that Judy did not even have its exact address. All communication between them was sent through a Whitehall address. 'Damn good,' Ross had said. 'I hope he's making something to blow them all to hell over there. At least they're not letting a brain like his go and rust itself on writing some stupid training manual—which would be typical of the mess they've made of everything. When this war's over, the real heroes won't be the guys with the medals, but the ones who made the better gun. If we hadn't got radar, this island would be finished now . . . but I don't recall them handing out any medals to the men who came up with radar.'

He had come back for Lloyd's funeral. 'Bloody waste of a good life,' was his bitter comment. 'What fool put a man with a speciality like that in a front-line hospital. These old men just don't know how to use their resources.' Margaret had been thankful when he left.

So her family was shattered and shaken, the whole structure thrown out of balance. She strove desperately to keep this centre here steady and peaceful, but the stresses and the pulls against it were proving too much, even for her strength, and the belief, never before challenged, that they would survive as a family. But at the moment her worst and most immediate worry focused on Nicole. Nicole was on her mind in every waking moment since the news had come—Nicole, who as yet, had not begun to accept it.

Margaret removed her glasses, and rubbed her weary eyes. She needed glasses almost constantly these days. A year of war had aged her in ways she hadn't thought possible.

Wilks tapped on the door and entered. It was strange how some of the old customs survived the great changes. Gone were his striped trousers and black coat. These days he wore a sort of all-purpose jacket of grey cotton, equally suitable, he had said when he bought it, for answering the door, or plucking a chicken. Margaret sometimes wondered if in fact it wasn't Wilks, rather than herself, who held the remnants of this family together. Wilks and, in her own way, Henson, who still insisted on teaching the children the manners of a more gracious time, which now seemed so far away it might have been a century ago.

Wilks made his usual half-bow, which wasn't at all incongruous even in that ill-fitting grey jacket. 'Lord Manstone to see you, Ma'am. I've left him in the hall. I'm afraid the drawing-room isn't——'

Margaret rose. Wilks had to be as aware as she who Lord Manstone was. People like Wilks and Henson had such excellent memories for such details.

'Please show him in here, Wilks. And I wonder?—do we have any biscuits for tea?'

'Miss Judith baked this morning, Ma'am. I'll prepare a tray, shall I?'

'That would be nice, Wilks. Thank you.'

Margaret had, of course, never met John Manstone. But she expected the good looks of the man who came into the small, cluttered room. She remembered the photographs of Nicole and his son, David, during the brief, notorious engagement six years ago. The father was an older, leaner, more worn version of that smiling golden youth of the pictures. He was wearing army uniform, and the insignia of a Lieutenant-Colonel.

'Mrs Fenton—good of you to see me. Perhaps I should have telephoned. But I came on an impulse. It's awfully hard to put an impulse into words on the telephone. I hoped I might see Nicole.'

Margaret was strangely touched by the way he said her name —not as if she were the strange and wilful girl who had left such chaos and hurt behind her when she left England; he said it simply, gently. At once, when only these few words had been spoken, she liked him.

She gestured him to a chair, making room on the big round table in the centre of the room for his cap by simply sweeping aside the clutter. 'I wish I could say she'd see you, Lord Manstone. It isn't just *you*——' She turned to him swiftly, in an appeal for him to understand. 'You see, since Lloyd was killed, she doesn't really *see* anyone. I could send for her, and I'm sure she'd come. But I couldn't say she'd see you, or hear anything you said ... She is ... she's frozen. She refuses to accept what's happened. By not admitting it ...' She shook her head, 'Oh, I'm sure you know. People like Nicole feel everything ... feel *too much.*'

He nodded. 'I've always known that about her. She has a strange power in that small body. One can see ... yes, I suppose one can see how she might wreck herself.'

He had gone far beyond Margaret's vague suggestion. She looked at him in alarm. 'But in time ... everyone accepts in time.'

'Only what we choose to, Mrs Fenton. Do you think I might go and try to find her? Perhaps she might talk to me if she didn't know beforehand that I've ...'

She sighed. 'Perhaps that might work. Whatever way you wish, Lord Manstone. If you could only get her to talk ... we'd be grateful, I do assure you.'

'Where would I find her?'

She shrugged. 'Frankly, I don't know. We're almost finished harvesting. We do it partly by machine, and partly by hand, with whatever help we can get from anywhere. But we've not let Nicole do any of that. It's hard work, and while she's very healthy, she's not strong—you understand. But she has some amazing gift with animals. Andrew, my husband, says he doesn't quite understand it. Nicole goes and does almost anything she wants with the horses—and yet she says she's frightened to death of them. That can't be the truth—they always know. And the pigs, and the hens. Can you imagine someone like Nicole milking cows, and cleaning out the sties? Well, she does. So you'll find her—well, somewhere. The stables, the sties. I notice she spends as long as possible out of doors. It's quite dark these evenings before she comes in ...'

358

'I'll find her, I'm sure. Thank you for telling me.' He left his cap behind, and seemed to go by instinct towards the kitchen, where Wilks directed him to the stables. 'It's all there, m'lord. The stables, the cow byres, and beyond that the sties and the hen-runs . . .'

Wilks clucked a little as he looked at the tray he had laid out. Well, he hadn't poured the water on the tea-leaves yet, so it wasn't wasted.

Not even Margaret's description had prepared him for what he saw. She was in the middle of the sties, raking the manure. On one side the individual sties were immaculate, hosed out, fresh straw in place. The others were waiting her attention. He heard the tuneless sound of her voice as he came nearer, a weird, hoarse song that she chanted to the animals.

'Nicole . . .'

She turned around. For a moment she seemed unable to focus clearly on him. Then a croaking whisper, '*You!*'

He moistened his dry lips. 'I came because——'

She flourished the rake at him. 'Don't tell me why you came. I don't need to ask. I know too well. You came to offer your sympathy. I don't want it. You hear—I don't *want* it! Why don't you go away? You can't do any good. No good at all, you hear! None! Go—go away!'

'Nicole, please. I thought just this once we might talk——'

'*Talk!* What's there to talk about? Lloyd's dead. What am I supposed to do? Sit there and drink sherry with you, and listen to you say nice things about him? What the hell do I care about that? You can't *do* anything. He's dead. Words won't bring him back. Why did you waste your time? Haven't you got a job to do? Everyone's got a job to do these days, even an Ashleigh. Oh, yes—I'm sorry. David did a splendid job. A hero. He knew what he was about. But don't—don't waste any time standing around here offering pretty words. Get on with your job—whatever it is. Get on with England's job. Stupid, isn't it? Neither Lloyd nor I are English. Neither are our children. But here we are. Landed with England's war. Stuck. I've lost a husband—a lover. They've lost a father. And we don't even *belong*! I've never belonged. Nor did my mother. And yet here we are, my children and I, and we've lost something we can't ever have again because Lloyd had some notion

359

about England. Some crazy, wayward notion——'

'Nicole, I'm not trying to say he'll come back, or he'll be replaced. I'm not trying to say you'll forget. That it'll pass. I just ... well, I just thought I'd come and say that he'd saved David, he'd given a certain kind of skill, and you should try to think of the other men he did the same thing for. His notion of England? All right—we need every kind of notion there is. Whatever draws men, whatever keeps them here, giving skills like this, they're needed. Every one of them. I came here because——'

She gestured again with the rake, and he was once more aware that she had kept the fence of the sty between them. While she had raged at him, the big sow had come to rub herself against the dirty trousers she wore.

'Oh, for God's sake, spare me the graceful speeches. So, he saved David. I hope he saved a lot of other men. That's what he was there for. I never understood why he had to do it, but that was why he was there. Yes, so you still have your David, and you want to say thank you. I know—Lloyd told me he was badly wounded. He isn't going to be that beautiful, golden boy any more, but you still have him. You *have* him ... and I have your thanks. It's not enough. It's not nearly enough.'

'You didn't know then? I thought perhaps ... well, I came over really to say how thankful I'd been to your husband even though in the end his work was lost. I sat there in the hospital for five days. I thought I might see my only child live to be a vegetable. But he spoke to me. He even joked. He was going to be all right. That's what I came to thank you for.'

'What do you mean—*was*? He's all right. He's going to live. Lloyd said he was going to live.'

'He would have. He would have lived quite fully because of what your husband was able to do. But you didn't know they both died in that bombing, Nicole? ... you didn't know that? I supposed you did. Why you would, I don't know. So many dead these days ... why should you pay attention, at a time like this, to the newspapers?'

'David? ...' she said softly, wonderingly, as if trying out his name. 'David is *dead*? Only about ten people died in that bombing of the hospital.'

'Lloyd stayed with him. His head was sandbagged to keep him from moving. Lloyd stayed with him. I suppose a nurse could have done that, but Lloyd stayed with him. Anyone who could walk was sent to the shelters in the basement. I went down there. And upstairs, David and Lloyd died.'

'Lloyd—Lloyd and *David*. Beautiful, golden David. He was meant to live. All these young men were meant to live. Oh, God, what are we going to do without all these beautiful young men? What ... what ... ?' She shook her head frantically, as if to clear a vision that had become blurred. The rake dropped from her hand, and the big sow scrambled back against the rail, snorting with surprise and anger. She took a few steps towards Manstone. The skin of her face seemed to cleave to the bones, so that, for these moments, it could have been an old, old woman who looked at him, an old woman with a stick-thin body, and black hair, an old woman who had once been beautiful. She reached the rails and her cracked hands with the ragged fingernails went out towards him. 'David ... David and Lloyd.' He could hardly hear the words through the tightness of her throat. Before she slumped forward, he saw the first shimmer of tears.

Later that evening, she miscarried of her third child.

CHAPTER 5

I

The autumn passed into the dark short days of winter. Strength returned slowly to Nicole; it seemed to her that her body had aged very swiftly in those terrible days following Lloyd's death, and the strength of which she had boasted had gone with the child she had lost. She felt herself to be useless, a burden on the little group at Fenton Field, and yet she seemed to have neither the will or determination to leave. She clung to this place and this family which in the end had been Lloyd's strongest loyalty. At times she doubted that she would ever return to America.

As the winter went on and she came out of her cocoon of self-absorption, out of the blank indifference of her first shock and grief, she woke to the fact that a new war had begun. While she had lain in bed or sat before the fire in the sitting-room, listlessly trying to mend and darn, new maps had appeared on the kitchen wall. As the weeks went by and she began to read the newspapers again, to be able to recognize what the maps represented, she saw what the new war was about. Once Hitler had conceded that the Battle of Britain had been lost by his Luftwaffe and the invasion postponed indefinitely, he had simply turned to an age-old strategy. His submarines would starve Britain into surrender. Now Andrew's maps included one of the whole North Atlantic, that sickeningly long, incredibly dangerous journey which merchant seamen must make time and time again so that Britain could stay alive. With the French Navy lost the British Navy was insufficient to provide enough escorts. The convoys were herded together, chased about by a few destroyers, and the Germans learned to signal their sightings, gather their own forces into the infamous 'wolf-packs' for their attacks. They were stunningly successful.

The letters from Boston arrived at Fenton Field. 'Nicole, surely *now* you must come back. There's still time. Uncle Pete can still get you a passage, and in any case most of the ships heading west are in ballast. They don't mind having passengers. But it has to be an American ship. It's too dangerous any other way ... Now, you're to get in touch with ...'

Nicole never took any notice of whom she was to get in touch with. She wrote to Liz to rent the house in Cambridge. 'I wanted to keep it open and free in case Lloyd should decide he'd done enough—or America came into the war and we all went back. I can't face either the journey or that house yet. Will you store the personal things?—you'll know which ones. And will you keep on having MacGinty? He's so old now, he can't have much longer. And try to find someone to use the house on the Cape during the summers—friends. I don't want it rented to strangers. It's a Fenton house. It has to be kept for the boys. Perhaps I should sell the Cambridge house instead of renting. Talk to Sam about it, will you, Liz? He's pretty good in the real estate market.' She added as an afterthought, 'I don't think I'll ever live in that house again.'

And yet what house, and where? At Fenton Field she was in a group thrown together by the fortunes of war. It was impossible now to imagine the ending of this war, this war in which Britain had nearly gone under, and might yet do so. So why did she wait here, linger on? The reason for staying was gone. And her children were beginning to grow up. Where would they grow up, and with whom? Constantly she asked the question, and each time put the possible answers from her mind.

Slowly, and with a certain mechanical efficienccy which sought to spare her body from the results of the punishment she had inflicted on it, she went back to some of the chores she had demanded. 'Nice to see you here again, Mrs Fenton,' Ben said on the first morning of that winter that Margaret had permitted her to go back to helping with the milking. The wound that had seemed fairly slight when Ben had returned from the voyages back and forth to Dunkirk had proved troublesome and resistant to treatment. An operation was scheduled when free space opened up at the hospital. Ben walked with a limp, and had been turned down by the Army Medical Board. Nicole had heard a story of someone in the pub commenting, 'Half your luck', when Ben had passed on the news. And Ben had knocked him down and been barred from the place for six months. That had been simply a gesture. The landlord let him back in again inside of a week. To the landlord of *The Falcon* Ben ranked with any man who had returned wounded from Dunkirk, uniform or not. It didn't matter that he was under age for drinking either.

It was strange to Nicole to wake from her stupor of grief and find Roosevelt elected for a third term. She found herself echoing sentiments she read in the newspapers. 'Surely now America will come in ...' But the British were still paying in precious and dwindling dollars for every ton of food or war material they bought and transporting it across the Atlantic in their own ships. She tried to stop herself from saying such things. It sounded too much as if she herself was not American. The darkest, coldest winter days of February brought the news that the US Senate had signed the Lend-Lease bill. Nicole had a long letter from Uncle Pete, weighing the pros and cons of this action and urging her once again to get on one of the few ships available to her. 'While there's still time, my girl. Don't know what that hothead Roosevelt may do, and if we come in, then *no* ship is safe on the Atlantic.'

She read Uncle Pete's words and did nothing about them.

And from the short dark days of February, the days lengthened into the longer twilights of March, and Andrew had a map on the kitchen wall of another area of the world none of them knew about. They had to learn the names, the locations. It was a map of North Africa. It happened that there the British at first faced the Italians, and in January they had taken Tobruk. Then in February a man named Rommel came to take charge and brought his Afrika Corps. The whole North African campaign was more than another sphere of war to those at Fenton Field; Ross had been sent to North Africa. Ross, still young, and as old as war can make men, was already a major and had received his MC.

And, as always, the lengthening days of March gave way to the chilly promise of April. And that in turn produced the budding of the hawthorn blossoms of May in the hedgerows. Nicole was returned in memory to the very first days, those lovely days of May, she had spent at Fenton Field.

II

In the house in Laurel Canyon Anna had the news, through the cutting service, of the death in Maidstone, England, of Dr Lloyd Fenton. The Boston papers carried a number of news items on it, and a number of obituaries. None of the items said anything about the plans of Dr Fenton's widow.

Anna found it hard to think of Nicole as a widow. She acknowledged that she herself had been widowed at an earlier age, but then she had never felt for Stephen as she had evidence of what Nicole felt for Lloyd Fenton. She waited through each week for more news—news that Nicole was returning with her two sons to Boston. Nothing came, and Anna began to doubt the efficiency of the clipping service. She went to the public library and checked herself all recent issues of Boston papers. There was no news.

From her own happiness with this man, Michael Ovrensky, whom she had married, for the first time she knew real pity for her daughter. Often, in those days, she stared at Mike as he took his leave of her and wondered how she would stand the advent of his death. She kept turning the thought aside, and still it persisted. This was like no other feeling she had ever had. Once she had, as a young girl, loved madly and without reasoning, a man called John Manstone. After that, she had given love to a man called Stephen Rainard because he had loved her and restored her. And then, beyond what people called the prime of her life, she had been given the gift of Michael Ovrensky, a man from her past, who had been a boy she had loved, a man she now admired, respected, and with whom she found sweet fulfilment of a passion she had thought did not exist in her. With Michael Ovrensky she shared a bitter-sweet love, a thing with its roots back there at Beryozovaya Polyana, a strong mingling of their different, but yet strangely shared experience. They had come out of Russia, and they lived an American life. They were exiles, and they found their home again.

III

Life moved on at Fenton Field at a pace that seemed to Nicole to have slowed perceptibly. It could have been that the tension of the first invasion threat was over, or it could have been the exhaustion of feeling embattled was beginning to tell. The weariness of struggling to overcome the shortages, the lack of help on the farm, was now a constant daily dragging reality. If any of the younger people about them had ever thought there was any glamour in war, the thought was now gone. They all lived a small, restricted life, and although none of them spoke the thought, because it seemed petty while men continued to die on the Atlantic and in the Western Desert, there were many times when they were bored with the sheer grinding routine of their tasks.

For Nicole there seemed no real break in those months, the months of spring that flowed into summer. When the telephone rang, her ears did not strain to hear who was calling. It would never be Lloyd. There was no leave to look forward to, no one to save up items of news for. She wrote her letters to the Fentons in Boston, determined to keep that link with America for her sons, but there was little to tell them. She wrote to acknowledge the many food parcels that arrived—strange how guilty they felt about a tin of jam at Fenton Field because it might have taken the space of a belt of ammunition.

'Eat it,' Andrew said authoritatively. 'You don't think they'd let parcels be sent if they didn't think civilian morale was important too? And England's not paying for all these bits of goodies. That counts, too. We'll all of us owe a big debt after the war for what comes in food parcels.' He put a little sugar in his tea. 'Here's to the Boston Fentons. Just thank God for them —and don't question the manna that falls from Heaven!'

During that spring Nicole travelled up to London to meet Charles, and together they went to Buckingham Palace, where Charles received Iris's posthumous award of the George Cross, a recently instituted award for civilian gallantry. It seemed a whole age ago since she had made her only other visit to this Palace. They stood in the long line of those waiting to receive medals, mostly servicemen, a throng of ordinary people, from every place in Britain, from Canada, Australia, New Zealand, some of them terribly disabled. It wasn't hard to see the future. She thought that never again would the lines of nervous, white-plumed débutantes form up. More than one sort of wall had crashed down when the bombers had crossed the English Channel.

After they had lunched on very slender rations at the Savoy, Nicole made her way to a firm of solicitors in the City. Just after Lloyd had been killed, she had received a letter from them, asking that she visit them at her convenience in connection with the estate of the late Sir Gerald Agar. She had supposed that it meant some small momento; Margaret had written for her that she was unwell, and unable to come at that time. During the winter months she had put it from her mind; there was enough sadness, enough pain. She still refused to believe what was said about Gerry's supposed collaboration with the Nazis, but she didn't want to face the cold reality of it again in the office of some unknown solicitor. In the spring they had written again, hoping that she could come to London, and failing that, asking if they could send a representative of their firm. Margaret had urged her to go up to London, both because Charles needed her, and the fact of Gerry Agar's death and its circumstances must be faced, just as she had had to face the fact of Lloyd's death. So she went, and a dry, papery little man, with the common look of weariness that Londoners wore, told her that although most of the estate of the late Sir Gerald had been entailed, and passed to his sister's oldest son, certain pieces of his personal property had been his to will specifically as he chose. To Nicole Fenton, *née* Rainard, he had left his collection of twentieth-century pictures.

Nicole had gasped, and the dry little man had peered at her over his glasses.

'You're familiar with Sir Gerald's collection?'

'I saw only a few of the pictures. The ones he had in London. I believe there were others in the country house ...'

'Indeed, yes. Well, they *were* there. Before war broke out, Sir Gerald had them all crated and sent to a farmhouse he owned in Wales. Very remote country, it is, I understand. Unlikely to suffer from bombing.' He went back to his papers. 'The list includes some by Pablo Picasso ...' He droned on through the other names, as if they were of little interest to him, mispronouncing some. 'Leger, Braque, Klee, Matisse, Soutine, Gris, Modigliani ... Miro, Chagall.' For the first time he ventured a personal comment. 'Sir Gerald had a rather peculiar taste in paintings. Now myself ...' He decided to forgo stating his own preferences. 'Sir Gerald's nephew, who also inherited the farmhouse, is willing that the pictures should remain in storage there for the duration. These are difficult times—difficult to arrange the movement of such things. There is an elderly caretaker in the place, and since it is very remote, three miles from the nearest road even, it is not being used for evacuees. They should be as safe there as anywhere in this kingdom, I should imagine. There are some fifty-seven paintings in all. I have had a list prepared for you. It was compiled from the list made by Sir Gerald who himself supervised the packing and removal of the paintings. He journeyed to Wales himself and saw them safely installed. I haven't had the opportunity to go there to ascertain that they are all intact, but I am assured the caretaker is a very trustworthy person. Sir Gerald's nephew is willing, as I said, for the paintings to remain *in situ*, but naturally he will require a small storage fee. It helps defray the expenses of the caretaker, you understand. Now, of course, if you want them taken somewhere else, you may make arrangements ...'

'I'll leave them,' Nicole said softly.

'Rather a nuisance for you,' the man commented. 'Such things are surely faddish, and cannot have much value—though I do think that Sir Gerald paid rather a considerable amount of money for some of his later acquisitions ...'

'I wouldn't doubt it,' Nicole answered.

She completed the formalities he required of her. 'Some day, when you are able to travel to Wales, I should be grateful if you could go and verify what is there against this list.'

'Some time ... yes.'

During the long slow journey back to Fenton Field, she thought of the events of the day, the moving little ceremony at Buckingham Palace, and the tears that had momentarily shone in Charles's eyes. And now this strange and beautiful gift from Gerry of his most loved possessions, this legacy which surely must have sprung from that chance meeting that afternoon in the Tate in the summer before the war. The words went on and on in her head 'the summer before the war ...' The time that would never return again. She hadn't now, the faintest idea of what she would do with this legacy, but whatever happened, she was determined the pictures would be kept together, and in defiance of what the world believed of the way Gerry had lived and died, they would not be slipped into the anonymity of an auction house and sold. Somehow, in some fashion, she would contrive to keep them together, and they should be known as the Gerald Agar Collection. She hadn't the least doubt that Gerry's taste had proved unerring. Some of the names were already great, though unknown to the dry, little man who ran Gerry's legal affairs. The others, in time, would become as well known as Picasso and Matisse. It only needed time. They would stay in the safety of their Welsh fastness until this was all over, and then she would consult with the experts on how this great work of Gerry's would be preserved.

She wasn't aware of it, but in those hours of planning on the journey back to Fenton Field, she had dared for the first time to look into the future, some purpose shaped in her mind. She had some task other than the tending of children and animals; this gift of awakening Gerry had also given to her.

Margaret noted the change in her face when she got back to Fenton Field that evening. She herself felt a faint repugnance at the thought of a legacy of this magnitude from such a person as Gerald Agar had proved to be. After the war, when it was revealed, when Nicole had to make decisions as to its future, all the old scandal of Gerry Agar would be revived, and with that, Nicole's name must inevitably be muddied by association. But listening to the note of excitement, the talk of the future, she was grateful for anything—even such a thing as this, which would make Nicole talk as if there was indeed a future beyond the next milking.

The other task which woke Nicole to life that year was the need to find some way to help Richard. He had been moved to the Moorfields Eye Hospital in London, and two operations had been performed. The sight in one eye had gone completely; in the second his only vision was of faint images, blurred at the edges, against a generally grey background. It was not enough, in the beginning, to allow him to successfully negotiate his way across a room. They told him he would learn, by experience, and as his confidence grew, to find his way around and past objects which he only dimly perceived. He would never read again.

He was discharged from the RAF, and he came back to Fenton Field. Potters was still used as a convalescent home. Celia was still at her post at Stanmore. Richard had curtly refused to allow her to apply for leave when he returned to Fenton Field. 'I'll have enough damn women hanging over me, won't I?'

Nicole heard him snap into the telephone on the day he left the hospital. They were providing an ambulance for his journey home. There would be help and instructions from a teacher for the blind whenever it was possible to arrange that. That, and a total disability pension, was his last contact with the service except for the summons to Buckingham Palace to receive his DFC.

He sent Celia and Margaret. 'I'll be damned if I'm going to provide copy for the newspaper sob-sisters,' he said. 'Nice tear-jerking sight. Brave officer with his white cane being led forward and having to be told which way to face so the King can pin the medal on. No thanks! Let my sweet, trim, efficient little officer wife do the honours. The newspapers can really wallow in the story of the brave little WAAF officer still gallantly doing her duty while her sham hero husband sits in darkness. The fact that she's an Air Vice-Marshal's daughter will just heighten the pathos. A family devoted to the service, through and through.'

'Oh, for God's sake, shut up!' Nicole had shouted at him. She didn't care that Wilks was in the kitchen at the time. They were used to saying exactly what they pleased before Wilks. The war had made him and Henson closer to them at Fenton Field than Ross or Gavin would ever be. 'I'd like to know who's wallowing in *what*! All this picture of the bitter, blighted cynic just doesn't impress me, Richard. What's wrong with what Celia's doing? Someone has to do it, and from what I hear, she's damn good at her job. Maybe it *is* in the blood, even if she doesn't like to fly. Are you going to make life hell for her because you've had something terrible happen to you? Of course it's terrible. You probably wish you were dead. But as long as you're alive, you'd just better settle for living. You see, we don't have much time here at Fenton Field. We work. It's dull, boring, dirty. We all look a mess—but you can't see that any more. All of us—*all* of us, will be helping in one way and another, Richard. The rest, you'll do yourself.'

'Listen to who's talking ... Why you——'

'Yes, I know. *Me*. I'm no example to hold up. I let go when Lloyd was killed. I let go and thrashed and kicked so much about what had happened to me that I lost Lloyd's child. I'll tell you something, Rick. I'd give anything I've ever had, except Lloyd himself, to have carried that child, and had it born. I lost two lives then, and I was a fool. What I'm saying ... what

370

I'm trying to say, is that I made a terrible mistake. Perhaps it was inevitable that I would make it. I was thinking too much of myself. Probably we all do that when the blow first hits. I'm telling you, Rick ... dear Rick ...' She stretched her hands across the kitchen table towards his, realized that he didn't see them, and so forced hers upon his. 'I'm telling you ... we're all trying to help you, but in the end you fall back on yourself. Let it in, Rick, let it in! Weep if you have to. Curse! Shout! Do anything but deny that it's happened. Because it has ... Nothing can ever undo it.'

'God damn you!' He stood up abruptly, jarring the table, upsetting his mug of tea, which spilled on to the floor. With a wildly thrashing movement of his stick, he made his way towards the door of the kitchen. Wilks reached it before he did, and opened it. Richard passed through, almost striking the old man with his stick, unknowingly. They heard him slashing his way along the corridor, hitting the walls to the left and right.

'Shouldn't I go with him, Mrs Fenton? If he's trying to go upstairs——'

'Leave him be, Wilks. He will learn the way very quickly. He'll learn to count each step. He *has* to. He'll fall a lot of times. We can't always be with him, every moment. And he doesn't want it. Just leave him be. He'll have to rage and shout and weep. He won't ever accept it. He'll just learn that this has happened to him ...'

She looked around the kitchen. 'Now, where are the beans? I was going to slice them ... I wish Judy would come in. She was going to do something to that bit of stew we have. I'd like it to be a bit festive for Aunt Margaret when she gets back. And Richard ... when he decides to come down. I suppose there isn't a bottle of wine ...? Oh, I'll tell you! We'll bring up a bottle of Gavin's Glenlivet whisky. I'll write him an IOU for after the war.'

In the weeks after that Nicole and Richard fought bitter battles over the piano. She tuned it for him, forced him into the seat, and dared him to play. 'Well—can't you do it? You never looked at the keys before. Can't you find your way? Can't you hear anything in your head that you know you can play—just the melody? Oh, come on! Damn it, you're a musician. What you can't hear in your head isn't worth remembering. Come on!

Come on, damn you. There's middle C. You can feel that. After that, the whole keyboard is yours.'

'And damn *you*!' he shouted back. 'I haven't laid a hand on the piano for years. I can't remember a bloody thing. So here's middle C. What the hell am I supposed to do with it?'

'Do with it? If there's nothing else to do, then play the C major scale. Both hands. That's a beginning.'

'*Me?* Back to scales?'

'Listen, Buster, as we say in the States—at times we all go back to the beginning. So, go back.'

She didn't know how to teach him. She had no way of knowing how to teach anyone who cannot read music. Each day she watched his more confident progress around the house, she listened to the careful, measured tread on the curving wooden staircase. Each day he gained some measure of independence, and had help along the way, whether he chose to acknowledge it or not. He had a curious ability to withdraw himself from the helping hand, to act as if it were not there, even when he accepted it. Mostly he suffered his dependence in silence. Wilks added to his formidable range of tasks by coming to shave and help him bathe each morning. Then that was left off as Richard began to get the feel of the razor against his skin without being able to see his face. The little dried nicks were the only evidence of his struggle. Everything took an inordinate length of time— to bathe, shave, dress, and finally appear in the kitchen for breakfast, unaware that it was already eleven o'clock.

'On no account ever say anything about the time—about his being late,' Andrew told them all. 'After all, what else does he have to do all day? My God, what *is* he going to do? There's all the rest of his life . . .'

Richard had started to venture beyond the relatively safe confines of the house. Often Nicole saw him tapping his way with his stick across the stable yard, holding his face upwards if there happened to be sun. Always now, the black labrador, Nell, was at his side. She was only two years old, one of the dogs that had been spared, at Judy's pleading when the war brought serious food rationing. 'We *have* to have some dogs. This is a farm. Between us we can surely find enough to feed her.' Nell had never become a working dog. She clung to the house and the people in it. She was not timid, but she did not want the life of the dogs who lived in the stables. And now it seemed that she had found her task, her object, in Richard. Soon after he had returned from the hospital, she had placed herself at his side; in the beginning he had tried to reject her, as if she were some other symbol, like his white cane, of his blindness. But she refused to allow herself to be rejected. She stuck to his side, and it was her need for exercise and fresh air which first drove him out of doors.

Nicole would call to him across the yard, telling him about the horses, their temper that day, about the state of the tack. 'That's something you could do for me—clean a bit of tack.'

He tended to turn away when a task was offered, thinking that it was done as make-work for him, and would have to be done over. 'What do you want me to do—start weaving baskets and making brooms?'

'It would be better than doing nothing, wouldn't it?' Nicole shouted at him. 'If you think you're going to be a grand gentleman sitting around while everyone else waits on you——'

Their quarrelling was usually broken by laughter. Nicole, being removed from the family, was the only one who could bully him into some sort of acceptance of his situation. When time permitted, she would take a walk with him and Nell. He even allowed himself to rest an arm on her shoulder for guidance. Nell was close by his leg on the other side, instinctively nudging him away from any obstacle. She would talk of the things she saw as they walked. 'You smell the hawthorn, Rick? It's so white, and yet when you stand back from it, it's got that marvellous pink flush on it . . .'

'What are you trying to do, Nicole—see for me?'

'Perhaps,' she admitted. 'But it's possible I'm really seeing them for the first time fully for myself. You're lucky in one thing, Rick. You have seen things once. How does one describe blue to someone who's never seen blue? And what colour is a sunset?'

A harried, middle-aged woman came to begin to teach him Braille. Nicole found herself learning also, so as to be able to help him. He worked hard at it, and his naturally good brain responded to the challenge. The response was that of a muscle left long unused. 'I think I might, I just might, be able to do something,' he said. 'I'd begun to think I'd spend the rest of my life listening to the radio, or waiting for someone to have time to read the newspaper for me.'

'Develop your memory,' Nicole said. 'Develop your sense of sound. I don't know how to translate music into Braille for you, but it must be done somewhere. You should be able to remember the sounds I play, and reproduce them ...'

They still quarrelled over his music. She bullied and goaded him on. 'Scales ... scales, Rick. Until you get your technique back you'll never get anywhere. Strengthen your hands—get your reach back. When the war's over, there should be some way to get you a teacher.'

'Damn little tyrant,' he answered. But the effort to help him drove her back to the piano herself. 'Listen, Rick ... *listen* ...' The vet, Mr Carbury, who had conceived an admiration for her, brought her some lanolin for her hands. 'The chemist makes it up for me,' he said. 'I hear you're back at the piano with Richard. That's damn good. *Everything* shouldn't be lost because there's a war on.'

One day the teacher brought a light cane-harness for Nell, with a raised handle that Richard could hold as he walked. 'She hasn't been trained, of course,' the woman lamented, 'but she seems to *want* to do things for you, Mr Fenton. Let her try ... There's no time now to train dogs for the blind, and no one to do it ...'

Help that Richard also seemed able to accept came, surprisingly, from Lord Manstone. Since the time in September when he had come to see Nicole, and in giving her the news of David's death had finally broken through her hard shell of remoteness, he had come frequently to Fenton Field. At first Manstone had stayed in one of the two rooms *The Falcon* had to rent, and then Margaret insisted he stay at Fenton Field. Lynmara had been taken over as officers' quarters for Hawkinge fighter command base; the Belgrave Square house was requisitioned for the Ministry of Information. 'There's Ross's room,' she said, 'He won't be using it for quite some time. And Allan's room hasn't been used since he was married, except when we had the evacuees here. It isn't luxurious, of course—and it isn't very warm. We've only limited hot water. But then, I suppose things aren't very different at *The Falcon*, are they?'

He had accepted with a curious readiness and humility. They found they hardly noticed his presence at Fenton Field. He would come for the few days of his leave, bringing his rations with him, and whatever small luxury he had been able to scrounge in London. He would appear in old trousers and sweaters and quite naturally he took over whatever task was to hand. He came quietly, and left quietly, always making his own arrangements about travel. They got used to his coming and going. Richard was even heard to ask, 'I wonder when John will be back again? He's the best newspaper reader of you all, do you know that? Charles is second best. I'm beginning to rate you all now. Nicole's the worst. Too impatient ...'

They knew the degree of acceptance John Manstone had attained in the house on the morning, at breakfast, when Richard said, 'Would you mind taking a walk with me, John? Nell's not quite used to this harness yet. I'd feel better with someone along with me.' Around the table the family glanced at each other. It was the first time Richard had openly asked for something to be done for him, with him. Brusquely, to hide his emotion, Andrew thrust the pot of marmalade towards John, oblivious to the fact that he had honey on his toast.

'Here—take some of this. The Boston Fentons are positively embarrassing in their generosity with food parcels ...'

During his next leave John Manstone managed to borrow a staff car and beg enough petrol to get to Lynmara. From there he drove to Fenton Field, and from the back of the car and the boot came some of the treasures of his cellar—fine old brandy, château-bottled clarets and burgundies. 'I stored it all in the chapel at Lynmara when it was requisitioned—boarded up the windows and the door so those chaps wouldn't know what was in there. Swore the gamekeeper to secrecy at the price of a few bottles for himself. I thought I was saving it all for David. I just didn't think about it until you mentioned the food packages from the Fentons in Boston. I suddenly remembered it was there, and there was nothing to save it for any more—and no time when it's needed more. So let's drink up. There's plenty more where that came from, if only I could get the transport.'

'*I* can get it,' Richard said promptly. 'I get an invalid's petrol allowance—didn't you know? If there's any more claret like this to be had, I'll pretend to be crippled as well as blind ...' It was good to hear him joking about it.

'Pity I didn't lay down tins of ham and all those sort of things

375

they sold at Fortnum's before the war. How *does* one provide for a war, I wonder?'

They were always, Nicole thought, talking about 'before the war' and 'after the war'—the second with a degree of bravado and uncertainty. There was a noticeable quietness about Ross and Allan. Their futures were question marks. And every time John Manstone or Charles left Fenton Field to return to London, no one was quite certain that they would return. The bombing had virtually ceased, and yet its threat was still there. So they drank the Manstone wine, and sipped the brandy that had been laid down for David, and they knew they were right to do it. It suddenly seemed foolish to set aside, to store up anything for a future that might not come.

Nicole noticed how little now they talked of the war news. It had been such a bad year, one whose events they tried to ignore, except that Andrew's maps would not let them. What was the use to talk about the chances of Ross coming home when Rommel had encircled Tobruk? Allan was locked in the fastness of hinterland Germany, and escape seemed impossible. He wrote that he was receiving further treatment for his leg. 'In heaven's name, what sort of treatment would he get in a prison camp?' Joan demanded. 'And he doesn't even say what's wrong.' She had turned into a gaunt, almost aged woman since Allan's capture. Most evenings she ate dinner with the family at Fenton Field; her children were there with their cousins all day. 'Might as well be in charge of a flock as one or two,' Henson said, but she herself looked worn and old. She no longer talked about going back to Boston.

Maps of Greece and Yugoslavia appeared when Hitler invaded in April. Then in May the Germans were in Crete. The maps on the wall became more military as John Manstone supplied some from his office in Whitehall. 'Maps we have,' he said with a touch of bitterness. 'What we need are a few victories.' He said this, indirectly referring to the sinking of the *Hood*. There was outrageous jubilation among them when news of the sinking of the Bismarck came to offset it. John Manstone came down that weekend, and insisted that they open champagne to celebrate it.

'I've hardly ever tasted champagne as good as this even before the war ... only once or twice ...' Nicole murmured.

John Manstone answered quite casually, and in a voice

loud enough for the rest of the family to hear, 'Well, it's a good thing you're drinking it. I got it in preparation for your wedding ...'

Nicole gasped, and then she smiled, realizing there was no malice in the remark. 'Well, why didn't you serve it when David finally did get married?'

He shrugged. 'I don't know. Perhaps I thought it was unlucky ... or something. And don't forget David had a big London wedding. The bride's parents saw to all that sort of thing. All I had to do was be present. My mother wasn't there. She died two months later. It's one of the things I'm glad of ... that she didn't live until the war. She couldn't bear to see Lynmara turned into a barracks. *That* would have killed her, even though she always thought of herself as a great patriot. But it wouldn't have extended to having young men playing darts against her precious panelling.'

'They're not? ... surely not?'

John shrugged. 'Why shouldn't they? Lynmara isn't anything special to them. Just a big house. Of course the Ministry removed all the furniture and pictures, had them properly stored. It's stripped bare. But the wear and tear of a lot of young men ... Well, there's nothing to be too concerned about. After all, when they went up in their planes it worked as much to protect places like Lynmara as a row of terrace houses in the East End. But fortunately, young men don't think that way. Their job was to shoot down German planes. They did it.'

John had a thirty-six hour leave on the day the news came that Germany had broken the non-aggression pact with Russia and had invaded the territory of her former ally. That evening, leaving Richard practising scales in the drawing-room, Nicole walked with John down the beech-lined drive of Fenton Field, along the road, heading for *The Falcon*. She hadn't realized that she was going to walk with him, that they would head for *The Falcon*. She still wore her working clothes. It was 22 June, and the summer twilight would stretch to its greatest length. Midsummer's Day.

She said, as they walked along. 'I drank the champagne of my own wedding—the wedding that never happened. What about David's wife? What about the girl he married eventually?'

'The girl he married?' John answered. 'I suppose I'd hardly know her if I met her in the street. She was—is—a conventionally pretty girl. Very pretty. She and David made an ideal pair, as far as looks were concerned. Perhaps they would have made a great pair for the rest of their lives. But David didn't live. She's gone back to her parents. Where else could she go, poor girl? Lynmara wasn't her home any more. They didn't have time to have children—at least, not much time. So ... she will marry again, if she's sensible and lucky. Marry someone she loves. She has nothing more to do with Lynmara, or the estate. It's all entailed. Only a son could have inherited. Now it will go to—oh, God, I think there's some distant cousin in Scotland, whom I've never met. Well—what does it matter?'

They were coming close to *The Falcon*. With the late twilight of this midsummer night, the windows were wide open. No black-out shades had appeared. The noise poured out in a kind of frenetic welcome.

'All these chaps in here—I'd imagine they've lost someone. The family's been altered in some way. It matters just as much if there's a terrace cottage to pass on, or a place like Lynmara. It's only a difference of degree, and that doesn't really matter any more. It hasn't mattered a damn since we went to war.'

They elbowed their way in. John took a couple of glasses and filled them from a bottle behind the bar. No one made any objection. 'Comes of being an old tenant,' he said to Nicole. He found some water, and topped up the glasses. Then they fought their way to a bench outside the inn. The noise receded a little. They could hear the birds calling to each other. From this bench Nicole could see the line of beeches planted inside the wall of the graveyard where Lloyd was buried.

'But it isn't all finished yet,' Nicole said. 'David's mother—*your* wife. You do remember what you told us that evening? About your wife?—David's mother?'

'My wife—David's mother—is dead.'

Nicole leaned back against the harsh, prickling rose bush that climbed the ancient wall of the inn. Its rejection jerked her upright. 'Your wife?—your wife is dead?'

'Is dead,' he said. 'After these long years of being half-alive, she is dead.'

'When?'

He shook his head. 'I have to say I don't know precisely. Yes, they showed me a record of her death. They showed me a place where they said she was buried. How do I know? I hear rumours now that I couldn't believe then. I hear all kinds of rumours. Before the war hardly any of us chose to believe them. We didn't think people were like that. In the last years they told me not to come to see her any more. It was useless. She was far gone in dementia. Hopelessly schizophrenic. The sight of me would either leave no impression, or trouble her more. So I stayed away. You remember where she was ...?'

The noise was spilling out of the bar. A few couples strolled out to enjoy the summer twilight air. They seated themselves on a bench across from Nicole and John. The talk drifted over. 'Damn good show we had at ...'

'Hell, that wasn't anything. You should have been ...'

In another group someone said quietly, 'I expect we might have to start learning Russian ...'

Nicole had never forgotten his description of the valley in Austria which was so beautiful, and for him the most terrible place in the world. 'I remember,' she said. 'The lake, the beautiful gardens, everything so serene and peaceful, except the people.'

'Do you remember the *Anschluss*—the union of Austria and Germany? The time that Hitler just walked in. No resistance was offered. It was all over in a day.'

She wrinkled her brow. 'That was ... was ...'

'March, 1938,' he finished. She had been absorbed in Lloyd, her own life, her children. It seemed a hundred years ago, and what had happened in Austria had happened in another world.

'I went to get her out,' he said, 'but I'd left it too late. My fault. I should have known. But not even the British Government took it very seriously. They didn't expect the German ultimatum—the take-over in a day. I had to wait in London while all sorts of papers were prepared by the Barrington solicitors. You see, they'd tied it all up so tightly that I had no right to go and remove my own wife from that place without the consent of the trustees. Old Barrington had tied the knot too tightly. When I got there, accompanied by someone from the solicitor's office, and a nurse who would help us move her to Switzerland, everything was changed. The Director who had been running the clinic was gone—Herr Director had been gone for six months. The staff was changed. Even the patients seemed to be of a different type. I got the impression that it had been turned into some kind of luxury prison for those who had offended the Party in some way—or highly-placed alcoholics who had to be watched. Cynthia was there under the name of Mansten—Frau Frieda Mansten. That was to protect David, of course. They showed me a certificate which stated that Cynthia had died of kidney failure about two months before. They showed us the place where she was buried in the local church-yard—a Lutheran church. When I demanded to know why I hadn't been informed, they shrugged. Herr Director had destroyed or taken away many files when he left. They did not know who Frau Frieda Mansten was. They even called her Frau Manstein. The solicitor demanded an official enquiry, and he got more shrugs. He would have to instigate proceedings in the Austrian courts. Yes, they had received a cheque drawn on an English bank, but the covering letter had not been self-explanatory. They had not known it was for the expenses of Frau Manstein. They would, of course, refund the money. To have an official enquiry into Frau Manstein's death would be more difficult. There would have to be proof of some real suspicion of wrong-doing. All that had happened was an administrative muddle which often follows the abrupt dismissal of the head of an institution. Perhaps out of spite, or out of fear of malpractice being proven against him, Herr Director had chosen to destroy many files. There had been serious allegations against him, they said. They also added that he had, of course, been a Jew.'

'My God ...'

'That was about all we could say. When we asked where we might find Herr Director, we were told he had killed himself shortly after his dismissal. The fact was that he was never dismissed. When Cynthia was put there, the place had been owned by him. It was simply a case of the Nazi take-over of everything Jewish. They were expelled from every position of power or trust. It could have been quite true what they said about Cynthia. Perhaps she did die of kidney failure. It might have been true that she couldn't tell them her true identity. But the fact is that the awful suspicion haunts me that they simply carried out the Aryan philosophy of the survival of the fittest, and the destruction of the weak links in society. Those who were mentally deranged were surely the weakest ... If that's what happened, then it was totally my fault. I should have faced the facts long before, and either taken her to Switzerland, or brought her back to England. David was old enough to be told about her, and tough enough to take it.'

He fumbled in his pockets for cigarettes, and there were none. 'But you don't *know*,' Nicole protested. 'That's just some vague suspicion . . .'

'It really doesn't matter whether it's true or not. I have to add that the Barrington solicitor didn't seem to give much credence to the theory. He was just furious that so important a person as Cynthia should have passed so completely from their control. But true or not, I'm still guilty, and I can't shake that off. It begins when you start to lie. I lied in that marriage to Cynthia. I lied when she began to be ill. I agreed to the lies Barrington wanted. I told myself I did it for David—and Lynmara. And now I've come to the point where none of it has been worth a damn. Whether I lied for my own sake, or for David's, I've got nothing left. I've got an empty shell of a house, and no son. I have no grandchild. The whole rotten cowardice of my life has come home to roost. How right your mother was to get away from me. Yes—I know I let her go. I hadn't the guts to even try to keep her. Look, I'd better get us another drink. I need it.'

He went inside, and finally managed to get the attention of the innkeeper, Fred. Two whiskies were produced. 'I haven't got any money,' John said.

'That's all right, Lord Manstone. I'll put it on the slate.' Fred rather liked Lord Manstone, principally, he supposed, because he had never acted like a lord. He liked him when he had stayed at *The Falcon*, and better when he started to bring Richard Fenton there for a drink during their walks together. Richard Fenton, Fred thought, needed bringing out. And it pleased him to see Mrs Fenton sitting out there in the evening sun. She didn't get away from that place nearly enough. He watched Manstone settle himself on the bench again beside her, and he wondered what on earth they had been talking about that made them both look so grave. People took the war too seriously, he decided. It was all right to be serious when you had to get on with the job, but when you were relaxing, you should forget the bloody war. He had given them two extra large whiskies, when whisky was hard to come by. He hoped he'd see Mrs Fenton smile before she left. Despite the fact that she was a thin little scrap of a thing and Fred liked something more substantial, Mrs Fenton looked really beautiful when she turned those strangely-coloured eyes on a man and smiled.

But Manstone brought the empty glasses into the bar alone, cadged some cigarettes from Fred, and the two set off to walk back to Fenton Field before closing time. They had sat silently on the bench all the time they had had their second drink.

They had started down the avenue towards the house before Manstone spoke again. It was as if they had been silently conversing all the time, and he simply added the conclusion to the tale. 'All the trusts that the Barrington estate had set up for Cynthia and David go on, but they've reverted for the use and upkeep of Lynmara. Barringon couldn't see that far into the future. Well, who could guess it? No one thought of me surviving both of them, or of David having no children. Well, they *thought* of it, but it didn't seem likely that it would happen. That distant cousin in Scotland is going to be the final recipient of all Barrington's flair for making money. There aren't any Barringtons for it to go to. Lynmara and the Ashleigh name was what Barrington wanted. The bargain did him no good, nor me, nor Cynthia. It didn't even do David's wife any good because he hadn't inherited anything to leave to her. She gets a small annuity from the estate, and that's all. *I* can't even make over anything to her, because I don't own anything outright. It's the damnedest situation, and I deserve every moment of hell I've had from it . . .'

She let him talk on, let him talk because she knew that he had to. When they reached the house, she brought a bottle of whisky from the store he had laid in, and took it to the wooden table under the big oak. The late twilight had finally come, the twilight of the longest day. She poured generous measures of drink into the two glasses. Across the lawn came the sound of the piano, stumbling, uncertain. 'Listen, Rick's trying to play some Chopin . . .'

'What was that damn thing you played that night?—the thing that Anna played?' He hummed a few notes of it.

'Für Elise,' she said quietly. They were both plagued by memories and neither would forget.

IV

Demands from the Boston Fentons for Nicole's and the children's return became more urgent. In July the Anglo-Soviet

382

Mutual Assistance Treaty was signed. The American Navy took over the British base in Greenland, and therefore took over the task of escorting and protecting their own supplies of lend-lease material as far as this point. In August Roosevelt and Churchill met and signed the Atlantic Charter at Placentia Bay. This last move made Uncle Pete choleric with anger. 'Blasted man will have us in a war whatever Congress does,' he thundered in a letter to Nicole. 'Now, listen, you get on home here, and quit this nonsense. We Fentons are a clannish lot, and we look after our own. You belong here, my girl. American, and a Fenton. Come home.' More persuasive was the letter from Liz. 'Nicole, don't you think it's time? The kids are getting older. Don't you think they should grow up here, as Americans? We all know how Lloyd felt about England, but in the end, and right down to the end, he was still a Yankee—a stubborn Yankee trying to shore up the place that we all came from. The kids ought to understand this, as well as just the English side of it. And I've been making enquiries. There's a very fine school for the blind here in Boston. Why doesn't Richard come over here? Being totally disabled, there should be ways around getting him a passage. But for God's sake, Nicole, don't leave it too long. If the States goes into this war, then that crossing of the Atlantic will be more dangerous than anything you've been through yet.'

Nicole read portions of the letter to Margaret. 'Do you want me to go? I'm a drag on you here. And it would be easier without the boys.'

'Nicole, there are reasons why we fight. The freedom to do what we want is one of them. To have you here—to have the joy of the children . . . If there's no future, what are we fighting for? If there's just going to be a rubber stamp which sends each and every one of us to some appointed place, to do some appointed task, then it's all useless. Well, yes—I know. You're going to say Richard didn't have a choice, or Ross, or Allan, or Gavin. Our men we give, for the time being. Not for ever. Unless they die, as Lloyd and David did.' She spoke now as if David had been part of the family, and she had never met David. But she knew his father.

'And Richard? What Liz says is sense. There could be training for him in Boston that he couldn't get here until the war's over. If he's left without a challenge, to have to fight alone for that long, he may give up. Would he go, do you think, if it could be arranged?'

'Hell, no,' Richard said when she asked him. 'What on earth would I do in Boston? If America's coming into the war, then I'd just be an Englishman cluttering up the scene. There are plenty of people in need of those services without a foreigner added to the number. What on earth would I do in Boston ...?' He repeated.

'I'll talk to Celia,' Nicole said. 'Perhaps she can persuade you that it might make sense. You'll rot here for the rest of the war. You know that, don't you, Richard? There's a limit to what anyone can do for you until you have whole-time teaching. And I mean everything. Braille, a properly-trained seeing-eye dog, your music ...'

'No one's going to part me from Nell,' he said. 'Forget that. And forget about talking to Celia. It's none of her business.'

'None of her business? She's your wife!'

'Not for long. We've agreed to all that. We'll be divorced as soon as it can be decently arranged.'

'What on earth for? Celia adores you.'

'Celia *used* to adore me. Have you really paid much attention to her lately? She's changed, hasn't she, my little Celia?'

'Changed ... well, outwardly.' Nicole shrugged. 'Who wouldn't? She's learned a new sort of life. She's got a job——'

'Exactly!' Richard snapped at her. 'She's got a new life, a new job and she's become a different person. We've switched roles, Celia and I. She used to be clinging and dependent. I suppose I liked her that way. I suppose I wanted to be sure that I'd always be the dominant one in the partnership. I wasn't looking for any challenges from a wife. It never occurred to me that *I* could become dependent on a woman. It never occurred to me that Celia could change into someone who will want to run my life when the war's over—the one who will make the decisions because she'll not only have the right to, but she's learned *how* to make decisions. So efficient and decisive, my quiet little Celia has become. The truth is—I can't take it. I might be able to take it from another woman, someone I hadn't been married to when I was top dog. What I've discovered, Nicole, is that I must have displayed a streak of the bully a mile wide to Celia. Somehow, I'm not able to ask her to forgive me, and to forget it. I can't take favours from her. I'm going to have to ask for so

384

many things as I fumble and grope my way through the rest of my life. And I find I just can't ask them from Celia. It never was much of a marriage, when I look back on it. My fault. I just took her for granted. So ... she won't be losing much. She won't have *me* tied around her neck just because she once used to love me.'

'Are you sure, Rick ...' She hesitated, and fumbled for her words. 'Are you sure you haven't invented this difference between yourself and Celia, forced a break-up, because you want to free her from any sense of responsibility towards you? Any responsibility *for* you. Are you sure this is what *she* wants?'

His unseeing eyes had been focused in the direction of her voice. Now he deliberately turned his head. 'Why don't you mind your own bloody business?'

She remembered how he had looked as she left him there in the sitting-room, the lines of his face spare and lean, his profile beautiful against the window, and his hands clenched in a kind of frenzy of uselessness, on his knees.

V

She found the item one day when she was reading *The Times* to Richard. It was small, tucked away at the bottom of the page, something a court reporter might have picked up during routine work. She was silent for a long time after she had scanned it, so long that Richard became impatient. 'What's the matter? Dried up?'

'No—it's ... Well, I don't understand it. This bit here. It just says *"Police last night arrested and detained a man who was about to board the Holyhead–Dun Laoghaire night boat for Ireland. He is Brendan de Courcey, son of the well-known owner and horse trainer of Clonkilty, Kildaire. He appeared before a magistrate this morning, was charged, and held on remand without bail. The court was held in camera, for reasons of security, the police said. Reporting restrictions were not lifted. Police describe the charge as 'extremely serious'."* That's all. That's all it says. My God, what can he have done?—or what's he supposed to have done? I wonder does he need a lawyer?'

'Leave it alone, Nicole,' Richard said quickly. 'Look, he has parents, a wife, other friends. He'll have his lawyer.' From his tone she knew he didn't want to talk any more about Brendan de Courcey, and she remembered it was Richard who had given her that strange item of news about Brendan, his odd involvement with a few rowdy IRA sympathizers. Of course it couldn't be anything of that kind, she told herself, but the thought nagged. Before the end of the day she had worried enough to try to get through to Charles in Whitehall—always her best source of information.

Charles sounded cautious when she spoke to him. 'Really, Nicole, I just don't know. I wonder why you think I can instantly get information about anything. There are plenty of things *I'm* not allowed to know ...'

'You'll try, though, won't you?'

He sighed. 'I'll try.'

He appeared unexpectedly at Fenton Field that next weekend. 'Just got twenty-four hours off. Thought it would be nice to sleep away from London for the night ...' The house in Elgin Square was empty, and now bomb-damaged. Charles used a service club as his living-quarters; Adams lived in the basement of Elgin Square, which was habitable, and had a job with the Ministry of Food. Iris's estate had been settled, and apart from a few legacies to her favourite charities, her fortune had gone to Charles. He found himself, unwillingly, a rich man. 'A bit late in life,' he had said to Nicole. 'There isn't much to do with it now.' So Fenton Field had become for him, as it had for John Manstone, a place of refuge. These two lonely men spent their spare hours hunting the almost empty shelves of London's shops for any item available without ration coupons. Strange presents turned up at Fenton Field. John Manstone made a hobby of charity bazaars; Nicole suspected that he often paid outrageous sums for second-hand items which might be of use. Charles had combed Elgin Square for anything serviceable, blankets, bedding, even Iris's clothes. Margaret rather unwillingly wore a fur coat that had belonged to Iris. 'I don't see how I can say "no" to something that keeps me so warm ...' she murmured.

Charles, at first, was evasive when Nicole asked him if he had had any news about Brendan de Courcey. 'It's hard to get the exact truth,' he said. 'I'd almost rather not speculate. We may all know a good deal about it quite soon. They can't keep something like that out of the papers for ever, not if the man goes on trial.'

'What do you mean?' Her tone was sharp with anxiety.

'Well, precisely *what* he took we may never know, or how he got it. But I have word from what we call "a usually reliable source" that he was carrying microfilmed plans with him back to Ireland. He even had a suitcase with a false bottom—the whole incriminating thing.'

'Brendan?—why? What were the plans *of* . . ?'

Charles cleared his throat. 'It's something so hush-hush that even if I knew the details, which I don't, I wouldn't be telling them to you—or anyone else. I could get only the vaguest notion of what it was. Some further development of radar—I think they're calling it centimetric radar or some such thing which will fit in smaller warships, and eventually, they hope, in planes. The only way to fight the submarines in the Atlantic. And if we don't beat the submarines, we could easily lose the war. The Germans aren't nearly as advanced in radar as we are, and that's what saved us last year in the Battle of Britain. Now it's the Atlantic. If the Germans knew as much as we do, they'd be making their own modifications. Preparing themselves . . . As I gather, it's an absolutely vital piece of intelligence. And some very advanced plans were found in Brendan de Courcey's baggage. We will probably never know exactly what those plans were—for security reasons.'

'But why would Brendan do a thing like that?'

'Ask me why a man ever turns traitor—who knows what goes on in their twisted minds?'

'But *why*? You think he was going to give the plans—or sell them to the Germans? Brendan's Irish—and Ireland's neutral.'

'But not all Irishmen are neutral. Some of them have very long memories, and some just plain hate the English. All the hundreds of years when Britain ruled in Ireland—all that bloody Partition business, and the Home Rule row. Oh, they're neutral, but some are stupid enough to think that a German victory would see their country free of Britain, and united again. They delude themselves, of course. Hitler would treat them exactly as he's treated every other country that becomes a nuisance. Don't forget, Nicole, that invasion, if it comes, could just as easily come through the conquest of Ireland, as it could be launched from France. They could come in the back door there ...'

She shivered. 'But since he's Irish, what will they do to him? Suppose he's found guilty ...'

'Unfortunately, if he's found guilty, they'll do more than lock him up. You see, there's that technicality of the Irish choosing their citizenship. They had the chance, when the treaties were signed, to opt for English or Irish citizenship. Brendan de Courcey remained English. He carries an English passport. And if he is convicted of spying against His Majesty's Government, then he'll be guilty of treason.'

'Treason ...' She whispered the word fearfully.

'The penalty for treason, Nicole, is hanging.'

She worked grimly on the hoeing in the vegetable garden on what had been the south lawn. Her back was to the orchard as she worked, and some disturbing sense made her keep glancing over her shoulder towards it. She could see the tree under which they had all sat that day when England had been new to her, a dream world opening up, with war only a vague threat posed by troublesome, pessimistic people like Gavin. That was the tree where Lloyd had dropped down beside her and told her that he meant to stay in England. The place seemed peopled with ghosts of past times, times when there still had been laughter. She thought of them all, the ghosts of that one summer. The faces and names came up, as if by a roll-call. Gerry dead, Brendan perhaps a traitor, Ross a hard-bitten veteran of two campaigns. Gavin lost in his research station and talking of being sent to the United States to co-operate on some project of advanced physics. Allan immured in his prisoner-of-war camp, suffering hunger and cold, and some leg injury that would not heal. Richard, shuffling around in his world of half-images in grey and white. David, beautiful, golden David, was dead. Lloyd, her only love, was dead, and his unborn child was lost.

She turned her back determinedly on the orchard with its too-vivid memories. But inexorably, as she wielded the hoe in the rhythm she had learned, the lines beat into her brain, lines learned long ago at school and which had never, before now, had reality for her:

388

The many men so beautiful,
And they all dead did lie ...

VI

It was a dismal autumn. The sinkings in the Atlantic continued, the Germans advanced steadily into Russia. The coloured pins on Andrew's map extended farther and farther into that vast space. Leningrad's land communications with the rest of Russia were severed, and in October the Germans broke through in the Crimea and attacked Moscow. The British began the fearful Murmansk run to bring supplies to Russia by a sea route which seemed to Nicole to take them virtually over the top of the world.

'I don't see why,' she said, *'we've* got to send supplies to Russia when we've got hardly any ourselves. *And* we've brought them across the Atlantic.'

'The Russians have manpower, and while Hitler's engaged on his Eastern Front, he's not likely to try an invasion of Britain,' John Manstone pointed out. 'We rarely do things for quite altruistic motives in war. I suppose we figure that it's better for the Russians to die than us. There are more of them.'

She looked at the confusion of the maps on the wall. The old maps of the Channel ports seemed to belong to another age. The maps of the Western Desert, and their unforgettable names like Tobruk and Benghazi. The maps of Greece and Yugoslavia. The maps of Indo-China, and something they called the Burma Road. 'How long can they stay out?' she said. 'How long can America stay out?' She saw from the maps the tide of war running wild all over the world. 'They can't stay out for ever.'

'It took a long time, last time,' John said. 'And we were nearly beaten before they came.' He turned away from the maps and looked at her directly. They were alone in the kitchen.

'Why don't you go back, Nicole? Why do you stay on here?'

'Because I'm afraid to go back,' she answered. It was suddenly simple to tell him the truth. She was not emotionally tied up with this quiet man, this strange and lonely man who had been able to tell her of his own guilt and shame, who had shared with her the sorrow of the death of his son. She could talk with him as she could with none of the Fentons, nor with Charles, because she did not need, with him, to keep up the façade of courage. It was odd how much they knew about each other, things in the past that no one else knew.

'I'm afraid that if I go back, I'll finally break. You know, I keep pretending that Lloyd isn't really dead. I'm still waiting for him to come on leave. We had such short times here together, that it isn't hard to kid myself a little that it isn't quite over. If I go back to Boston, I'll end all that. I'll have to admit finally that he's gone. While I stay on here, I drift ... I live from day to day. I do what chores I can, help where I can, and I let the future take care of itself. To go back to Boston is too much of a decision for me. What's for me there? You ask—what's for me here? Well, I don't want to know ... I just let the days pile up, and one day I might have the courage to make myself believe that Lloyd is dead, and *I* have to do something about the future. The decisions now are small ones. I take one step at a time. I'm like an invalid learning to walk again. No one expects much of me. They're used to me here. They understand the way things are. If I go back to Boston, I'll have to be the brave little widow. I don't think I can play the role—not yet. If they were at war themselves, they'd all be so busy that maybe I'd be able to slip back in without anyone making any fuss. But here ... well the life here is like an old shoe, and I fit it.'

'But Dan and Timmy? You're going to have to make decisions about them.'

'They're such babies yet. Well, Dan's not such a baby. He's starting at the Dame school in the village after Christmas. Did I tell you that? He and Alistair are going together ... That was another decision made for me ...'

'But are they going to grow up British or American?'

'You sound like Uncle Pete. He can't bear the thought that good Fenton material might be getting watered down over here. He's made a real case of it. He's sort of fixed on Richard as the real hook to bring me back to Boston. He says Richard *must* come to Boston. He can have the finest teaching. He, Uncle Pete, will personally see to it. Richard can live in his house. It seems Richard can have anything he wants, so long as he brings me and the boys along with him.'

'And don't you think Richard should go? He would have much more to do than he has here ...'

'I know it. Now don't *you*—for God's sake—don't *you* start putting pressure on me. Even Uncle Charles tries. I *know* he doesn't want me to go, but he feels it's his duty to urge me to. He says I should do it for the boys. And I think it won't hurt the boys for a little longer to have things a bit hard. A year in a village school won't hurt Dan. Timmy's thriving on his baby rations. He looks like a lean little tiger. What's *wrong* with my staying here? Why is everyone trying to get rid of me?'

She turned away from him, 'Oh, damn, it's getting dark already, and I haven't fed the hens. Help me get the black-out frames up, will you. God, how I hate these early twilights. I hate the thought of the winter to get through. It's only November, and I've been getting up in the dark for weeks. I hate to think about January ...'

'By January you could be back in Boston.'

'Are you trying to push me too?' she said angrily. 'Leave me alone, will you?'

She left him to put up the black-out frames alone, and stamped outside. Damn them all, she thought. The forces that pushed and pulled each way. Was she really, she wondered, holding Richard back here? Would he go if she agreed to go with him? She felt useless, and alone, and guilty. Guilty of what? Guilty of drifting, of letting events carry her along. Guilty of keeping her children in what was thought to be a place of danger. Guilty of putting off the return to that empty house in Cambridge, Massachusetts, the house that she and Lloyd had made together, the house where she could never possess him again. She did not think it was that grave in the churchyard, along with the English Fentons, which held her. She seldom went there, nor did she feel it a place of pilgrimage. She was conscious that she did not mind, though, that Dan was starting school in the village where his father was buried. She did not mind her children growing up in a place where what their father had done was a respected and admired thing. In Boston they might think that Lloyd Fenton had been an idealistic fool; in England he had been a hero.

These were the things she could not say in the letters to Liz and Uncle Pete.

CHAPTER 6

I

The planes came in low at Pearl Harbor very early on that Sunday morning, and the first blips on the radar were reported; there was, however, no duty officer to act on the report. It wasn't until the sounds of the explosions in the harbour, where the strength of the American Pacific Fleet was anchored, began to roll through the valleys of the island that anyone began to take notice. The news was beamed out immediately to the mainland United States. Radio programmes were broken into to give it. An excited, almost incoherent gabble of voices tried to give each detail as it was received. Out of the confusion, only one thing was clear. The United States had been attacked by a force of Japanese bombers. The losses were very heavy. It was almost, but not quite, a mortal blow.

This was what Anna and Mikhail heard as they switched on the bedside radio. They were two hours ahead of Honolulu time. Mikhail had been to the kitchen and brewed their strong, hot tea. It was strange how they both preferred it to the American coffee which had for so long been a staple of their lives. But this was Sunday morning—the morning to sleep late, to lie in bed, to drink tea slowly, to make love, and then, as an afterthought, to switch on the radio.

They gripped each other, as many people did that day, on hearing the news. Mikhail slammed his hand down on the bed. 'Anna, they have to find me a place. There has to be one for me.'

'For *you*! You're crazy. You're too old.'

'You can't be too old when you can use your hands like I use mine. I can fix any engine that exists. Any fool can drive them. It needs a genius to fix them. I tell you, Anna, there has to be a place for me.'

She looked at him, and the coldness froze her face and her voice. 'You mean you want to go off somewhere—go off and fight?'

'*You're* crazy. No man wants to go off. No man wants to go off and leave what I've suddenly got. Not when I've got something I never expected to have. I've got you, Anna. I've got a life. I thought it was all fixing engines. If I have to go back to fixing engines for a while, just so that I can come back to you, then I'll go. The sooner the better. You know, in Russia we hung about a lot. We talked. We wasted time. We said how it would be in the future. Well, here in America this whole country has done that in these last years. We always knew it would come, but we didn't want to think about it. Not plan about it. Now it's here. So—for a while I have to go and fix engines, motors, anything that needs fixing. I don't pretend I'm still that young kid who rode a horse for the Tsar. I'm not going to win any medals, Anna. I'm just offering to fix their god-damn engines and get it all over with, so I can come back to you and get on with being the biggest Ford dealer in L.A. Don't you ever forget it, Anna. The biggest Ford dealer in L.A.'

They made love as if it was for the last time. It wasn't the last time. He was too old to be taken into any fighting services. He would hold no rank or command. He eventually got himself into the Navy as someone who would hold a shore job, and one day found himself steaming out of San Francisco on a battleship, bound for the South Pacific. He was there purely to fix the engines which went wrong, to see that the bulldozers which levelled the airfields would function, to command the crew of young men under him. He was part of a Construction Battalion. He was part of the follow-up of Guadalcanal. When the cable reached Anna a little more than a year later, she went to meet him in San Francisco. She wasn't prepared to see him come down the gangplank between crutches; he paused to wave, nimbly balancing on one crutch. On the dockside, he swept her between his arms. She felt his weight on her. 'Oh, God, Anna Nikolayevna, am I thankful to be home. I found out I wasn't a hero. Some fool says he's going to pin a medal on me, but all I want to do is get back to being the biggest Ford dealer in L.A.'

It wasn't until they drew apart, and she found herself trying

393

to fall into step with him, that she realized that the lower part of one of his legs was missing. 'Oh, hell, Anna—what does it matter? I've still got my hands. I'm still a genius with an engine ... I came back, Anna. And I'm going to stay.'

II

When the news of the bombing of Pearl Harbor reached Boston, it was lunch-time on Sunday. The cook at Peter Fenton's house came rushing into the dining-room, a place she never normally appeared. She had the radio on in the kitchen. 'The Japs have bombed a place called Pearl Harbor!' she shouted. 'They say the Navy's destroyed! Thousands killed! Does this mean we're at war, Mr Fenton?'

He put down his napkin and his face was grey as he considered the news, then the colour began to mount in it as the sense of outrage and anger grew. 'This country is not at war, Hetty, until Congress says it's at war. But yes, I guess you can count on it that we're at war.'

He didn't finish his meal. He went to his study and took a cigar and brandy, and listened to the bulletins for himself. While he listened, he heard his own voice muttering in between the items of news, the fresh details that kept coming. 'That man,' he said softly, with all the force of his dislike of the American President, 'that man and Churchill have cooked this up between them.' The thought was illogical and malicious, and in a calmer moment he might have acknowledged it. But he was not calm. One of his first thoughts, after the news, had been to count the heads of his grandsons and grand-nephews who might be expected to join in this war, which he had feared for so long. How many would live, and how many would die? He thought of Lloyd Fenton, already dead in this cause. He thought wistfully of Lloyd Fenton's wife. 'Too late for her now,' he muttered. 'She won't come now. I'll never see her again.'

III

It was just before six o'clock that winter Sunday when the news was flashed across the Atlantic and reached Europe. At Fenton Field they had gathered, as usual, in the sitting-room, to hear the six o'clock news bulletin. John Manstone had a weekend leave and he was with them. Nicole had just come from helping Henson supervise the children's supper in the kitchen. She watched nervously as Richard went through the tricky process of pouring drinks. The whisky was so precious, and they always feared he'd spill it, and sometimes he did. But no one ever kept him from the task.

The first news was very sketchy, and Nicole did not grasp the meaning of the first words of the bulletin. '. . . reports an air attack on the American Naval Base at Pearl Harbor, Honolulu. Few details are available at present, but it is believed that at least one battleship was sunk, and others damaged. There are reports of many casualties . . .'

They listened in complete silence. They listened until the end of the bulletin, all the items of home news. There was some comment on the fact that Britain had declared war two days ago on Finland, Hungary and Romania. Nicole wondered what good that would do anyone. They heard the first suggestion that the German tanks were stopped in a 200-mile semicircle around Moscow. It was not until the long winter was over that they realized that this event had almost as much significance as that sketchy account of a bombing raid on Pearl Harbor.

By nine o'clock the news was firmer. The battleship *Oklahoma* had capsized, the *Tennessee* was on fire. There was even a suggestion that four of the eight great battleships which rode together in the harbour that morning had been sunk outright and two more extensively damaged. The number of casualties could not yet be estimated.

They had waited almost in a state of suspended animation until this later bulletin, hardly daring to trust it, knowing what it meant, but not wanting to rejoice in the horror and devastation which had been visited on the unprepared giants of the American Navy.

It was Nicole who broke the spell. She had been down to the cellar and come back with a bottle of Gavin's Glenlivet. 'I've left him another IOU,' she said to Judy. She went and poured two fingers full into the glasses which had been washed and returned to the side dresser.

'Well, I'm the only American here, so I'm the one who can say it. It's come at last. *We're in!*' She handed the glasses around. 'I suppose I'm drinking to Lloyd now, and wishing there hadn't been so many times I'd doubted him, doubted that this day would finally come.' She looked at Margaret's troubled, anxious face. 'I remember when we were all here, listening to Chamberlain telling us we were at war with Germany. We drank to victory. But Aunt Margaret was right. What we need is peace.'

She took a long pull at the whisky; for a moment its strength caught her breath, and then the healing warmth crept through her. 'By God,' she said. 'By God, Uncle Pete's going to be mad!'

And then she said good night and went to bed. But she lay wakeful in the darkness of her room. Her heart seemed to beat more rapidly, and she was restless. The event had come. The time of waiting was over.

IV

The plane was only a small one of the Luftwaffe, and its mission was to fly a German general from a meeting at The Hague back to his base near Calais. He had with him two of his staff members, and the plane carried one gunner. They took off into the gloom of the December night; the flight plan was to keep along the coast all the way, making the most direct route to the airfield near Calais. There was supposed to be a total black-out of all the coastal towns, and right into the heart of France and Germany, but as usual it was not completely effective. The dull waters of the Channel glinted on the right, the faint glow of the coastal cities on the left. There was a low cloud which partly obscured both. They flew in and out of it, bumping a little as they encountered the turbulence.

The pilot never saw the little coastal freighter which had heard the drone of the aircraft engines above. It was low-flying. On the ship's radio they had received the news of Pearl Harbor, and while they guessed that they now had a new ally in Japan, they also would have a new enemy in America. They were not now so certain as they once were that the war would soon be over, and victory just a matter of time. They were nervous and apprehensive that night, and they did not first check with their radio coastal control as to the identity of the plane above them. The gunner believed he saw the hated marking of the RAF, and he fired. Afterwards he claimed he had had a hit, but the plane continued on, changing direction and heading back towards the coast of England.

The windscreen was crazed, and the pilot hit. He could feel the warmth of his own blood pumping out of him, and in a very few minutes he began to feel the cold and the faintness. The instruments didn't register, the compass and altimeter swung wildly, uselessly. The three army men crowded towards the cockpit. They were as helpless as this piece of machinery which suddenly would respond to nothing the pilot did. His hands were on the controls, but he could barely hear the shouted commands, instructions, orders from these men who couldn't fly. At the rear the gunner lay tense, waiting for another burst of fire from below. They were far out over the channel now, the black waters slick and oily. He had not even seen the source of the AA fire which had hit them.

The pilot died just about when the craft crossed the English coast. They met a full barrage of AA fire, and flew on serenely through it, untouched. By now the general had realized which coast they had crossed. He had given up his attempt to shake life into the pilot; he had given up cursing his aides because they were soldiers, not airmen. He was attempting to destroy the papers in his briefcase.

They were past the coastal searchlights and the balloon barrage. The plane droned on over the quiet countryside, slipping past the inner defences. Those alive in the plane could sense that they were very low, too low to parachute. It was seven minutes since the craft had been hit. They hoped that when they came down it would be into a field of plough or a pasture. But when they hit, it was a building, and the plane exploded on impact.

V

The lonely ringing of the telephone downstairs roused Nicole to full wakefulness. How terrible the sound of a telephone ringing in the lonely hours of the night was when it could bring only bad news. She fumbled her way into the dressing-gown and started downstairs. Was it Ross? ... Allan ... ? Was it Charles? Margaret was at the telephone before her. She heard her terse, strained voice. 'Yes, Lieutenant-Colonel Lord

Manstone is staying here. Do you want me to take a message? You'll hold on ... Very good.' She turned to Nicole. 'Quickly, bring John.'

But he was already at the head of the stairs, in his dressing-gown, his hair rumpled, his face heavy with sleep. Andrew was behind him. Even Richard appeared at the door of his room. 'What time is it?' he demanded. 'It feels like the middle of the night to me. What's wrong?'

John had taken the telephone from Margaret. 'Manstone here. Yes ... yes, it's *you*, Beggs. Yes, I left the number ... What's the trouble? What ... what? Yes ... yes, I understand. I don't know if it will be possible. I'll see ... I'll see. Yes, thanks for getting in touch. Good of you.' Then, finally, in a lower key. 'Yes, I understand how you feel. Thanks very much ...'

He replaced the receiver. Wilks had appeared along the passage leading from the kitchen. He was bundled in an old, heavy dressing-gown. 'Is there anything I can do, m'lord?'

Strange, Nicole thought, how it was people like Wilks who could always ask the question, and never seem out of place. 'I don't think so.' John's voice was almost absent-minded, as if he really had no answer to the question. 'There's nothing much any of *us* can do. It's up to them ...'

Nicole moved towards him and shook his arm. 'For God's sake, wake up! What's happened? *Can* we do anything?'

He shook his head in a dazed fashion. 'No. Nothing. That was Beggs, the steward at Lynmara. It seems that ... well, a plane has crashed, a small plane has crashed into the house. It's on fire.'

'Lynmara?—Lynmara's on fire?' She stepped back from him. 'Oh, God. Not that *too* ...' She didn't herself quite understand what she had meant by saying that. The idea was terrible to her, as if all the senseless waste of this war had found a gathering point in the destruction of a house she had loved.

'Let's go,' she said to John. 'You have to be there.' She turned to Andrew. 'John can borrow the car, can't he? Is there enough petrol in it, do you think?'

Andrew nodded. 'Enough, I'd say. You'll probably find someone to help you out with a bit of petrol when you get there. I've a few coupons.'

'I've a few more,' Richard said.

John was shaking his head. 'What's the use? My being there can't do anything. Either they can save it, or they can't. Beggs said the equipment from Hawkinge is helping the local fire brigade.'

'For heaven's sake,' Nicole cried at him, shaking him again. 'Lynmara is burning! You at least owe it to the people on the estate to *be* there. You owe it to your family——' She stopped. There was no family.

He was looking at her. 'You'll come?'

'Of course I'll come. I'll be down in five minutes.'

Wilks was already padding back towards the kitchen. 'I'll prepare some sandwiches ...' They might have been making plans for a picnic, Nicole thought as she pulled on her clothes.

Her own sense of urgency seemed at last to have communicated itself to John Manstone. He was waiting with the motor running when she took the passenger seat, Wilks's hastily bundled-up pack of sandwiches in her hand. They spoke very little during the journey; he seemed to give all his concentration to the road, driving fast in the dark and narrow lanes of the countryside, with only the tiny slit beams of the black-out headlamps to light their way. It occurred to her how well he did it; how much in control he seemed now, once the action had been decided on. He seemed to know his way along all the back roads. Only once or twice did he pause and hesitate at a road junction; there was little in the way of signposting left after the invasion threat of last autumn. They moved quickly across east Sussex and into Kent.

She thought about it as they drove. She thought about the house, how beautiful it had been, even in its great size. She wondered how much would survive. Would the great hammer-beam roof of the hall go to the flames?—would the Grinling Gibbons staircase go?—the famous panelling in the Long Room. And the precious silk-lined rooms, the Red Room and the Green room? Would the beautiful carved alabaster chimney-pieces of the Long Room go crashing down through the burning floor? There was a light wind which moved the boughs of the leafless trees above them as they drove. Which way was it blowing?—how strong was it? The night was cold; a light cloud moved before the wind. Sometimes she could see the stars. A plane—what plane? Whose plane?

Sooner than she thought they topped a rise in the downs and saw the glow in the sky. It was faint, as if a small village, lighted as in pre-war days, was tucked in the hollow down there. The sight of it seemed to galvanize John. His foot went down hard on the accelerator. They rocketed at a dangerous speed along the last of the roads that led to the big main gate she remembered. He screeched to a halt at the lodge. A faint light came from a window where a black-out curtain had been left partly open. He shouted something to a woman who came to the door, and then they were racing along the drive between the bare oaks and beeches of her memory. And there was the house.

The sight of it seemed to destroy his sense of urgency. The car slowed almost to a crawl as their eyes probed the scene. They knew what they were looking for. The glow was there, but the front of the house was dark—silhouetted against the light that came from behind. For the moment their straining eyes could not see whether they looked at a building still intact, or a dark and gutted ruin. The chimneys stood out against the glow. The line of the roof seemed still to be there.

'It's the North Wing,' he said. 'The Georgian part ...'

They had reached the first of the lorries which had come from Hawkinge Air Base. John pulled off on to the verge of the drive. They walked the rest of the way, up the stairs to the terrace, along the whole lovely South Front, around the West Wing. There was fire equipment pulled up on the terrace itself, and firemen worked with hoses playing water on the roofs. Windows were broken to allow the streams of water to get in. There was a continuing sound of chopping, as firemen used their axes. There was the deadening smell of smouldering wood.

They stood and looked at the North Wing. Here the roof was gone, and the fire still burned. They could see all the interior as if someone had placed a light at each window. But the worst of the fire was gone, its force spent. The water continued to pour in from the hoses, but it played on wood that was giving up its dance with death. It was charred and blackened, and in parts it only smouldered.

At first no one recognized Manstone. He and Nicole were just part of the onlookers who had gathered. The hoses were tangled everywhere. An irritated fireman ordered them to stand back. Finally, a man in the clothes of a farm-worker saw Manstone.

'It's you, m'lord. Wondered if you'd get here.' He put his fingers to his lips and gave a loud whistle. 'Hey, Bill—fetch Beggs, will you? Here's Lord Manstone.'

They were surrounded very soon. Beggs was there, trying to tumble out the story of what had happened. Then there was a Wing Commander who had used the bedroom which Manstone himself had used. 'Back luck,' he said. 'Rotten bad luck. Plane came from bloody well nowhere. Small plane—German. Must have been wildly off course. I've had reports from the batteries at Dover and Folkestone that a German plane came over very low. They don't think they got a hit, though. Can't say what brought it down. There are a few bodies in there, somewhere. Look, there on the other side you can just about make out the fuselage. I think we lost about three of our chaps. We've done a roll-call, and unless they're out without permission, then they're dead. It was pretty hot here a few hours ago. Well, I suppose you're lucky. If it had happened when there was a raid on Hawkinge, or any of the towns around here, you wouldn't have had all this equipment available. At least they've saved the older part of the house. It's pretty wet though. Hard to see how bad the damage is until it's light.' Nicole watched the Wing Commander's face in the last glow from the fire. He had a clipped moustache, and a scar which ran through one eyebrow. He was wearing his uniform over pyjamas, his cap with insignia pulled firmly on his head. He was puzzled by Nicole's identity, and since Manstone had not introduced her, he gave his report directly to John, avoiding her gaze. He was attempting to make a military assessment of what had happened, and trying to conceal that he was itching for the dawn himself to see what of his own possessions had escaped those penetrating, destroying jets of water. 'Damn lucky the river's so near. The boys had the pumps down there within minutes. Without that full pressure of water the whole house would have gone. At least the best parts are still standing . . .'

At intervals during this John had murmured, 'Yes . . . yes . . . They've done a wonderful job. Very good of them. Very good . . .'

The Wing Commander concluded, 'Look, I'm ducking over to Hawkinge. They'll billet us there temporarily. You can get a bite of breakfast there, if you want ... I'd just leave it to the fire chaps now, if I were you. They'll stay here until the very last of it's out. Can't take a chance on a spark blowing on to the other roofs ... I've sent off all the men who were here. I expect they'll be back later to see if there's any of their gear they can salvage. Just as well it was that wing ... the rest would have gone like tinder. That old panelling ... dry as a haystack. We would have lost more men ... You all right, Lord Manstone? Look, why don't you both come over to Hawkinge right now? I expect you could use a drink ...'

'Very kind of you,' John said, as if he really hadn't heard what was said. 'Very kind ... But I think I'll hang about a bit. A few people here I know. I'd like to say hallo to them. They wouldn't understand it if I left.'

'Yes ... yes ... of course. Naturally. Well, come over when you're ready. I'll tell them to expect you. Bennett's my name. Awfully sorry, again. Rotten luck ...'

They sat finally on the steps of the chapel and ate Wilks's sandwiches. There had been a dozen offers of breakfast from various people, none of which registered with John Manstone. He had thanked them all, and had forgotten them. He had, however, remembered to ask for the key of the chapel from Beggs. They sat on the steps with Wilks's sandwiches, and the finest brandy the torch they carried could discover.

The glow had died and gone. In its place was the slow blanching of the winter sky which heralded the dawn. Above them, once again silhouetted against the eastern sky, the outline of Lynmara began to take form and substance.

'Well, there it is,' John said. He passed the bottle of brandy to Nicole; they had no glasses or cups. 'The life and death of a house. I suppose it was worthwhile to be in at the end ... but since it was death, I don't really know why I came.'

'It's not dead.' She took a long pull at the brandy bottle, and then set it carefully down on the steps between them. 'It's damaged. Wounded ... if you want to call it that. It's far from dead. One wing is gone ... for ever. Perhaps no one regrets that. It was the least beautiful part of Lynmara. It can be dispensed with. The rest ... it will need repairs. It will cost ferocious sums of money to repair the damage the water did. The pictures are safe, the carpets, the tapestries. They say the panelling is still intact, except where the firemen chopped through. The staircase is still standing. What is needed is will and energy to put it all back in place again.'

He shrugged, and reached for the bottle again. 'And why? Why should I? This house has taken a high price from my whole life. Why should I give the last years to it? For whom? For some cousin I've never seen? I have no son—I have no grandson. It would be only for me—for my own satisfaction. And I can't find any satisfaction in doing it for myself.'

She turned and took his arm firmly, so that he was forced to shift his gaze away from the dark pile on the skyline which grew more distinct with the advancing light.

'Then I have a proposition to make. A proposal. Marry me. I'll give you sons to build for. I'll give you a reason for building. Remember you once dreamed of the sons my mother would have given you?—the young Tartars to run the corridors of Lynmara? Well—I'll give them to you. You want a reason for going on? I'll give it to you.'

'You . . .? *You!*'

'Why not? Have you any better plans? I haven't any. One thing . . . you do know I don't love you? That is clearly understood. I've only loved one man. I still love him. But he is dead, and I am not. I have something to do with my life. So do you. For one reason . . .' She nodded towards the pile on the skyline, where the rosy brick was beginning to emerge in the grey of the dawn. 'For that. Good enough? I will give you all of my devotion and energy, and whatever skill I have. I will give it to you and your children. I will expect the same from you. Everything . . . everything. Is that a kind of love? Perhaps it is . . . Both of us could do worse.'

They sat there and ate the sandwiches and drank the brandy. The low cloud gave way before the light wind, and Lynmara was revealed in the first light of a winter sunrise.

Epilogue

February 28th, 1974

Nicole came up by the back stairs, and so avoided seeing any of her children until she was dressed and ready for them. The back stairs were very convenient. She and John had never rebuilt the North Wing, the one so badly damaged on the night the German plane had almost destroyed Lynmara. The space made by demolishing the North Wing had allowed such things as new kitchens and staff rooms, and these stairs, to be built. Lynmara was easier to run than in the old days, and it needed to be. She used to smile when she listened to John trying to count up how many staff his mother had employed.

She carefully creamed her face, and took a long time soaking in her bath. She needed the hot water to help relax the arthritic stiffness of her hands and knees. It had been one of the bitterest things to accept, this attack on her hands. When she found that she no longer could play the piano well, she stopped playing altogether. 'Music was not meant to be played badly—for *exercise*,' she had snapped at the doctor who had urged it on her. She knew she was often bad-tempered these days, especially since John had died. She even wondered if she seemed, in some people's eyes, to resemble that formidable old woman she had so much disliked, John's mother. If the arthritis grew much worse, she would have a stick to walk with, and the resemblance might be greater.

She applied her make-up carefully. Her skin was still white, and comparatively unlined. There was still the foundation of blackness under the streaks of pure silver in her hair. She twisted it into the French knot she always wore. That task also was growing more difficult.

Her skirt was black, of finest French velvet, and with it she wore a black silk blouse, high at the throat. Then she sat with her jewel case open before her, making a careful selection of what she would wear.

The pieces represented milestones of her life. The important jewels, among them the Manstone sapphires, had gone to the wife of Thomas, the eldest son of her marriage to John, after John had died. She still found it hard to think of herself in the role of the dowager Countess of Manstone—that another, a much younger woman, held the title. The emerald ring represented John's gift to her at Thomas's birth. There had been emerald earrings when Peter had been born, an emerald and diamond cluster for George's birth, and when at last there had been that lively, precocious girl, Judith, a necklace of emeralds and diamonds. The Barrington trusts, she thought, had provided for many things that perhaps Lord Barrington had never intended. In the jewel case were also the pearls that Iris had once given her, and which had been given back, the sapphire and diamond brooch which had been meant as Iris's wedding present. These she had been given by Charles when she had married. It had eased her sense of guilt a little to know that Iris had never sold the jewels that represented that one summer of her niece's rise and fall in London society. Among the jewels were Lloyd's wedding ring and the single diamond he had given her from the small Sussex jeweller. These now were never worn. There were the garnets which perversely she loved best of all. And there was the little gold horseshoe on the thin gold chain. *Good luck. Lucky.*

It was strange to think that none of her children, the children she had promised to John, had actually been born at Lynmara, except Judith. Lynmara had not been handed back to them until after the war, when the long work of restoration had begun. How she and John had worked at it—living uncomfortably in various parts of the house while the work went on around them. But at last it was done, the damaged woodwork restored, the floors strengthened, the chimneys rebuilt, an enormous central-heating system installed and disguised behind grilles. They had brought workmen from Italy and France, they had combed Europe for restorers for the painted ceilings; the silk for the walls and hangings had been woven in Lyons. The day had come when the pictures had come back from storage, then had come the summer night of the first great party at Lynmara. There had been those who told the story of how this present Countess of Manstone had almost married her husband's son. But it hadn't mattered very much. It was not the scandal it might have been. The world had changed very much, and people had admired Lynmara, and wondered how long it could survive.

It had been a surprisingly serene marriage. She and John had united in this one great project, and while they had argued about the details, they had never been unsure of the purpose. To Lynmara, to John and his children she gave an unstinting devotion and energy, and her reward was the solidity of accomplishment. Her two Fenton children had become almost John's children, though she had never allowed him formally to adopt them. 'Their name must remain Fenton,' she told him, and he had conceded her point. 'I will advise them,' she said, 'when the time comes, to keep their American citizenship.' To reinforce that, she had taken all six children for many summers to the ramshackle house on Cape Cod. She had seen Uncle Pete once more before he died. Her children had played with their Fenton cousins, and the Ashleighs had mixed with supreme ease. During adolescence and their early twenties there had always been one or two Fentons at Lynmara—Fentons attending school or university in England, Fentons taking post-graduate courses. All of her children, on completing Cambridge, had spent a year at Harvard. They all now wore a smooth, international look; they knew the world they had inherited, and its changes. They made their way surely.

'And where are the little Tartars you promised me?' John had once teased her. 'My only complaint about all our children is that at times they're just too well behaved.'

'They've all got guts,' Nicole had retorted. 'They're just too clever to let anyone know when they're angry.'

So she had shared the life and the house of John Manstone, and it had been a successful partnership. Their children had given them a great party at Lynmara for John's seventy-fifth birthday. His face was glowing as the house had come splendidly to life, his spirits had matched its radiance. 'It's as I've always wanted to see it,' he said to Nicole as they waited for their guests. 'It's a happy house, filled with our children. It's now what it never was when I was growing up, or in David's time. I've almost forgotten how sad and lonely it often seemed. How beautifully you've managed it all ...' And then he had tucked a stray curl back around her ear, and used the excuse to kiss her. 'But then you always were a managing little minx.'

He had died serenely seated in a chair on the south terrace on an autumn afternoon last year while she had dead-headed roses in the beds below. He had been eighty-one years old.

And so, last year, Thomas had become Lord Manstone, and technically the house now belonged to him. She had made some vague offer to move, so that he and his wife could have it, but she knew she had no intention of moving. Let them put up with an arthritic old lady because without her there would have been no house to inherit. But they seemed in no hurry to take up residence. They liked their London house, and their retreat in Scotland. They continued to treat Lynmara as a convenience for weekends. But she knew they were planning something. They were all too quiet, her children.

Then the letter had reached her from Los Angeles. She had said nothing of it to Thomas, or to Dan or Timothy, the ones she confided in most. She had merely said she was going on a visit to the Boston Fentons, and that had been partly true. From Boston she had flown to Los Angeles, and had been met by one of the senior representatives of an eminent law firm.

The revelations had begun then. She had been driven to the house in Laurel Canyon. It was no bigger than when Anna had first bought it, a small, modest house on five acres in the middle of the houses of the rich. She had walked through the few rooms of the house, and come back to the living-room, the room with the books in Russian, the samovar, the jewelled icons. The man who had come to meet her was almost her own age, old enough to have known her mother for many years. 'Can you tell me what she was like, my mother?' She thought how strange it was that Anna had died so soon after the death of John Manstone, her first love.

'Your mother, Lady Manstone, was a splendid woman. If you don't mind the expression, she was a real character. Take this house—we always pointed out to her that she was paying enormous taxes to hold five acres here, and a house that was not— well, let us say, commensurate, with her wealth. She declared that privacy was her one luxury, and she would keep her five acres, and her small house. It didn't matter, and not many people knew that she owned some of the choicest pieces of Los Angeles real estate. That acreage out in the desert ... she bought it at a time when no one wanted desert land. When they did want it, it was worth millions. Those pieces she bought in

San Diego before the war. They turned to gold. She had a genius for real estate ... a very long vision. She came out here when this city was scrub land and bean fields and orange groves, but she was able to see it the way it is now. She was always at least ten years ahead of where the next area of development would be, and sometimes, like the desert property, she was a generation ahead. But I guess she had a real genius with money. It took lots of guts, Lady Manstone, to buy stock during the depression, but Mrs Ovrensky did. Just that purchase of IBM stock alone would have made her rich ...'

'And the man she married?'

'Well, he was one of those guys we all sort of love, the sort of person you call "a prince of a man". And the funny thing was that he really was a prince, only no one knew it until after he died. They were both American citizens. They never used the title. But it was there, and I never knew it until I went to help her register the death. But in fact, it didn't surprise me. He was a gentleman, and while that's an overworked word, I can't think of a better one for him.

'He built himself up until he became Los Angeles's biggest Ford dealer. I think it had always been his ambition. He served in the Navy for a while, and lost a foot. Your mother carried on the business with whatever second-hand stuff she could get during the war, and had it waiting for him when he came back. He became the biggest Ford dealer because everyone knew he was a nut about engines. He always paid top wages to his mechanics. He only wanted the best. Every new car he sent out had been so thoroughly checked he never had a dissatisfied customer. If you had a complaint, Mike—everyone called him that—would attend to it himself. If a mechanic was sloppy, he fired him. And he could always prove his point by being able to strip down an engine and put it together almost blindfolded. He had a favourite expression about engines—perhaps it was the first Americanism he ever learned. "It should run as sweet as sugar." By all logic he was too honest to have been as successful as he was, but there was some magic in his personality that brought people to his place in droves, so the extra money he spent on servicing cars was made up in sheer volume of business. Come to think of it, Lady Manstone, he was my idea of what a prince should be. He was never cut-rate ...'

She turned to face him, wanting to see his face as she asked the question. It was November, and for her, unnaturally hot. The smog hurt her eyes. She was tired after the plane journey, but she could not bear to delay any part of this new discovery she was making.

'Do you ... perhaps it's not a question I should ask of you. But I would like to know. Do you think they were happy together? My mother and Michael Ovrensky?'

'Happy? Lady Manstone, with all respect, use your head. To the few people who ever were allowed to come here, your mother and her husband were a legend. You see this little house? Comfortable—nice ... but by Los Angeles standards, it's hardly more than a shack. You saw that vegetable garden? Mike worked in that almost to the day he died. You see these rooms? Very simple. Only very happy people, who are also very rich, can afford to be that simple. They had something going for them, those two. None of us ever quite understood what it was, but I'll tell you one thing—we envied them, and it wasn't because they were rich.'

She had asked to be left in the house for a while. He had promised to send back the car for her later. The woman who had cleaned, and in later years, done some cooking for Anna had come, and she had made her a simple lunch. The lawyer had left the keys of Anna's cupboards and files. It was here, as the afternoon heat settled on Los Angeles, that Nicole found the envelopes full of clippings. Almost every year of her life since she had last seen Anna was charted here. The envelopes were marked with dates. She saw the old photo of herself from the *Tatler* seated at the piano. There were pictures of herself and David at Lynmara. There was the announcement of her marriage to Lloyd, the announcement of the births of her children in Boston. There were the obituaries of Lloyd. There was the announcement, which must have come as the greatest shock of all to Anna, of her marriage to John Manstone. The births of each of John's children was known to Anna. There was the big newspaper coverage of the first great party they had given at Lynmara when the restoration was complete. And how had she found out the sort of degrees her children had got at Cambridge? It was there, in Anna's handwriting, growing a little stiff and crabbed with age. She must have taken great pleasure in the double First Judith had won. It was underscored heavily. She sat there all afternoon with the cuttings and the photographs, and tried to see it all through Anna's eyes.

She had heard the terms of the will; from them she knew that the use she had made of these years had pleased Anna. 'To my beloved daughter, Nicole, Countess of Manstone, I give, devise and bequeath my entire estate ...' Nicole wished that, apart from the millions of dollars that that represented, there had been a letter from Anna, but there was none. Perhaps she had been right. The events of the years spoke for themselves. Then she came on the packets of letters Mikhail Ovrensky had written from the South Pacific. She held his photograph in her hand. There were the yellow sepia-tinted photographs of the Ovrensky children at that place called Beryozovaya Polyana. Among them, she could single out her mother's face when she had been a child, growing up with them. She wondered if any of the members of that great law firm who had helped her mother knew that the prince she had married had been her childhood playmate. She doubted it. She had pieced together the story of Anna's early struggle in her small real estate office. She saw photographs of *Mike's New and Used Cars*—each time the showrooms getting bigger, the lines of parked cars longer. They had come out of the old world of Russia in the last century, and they had conquered, in their own fashion, this new world they had embraced. And she knew from the letters that they had loved each other. With all this there had been no need for her mother to write to her; the story told itself. She felt that Anna had known that she would make this long journey to Los Angeles to see this place for herself. With a kind of reverence she replaced the stiff, browning newspaper clippings, the photographs. They would come back to Lynmara with her.

She dragged herself back to the present from the remembrance of these things; she finally made her selection of jewellery, and prepared to go downstairs. She had asked that drinks be served before one of the fires in the Great Hall. It did not hurt to keep her children waiting, surrounded by the portraits of the Ashleighs, to sense again what their legacy was.

On the way along the corridor she glanced from a window down to the lighted area that showed through the skylights of the new structure which had been built on the site of the old North Wing. No doubt Judith had been there. It was the last piece of work they had completed at Lynmara, and it housed the pictures which had been left to her by Gerry Agar. It was thought faintly unpatriotic of her to have named the collection after its original owner—a man believed to have been a collaborator with the Nazis, a man whose cousin, Brendan de Courcey, had been hanged for treason. But she had never cared what people thought, and to do her justice, neither did Judith. She took enormous pleasure in that collection. 'How brilliant he must have been, Mother,' she said. 'Just imagine putting it all together—and only the very best examples of their work. Imagine leaving it to you. Was he in love with you?'

'I wish I could say he was. I never knew.'

Judith had looked at her oddly, but asked no more. 'At the prices these artists are fetching at auction these days you know they're worth a king's ransom, don't you?'

'Why do you think we built such a secure place for them? It's fire-proof, and, they say, burglar-proof. I'm not a fool.'

'No, Mother—you're not a fool.'

Her steps slowed perceptibly as she neared the end of the corridor, and she could hear the low murmur of voices in the hall below. In the darkness she leaned over the balustrade and looked down at them—at her children, and their wives. Judith wasn't yet married. Nicole thought she was the sort who might have many lovers, and perhaps never marry. She had particularly asked her not to bring a man with her this weekend. 'It is for the family only,' she had said.

She sought Thomas's face among the gathering. Thirty-two, he was, and the new Earl of Manstone. His half-brothers Dan and Timothy had always been close to him. Dan had done extremely well in the City, and it was his tips which propped up Thomas's quite modest fortune in the years while he had waited for his inheritance. Timothy, to everyone's surprise, had joined the Church. He was what they now called 'trendy'. He was quite famous as a television personality, giving the modern version of religion, writing books which got him into trouble with his bishop. People had tipped him to become a bishop himself. Nicole wondered how many remembered that he was still an American citizen. Peter was making his way, slowly, determinedly, up the Army ladder. George had headed his own public relations firm, was a journalist, and almost as frequently seen on television talk-shows as his half-brother. It was he who, Nicole thought, would quite soon face Judith across the aisle of the House of Commons. He was as passionate a Conservative as she was a Socialist. Yes, her children were doing very well. But she wondered if they were all quite honest in acknowledging how much the background of Lynmara had helped them in the climb. Judith refused to use her courtesy title of Lady Judith. George did not at all mind using his; being a younger son of a peer would not keep him out of the House of Commons, and it was a useful handle.

Worldly, sophisticated, quite brilliant in their own fashions were her children. But they were beginning to be aware that Lynmara was an anachronism in this day. A part of England, yes—but was it a part they could afford to keep? Nicole was aware that a weekend guest Thomas had brought down about six weeks ago had been the American representative of Middle-East oil interests. She suspected that Thomas had brought him with the idea of dangling Lynmara before him as a potential showcase for the company, a place where they might entertain, a valuable piece of real estate to hold for the future. The spectre of the still unpaid death duties which the death of his father had brought on the estate, loomed before him. The Commissioners of Revenue were in no particular hurry, and in the few months since John had died, his children were only beginning to learn the intricacies of the Barrington trusts. All they knew of Cynthia Barrington and her son David were the portraits of them which hung in this hall—that and the vaguely legendary name of Lord Barrington, self-made millionaire, which still circulated through the City.

No one understood better than Nicole that the estate was entailed, and that Thomas was the heir. What was not yet untangled was how far the Barrington trusts reached, and how much they had been diminished through the years. As long as John had lived, they had been secured for Lynmara by his presence. No one yet knew if they had provided for a succession which did not come through Cynthia Barrington, or through her son, David. There was a wicked legal tangle to unsnarl.

Who could afford a house like this any more, they asked? And she asked, 'Could England afford to let it go?' She was prepared to listen to almost everything. She would let the public walk through each day, tramp along the Long Room, look at the Turners in the Great Saloon, view the Gerald Agar Collection. She would do anything, but she would not let Lynmara go.

Her arthritic hand touched the banister only lightly as she began her descent. Let them not see her leaning or faltering. Gradually, as she came down into the light of the Great Hall, the talking stopped. The heads turned to look at her. She brought with her the knowledge and the strength of her mother, the woman who had almost been the mistress of this house a long time ago. She brought with her the fighting power of the money that Anna and her husband had earned. And the jewellery she had chosen to wear on this night was the simple gold chain with the upturned horseshoe, and the great diamond-studded star, which had been among her mother's possessions, the Grand Cross of St George, awarded to the father of Mikhail Ovrensky by the Tsar of all the Russias.

She believed that she brought equal forces to battle with her children.